RIDING THE
HIGH ROAD

RIDING THE HIGH ROAD

Written by

Penny Frances

First Published in 2023 by Fantastic Books Publishing

ISBN (ebook): 978-1-914060-52-6
ISBN (paperback): 978-1-914060-51-9

For my son Jacob

Acknowledgements

This book has been a long time in the making, and would not have been completed but for the support and encouragement of many people.

First thanks must go to members of my writing group past and present: Judy Harris, Sara Gowen, Nicky Hallett, Jenny River, Chlöe Balcomb, Corinna Flight, Julia South, Rita Willow, all of whom have been present at various stages from the very beginnings of the first draft, giving their insightful and constructive feedback chapter by chapter, as well as encouragement to keep going and to accept requests for re-writes from agents and publishers as an opportunity to improve. Thanks also to Jessie Greenfield for reading the manuscript and giving her insight as a young person from an LGBTQ+ family. Special thanks to my lovely writing buddy Lesley Ali for her friendship and encouragement over many years. Thanks are due to Sheffield Hallam Writing MA, and in particular my tutor for the novel unit, Lesley Glaister, for giving me the confidence and stamina to persist after the near misses in getting my first novel published. More recently I thank Beverley Ward and the members of the Sheffield based Writers Workshop for helping me re-connect with Sheffield's writing community and offering useful advice on broadening my publicity and social media reach.

Many thanks also to Fantastic Books for taking on this book after many years of submitting. Their reader reports, initially of the first chapter and synopsis, and then of the full manuscript, were detailed, constructive and encouraging and, despite pushing me through two re-writes, did undeniably result in a better book 'well up to publication standard'. Special thanks to Anne-Marie Strand from Fantastic Books Publicity and Marketing for keeping me on board by being honest about expected long waits for editors' responses and for her prompt and reassuring responses to all my queries. Their detailed publicity questionnaire has also helped me focus on the steps needed to the ensure maximum reach to potential readers of the novel.

Finally, special thanks to my family. To Richard who has been both sperm donor and exceptional dad to my son Jacob. To Jacob and my stepdaughter Laurel just for being their uniquely wonderful selves and, along with their friends, keeping me connected enough to be able to write from the point of view of the young people in the novel. To my sister Jane for her continued encouragement and publishing expertise. And extra special thanks to my husband John for believing in me, and without whose loving encouragement, constructive suggestions, and invaluable knowledge of all things motorcycle, this book would undoubtedly have been the poorer.

Extra Terrestrial – *Gethin*

Somehow, I know before we start that my eighteenth will be a disaster.

It's not so much Mum's choice of a birthday treat – as in dragging my wasted self for a late lunch at the new café down the road. OK, it's not the coolest venue – the women all long grey hair and old hippy clothes; balding blokes in slacks and sandals; kids in home-made tie-dyes – but I'm happy to make the most of it, especially when I find it's actually not vegetarian.

And Mum's making an effort too. All done up in her new floaty top and plummy lipstick, twitching to hide her upset when I order the Pure Ground Steak Burger Special. I do good at acting surprised when the waiter pops a bottle of Cava.

But something about Mum is more edgy than usual. It breaks through in literally seconds with her stressing about her art installation, how she's losing faith in it, but I wouldn't understand. Then she uses this to justify her closing performance at my party last night, in a passive aggressive apology for screaming at my friends when she came in late from her studio.

'Well, it was just the run-of-the-mill drug-fuelled orgy,' I try a joke.

'Not in my bed!' she snaps.

'Aw, come on, Mum. You used to have a sense of humour.'

Let's face it, my relationship with Mum has been at breaking point for a fair while. Somehow, we know not to push it and we finish our food in silence. Just as well the restaurant fans are cooling the heavy hot air between us. Then Mum takes a decisive breath, like she's starting over, suggests another bottle of wine while I open my presents.

Her gift to me is an iPhone, all boxed and beautiful, and I am genuinely touched. As in it's been the most basic of mobiles up to now, and she's far from loaded. Then there's a card from the grandparents, sporting a cheque for a cool £500. We retreat for a few brief moments into some safe shared anecdotes about their ridiculousness. But then Mum tenses up again, shoving a card from Karen at me.

Karen was kind of like my auntie after she and Mum split up.

'I haven't seen her for ages. Since she took me bowling and shit,' I say, shaking out the quite acceptable £40 cash.

Mum starts on about how Karen was like the runner, between her and my sperm donor. She actually smiles when I share a sudden image of Karen in spray-on pink Lycra carrying a test-tube of spunk between her bouncing bazookas. She tells me Karen met the guy through her work, but Mum never knew who he was.

'So, I could get the dirt on him from Karen?'

I may be mildly curious at this point, but I'm still not prepared for what's coming.

'She got him to write some basic facts about himself, you know, for you to have when you grew up?' Mum looks at me, all blue-eyed saucers.

'She's got something written about my dad?'

Mum winces at the dad word. 'To tell you the truth, I'd kind of forgotten about him until Karen sent it. But we can look another time.' She chews her lip, looks down at her glass.

'She's fucking sent it? Have you got it with you?'

2

I lean forward to snatch her bag, but she grabs hold of it.

'Come on, you've told me about it now.'

There's a photo clipped to the letter of a guy in a biker jacket. Thirty-something, all straggly brownish hair and stubbly chin – looking like he's been caught out somehow. His name at the top: *Don McCalstry.*

'You are joking me,' I shake the photo at Mum. 'That's him?'

'I've never met him, Gethin. What does it say?' Her bony shoulders are sharp with tension.

It's not so much a letter as a list of vital statistics. I start reading out loud. '*Date of birth 6th May 1965.* He's a lot older than he looks.'

'It was taken nineteen years ago, remember.'

'He'll be even better looking now then! Height 5ft 10, weight 12st 7. OK, not too much of a fat fuckeroo…Oh, look, family health history: mother died of cancer, grandmother of heart disease, father suffers from asthma, mother had bouts of severe depression. Hey, bundle of laughs.' I feel my voice shake as I speak. Why the hell is this getting to me?

'It's stuff you may need to know, isn't it?' Mum's soft tone irritates me to fuck.

There's some blurb under the health bit. It goes like this:

'A bit about myself? Guess I'm something of a loner. Motorcycle mechanic, spending all my money on classic British motorbikes and associated memorabilia (if only there were a job in that…). Born in Lochgillan, NW Scotland, but moved to Glasgow when I was a kid. I escaped to Sheffield in 1982, but I've a yen to return to my ancestral home. See out my days roasting small mammals and blaeberries in a cave on the loch side, perhaps?

'Fucking laugh a minute. Greasy biker, lacks social skills, would NOT like to meet?'

Double frown now from Mum.

'Oh, Mum, fuck's sake!'

'Gethin, please, stop swearing, will you?'

Deep breath. 'OK, have I ever had a problem with how I was conceived?' My voice strains with the effort of trying to calm it down. 'You're a lesbian who wanted a child, so you found a sperm donor. I'm not exactly complaining, am I?'

'You always seemed proud to be different, I remember you telling people…'

'Maybe you were proud of being sooo alternative. To me it was no big deal.'

Mum shrinks back, like I'm about to slap her. I can't seem to stop this coming on all aggressive. Something about this whole thing I just don't need right now.

I lay the letter down as Mum does that sigh thing designed to get me, but I'm braced against its force.

'It's not just your conception that was important to me, but bringing you up to question things, to have an open mind, you know?' she says quietly.

'Until I chose to drop out of sixth form, is it?'

Mum bites her lip, all traces of lipstick gone now. 'It's just, you used to be so into everything…I find it hard, you doing nothing.'

She's sounding close to tears, and this does pull me back. I refill our glasses and try to think what's getting to me. I get a flash of this poster of hers by some 1920s German feminist. A collage jumble of heads and giant cogs with words like ANTI and DADA.

'You know that Dada picture?' I start.

'Ah yes, the Hannah Hoch?'

'There's a tiny line of random people trying to dance their way out of the crushing machines and those, like, faceless robots.'

'A bit like my dancing Greenham women pictures?'

'You've surrounded me with those images, and I'm not knocking it…' I struggle to hold onto my point.

'You had so many questions,' Mum interrupts.

'So why be surprised that I have a problem slotting into the shit world you taught me about?' I try to keep my voice gentle. 'As in the little people don't get out, do they?'

'They don't give up, that's really not what I taught you.'

'You had hippies and punk and music that meant stuff… that faith that things could change? But none of it exactly made any difference, did it?'

Mum takes a big breath. 'So, you lie down and do nothing? Stop wanting to know?'

'No, it's like *The Matrix*. I choose the Red Pill, remember?' I smile in a snap decision to pull away from this argument.

'Just waiting for Trinity then?' Mum says in a fair effort at lightening up.

I make a show of hopeful looking around, then shrug. 'Oh well, can I have pudding instead?'

'Blue Pill pudding?'

'You reckon? I'm not eating Zion gunk on my birthday.'

I think about *The Matrix* thing while scoffing sticky toffee pudding. Mum takes delicate mouthfuls of lemon parfait and I catch her shooting a glance at the sheet of paper. She looks up quickly with a guilty smile. Proper proper irritating.

'It's not that I don't want to know how things actually are.'

I lay my spoon on the empty dish. 'I get on at my friends for being pig ignorant, I hate all that.'

Mum nods, lips pursed.

I pick up the letter, glance at the smug CV. 'Did I ever complain about not having a dad?' My heartbeat pumping again.

'No. Gethin, come on now.' Mum's pleading is petrol on the flames.

'How long have you known about this?' My voice hoarse and strained.

'It's just you haven't asked for so long…'

'What fucking deal did you do with the jerk?' I bang the table with a jangle of cutlery.

'Gethin, please!' She nods towards some disapproving grey-slacks.

'You've always insisted on the truth, haven't you Mum? Mum?'

The tie-dye children get ushered to the door, the guy in charge stares from his corner.

'Gethin, you're really not listening,' Mum does controlled calm like I'm a kid in a supermarket kicking off for sweets. Not a chance of it working now that the lid's blown.

'So, how come I never knew about this?' I'm half out of my seat now, waving the paper at her. The owner guy's walking over and Mum shoots him a glance, puts her hand on my shoulder.

I shake Mum off as my chair clatters to the floor and I make for the door.

'Why would I want this tosser from outer space thrown at me now?'

Spanish Omelette – *Jez*

'Is that you, Jez?' Ken's cracked voice calling.

'No, it's Angelina frigging Jolie,' I holler, kicking the kitchen door open.

He's as I left him. Hospital bed in the corner, clutching cold coffee. I squeeze past the table that's too near the door. Moved to make room for the bed. Try suggesting he sleep in the living room? Oh no, he'll not be shoved out the way.

Park the bags and stick kettle on. Sweating cobs. Accrington air today thick enough to slice. Right sickly smell about him as I uncurl his bony yellow fingers from the mug. He brushes his hand over mine, rheumy eyes filling. I move to the kettle. Do not go Sentimental Dad before I'm even sat down. I open the Kenco and make us both a cup. Hand him his, black and strong.

He nods his thanks and I go back to the shopping.

'What the jeepers is this muck?' he croaks. Ah, Grumpy Git, that's more like it.

'Rich Roast.' I shake the jar at him. 'Makes a change from Tesco Bloody Value.'

He slops the coffee with his usual rant about me squandering his money on fancy goods. Collapses into a dry coughing fit at the sight of the Chocolate and Orange Cookies.

I take his mug and tip the coffee between his grey lips. He splutters, spraying my hand.

'I don't like to buy a large jar neither. Know where I am with a small one.'

'Here, try a cookie. My treat, so's the coffee.' I dump the change and receipt on the cabinet rammed beside the bed. 'Check, if you want.'

He licks at the chocolate on the biscuit. 'Too rich for me. Don't need your bleedin' charity neither.' Another lick, and another.

Unpack the shopping into the fridge and rickety cupboards. Everything minging with grease and a coating of nicotine yellow. Could lick the walls if you ran out of fags!

Back to my coffee. Flick though the *Bike* magazine, my random grab in Tesco.

'What you got there?' Chocolate round his mouth, no sign of the cookie.

I show him the fuck-off sports bike leaping off the cover.

'Unusual read for a lass like you?'

'And what would you expect?'

'I dunno, one of them celebrity fashion magazines.'

Look down at black top with ripped off sleeves, combats and pink Docs. 'And I look like a slave to celebrity fashion?'

'Pesky motorbikes…'

I skim an article about touring the north of Scotland. Superbly twisty empty roads, and not a speed camera past Inverness…

'Roll us a fag, love.'

It's just gone three. Cigarette, then afternoon meds. Routine set for a lifetime in just over three weeks. I find his illegal import Old Holborn. Make the thinnest possible fag.

'You're right lucky I turned up. Can't see social services rolling you fags.'

'Don't need bleedin' social workers. Don't need you neither.'

'No? I'll just find my dream bike and bugger off up the top end of Scotland, shall I?' I fish out my fags, light us both up.

'What sort of bike could *you* dream of?' He coughs with his first drag.

I flick through the glossy pages. Sexy curves of a Yamaha V-Max catch my eye. 'There. Just a question of, like, sixteen grand and a crash course in how to ride the fucker.'

'Crash course'll be about right,' he wheezes.

I tell him how Foster Bruv Martin got me well into bikes, then how Boyfriend Stan used to let me blast his Honda CB500 over the moors. Was that the most powerful buzz ever? Shame it wasn't so simple with the boyfriend.

'Well you can be off whenever you please.' Ken strains for the ashtray.

I shift the trolley table across the bed, and he focuses on flicking his ash.

'Tempting,' I say, 'but I'm not one for making plans. Like, did I plan to come here?'

'So, what brought you nosing your way into my life?'

Here we go again. 'The search for adventure?'

'Your mum turfed you out, more like.'

So, back on repeat, I tell him again how Mum needed me to clear out my room for a new foster kid. At twenty-three years old, I was only like, home between jobs.

'Nice kind of mother you ended up with. She chose to adopt you, didn't she?' He bangs the bed with his fist.

Deep drag on my cigarette, exhale slowly. Pull back from pointing out it's hardly his place to criticise my mum. Don't rise to that one, girl!

'Won't be keeping you long…doctor gave me six weeks and that were…'

'Four weeks and five days ago? Don't worry, I'm not in a hurry.'

'Bugger off whenever it pleases you. Just like me bleedin' proper kids.'

'And I'm not a proper kid, am I?' I go to the drawer for his medication. Slam the bottles on the counter.

'You know what I'm on about.' He closes his eyes.

I lean back, calm my breathing. Getting upset is helping how? The proper kids don't even know he's ill. The argument is just part of the routine.

Count out his meds. Pour a shot of Teacher's in the stained cut-glass tumbler. How much fuss was there letting me near the whisky? Dragged himself to the locked cabinet until I persuaded him I don't even like it. All about me subtly doing more and more.

I put the drink and pills on the table. Flick the ash off the fag, put it back between his fingers.

'Don't deserve a lass like you.' Eyes filling with gooey tears.

'Fuck's sake, Schmaltzy Daddy don't suit you.'

'Social workers traced me when Alice died.' He clutches at the whisky glass with no attempt to drink. 'I'd no idea she'd had a kid, Jez.' His body rigid as he tries to sit up.

'It's alright, Ken, we've been through this.'

I feel the hard knob of his shoulder bone as I rearrange the pillows. He stares ahead, breathing jerky. I rescue the biscuit squidged down the side. He hardly touched his breakfast, either. I'll ask Sandy to help me change the bedding later.

He tries another suck on his dead-looking fag. I take it from him and get it lit again, guide it to his mouth for the last drag. His lips like sandpaper against my fingertips. He coughs out the smoke in a terrible rattle. Reaches for the water bottle and pours a bit on his lips and down his front. Leans back clutching both bottle and glass.

'This place goes back to the Corporation when I'm gone,' he carries on.

'Here, have your meds, will you?'

'You can't wait for me to nap. With your fancy coffee and motorbikes.'

Wey-Hey, we're back to normal.

I take the fag-end and water. Put the beaker of pills in his hand. He pops a pill, then downs a sip of whisky. The power of routine! Another pill, another sip, emptying the beaker. He lays his head back. Eyes shut. His skin is right thin and papery over his thick-set face. You could stick your finger through it.

'You was already settled with that foster family and they wanted to adopt you,' he whistles a whisper, clenches his fists. 'I was, divorce, nowhere to live, proper kids turned against me. I would've took you…'

'I never knew owt different.'

'Makes you wonder though, don't it?' He opens his eyes, bulging like marbles in their dark sockets.

'Things were as they were, Ken.' I move to the sink.

How routine is this conversation? Refuse each time to get into What Ifs. Now I catch myself wondering how would I have been like brought up by him, his proper kids, all that?

'Sixteen grand on a bleedin' motorcycle? To get splattered across a blind corner.'

'You think I've got sixteen grand? Go to sleep.'

I rinse out the pots, listening for his breathing to steady. But it gets raspier, more uneven. Forcing me to look over.

'Spice rack,' he waves like a maniac at me.

It's one of them seventies orange-varnished jobs loaded

with bottles of faded spices. Welded to the wall with the grease like everything.

'It's behind it,' he gasps, falling back on the pillows.

'It's behind you!' I do panto, looking closer at the rack.

Then I spot a small grease-coated envelope stuffed behind the oregano and paprika.

'I want you to have it,' he says.

It's a fuzzy old Polaroid of a young woman with bleached blond hair piled up. Pale thin face, like she's sucking her cheeks in. I lean back on the kitchen counter. Stare at the heavily made-up big grey eyes. They look caught unawares. I feel my breath squeezed, tight in my chest.

Ken beckons me over. Squints at the photo, then at me.

'Pretty lass, she were. Delicate, like. You get your big bones from my side.' He gives a wheezy chuckle.

I laugh with relief at his daft insult. Tell him how the social workers couldn't believe I was such a chunky baby – apparently, they joked I'd been swopped at birth. That shadow-life I sometimes day-dreamed – my real parents bringing up some pale little wench who had stolen my life.

I lay the picture in the pages of my magazine and open the fridge. What to cook?

'I kidded myself on I were looking after her,' Ken starts rambling. 'Helping her back home, she could hardly stand.'

Sausages, peppers, eggs…

'I should've known better, I were married with kids, made it plain to her.'

'She asked you in and got you dancing.' I repeat the story he's already told me. With her flimsy green dress and scratchy Whitney Houston *Greatest Love of All*. Now I can put a face to this corny movie twisting my guts.

I pick up the sausages. Study their label without taking it in.

'What else did you buy on this spree of yours?' His eyes open just a crack.

'Caviar, oysters, truffles. Make a change from chips and egg?'

'You can please yourself, I'm not hungry.' He sinks back into his pillows.

Did Sandy say he would lose his appetite, as well as sleeping more? Something's got to tempt him.

'It were like she were trying to wipe everything out. And the bloke in me, couldn't help mesen. Sickened me forever the regret of it.'

'But if you hadn't, there'd be no me.'

He nods, pulls the sides of his mouth down. Hard to see he's right pleased at this idea.

'I never saw her again. Someone else were renting the bedsit. She were never in the bar, I looked, over and over.' His voice shakes like I've not heard before.

'Ken, get some rest.' I go to stroke his arm, solid under the papery skin. He's right about being big boned.

He opens his mouth and starts to snore. Tobacco stains on his bottom teeth. White fuzz of his tongue.

Retreat to the fridge.

Colour's what we need, that's why I bought peppers. Peppers, eggs, potatoes, Finest Sicilian Sausages. We could go Mediterranean.

'I know,' I slam the fridge door. Could even chuck in herbs from the spice rack.

His hands twitch on the duvet. Breathing settled to a regular rasp.

'Spanish omelette,' I announce.

Go Down to the Woods – *Gethin*

Francesca crashes through the thicket, bashing her rucksack against the overhanging branches, texting as she goes.

'For fuck's sake, where the hell are they?' She swings round to belt her bag into a young silver birch.

'What's with the big hurry?' I push through behind her as the birch branch snaps back in my face. 'It's only six o'clock, chill out.'

I follow her through a narrow space between two holly bushes. Trip on a bramble and get catapulted into a clearing, breaking my fall on the nearest available object, as in the bulk of Jarvis' back. He tips over and I land splayed on top of him.

'Fuck, I was making a spliff, Dickhead!' Jarvis jerks to roll me off him.

'Sorree!' I jump up and Jarvis frowns, brushing off the dusty earth. I peer at the ground to pick up bits of what could be weed.

'No worries. I'll start again.' Jarvis turns his saintly smile on. He's the weirdest, like all sparking anger ready to explode something massive, then puff, back to nothing's-gonna-bother-me Jarvis. Tucking his hair behind those big bulgy ears, he starts on another doob.

I stand for a minute and look around. There's a fire-pit of burnt-out cans in the centre of the clearing; a few half-charred logs to sit on; patches of parched grass and nettles around the edge. I feel relief literally pulsating through me. I'm here, with the gang, at last.

They've got a tent up on the far side and there's movement in it. I stroll over and bend to unzip the door just as Emily pops her head out and screams.

'Oh My God! What the hell are *you* doing here?' She crawls out, pointing her chin at me, accusing.

I am so not over Emily, though it's been a good four months since she literally dumped me by text. She's been nothing but mean to me since, but it still cuts me up how I've lost that sexy, sparky girlfriend, however screwy, which she was, is, totally, screwy.

'I'm, like, just a couple of hours early…' I mutter.

'Gethie's mummy upset him,' Francesca says, slinging her arm round me.

'How can Pat upset anyone?' Emily shakes her head.

Emily loves to put my mum on some pedestal. Like when she's told Mum how her mother neglected her, reliving her youth with numerous lovers. All about how lucky I am.

'Yeah, don't we all know you have the monopoly on difficult mothers?' I say.

'Ooo!' I hear Fran as I walk back towards Jarvis.

How is it Fran can be a good mate one to one and then such a twat to me in company? Don't need the girls winding me up like this.

'We could do with a fire.' I gather some random twigs.

'Ben's gone for wood.' Jarvis beams at me.

'Ben's here? Awesome!'

I walk towards the sound of breaking wood. The evening light is metal-heavy with the heatwave that looks like breaking soon. The trees glow luminous as I breathe in the scent of vegetation, shake my shoulders out. I will feel that relief.

15

'Hey, Gethin! Sick!' Ben drops the pile of branches he's carrying, dodging them with his pink Converses. He ruffles his hand through his tight dark curls, then grabs me by the T shirt and plants a whopping kiss on my lips.

'How's the gorgeous birthday boy?' He takes my arms and bends them straight out from the elbow. 'Here, butch bro, have a present!' He loads up my arms with wood and picks up the remaining few branches. 'Any birthday surprises?' He kicks me lightly on the arse and I set off down the path.

'Don't talk to me about surprises!' I shout over my shoulder.

Back at the camp, Emily is helping Francesca with her tent. It is so Fran: orange with big white daisies. I dump the wood and Jarvis passes me the spliff. I watch Emily walk across from the tents, her blond ponytail catching the light. Does she have to keep looking so cute? I take a few drags then pass the spliff to Ben. Squat down to break small twigs for kindling.

'Aw, Ben, you should see Fran's tent. She's got like raspberry muslin drapes, and lemon-yellow cushions.' Emily laughs.

'Fabuloso, good enough to eat,' Ben camps it up. 'I hope I'm one of the girls for the sleepover tonight.'

'Totally!' Emily smiles as she whips the spliff from Ben and moves towards me.

'Did Francesca tell you her parents are getting married?' Emily says, frowning as I look up, like it's a massive effort to talk to me.

'What? You are joking me. Grace and Sebbie?' I can't help being interested. 'Have you heard my mum on the subject of Sebbie? He's not exactly marrying material.'

Francesca comes up to poke me in the back. 'It's not decided yet. But I think he really wants to, and he's always been my dad.'

'Of course, he's your dad...' I look up at her glare and decide to drop it.

'There's no *of course* about it,' Emily piles in. 'Like my mum when she ran away with lover boy.'

'Yeah well, that's different.' I swear if I hear another thing about her mum...

'How's it different?'

I wave her question away. When Emily's mum moved to Spain and she was forced to live with her dad, I tried to support her, then got dumped for my trouble. I so don't want to talk about it. I turn back to the fire as Jarvis dishes out cans of Red Stripe. Cheers. Nice One.

'Anyone got any scrap paper I can burn?' I call out.

People pat their pockets. 'No, sorry. Nope.'

Fran runs to her tent and comes back with an A4 printout. 'Exam timetable!' She does a joyous dance as she waves it in my face. 'Yesterday was my last one! Let the non-stop partying continue!' She opens her can with a flourish.

'Hey, I've still got my higher maths to come.' Ben shakes his head, like in mock worry, but you know it is actually real.

'Come on then, I'll practice you.' Jarvis taunts. 'Pi to fifty digits.'

'Oh please!' Emily sticks her nose in the air.

But they're off, Jarvis and Ben replaying their famous Pi fight with Fran egging them on. Was there really a time when this was my world? It wasn't even that long ago.

'...932384,' Jarvis is already about twenty digits in. 'What's next, Ben, for your A in maths?'

17

'I have absolutely no idea, mate.'

'Aw, you'll just have to join us wastrels,' Jarvis smirks.

'Oh, as if!' Emily says. 'Ben will get straight A Stars for sure, and Fran's gonna hit the grades for her design course.'

'Celebrations all round!' Jarvis lifts his can. 'Even I'm going to Off The Record studios in the autumn.'

'Are you?' I say, looking round at the others to share my disbelief.

'Apprenticeship in sound engineering.'

'Fuck, Wasteman?' I say. Jarvis has earned his nickname with serious levels of inactivity. 'I'll be the lone stoner!' I light Fran's exam timetable and stuff it under the twigs.

'It'll just be me and you then, Geth,' Emily says as I give the flame a blow. 'Without a future.'

I feel the dead weight of her words and remember how I was also blamed for her dropping out of college. The fire whips through the paper and fizzles out. I sit back on my heels, head drooped useless. Listen to the cackle of a bird in the trees.

'Here, use this.' Ben pulls a Metro out of his bag. 'Forgot I had it.'

'Ah, did you see that about Selena Gomez's boob job?' Emily starts them on a load of celebrity gossip drivel.

I tear out a page with a picture of a couple of dusty boys scrabbling about in burnt-out ruins in Gaza.

'Is she going out with Justin Bieber or not now?' Fran carries on.

'As if any of that bollocks is news,' I say. 'Does even one of you have a clue about Gaza, for instance?' I scrunch up the picture, shove it under the twigs, light the paper.

'They will blow each other to fuck whatever.' Jarvis pulls his call-me-stupid look.

'Well, that does seem the way in the Middle East,' Emily adds.

'If you knew what a bunch of ignorant fuckeroos you all sound…' I chuck some more twigs on the fire as the flames flicker through. 'Back me up, Ben?'

'I'm with you all the way, mate.' Ben does care at least. Not surprisingly, his dad being an Iranian refugee. He takes a breath, holding his shoulders tense. 'But I guess the guys are taking a holiday today, so…'

'Yeah, take a break from Negative?' Francesca lowers her face with a pleading smile.

I feel bad instantly, Fran has just finished her exams. Negative is practically my middle name with this crowd. Still, I resent having to listen to such thoughtless crap, and then having to feel bad about it.

I feed the fire some bigger sticks. Get my face to the ground and blow; hear the crackle of the spreading flames.

'Hot Breath Geth,' Ben says eventually.

'Nice one.' Jarvis lights a freshly rolled spliff.

I sit back, take a couple of sips of beer, then I'm up again, breaking up more wood.

'Hey, chill out now, man.' Jarvis gestures to me with a wave of smoke.

I hesitate, still not happy, then I reach for the spliff. 'OK, I am that shallow: bribe me with drugs and I will lighten up.' I treat them all to a mega grin.

'Yo, bro!' says Ben. 'Tell us about your birthday surprise.'

'Surprise?' Emily accuses.

The evening sun breaks through the heavy cloud, lighting the swirls of wood smoke. I take a breath. Is this why I'm still feeling so wired? I start to tell them about Don's letter, hoping I can get it out my system.

'Whoa,' Ben speaks for them all. 'You have a dad?'

I pull out the envelope and hand it to Ben, signal the OK for him to open it.

Ben's eyebrows twitch as he reads, suppressing a giggle. He looks up and mouths Oh My God.

'Let me see!' Emily grabs the letter and Francesca comes to look with her. More gasps and OMGs. It's almost gratifying.

'That's your dad?' Emily's eyes couldn't get rounder.

'Have a look at this.' Fran squeezes herself next to Jarvis on his log.

'It's the weirdest, to think of him as an actual person,' I muse. 'As in living a life somewhere, like totally fucking oblivious?'

'You've got a dad, Gethin.' I swear Emily's eyes are filling – maybe it's the smoke.

'He's not a dad. Fuck's sake. It's like some seedy internet dating blurb. Fun times for the future roasting blaeberries? What the hell are blaeberries anyway?'

'The bikes sound pretty sick,' Ben chips in. 'All sexy leather and shiny chrome?'

'Wallace and Gromit sidecar?' Fran adds.

'You could find him,' Emily pipes up.

'No way! Shut the fuck up, the lot of you!' I shout.

'He must have cared, why would he write that for you?' Emily keeps on, regardless.

'I can't get my head round him existing, never mind if he gives a toss.' I rub my hand over my eyes. The image of him in that photo sticks, as if he's been created fully malformed.

'You must find him, Gethin; it would make such a difference for you to have a dad.'

'Bollocks Emily.'

Nobody says anything. I break some more sticks, the sound of the wood cracking magnified. The sky darkens heavy purple as the sun disappears.

Jarvis lopes over to me with the letter.

'What do *you* think, Jarvis?'

'Don't get me on the subject of dads.' He grimaces, holds the letter above the fire.

I can see the heat waves rising, the paper starting to curl.

'What should I do?' my voice strains to get the words out.

'Simples. You've just turned eighteen. And you need another parent?'

He's right. Just think of *him* stuck with a stepdad he can't stand, his real dad making an unwelcome appearance literally three or four times in his life. And Emily left to deal with her depressive father on her own. Who needs it?

Blood banging in my eardrums. I glance around the fire: Emily leaning forward, a wired spring; Ben's face pulled sharp by a frown; Fran's questioning eyebrows.

'Yeah, what do *I* need with some anti-social cave dwelling old biker daddy?'

Jarvis lowers the letter nearer the flames, expression deadpan as only Jarvis can do.

'Go on then,' I say.

He looks at me again, but I don't flinch. He's about to let go when Emily jumps up and snatches the letter.

'No! You can't let him do that, Gethin.'

She hands me the paper, all eyes on me. Rumble of thunder in the distance.

My heart thumps as I stare at the letter, my alleged dad's

21

picture clipped to the top. I'm stunned by the force of my reaction.

'OK,' I say, faking a lightness I don't feel. 'It's not as if burning will actually stop him existing now?'

I fold the letter and put it in my pocket. Hold my hand out to the first heavy drops of rain as the thunder breaks again.

A Different Conception – *Pat*

The waterlogged haze fills the streets outside my bedroom window, my eye tracing pictures in the salmon pink dissolving streetlight. It must be nearly ten, just the odd swish of a car punctuating the stillness at the end of this June day.

I look at the forgotten collage spread across the worktable. Unearthed in a frenzy of displacement junk-clearing after the debacle of Gethin's birthday lunch, now it tortures me with his rose-tinted childhood. All I need with one day to go before my submission deadline.

The collage is an eight-foot-long piece of calico sewn with a trail of Gethin's life. Starting with the ten-mil syringe of his conception; the twenty-week scan; Gethin minutes old with his screwed-up face in that mass of dark hair and those big red baby balls. Then it spreads wider: his first pair of shoes, lock of hair; Gethin and Francesca in the double buggy with holly piled high in the rain cover. I added to the collage over the years: Gethin as Pied Piper in the school play; his drawing of the cat in a space helmet in its fiery rocket; clippings from his Horrible Science and astronomy magazines. Every time he had a clear-out, I stole the icons of the just-gone days. He knows nothing about it, but would he even care? At least these days I have a wider focus for my art, which is really where I need to be right now.

I turn back to the sketches for the installation. If only I could recapture the buzz of those first drawings. Experimenting with a 3D setting to explore the contradictions of contemporary political art. So excited to be accepted for the *Cuttin' Edge* exhibition after all those years of isolation and rejection. And now the crashing doubt.

For this, Gethin's eighteenth became incidental. Leaving him to his party while I worked in the studio, coming home and picking my way through the bodies. Losing it as I turfed a couple out of my bedroom. His friends edging their way to the door, and me screaming at him to stop shouting.

'*You're* shouting, Mum.'

By the time I'd finished, the friends had gone, he'd stormed off to his room, and I was left with the dregs of their strange drinks, wondering what happened when my son grew up.

I hear a step and jump up, expecting Gethin. But it's Grace peeping round the doorway, her dark bob framing those wide mascaraed eyes and luscious red-lipsticked mouth.

'The door was open, I was calling. Are you all right, babe?'

'Apart from throwing myself into this sentimental diversion...?'

'Wow!' Grace comes to get a closer look at the collage. 'Babe, only you would think of such a beautiful thing. Look at that!' She points to the picture Francesca drew of them hollowing out a pumpkin, sewn in next to the chewed end of a severed latex finger.

'It was your idea, as I remember.' I lean into her, a surge of gratitude that she's here. 'I was going to do some Bayeux tapestry thing about Greenham, but it didn't happen, and when Gethin was a baby you suggested I use it for a record of my journey with him.'

'Did I? But it needed your gorgeously creative self to make it.' Grace puts her arm around me.

'You convinced me it wasn't pure self-indulgence. *A Different Conception*, you called it.'

'I always thought it was something to shout about, the way you had Gethin.' She turns to look at me, that beautiful smile.

I can't help smiling too, especially when Grace catches sight of the syringe.

'Oh My God!' She points in an exaggerated gesture. 'Babe, I thought you extracted the sperm with it, needle and everything!' She claps her hand over her mouth.

I snort my laughter as I remember explaining the mechanics of self-insemination. She'd talked me into going to the pub after ante-natal class, saying we were officially allowed two units a week.

'I was intrigued by you saying you'd chosen to be a single parent. The rest of them annoyed me in their cosy coupledom.' Grace squeezes my arm.

'Aw, remember when we bumped into each other again after they were born. Me with my ancient gabardine pram,' I start.

'Babe, it reminded me of pushing my little brothers and sisters in just such a thing!'

'We went back to yours for a coffee, remember? Exchanging life stories in about half an hour.' I loved Grace right from the start, and she was totally unfazed by my lesbian lifestyle. She's a good ten years younger, but we practically raised those kids together.

'All that time gone by, look!' She to points to the lacy cap that she knitted Gethin. 'Do you remember everyone thought he was a girl?'

I nod, suddenly choked with the loss of those simple times. I glance across to the junior school days: Sheffield United badge from when football ruled, then his Top Gear cool chart. That tinge of guilty disappointment at how boy-orientated he'd become.

'I had such ideals of bringing up a child, you know, to value themselves and question the status quo.' My voice chokes as I say this.

'And that's exactly what you did. Gethin's a credit to you. He's open, sensitive…'

I nod unconvincingly. 'He won't talk to me anymore.'

'And he's growing up, feeling a bit lost. Show some faith in him.' Grace stiffens her shoulders and moves along the collage.

I take a breath, hold back the protest I feel at this. She thinks I have no faith in him?

Grace unrolls the end of the calico and points to the picture of Gethin and Francesca at the school prom. So beautiful. I bite my lip as she looks up at me.

'It just shows how I directed all my creativity into him. Quite unhealthy, really.'

'Aw, how can that be unhealthy? You should finish it, take it up to eighteen.'

'He won't want it – all he does is rage at me.' I feel my voice swell with resentment.

'You should hear Francesca when she gets going. Believe me, he will treasure this.' She pauses at the last picture of Gethin waving his GCSE results with that loony grin. 'Look at him there, so pleased with himself.'

'But there's been nothing but torn Rizla packs for the collage since then.'

She pulls back as if shocked at my tone. 'How about a Champagne cork from his party?' she says, forcing a lightness.

'So, perhaps I should have cracked the Champagne at midnight instead of spending half the night at the studio and coming home to yell at his friends.'

'I can see that might piss him off.'

I look at the picture of Gethin a couple of years ago in that shirt with the blue roses I gave him. It's my fiftieth and he's got his arm round me, glass of bubbly in the other hand. I sigh, remember how we'd argued the day before. Grace touches my hand.

'We had Cava today when I took him out for lunch,' I say.

'There you go, cork from his first legal drink.'

'Just drop it with the collage, will you?' I yank the end of the calico away from her.

She takes a step back, picks up her bag and turns to face me, hands on hips.

'I don't know what's got into you these days. I've hardly seen you, so I thought I'd pop in and see how you're doing, drop off a card for Gethin, and I get my head bitten off.'

'It's just, Gethin's not here, Grace.'

'They've gone out camping, Fran said. But it's hardly the point.' She fiddles with her bag clasp.

'No, I'm sorry,' I try to explain. 'He stormed out of his birthday lunch and I've been so deflated and pissed off with him, to tell the truth. I should be focussing on my installation.'

Grace lets out a heavy sigh. Steps towards me and touches my arm.

'You're upset, darling. Shall I make us a coffee, love?'

I blink back the tears that spring from nowhere. I don't deserve her kindness.

'Hey babe, you want to hear my news?' Grace sits at the kitchen table rolling a joint. 'You all right with this?'

'Of course, it's what I expect of you.' See Grace and the chance of a smoke: the idea of both generally cheers me up.

'Anyway.' She fits the roach, running her tongue over her top lip. 'My news?'

'Go on then.'

She lights the joint with a flourish. 'Sebbie has only asked me to marry him.' She takes a toke, then exhales as a grin spreads over her pretty cheekbones.

'No! You are kidding me.'

'I swear, down on one knee, diamond...' Her smile is straight from a teen magazine.

I sneak a glance at her left hand, but there's nothing. Of course, she wouldn't.

'I said I need to see some commitment. My priority is Francesca, I'm in no rush...'

'You told him no, right?'

She passes me the joint. 'No, babe, I didn't.'

I take a puff, nicotine dizzy as I sip my coffee, totally at a loss for what to say.

'I know what you're thinking. But he says he wants to try; he's agreed to go to Relate...'

'Oh, he'll say he wants to be with you until you expect something of him, then he'll be out the door with no explanation.'

'But I play a part in that as well, and if he can acknowledge he's got a problem...'

'It's total crap, Grace, and you know it.' I feel so angry and upset with her, I don't know what to do with it.

She pulls herself up, tidies her bits of roach card. 'You could have a bit of faith in me too, you know?'

'After twenty years and a child? Really?' Sebbie has been a point of contention between us before. I have never got why she won't cut free from their endless can't-live-with-can't-live-without cycle.

'The child is grown, and he's always been her father.' Grace packs up her little smoking tin.

'All those times he's let you down?' I think about Sebbie too busy playing pool to take her to see her dying father. Or when Francesca was in hospital and he wouldn't fetch some ice cream. Like a child having tantrums, refusing to make up for months on end. Then finding his sweet side and charming her into giving it one more chance.

'Babe, he knows he needs to change all that.'

'Well, I thought you had more sense,' I say, passing back the joint.

'No, babe, you keep it, I'm off.' She pulls her bag to her shoulder.

'Don't go, please, I'm sorry, really.' I feel the panic rising again. 'Gethin's gone, Grace, I don't know what to do.'

'He'll be back.' She turns towards the door.

'I upset him, really badly.' I feel the tears again, emotion intensified by the dope.

'You're not the first parent to scream at a bunch of teenagers.'

'Please, I'll make another coffee.' I can hear the whine in my voice.

She stands fiddling with her bag strap, takes a glance at her watch.

'Well OK, but you need to get off your moral high-horse, babe.'

So, I make us another drink and sit down to tell her about Gethin.

'He says I've been on at him, but maybe getting off his arse is the cure for that?'

'Did you not lay off for his birthday?' Grace frowns at me.

'Of course. We had a slap-up lunch with a load of wine, maybe too much wine…I bought him a bloody iPhone.'

'iPhone cool, no?' She nods her approval.

'But then, you see, there was this letter Karen gave me for him.'

'Karen? Wow! Blast from the past?'

I remind her how Karen had sorted out my sperm donor. 'I never even knew his name and I was more than happy with that. I wanted a child all by myself, although Karen had a lot of involvement to start with, as you know.'

'He was always your son, darling.'

I nod as I pull myself back to the point. 'I knew a couple of women with donors who played Daddy to their kids, but to tell you the truth, I didn't want some random man's involvement. I would have been happy to pay a sperm bank.'

I explain how Karen found this bloke from her work who agreed to be a non-involved donor. 'She got him to write a few details about himself for Gethin to have when he grew up. It seemed better for the child than total anonymity, or at least, Karen thought so.'

'She could have been right. Kids like to know where they come from, don't they?' Grace smiles as she passes the joint.

'Gethin wasn't so pleased when I gave him the sperm donor's letter this afternoon?'

I take a deep puff and feel a lurch of panic as the dope takes hold. Not really the relief I was hoping for. I pick up my coffee and slop some over the table. Jesus, what on earth is the matter with me? Grace stares at me impassively, or critically is what it feels like.

'The thing is the letter was never my idea. I did mention it when Gethin was little, but after we'd established how he was conceived, he didn't seem interested in the donor.'

'So why did you give it him?'

'Karen sent it to me just before his birthday. Once I had possession of it – I couldn't withhold the information, could I?'

'Not sure I'd have picked handing it over straight after the iPhone.'

'You think I planned it that way?' I snap.

'OK babe,' Grace waves her hands in a calm-down gesture. 'He didn't take it well?'

'He caused an almighty scene and stormed out of the café.' I describe him pushing me away as his chair clattered to the floor, my every nerve sharpened, the café owner stepping forward. 'I don't understand this rage coming out of nowhere, Grace.'

'Babe, it's probably best you take a break from each other.'

'What do you mean? Am I so hard to talk to?'

'You're not even looking at why he might feel so angry.'

'And you can see that?' I tense against the rising fury.

Grace pulls herself up. 'I can't talk to you like this – you know how I am?' That sweet apologetic smile. She has told me that confrontation reminds her of her dad when she was a child. Is that really what I'm doing now?

I take a breath, still desperate to keep her here. 'I'm sorry, we'll change the subject.'

'No, babe, like I said, I just popped in.' She walks to the door, turns to force a smile.

'It's my submission deadline on Monday, the show opens on Friday. I feel all at sea...' I'm annoyed at how pathetic that sounds, but I can't bear her to go.

'Then focus on it. It'll work out with Gethin. Good luck with the installation, babe.'

No tomorrows – *Jez*

The clock ticks through the numbness as I sit. Hands wrapped round the cold coffee mug. The world has dropped away – only the bed and the chair, pool of light from the lamp. Cool smoothness of the mug. Line of my combats against the dirty cream bedspread. His face on the pillow: grey line of square chin, hollow cheeks, dark eye sockets. How long since that last quiet breath? The clock ticks but time doesn't move.

Still I'm convinced I see his chest rise under the covers. Hold my hand to his nose to be sure. Can't believe he won't wake up and shout me to roll a fag to hang between his dried-up lips. Moisten his mouth with whisky ice-cubes. That time last night when he suddenly stirred, staring at me with opaque blue eyes, like he was right far away trying to locate himself. I held his hand. Wondered how that could possibly help.

I look at his face again, the lines of his life somehow smoother. He's not there anymore. I'm like watching myself watching.

Shiver through my body – am I cold? What did Sandy say to do? Phone the doctor? I've been sitting here all day and half the night. His rattling breath the only sound for hours, getting quicker, slowing right down until finally there wasn't another breath. I don't know when I made the coffee – black, like it was for him. Something like fear rises through the numbness – clench my teeth to keep it in. My hands are cold, but I'm breaking sweat.

Look at the clock: two in the morning. What time did he die? What if it was like an endless agony when time has no meaning? Fear rises again – call the doctor. I key the number without thinking. Count the rings, one, two, three, four…

'Hello?' Her worried voice.

'Mum?'

Running through trees towards the duck pond. Ken chasing me, howling like a demented dog. Down the grassy slope, his rasping breath behind me. Slip and fall on muddy grass. He pins me to the ground, face waxy yellow, breath hot and sour as he plants a wet kiss on my cheek. No, Ken, get the fuck off me!

'Woof, woof.'

I wake with a jolt and it's a scrawny boy licking my face.

'What the hell?' I push him off and he pulls himself up to kneel beside me.

'Woof.' He cocks his head, tongue hanging out.

I rub my eyes, working out where I am. On the settee at Mum's? The boy pants and paws at my arm. He's about eight, all matted curls and cheekbones poking out of a greyish face. Pond-water eyes. I pat him on the head. The dream-sense still live – Ken reincarnated into this mad boy-dog? I push my feet against the arm of the settee to stretch out. How familiar is this room with the worn flowery carpet, grubby mint-green walls? The dancing elephant batik hanging over the litter of photos and homemade ornaments on the mantle-shelf. Stuff everywhere. And in the corner a new widescreen telly. Dad's latest dodgy deal?

The boy-dog barks as the door opens.

'I see you've met Joey.' Mum hangs on to two cups of hot tea as Joey bounds on all fours towards her. He's got a brown furry tail sewn into the back of his jogging pants. He rubs his head against Mum's pyjamaed legs, woofs as she nods at him.

'Let me put this tea down, Joey.' She hands me a cup, sits on the edge of the settee. Adjusts her old red dressing gown. Joey leans against her thigh as she strokes his hair.

'Your latest foster?'

'Been here two weeks, haven't you Joey?'

'What's with the tail?'

'It helps him put his trousers on the right way round.' She laughs.

I notice his Action Man T shirt is on back to front – six pack hanging limp from Joey's bony back. Mum sighs, looks over at the DVD clock. It's only 7:15. Joey curls up on the furry blanket lying by the settee.

'That's right,' Mum says. 'Joey have a doggie-nap.'

'What day is it?' I ask.

'Wednesday. He's off school for an inset day. But no lie-ins at this joint, I'm afraid. You could have a sleep in my bed, the little ones will be down soon.'

I shrug. Sip my tea. 'How come you've got the girls?'

'Sonya and Ron have been working flat out on this house they're doing up. They need to get it on the market.'

'Working all through the night, were they?'

'So I believe. Jez, why didn't you tell me about Ken before?'

'I called you last night?'

'But, what, four weeks with him? I thought you were off job-hunting up the coast.'

'And you could do what with two toddlers and a boy-dog in tow?'

Mum bites her lip. 'I could have talked to you.'

'Talked me out of it, more like.'

She takes a breath, holds it. Joey gives a little whimper. She pats his head, and he settles back down. 'That's hardly fair, Jez,' she says, quietly.

She's right. She's always been open with everything she knew about my parents, how I could find out more. But now she's upset with me, it makes me mean.

'It's only, I thought you'd decided against finding him, after you contacted the agency last year.' She still sounds right hurt. 'But you know I would have supported you whatever.'

'Well, I read the agency letter again when I was clearing my room last month, so I thought, might as well see him as I had nowt else to do. It's not far to Accrington on the bus.'

'So, why move in? It's a lot for a girl your age, all on your own like that.'

'Look, I called you last night. Be glad about that.'

'Oh Jez.' She gives my hand a squeeze.

Joey spins away into the middle of the room, chasing his tail and barking. The door opens and Cherry comes in clutching a tatty ball-gowned Barbie. She stops as she sees me.

'What are you doing here?'

'I could ask you the same.'

She screws up her face and looks at Mum. 'Poppy wants to get out of the cot, Grandma.'

Joey's barking gets more frantic as he whirls around.

'Shut up, Joey!' Cherry screams.

Mum puts her hands over her ears. 'Don't shout, Cherry. What have I told you?'

'You should tell him not to bark.' Cherry pulls her Barbie close.

Mum catches Joey by his arms. He barks in her face. 'Come on, let's put your programme on and I'll make some breakfast.' She grabs the remote as Joey starts spinning again. 'Joey, sit!' Best dog trainer voice, pointing at the bean bag in front of the telly.

The DVD whirrs into action with a Special Edition Cruft's. Joey woofs happily and lies staring at the screen.

Now there's a banging and screaming from upstairs and Mum hurries out of the room.

Cherry pulls a smug grin at me. 'Why are you sleeping on the settee?'

'Because, funnily enough, there are no beds left in this mad house.'

'I'm not mad.' She sticks her button nose in the air.

'But you're in my bed.'

She screws her brow trying to think of a good answer. Mum comes in carrying the tear-stained two-year-old. She plonks her down with a kiss on the head. Pulls out the old garage and box of cars. Poppy grabs the battered London bus and sticks it in her mouth.

'No, Poppy!' Cherry rushes over to snatch the toy.

'Will you two play nicely while I get everyone's breakfast?' Mum shoots Cherry a stern look.

I swear Mum's more stick-insect than ever, with dark shadows under her eyes. And that aubergine hair colour does her no favours.

'Coffee?' she asks, taking my cup as I pull the sleeping bag over my head.

The settee smells of stale milk and crumbs – takes me back to days off sick from school. Making the most of a sore throat while Mum brought me ice-cream. The only time I ever had her to myself. Sudden ache for that rare cocoon. Like there's any fucking chance.

As if to prove it the door opens again.

'Such a racket, no way can I sleep.' Aisha squashes in by my feet on the settee. Arranges her laptop over her furry dressing gown. 'So, what the heck are you doing here?'

'Just crashing like for a few days,'

'Moving back in, more like.' She flicks her silky black hair and clicks on her computer.

'Not if I can help it.' Sudden churning panic that I have no other plan. Pull my knees closer into me.

Aisha shifts, reaching behind her to pull something out. 'Oh My God, how long have you had this old thing?' She holds the stuffed tiger upside down by his tail.

I reach for my Zooey. Did Mum tuck him in with me last night? Aisha pulls back and sits him on her laptop. His fur is matted and worn, ears flopping onto his sad face.

I remind her he's called Zooey because Dad bought him for me on a trip to the zoo after I was adopted. Feel a sudden soppy surge for my faithful companion who went everywhere with me.

Aisha holds him up, pulls her face to that pouty kiss pose before handing him back. 'Sweet,' she says, like she actually means it.

'I thought you were like working at that hotel in Skeggy?' She says after a couple of minutes on the laptop.

'That finished a few weeks back.' Seems like a different time-zone.

'So, what have you been up to, then?' She looks at me, shaped brows raised, smudge of yesterday's make-up round her dark eyes.

'Not a lot.' I pull the sleeping bag round my head again.

The girls are still playing with the garage.

'No, Poppy, this pink shiny one is mine. Aisha, make Poppy give me my car.'

'Oh, let her have it a minute for fuck's sake.'

Cherry gets up. 'You said a very rude word, Auntie Aisha. I'm telling Grandma.'

'Off you go then,' Aisha smirks. Cherry storms out while Poppy slavers over the car.

'At least that DVD keeps Joey quiet,' Aisha says. 'No fucking chance of any revision in this loony bin.'

'Catch up on your Snapchat, more like.'

Aisha swings the computer screen round to shove it in my face. The page titled GCSE Chemistry Revision Notes: Atoms and Atomic Structures.

'I'm predicted like A Stars in most subjects, especially science,' she brags.

'Smashing it!'

'I'm going to be a pharmacist, init? And I don't mean like a chemist shop assistant.'

'That'll come in handy for clubbing.'

'No way, Jez!' Smudgy eyes wide at me. 'I'm getting a good job and a flat of my own, right? No dossing on settees for me.'

Aisha types into her revision website, silver nails flashing. 'Did Mum tell you, Dad's back this weekend? He's finished his contract or whatever?'

'Is he?' Not right interested just now.

'Sonya's creating about how he uses Mum. Says he should like take her on holiday.'

'Maybe he should. How whacked out does she look?'

'She wouldn't go anyway. Not with me doing exams, and Joey and all.'

'Well, she always cheers up when he comes. I think it's best to leave them to it,' I say.

'Same,' Aisha says simply, back on her revision.

Close my eyes, count to two.

Cherry shuffles in carrying a Thomas plate loaded with toast and Marmite. Mum follows close behind with a tray.

'That's right, nice and careful. Now you and Poppy sit and share this toast.' She puts the tray down and gives them both a sucker cup. Hands Joey his Action Man plate.

'Has it got marmalade?' Hey, the boy-dog speaks.

'Best marmalade for best Joey.' Mum passes me my coffee and lowers herself into the armchair by the gas fire.

'I need a fag,' I say, starting to shift.

'Have one in the kitchen, if you want. We can grab a chat.'

The doorbell rings. 'What now?' Mum frowns. 'Get that, will you, Aisha?'

'Mum, I'm revising.' But Aisha shuffles off in her ridiculous Dalmatian slippers.

'It's only me.' Sonya bustles in. All flowery maxi dress and strappy sandals. Just the thing for DIY.

'Mummy!' Poppy lifts her Marmitey hands. Sonya dabs a little kiss on each of the girls.

'I just came to drop some clean clothes round.'

'But I thought you were taking them this morning.'

'The estate agent's coming on Friday. We need to get it finished, Mum.'

'I've got Joey to get to school tomorrow. And I wanted Jez to have the bed tonight.'

Sonya looks over at me. 'What are you doing here?'

'Nice to see you too, Sis.'

'Jez's been through a tough time; she's been …'

'Mum, no.' I nearly spill my coffee.

'Jez? Hard time? Run out of settees to doss on?'

'She was working at that hotel in Skegness. Hardly her fault the owner went bust.'

'It's OK,' I say. 'Sonya thinks I'm a dosser who doesn't give a shit. And she's right, I don't give a shit what she thinks.'

'Will the pair of you…' Mum raises her arms and bangs them down on the chair.

'Mum, I'm not here to argue,' Sonya says. 'If you can have the kids one more night…'

I pull myself out of the sleeping bag, Sonya screwing her nose at my crumpled combats and T shirt. Give her the finger as I stumble to the kitchen.

I clear a space among the toast crumbs and piles of bills. Grab an old saucer for an ashtray and light up. Sun pouring through the French windows. Shut my eyes against the brightness. Green shapes of the diamond windowpanes dancing. Flash of an image of Ken zipped up in the black bag over the stretcher when they came to take him to the morgue. Standing him on end to get him out of the door. Think of him lying on a cold slab on his own.

I lean my head on my hand, feel the sun hot on my hair. I want to be left alone, or maybe just with Mum. Zero chance of that.

I raise my head to flick my ash. Things could have been a right lot worse. Like being brought up by Ken with his nasty proper kids as siblings. Will they turn up now, have a sniff around, organise a funeral or something? Can't even think about it. Just want to be back fixing Ken whisky ice cubes while he mithers at me.

Jump as my phone beeps. Reach into my bag and open the text.

Hi Jez, so sorry to hear Ken passed last night. Hope you OK, I been to house but you not there. Ken give me letter for you. Can we meet up? God Bless, Sandy x

I stub out my fag, walk over and open the French windows as Mum comes in. I lean against the frame, the air soft and warm on my face. She puts her hand on my arm.

'Why don't you go and lie down. Sonya's gone and I thought I'd take the kids to the park. We can have a good chat later.'

'I've got to go out now.'

'But you need to rest.' Her face close up looks totally shagged. All under-eye bags and deep frown lines.

'You're one to talk,' I can't help laughing. 'When did you ever rest?'

'I'm used to it. And I haven't been through what you have.'

'I have to sort stuff out at Ken's before the Council come to clear it.'

'Can't that wait a couple of days? I could help you while Joey's at school.'

She steps down into the garden. Sits on the old bench that Martin and I rescued from a skip years ago. Pats the seat beside her.

'Let me get my fags.'

I go back to the table and look at my phone. If I leave in fifteen, I'll be in Accrington for elevenish. I send a quick text to Sandy and go back out to Mum.

'I'll go after I've had this,' I say, lighting a cigarette.

Mum sighs. 'Martin's up from Birmingham this week. You could pop and see him, perhaps.'

Am I tempted by a ride out on Martin's bike? Not right now. 'Maybe later.' I shrug.

'Hasn't Ken got his own kids?'

'Yes,' I glare at her. 'He called them the *proper kids*.'

Mum drops her head, reaches out as I pull away.

'I'm not a proper kid? Never was, was I?' I take a deep drag and exhale it fast.

'You're upset, love. But you must know you were always a proper kid to us?' Mum says slowly, leaning forward to grab my hand. I tense against her touch. 'In some ways you were never a child at all,' she adds.

'Maybe I didn't get a chance?' I catch the sulk in my voice.

She strokes between my knuckles. Her fingers dry and rough, raised veins and liver spots on the back of her hands.

'Of all the children I've fostered, and my own, which includes you, of course, you were the one to bring yourself up.'

'Maybe I learnt that with my real mum.'

'*Real Mum? Proper Kids?*' She smiles up at me, like I'm to know she's not upset.

Flash of the image of my 'real' mum. Not the photo, but the hazy silhouette of a woman on a green settee in front of a plate-glass window. Dark wavy hair, pale moon face, big coat. That same face coming in and out as I was pushed on a swing. Back in my sub-memory before she died. It doesn't fit the photo. I reach for my bag, wanting to check.

Why am I getting into this? I look at the time on my phone. Take a slow breath.

'The point is, right, Ken's kids haven't been around. He said they like lost interest after he refused to buy his Council house. But they'll probably show up now he's dead and I want to get my stuff out first.'

I stare out at the weed infested patio, push-along car lying on its side. The Wendy house Dad built, faded swirls of his painted flower pattern. Empty bird feeder on the washing line pole. All so familiar, but like unreal. The colours too bright so soon after Ken's death.

'You'll come back later, won't you? Dad's home soon, he's been asking after you.'

'Yeah, I'll be back. See what new recipes he's got up his sleeve?' Picture him sweating the spices, not just Indian, but Chinese, Indonesian, whatever his latest craze, until he's off and away again on some new dodgy scheme.

'I don't want him to know about Ken, right? Not yet anyway.'

She nods, leans to pull me into a hug. The simple thing of a hug from Mum. I can take that, I do. Inhale the smell of her sandalwood soap.

There's a crash and screams from the living room. Mum pulls away, wiping her eyes as she rushes through.

Sandy's looking at her watch as I arrive hot and sweating cobs.

'Sorry, the bloody bus was twenty minutes late. Frigging hate buses.' I wipe my face with my T shirt. Exposing tatty black lace bra.

'Hey, don't get me excited.' Sandy's cucumber crisp in her nurse's tunic. Black hair braided tight round the sides of her head, like innocent Jamaican schoolgirl, for all she's nearly fifty. I feel right manky beside her. Change of clothes could have been good.

First time I met her she was with that puffy old nurse who

was all sniffing at the minging kitchen. Sandy was the one who properly got Ken. She visited on her own after that.

She fishes a letter out of her bag. 'He insist I give you before they clear out the house.'

'List of complaints?' I study the envelope: TO JEZ written in wobbly capitals.

She smiles. 'He was one grouchy ol' bugger, but thought the world of you, turning up caring for him.'

'I preferred him complaining. Maybe it's genetic – I'm not one for getting right sentimental.'

Sandy looks at her watch again. 'Got to go, darling. But I'm happy now I seen you. GP say his daughter been informed and she probably on her way from down south. You going to be OK, darling?'

Stomach lurches at the thought of the proper kids turning up. So not up for them finding me.

'Do me a favour, Sandy? Don't give anyone my number. I don't want to be part of no family re-non-union. I'll just grab my stuff, stash away the valuables!'

'You be lucky!' She laughs. 'Well, I won't say I seen you or nothing. What you planning now for yourself?'

'Doss down at my mum's? Wait for the next adventure?'

'I hope it more joyful. God Bless, Jez.'

It's minging unwashed clothes, burnt fat and stale fag smoke. One night away and I'm not used to it. The blind's still drawn, the light dim. I avoid looking at the empty bed. Stick the kettle on and wash a mug. The room just as it was, but his absence like a layer of dust suffocating the life out of everything. I'm hardly breathing. The water stirring in the kettle is the only movement.

I take my coffee and sit at the table. The motorbike magazine where I left it. I can hear him ragging me about it – another life ago.

I open the letter, my movements slow, like someone else is making them. The handwriting is shaky and a weird mix of capitals and lower case. Tiny silver key taped to the corner.

Dear JEZ,

I'm not MUCH one for Words but you BEING HERE in my last Days. It Has meant a LOT to me. I've left You my treasure BOX under the Bed UPstairs. DON'T let on about IT, Just use it to ENJOY Yourself.

Never FORGET your Old DAD, KEN.

I stare at the letter, hardly taking it in. Seeing his writing like that, hand scratching across the page as he's propped up in bed. How long would that have taken him? I scan the letter again. What kind of treasure could he have? His dad's old war medals? His mum's rings? Ancient bottle of whisky? No chance!

That feeling of it being someone else pushing open the bedroom door, slinging the bedclothes back on the bed, peering underneath it. Piles of dust balls and just the box. Dark wood like about a foot wide with gilt trimmings. I pull it out and the dust billows into the room. Brush it with my T shirt and give the corner trimmings a rub. It's like a kid's treasure chest with the curved lid and a gilt clasp with a tiny padlock. Solid with the weight of something. I take the little key and open it.

The box is lined with purple velvet. A scroll of papers tied with a ribbon. I lay them to one side and there it is, gleaming in the dull light, stamped with Roman numerals and hallmarks. The size of a large bar of chocolate.

Cool solid weight. Heavier than chocolate. Rub its smooth surface against my cheek. Bite it like some Jack Sparrow testing his loot. I move towards the window, stunned with disbelief as I run my finger over the embossed stamp and letters that confirm:

1 kilo

Fine Gold Bullion.

Wrong Move – *Gethin*

Francesca throws her pizza dough onto the round baking tray, then watches me trying to pull my wonky oblong into a circle.

'Frankenstein pizza?' she teases.

I sling the dough on my baking tray and glance up at her mocking eyes. Am I blushing, of all things? Look away.

'Hey!' She moves to the fridge. The brushed steel of the door reflects the deep red of the walls as she holds it open. 'Remember we used to make monster pizza with Pat at Halloween?'

Instant flash of me and Fran standing on our plastic stools, carving bits of pepper into teeth with knives that weren't sharp enough.

'Let's see, we've got cherry tomatoes. Courgettes.'

'I'll have courgette for my eyes, slice of olive for the pupil.'

'These stuffed green ones, like bloodshot! Mushrooms?'

'For noses,' we both say, giggling as we remember how we'd argued about mushroom noses.

'It was my idea, you were going to have a tomato,' I start.

'You ate my mushroom nose.'

'You stole my idea.'

'I'm going to get you back!' She pinches my nose, pretends to pull it off, holding the tip of her thumb between two fingers, putting it in her mouth and chewing.

I grab a mushroom and try to squash it into her nose. She gets hold of my hands and we wrestle for control, laughing our tits off. Our heads touch and she looks up, all shiny cheeked with laughter tears. I release my hold, suddenly awkward.

Fran starts spreading tomato sauce onto her pizza base as the doorbell rings.

'Get it will you, Geth? Probably Mum forgot her key.'

I walk down the corridor, see the outline of a blond head through the stained-glass panel. Looks like…

'Emily!' I say as I open the door. Taking a direct hit from the afternoon sun, all I can see is the shine of her hair. I shield my eyes. 'Fran's in the kitchen.'

'I'm not coming in.' Her voice is tight as fuck. 'It's you I've come to see. Pat said you might be here.'

'OK,' I shrug in an effort to control my banging heart, shift so the sun's out of my eyes.

'I thought I could help you, you know, talk through this stuff about your dad. After all, with my experience…'

'Your what experience?' Just her superior tone demolishes any hope that she wants me back.

'Why so negative? Pat hasn't heard from you for three days now.'

'And?' I feel the anger rise.

'Why are you punishing her?'

'Look, Emily, as you're so pally with my mum, you can tell her the self-righteous messages aren't helping. *You have no right to behave like this however upset you might be!*' I do a mean imitation of Mum's voice in a rough summary of her recent text.

'Your mum's the nicest possible, you don't know how lucky…'

I shake my head. Open mouthed. Stunned. How dare she

gang up with Mum against me? How dare Mum? I whip out my phone and get Facebook up. De-friend Mum and wave the screen at Emily.

'There, no longer friends with my darling mother.'

She folds her arms tight across her tits like armour. 'Well, you've got Fran now, I always thought there was something between you two.'

'What the fuck?' Literally reeling from this shot.

'All this, like brother like sister bollocks? You should see the way she looks at you.'

'And this is your business how?' My voice is a hoarse whisper.

'So, you don't deny it?' She pulls her lips tight like she's scored a point.

'Deny? Of course, I, fuck's sake Emily.' I hold my head in my hands. What happened to my beautiful sweet girlfriend?

'I'm sure you'll both be very happy,' she carries on in her shitty little smugness.

'Oh, do fuck off. I literally don't know what planet you're on.'

'Fine.' She turns to go. 'I thought we could be friends.'

'So, be friendly, bitch.' I shout as she scuttles away. I slam the door shut, lean against the wall to steady my racing heart.

I try to keep my face neutral as Fran looks questioning.

'Was that Emily? Why didn't she come in?'

'Oh, she was in a hurry,' I mumble, spooning the tomato on my pizza.

'Well, what did she want?' Fran moves to the sink. 'Gethin?'

'Oh, she, she actually wanted to pick up?' First thing that comes into my head. 'You know, as in weed?'

'Emily's coming to my house to score? That is so not on.

Did you tell her she could?' Fran doesn't wait for me to answer, goes straight into a rant about how people might think her mum was dealing! Why would anyone think that?

'Emily just thought I might have some…' is my weak response.

That dread feeling, like the time I blamed that kid for tearing the picture of the spaceship out of the school library book. What was I thinking saying Emily came to pick up? Dickhead!

'You were shouting, what was that about?' Fran moves towards me, wielding her knife.

Talk about digging a hole. I move back a step.

'Fran, please, I just told her to go away. Really, it's not such a big deal.' My calmest calming voice.

'Ha ha, big deal, very funny.'

I duly groan at the bad joke. Fran turns back to her pizza. Maybe I'm off the hook, if I can stop talking like an idiot.

'Look,' she says after a few minutes. 'Spiky teeth.'

'Epic, can I have a bit?'

She hands me some pepper and I cut a couple of yellow squiggles.

'Snot for nose.'

'Ew!' She frowns proper disapproval. Guessing she's still mad at me?

I lay half a mushroom in the centre of the pizza, position the pepper snot. Start cutting courgette eyes.

'I think Emily's jealous, that's why she wouldn't come in.' Fran slices a stuffed olive.

'Jealous?' I feel myself flush red as the pizza-face.

Grace comes in just as our creations are ready for the oven. She dumps her shopping and comes up behind Fran to give her a hug. She's like half Fran's height now, standing on tiptoe to see over Fran's shoulder.

'Wow, monster pizzas. Fabulous!'

Fran stands back, all admiration. Hers looks designer scary with its jalapeño olive eyeballs and spiky pepper hair and teeth. Mine looks a pile of crap, of course, but I don't compete where art's concerned.

'We used to make them like this with Pat when we were little,' Francesca explains.

'She always out-did me on the home-baked mum front.' Grace finishes unpacking M&S ready meals and slams the freezer door shut. 'I've just bumped into her, as it happens. On my way back from meeting Seb. She, of course, was stunned to hear he'd turned up at all?'

I tense up. 'Yeah, Fran said you're getting married. Mega pleased for you.'

Grace shoots a killer look at Fran, who literally flinches with the impact.

'Mum, I didn't say,' Fran passes the glare to me with interest.

Oh Fuck, Here I Go Again.

'Sorry, I think it was Emily mentioned it. I didn't think…'
When in doubt, blame Emily?

'I only told Emily that Dad asked you.' Fran slides the pizzas into the oven.

'It's not a state secret or anything, babe.' Grace moves to put the kettle on. 'But I could do without the world and his girlfriend either marrying me off or telling me I'm wasting my time, when we're just after a bit of space to work things out.' She gives us both a stern look.

'Anyway, whatever, I hope it works out for you and Sebbie,'

I say to fill the awkwardness. 'I know Mum has her views, but that doesn't mean…'

'It's OK, Gethin.' Grace spoons some coffee into a mug. 'Pat is just Pat. She wants you to get in touch, by the way.'

'And she's mentioned how she produced a letter from my sperm donor with literally no warning at my birthday meal?' My voice rises with irritation.

'She thinks you need to talk, that's all, love.' She finishes making her drink, leans up against the counter.

Grace is a cool lady, and you can forget she's your mate's mum as well as your mum's mate. No chance of that now, however.

'I can't talk to her. There's no point,' I start.

Grace runs her hand through her silky dark hair. 'Well, I think she wants to try, maybe?'

'Ever since I dropped out of sixth form, it's like, Oh Gethin, why won't you *talk* to me. But then I told her one time I was thinking of getting a job in a shop and she's like, is that how you see your future?' I kick at a piece of mushroom on the floor. Centre it with a tile and squash it with my foot. 'She's never got over me ditching this bollocks about being an Astrophysicist. Pretty much because I liked mapping stars and read that Stephen Hawkins when I was like twelve?'

'Hey, you were really keen. All about red shifting galaxies and shit,' Fran interrupts.

'I'm not saying it's not interesting,' I squish the mushroom harder. 'Just don't necessarily want to be the next fucking Einstein. Could be I'm just not enough of a boffin, know what I mean?'

Grace puts a hand on my shoulder. 'Come on, love, no need to shout. Pat's been really stressed, you know?'

I stiffen under her touch, I didn't realise I was shouting. I want to shake her off. I take a breath, try to calm my voice.

'She's stressing all the time. It's like, Oh Gethin, we must *talk*, then she's like five hours in the studio and when she gets back, she's in my face again. The other day, she actually asked why I don't get a job in a shop? Fuck's sake. Then, totally out of the blue, she chucks a non-existent dad at me? Well I don't want to know.'

Grace lets go of my shoulder and moves to get a cloth. She pushes my leg away from the mushroom and wipes it up, then rinses the cloth. I stand there feeling an idiot. Look up at Fran who gives a sympathetic nod. I want to hug her, then I think about what Emily said and look at the floor again.

Grace takes her coffee and sits down. 'Why not just write to her?'

'Well, it's not like I've gone far. Obviously can't just stay here forever?'

'You can stay as long as you like, sweetheart,' Grace interrupts.

'Whoa, I so wasn't angling for that.'

'I know. But I'm saying it's OK.'

'Yeah, well, thanks.' I feel thrown by this offer taking the wind out of my rant.

'The point is you need a break. Write and tell her you want to sort yourself out and it's best you do that away from her for a bit.'

Can it really be that simple? I scuff my shoe against the side of a tile. I feel all mixed up, with no idea what to say.

The timer goes on the cooker. Fran takes the pizzas out and the smell of fresh baked dough sets off about a million taste buds.

'Perfect monster pizzas!' Fran puts her arm round me. Her

hair smells of fresh apples. I look down and catch a glimpse of white lace edging the soft line of her breasts. Hold my breath. It's Francesca, for fuck's sake.

'Gorgeous.' Fran says, brushing my bare arm as she moves back to admire the pizza. 'Let's take this upstairs and listen to that Katy Perry I downloaded.'

Grace leans back in her chair. 'Think about what I said, Gethin.'

Francesca's room is a weird combination of familiar and new. All budding interior designer, with stripy silk cushions piled up on the futon and coloured Japanese lamps. But the big old armchair is still there beneath its new throw, where we used to snuggle while Grace read us a story.

Now we sit on the futon leaning up against the cushions with our pizza – Fran's laptop between us playing Katy Perry through its tinny speakers. She has like this perfect designed bedroom, but nothing approaching a decent sound system.

But the music does fill the gap between us chewing and we don't say a lot for ten minutes or so. My head's full of what Grace said. Why not? Take a break from Mum? Liking the sound of it, allowing the feeling of a weight lifting.

Fran leans over to put her empty plate on the floor, her hair brushing my arms. I make myself carry on eating as she looks at me all fondly, then laughs as she settles back against the cushions.

'Do you remember our sleepovers? When I had that platform bed and you slept on the mattress underneath? I'd tell you there was a ghost's shadow lying flat up against the bottom of my bed and you were totally terrified.'

55

'Too scared to move. But then I'd say that the ghost was sliding through the mattress to get you?'

Fran shivers. 'Still gives me goose bumps. Happy days!'

I munch into the last slice, nod at her. She leans forward, looking thoughtful at me.

'Did we ever even talk about who your dad was?'

'It was so not an issue. As in I vaguely remember telling kids at school that my mum got some sperm from a nice man or something.'

Fran says she thinks she always knew that, and I point out it's not like it's so unusual. There was a kid in our class with two mums, whose dad may have been gay, but we didn't think about it. Then I remember when we first did sex education in Y3. How I felt right smug when the teacher explained how babies were made. Like I had this great secret – I could tell her no, not all babies are made that way.

'I don't remember that,' Fran says.

'I didn't say it. Just liked the idea that I could.'

'Oh My God, I've just remembered.' Fran bursts into fits of giggles. 'Gethin, Son of Alien!'

I look blank at her, delayed memory reaction.

'You know, we had one of those like grow-in-an-egg alien things? We decided,' she pauses, clutches her stomach. 'We decided it was your baby.'

'Cos my dad was an alien, is it?' I catch Fran's giggles. 'Son of Alien!'

'We made you antennae out of Christmas reindeer horns.'

The giggles subside as I scoop up the remaining crumbs from my plate, thinking about Don's letter, how it won't let me rest.

'It is just the weirdest, the thing of him suddenly existing,' I mutter.

Fran takes my plate and shifts to lie on her side looking up at me. Her dark long hair trails along her neckline, moving up and down with her breath. I focus on the pyramid of coloured storage boxes opposite the futon.

'I guess you didn't need him to exist,' Fran says. 'You were always so close to Pat, like she was maybe enough?'

The top box of the pyramid is slightly off centre – I want to get up and straighten it.

'Gethin?'

I look back at her, try to think about what she's saying.

'Yeah, we were close. We talked a lot and I used to tell her everything. If I ever did anything wrong, like at school, or did something mean to another kid, I literally couldn't rest until I'd told her about it?'

'You told her when we drank that Calpol. I got in such trouble with my mum.'

'I couldn't stand the guilt. Telling her was, you know, like a cream of tomato soup and hot chocolate type of feeling?'

And it comes to me, when I was about eleven, totally screwed with guilt over porno fantasies about women, any woman. After all she'd drummed into me about sexism, there was surely no comfort from Mum on this one. But I can still feel the floods of relief after I blurted it out, and she said it was actually all normal, the main thing was what I did, not what I thought. I kept pushing it, telling her more and more stuff, but I didn't manage to shock her at all.

Fran touches my hand, making me jump with a resurge of eleven-year-old sexual guilt.

'Chill, Gethin! Just wondering what happened with you and Pat? Nothing more to confess?'

'Huh? Guessing there's a limit to how much a dude wants

to spew out to his mum? When hanging out with your mates in a rainy park becomes the most important? Worship of da holy weed!'

'Oh My God, you guys taking pictures of piles of bud, like it was the most amazing thing?' Fran grins at me.

'Yeah, man! That was Lenny and Frank, like sending each other competitive photos. I didn't have a camera phone, remember?'

Fran agrees that Mum was always a bit tight about anything involving a screen, and I remind her of how much grief I had to give Mum before she finally got me a second-hand Xbox. Literally crying when I opened it. Even then, I spent most of my time round Lenny's, because his mum let us eat pizza out of the box while sitting in bed playing Grand Theft Auto.

'I dunno.' Fran frowns. 'Pat was such a lot of fun when we were kids.'

I nod, thinking of trips to the space museum, costumes for Halloween, building dens in the woods. 'But that was the thing: she couldn't deal with fun-loving boy morphing into moody teenager.'

'Maybe it's harder for a single mum with a boy? You know, with a girl, there's always clothes and make-up.'

I laugh at the idea of Pat as a clothes and make-up type mum. I tell Fran I'm thankful that at least she's around less, since she started with her studio. Remembering how I had to literally talk her into it, saying I'd be full-on with my GCSE revision and shit. She liked that, of course. But I was glad to be out of the spotlight.

'She's so intense, my mum,' I add. 'Grace is a lot more chilled.'

'Oh, that's just what you see – she can give it some too.'

'Mum used to be all, whatever makes you happy,' I carry on. 'But when I told her I didn't want to do physics any more…it's like, you know, all about freedom and democracy, but, Oh, No, we didn't mean vote for *that!* And this thing about my sperm donor? It totally wasn't an issue but now she's made it one. I want to let Jarvis burn it, but it burns me instead, through a hole in my pocket.'

I pull out the letter from my jeans, bringing Gran and Granddad's card with it.

'Hey!' Fran looks at the picture of a skateboarding kid with a mobile phone. 'That's never from your dad?'

'Ha! No, that's from my grandparents who also gave me this!' I pull out their cheque.

'Wow! Five hundred smackeroonies!'

'I keep forgetting to pay it into the bank, shows how stressed out I've been?'

'You could have a holiday, Geth. Really get a break?' Fran looks at me, eyes all shining.

She is beautiful, I've always known it, but I've never quite seen her like I am today. I think again about what Emily said and shift position to hide the surge in my groin.

Fran takes this like a cue to turn and face me as Katy Perry sings *Spiritual.*

'You know, Mum already asked me how I'd feel about you staying longer? And I thought it's been ages since our sleepovers, but these last couple of days it's felt totally so normal to have you around.'

She squeezes my hands and her smile goes through me. I lean forward and stroke a strand of stray hair behind her ear, pause to feel the smooth skin of her neck, not stopping to note the puzzled look crossing her face as I pull her head

59

towards me and kiss her slowly, shifting my body closer, her breasts soft against my chest, my tongue sliding between her opening lips.

She sits up, pushes me back, takes a gulp of air. 'What the Fuck? Gethin?'

My blood drains as I shift away from her. 'Sorry, I thought you, it just seemed…'

'But we've always said that would never happen, we're like siblings, it would seem wrong?' She's up on her feet now, glowering down on me.

'I dunno, being around you more, I thought…' I can feel myself physically grovelling on the futon. Fuck. Wrong. Move. Big. Style.

'We said we can't imagine fancying each other.'

'Did we? When?'

'Oh My God, Gethin, ages ago?' She's got her arms crossed over her chest, shoulders tensed.

'Why would we say that? I mean, it's not like we're both ugly or…'

'It's a No, Gethin. Such a definite No. Jesus!' She shouts in my face, then takes a step back, blinking hard.

As if I'm arguing with her. As if I want to upset her more. Could I be more of a fucking idiot?

'I'm sorry, really. Just forget it, please?'

She tugs hard at her hair, shakes her head at me.

I sit and mess with Gran's card. Oh God. Gotta get out!

'Listen, Fran,' I shuffle to the edge of the futon. 'I think I told Ben I'd pop round tonight?'

She nods, biting her bottom lip. 'It's OK, you don't have to go.'

But it's not OK. I get up and stumble towards the door, grabbing at the handle which I somehow can't shift.

'Here.' Fran opens the door for me.

'Thanks.' I hurry across the landing to the stairs. By the time I think to look back she's closed the door.

At least I got out before Grace saw me, I think as I pace down the street, pulling on the hoody that I grabbed from the hooks in the hall. I pull out my phone to ring Ben – he's going to have to be OK with me crashing on his floor tonight. Maybe we can hook up with Lenny and Frank? Boys Night In, smoke a bud, shoot some FIFA.

Another text from Mum: Gethin, let's stop the silliness and try start again. Just want to talk. Purleeese! Mx

Something about that ridiculous *Purleese,* like she's way down wiv da kidz. Mum, Fran, Emily. Too many women fucking with my head! I type my reply as I hurry along.

Bit late now Mum. Back off! De-friended on Facebook btw L

Press send, then dial Ben.

He'd better not have no issues with me!

Homestay – *Pat*

I push open the meeting room door to a blast of stale air stirred by the fan. The others are slumped around the table.

'Hi, I forgot we had a meeting.' I plonk myself next to Charlie. He's busy texting but pauses to smile at me.

'Jeanelle's not here yet, probably held up with something important,' Rehana raises her eyes.

'It's unprofessional conduct when I'm five minutes late for my one-to-one,' Pauline moans. 'Even though I was dealing a difficult customer.'

'Well, it's good to be back.' I fan myself with a pile of agendas. 'Still no sign of the air conditioning being fixed?'

'Now you are being funny,' Pauline says. 'So how was your time off?'

'Yeah, Pat.' Charlie looks up. 'How'd the show go?'

'Oh, it hasn't started yet, I was just setting up. But I'm not sure I'm fitting their concept of Cuttin' Edge, you know?'

Charlie says I would say that, as I explain how it was billed as a venue to showcase art that's marginalised by commercial galleries. 'But it's mostly what I call Conceptual Bollocks, to tell you the truth. I don't think I'm obscure enough.'

Charlie, seemingly undeterred, asks when they can we get to see it. I tell him when it opens, with serious stomach clenching at the idea of people from work looking at my art.

Pauline starts on the next sore point. 'So how was Gethin's birthday?'

'Crap.' I shoot her a Don't Ask look, which she chooses to ignore.

'What's it like then, to have a grown up for a son?' She smiles in that cutesy way of hers, with her even teeth and pearly pink lips.

'Like I've lost a child?' I say, shocked by the truth of this.

Pauline's smile snaps shut as she pushes back her chair and walks out of the room.

Rehana fiddles with her purple headscarf. Charlie raises an eyebrow at me.

'What?' I say.

'Pauline is sensitive, you know?' Rehana says gently.

'Well, I'm bloody sensitive, she insists on asking when I've already said it's crap.'

Rehana flinches at my outburst. I can't say anything right in this place.

'She had a miscarriage, didn't she, Pat?' Charlie says.

Deep breath. 'OK, fair enough. I'll go and apologise,' I say, feeling both ashamed and resentful.

Perhaps Charlie sees this. 'Leave her be for a bit,' he says as his phone beeps a text in. 'Oh Jesus, what now?' He reads the message. 'Sorry.' He grimaces. 'Just Ex Number One telling me what to say at Chloe's school review today. Not that she'd dream of turning up.'

Rehana giggles. 'I thought she was really keen, making notes at parents' evenings.'

'No that's Ex Number Two with Danny. She draws up a list of targets for him that I'm supposed to enforce. Ex Number One doesn't do school meetings. She just likes to write stroppy letters and then I have to go and fight it for her. Hey-ho, c'est la vie. Oh, for the life of the single parent, eh Pat?'

Charlie's grin disarms me, and I nod my agreement. It's my single parent soapbox. You get to make all the decisions, none of this quibbling over every mouthful of chocolate cake that two parent families get into. I didn't live with Karen when Gethin was little, but I was happy to have her support, the best of both worlds, perhaps. How did that change to feeling she was constantly sticking her oar in, judging my parenting? Telling me I was too possessive when I didn't want Gethin passed around her streams of friends all wanting a slice. How I was making a rod for my own back letting him sleep in my bed. And now, years later, when she's hardly made any effort to see him, she slings this letter at us. I'm meeting her at lunchtime and I've really no idea what I'm going to say.

The thick air stirs as Jeanelle makes an entrance with her usual flurry. Today she's ushering in Hussain complete with flipchart. She holds the door at a half profile angle, her dyed black hair curling just so over her bare tanned shoulders, her cotton shift dress hitched well above the knee: look at me, still sexy at fifty! I catch Rehana's eye and she looks down to suppress her grin.

Hussain stands just inside the door: his grey suit hanging off his slight frame, eyes darting. Our new Apprentice aka Jeanelle's personal dog's-body.

Jeanelle waves Husssain to set up his flipchart in the far corner. Charlie jumps up to give him a hand.

'Uh, hmm,' Jeanelle signals for him to stop. 'This is a development opportunity for Hussain.'

Charlie raises an eyebrow and sits down, leaving Hussain to battle on. He gets the stand up but struggles with the paper. He's been given a pad with holes in the wrong places.

I get Blu-Tac from the cupboard and offer it to him. He takes it hastily and sticks the paper up while Jeanelle glares at me.

'Right, I'll just get Pauline then.' She sends me another look as she exits, re-entering a few seconds later steering Pauline to a chair.

Pauline looks down at her hands. Oh, God, I feel mean, why on earth didn't I apologise?

'Now,' says Jeanelle. 'I've asked Hussain to help with an exercise on customer relations. Something for him to capture for his NVQ.'

Hussain grins, awkward.

'So,' Jeanelle casts her eye about, 'Rehana. Give us a scenario where you are the customer making a phone call.'

Rehana frowns, desperately thinking.

Jeanelle cocks her head. 'Anyone?'

'Phoning the bank?' Charlie offers.

'Excellent, an experience we all share. Hussain, write, *Customer Experience – Phoning the Bank*. Rehana, what's the first thing that happens when you phone the bank?'

'Um, there's like an automated voice telling me to key in my bank account number....'

Hussain starts writing – *automated voice*.

'Yes, yes,' Jeanelle waves impatiently. 'But when you get to speak to someone?'

'They say, good morning Miss Ahmed, how can I help you?'

'Yes, but before that?' Jeanelle's irritation increases visibly.

'That's what they say at my bank,' Rehana whispers.

Hussain writes: Good morning Miss Ahmed, how can I...

'Hussain just stop a minute. What is the FIRST THING

they say when you phone the bank.' Jeanelle's practically jumping in her seat.

We look around at each other, completely clueless.

Jeanelle lays her hands flat in a gesture of calming. 'The point is, they will ask for your details before they ask what you want. This is a typical customer experience.'

'And it's one everyone hates. Are you really suggesting we use the banks as a model?' I ask.

'The Council now insist their staff have the same script for answering the phone.'

'We don't even work for the Council.'

'I think you'll find they hold the purse strings,' Jeanelle's smug reply.

'Not for much longer by all accounts,' Charlie mutters.

Jeanelle stiffens. 'We need to come into line on this. I'm suggesting 'Good morning, you've reached the Homestay Helpline, Jeanelle speaking. Please can I take your details before we start.' Then you get their name, full address, telephone, email, date of birth, ethnic origin…'

'We're talking about vulnerable people who we're trying to help stay in their homes. Let them ask their question, reassure them we can help, then take their details.' My voice getting louder.

'We're wasting our time,' Jeanelle says. 'I'll email the script and will expect it to be used as from Monday.'

'It's bollocks, come on.' I look round the table. Nobody says anything. As per bloody usual.

Jeanelle folds her arms. 'Right. Item 2. Future Funding Opportunities.'

Item 2 sets Jeanelle on ten minutes of SMART Thinking, Income Diversification, Revisiting our USP and no actual substance. I drift into thinking about meeting Karen. Why didn't she talk to me about Don's letter, instead of sending it with the birthday card like that?

A pause in Jeanelle's drone alerts me to her beaming her frosty smile, as if expecting applause.

'Can I ask what time we're finishing?' Charlie looks at the clock. 'I'm due at Chloe's school review in forty minutes.'

'I'm meeting a friend at lunchtime, so I need to go soon as well, really,' I add.

'If we can get on with the agenda, I'm sure you'll both be on time. Now Item 3, Mission Statement.'

'Before that, can I ask if there's any news on the contract with the Council for next year?' I say.

'I was coming to that in Item 4, General Updates.' Jeanelle sifts through her papers.

'It's a bit relevant to future funding, isn't it? All this talk of diversification – is our contract secure or not?' I say.

Silence. Jeanelle leans her head on her hand.

Charlie nods his approval. 'I think it's a question we'd all like answering.'

She takes a breath. 'OK, are we in agreement with bringing this item up the agenda?'

Just the faintest of nods from the others.

'The latest communication, and I stress, it is only a preliminary briefing to the chief executives of voluntary sector providers of Council contracts, which will form the basis for a consultative document…'

'What does it say?' Charlie emphasises each word.

'The recommendation is that some of the non-statutory

contracts be absorbed within existing Council services. In our case this would be their Equipment and Adaptations service.' She stops abruptly. Studies her agenda as if it held the meaning of life.

Everyone exchanges glances of disbelief.

'And you thought you'd drop this on us as General Updates?' As per usual it's me saying what everyone else simply thinks.

Jeanelle purses her lips. 'As I have said, it's a preliminary. I will keep you informed of any firm proposal. In the meantime, we need to keep positive, so let's plug on with our revised mission statement.'

I can't take any more, the blood boiling in my ears. I look at the clock: 12:05, I'll have to leave if I'm going to make it to see Karen.

'Pauline suggested Keeping Sheffield Homely. What about anyone else?'

I look up into her sickly smile and feel my fingers clench into a fist. I stand up, pushing the chair back to screech on the laminate.

'I'm sorry, I've really got to go.'

Jeanelle's grass green eyes widen as she opens her orange lipsticked mouth. I'm out before she has a chance to say anything.

I run down the street, blinded by the harsh sunlight, sweat and hot tears. Fucking bitch, fuck her, fuck them all.

A man's face in front of me, Arab complexion. Wearing a stripy cotton cap, wire rimmed glasses slightly askew, his hands held up in horror.

'Sorry.' I dodge past him. What's the matter with me, cursing out loud?

I turn the corner towards the cathedral, the café's just in sight the other side of it. Slow down, catch your breath. Think.

My phone rings as I cross the cathedral forecourt. Emily.

'Hey, Pat, how are *you*?' That forced familiarity I remember from when she was going out with Gethin.

'Emily, I can't talk now, in a hurry.'

'Just wanted to tell you I saw Gethin at Fran's yesterday. I can't believe he's being like this, he de-friended you in front of me.'

'What?'

'I wish I could help him, you know, this stuff with his dad, it'd be awesome if he could find him.'

'Find him?'

'Totally. Find himself as well?'

'Emily, I need…'

'Yeah, sorry, I'll stay in touch, shall I?'

I pause at the café entrance. It really might be better for her to keep out of it.

'Emily,'

'No worries, I know, you're busy. Bye for now.'

'Jesus, Pat, look at the state of you?' Karen sits in the corner under the Chagall print. Cool as his lilac-pale sky, clothed in sea-green muslin, her round face framed by those fading orange hoops of hair, plump arms resting across the platform of her breasts. 'You didn't need to rush.'

I catch my face in the mirror on the other corner wall: all red and blotchy, hair soaked with sweat. I feel like a monster.

'I got you your usual.' Karen gestures to the cappuccino and iced water.

I grab the water, gulp half of it down, feeling the cold sharp on my teeth.

'What is the matter, Pat?'

The heat rises in me. I take a gulp of coffee, slopping it into the saucer.

Karen reaches to put her hand on mine. It's cool and dry on my clammy skin. I look into those swirls of grey and violet eyes, the eyes I gazed into with longing over 25 years ago. Then she blinks and I'm back.

I pull my hand away and drink some more water, the ice clinking as my hand shakes.

'You really couldn't leave well alone, could you?'

'What?' Karen frowns.

'You think you know what's best, but you know nothing.' The words spit out like they're not mine.

'Pat, please, what are you talking about?' Karen's voice is quiet and measured, teacher with a bunch of five-year-olds. It does nothing to calm my thumping heart.

'Ask me how Gethin's birthday went, go on.'

'Well, I sent him a text, but he didn't reply. I wanted to pop round, take him for a drink even.'

'He's gone, Karen.' I feel the tears pricking, trembling in my voice.

'Gone?' She leans forward, anxious now.

'It was the last I saw of him, shouting and waving the letter. I'd ordered champagne and everything. Well, Cava anyway.'

Karen stirs her hot chocolate. 'Pat, please can you start from the beginning. I do not know what you're talking about.'

'Really? You don't remember deciding unilaterally that Gethin should have details about his biological father?'

She stirs her drink again, as if it's the most important task in the world. 'I've only ever wanted the best for Gethin. All I've done is tried to support you.'

She looks hurt now, that way she pulls her arms tighter around her. But her hurt doesn't match my anger, I don't believe in it.

'You didn't want kids, that's what you told me twenty years ago. But you couldn't leave me to it, could you?'

'Pat, please. What the fuck is the matter?' Her voice is a stagey whisper.

'I'm telling you, aren't I? From being the least judgemental person ever, suddenly you knew best about everything. I shouldn't let him have MMR, I should involve you in his parents' evenings, even after we split up. Why didn't you have your own bloody kid?'

Karen puts her head in her hands. When she looks at me there are tears in her eyes.

'I tried to have a child, about eight years ago. I didn't tell you, didn't tell anyone,' she says so quietly that I'm not sure I heard it.

I stare at her pale round face; there are deeper lines around her eyes that I haven't noticed before.

'You what? Why on earth didn't you say?'

'I don't know. I suppose I didn't want a public disappointment.'

'Public? Hello, this is me, Pat? It's hardly a bloody press release.'

Flash of memory of when I first met Karen. Dykes Against Clause 28 emblazoned across her chest, so bright and friendly to everyone, as if she never expected the slightest hostility. She'd have old ladies taking stickers for their shopping bags, young lads laughing as they signed the petition.

'You know, I remember you as totally open with everyone, then you don't tell *me* something as important as that? I can't get my breath.'

'We weren't together by then, and I felt like keeping it private,' Karen says quietly.

I slouch forward onto the table, suddenly deflated and exhausted. Remembering for the first time in ages those early heady days with Karen. The Manchester Clause 28 demo: spring sunshine, colour and noise, Karen's bare arm through mine… *We're Here, We're Queer…* peachy softness of her skin, scent of clean sharp sweat and coconut, riding the whistling chanting pride of it all to sleep together that night. How did we get from there to here?

Karen strokes my hand. 'I'm sorry, Pat. Not the right moment to bring that up.'

'I felt you withdrew from Gethin after we split up. Now I'm wondering, was that why?'

She shakes her head. 'No, it was just, he didn't want to stay at my place, it was difficult to keep connected.'

'He said there were always loads of jokey women around. As if you couldn't cope with him on your own,' I say, gentle as I can.

She takes her hand back. 'He was bored, mainly. It was better when I started taking him bowling.'

'That was a while ago, you hardly see him these days.'

'He's a teenage boy, he's not that interested,' she says, a hint of exasperation. She scoops out a piece of marshmallow from her drink.

'Well, I'm truly sorry you couldn't have a child. I wish you'd told me.' I take a sip from my coffee and feel its milky warmth in my empty stomach.

'I wish things could have been different. But I still don't understand why you're upset with me now.'

'You forced that letter from Don on Gethin,' I say slowly.

'Pat, we both acknowledged that as I couldn't un-know who the donor was, it would be good to get something for the child in his own words. It's just not true that I forced it on him.'

'I remember when Gethin was about six, asking if he ever wondered about the kind man who donated sperm for him. He just looked puzzled, said no, and changed the subject. I couldn't help feeling gratified that he seemed to have no need of a father figure. As far as we were concerned it was just me and Gethin. That's all I ever wanted it to be, you see? And I forgot about the letter, really.'

'You used to talk about needing men involved in his life. Remember the Rail Mole Model?' She smiles at me, her full lips spreading.

I have to laugh. 'I couldn't say male role model.'

'You drew that sketch: the mole skating on railway lines shaped like a men's symbol, wasn't it?'

I nod. And it's true I used to wrestle with the notion that it'd be good for Gethin to have more male influences, while doing little about it. But that wasn't about the donor, was it?

'You should have talked to me about the letter. You just posted it along with his birthday card.' I say, determined to get back to my high ground.

'I texted you about it a few weeks ago, offered to meet up. You said you were too busy.'

I tense up against the accusation. I'd forgotten about the text. And when I got the letter with her card, I just shoved it in my bag. I take another sip of my coffee, deflated again.

'You didn't have to show him the letter,' Karen continues.

'But once I had it, you see, I had no choice. How could I knowingly hide it from him?'

'Which has always been my point. We can't undo the information we have.'

'And that's why I'm angry you suggested it in the first place.'

'And if I hadn't found Don there'd have been no Gethin. Maybe he'll thank us both in the end.' She lowers her face to look at me, school teacherly again.

'Now I'm told he's off on some idea of finding his ideal daddy.' I shake my head at her. 'He doesn't want to know me anymore.'

'You're upset, that's all. Why do you think he was so angry, anyway?'

I can see Gethin in the restaurant, white faced with rage, shaking the letter at me.

'He said I hadn't been truthful with him, that the last thing he needed was some fucker from outer space fucking his head up.' There's a niggle trying to surface: maybe he's right. I had kept quiet about Don, perhaps hoping he'd disappear. I bat the thought down. This is not my fault.

'So, what makes you think he wants to find him?'

I shake my head. 'Probably just to get at me. His ex-girlfriend seems to think…'

'He needs time.'

'That's just what Grace says,' I snap, annoyed at this pat response. 'He's staying at her place – no doubt she's being very sympathetic. She's pissed off because I'm not falling over with joy at the idea of her marrying that waster.'

'Grace, marrying Sebbie?'

'Don't go there!' I can feel tension rising in me again,

remembering how Grace was when I bumped into her yesterday. Perfectly civil, promising to take a message to Gethin, but leaving me feeling I have no-one left to talk to.

'You need to look after yourself. You're so wired, it's not helping anything.' Karen reaches for my hand again, but I pull it away. She's right, I am wired.

I look at the clock above the door. It's nearly one.

'Oh, God, I can't face going back to work. I walked out of the team meeting after Jeanelle casually mentioned we're probably losing our funding.'

'So, ring in sick.' She pauses. 'Maybe you should go to the doctor, get something to help you calm down.'

'You think I'm mentally ill?' My heart thumps with my indignation.

'Pat, I'm just worried about you. I need to go back to work myself now. Why don't you go home? I'll call you later.'

'I'm not your bloody pupil. My art's being scrutinised, my job's on the line, and my son's eighteenth birthday has been ruined.' I stand up, blood pounding in my head, and pull my bag over my shoulder. Ignore that patronising concerned look of hers and leave.

Take the high road – *Gethin*

Today is up there for Most Pointless Day Award, and there has been some competition. Ben may have been cool with me staying last night, but it being the evening before his last exam (totally didn't remember that) pretty much kicked off the spare part feeling. The novelty of free games on my iPhone wearing thin as I sprawled on Ben's bed while he churned out incomprehensible maths formulae on scraps of paper for literally three hours. As if I was part of that world just over a year ago! Though when Ben adds the tunes of Mykki Blanco, his latest gay hip-hop idol, it's like he's going for some unique Iranian camp geek award. I tried to doze after he left this morning, but I was too wound up by the sounds of his mum and the kids she looks after. Seizing the moment when I heard them go out to get out myself.

My feet ache from hours of aimless wandering through the park, up the river, down the ring road into town, out the other side past cafés and takeaways. Spending a fiver on a greasy kebab I didn't want, binning most of it and wandering on out through the woods then cutting through suburban houses to the top entrance of the park again. I check the time: six o'clock. I start to head back to Ben's, same old riff in my head as I go.

Fucking Useless Waste of Space. As if I was such a dickhead with Fran? Just when Grace said I could stay a while. I should go back home except it's obvious Mum's got it in for me. Clearly, I am a Number One Useless Fuck. I charge along the path literally kicking myself. Lose my balance and nearly knock a little girl off her bicycle.

'Sorree!' I hold my hands up to her glaring mum as I loop a wide curve away from them.

'What's wrong with that man?' The girl's perky voice.

'I think he's drunk too much.' The sharp tone of the mum.

I wish! Perhaps Ben will go halves on some vodka?

Ben's folks live in a small terrace round the back of the bus depot. His mum's a childminder and the whole place is rammed with kids' stuff. I can see Ben and his dad through the window sitting either side of a Fisher Price garage with toy cars scattered across the carpet. Ben waves me to come in; I squeeze through the gap between the door and the sofa and stand like an idiot.

'Get them packed away, will you?' Ben's dad waves from his chair as Ben gets down on the floor, throwing cars into a plastic crate. 'Make yourself a tea, Gethin, or there's some of this stuff in the fridge.' He points a can of Mango Rubicon at me.

'Thanks,' I smile at him. Ben's dad, Rahim, is the nicest guy. Dead friendly and natural with you. I fetch a mango drink and make my way back to the sofa, literally aching for the chance to sit and chill for a bit.

'We were just having a celebratory drink before Ben goes off to work in that club of his.'

'Celebratory?' I say, stupidly.

'Last exam? Hello?' Ben slings himself back on the sofa.

'Yeah, sorry. It's like, yesterday everyone started their A levels. What happened?'

'It may have gone fast to you, but I assure you…' Ben mimics wiping sweat off his brow.

Feeling left out of the A level experience, is it? Out there! As if I wanted to be swotting and stressing with the rest of them.

'So, you're celebrating by going to work?' is all I say.

'Needs must.' Ben shrugs.

'Needs, my arse,' Rahim retorts, and I smile at how mad that sounds in his Yorkshire Iranian accent. 'He's taking home more than the rest of us put together. Which isn't hard with me earning zero.'

'I pay my way,' Ben says.

'Oh, you know we're grateful for it, Behnam.' Rahim uses Ben's full name, as if to show he's serious. 'But I need find something before you go to university.' He pulls a worried smile. He's a skinny guy with a fair amount of dark curly hair. But his deep-lined face underscores his age.

'Dad was made redundant six months ago now,' Ben says.

I nod, remembering him saying how Rahim was like a horticulture student in Iran, and part of the socialist opposition to the Shah. When he came here fleeing from the Ayatollah, he landed up working in the parks for years.

'There's not a lot of jobs for an old parky like me,' Rahim says. 'I might register for the childminding alongside Janice. But we're not convinced there'll be the work for both of us.'

'People will pretty much always need childminders, won't they?' I ask.

'Not if they can't find a job.'

'Yeah, sorry, it's hard,' I say, feeling an idiot.

'Ayee, it'll work out.' Rahim waves his drink to dismiss the subject. 'We're celebrating, remember?'

'So, what are you up to, mate?' Ben asks. 'I think everyone's down the Harley tonight.'

I take a breath, my shoulders up around my ears, lips tight.

'Worried about bumping into Fran?'

I nod.

'You are such a stupid fuck, you know that?' Ben rolls his eyes.

'Tell me about it!' I sink down the sofa.

'Aw, come on, son, leave the boy alone.' Rahim frowns his concern, making me feel actually OK to talk about it.

So, I start on a rant about how I literally can't do anything right and everyone's lining up to make that crystal clear and now I prove my total uselessness by making a pass at Fran, who I was pretty much brought up with. Plus, all my friends taking off for new lives at uni or whatever, leaving me with not a clue what I want to do.

'Well, beating yourself up won't help. You need a break, my friend.' Rahim nods slowly.

'That's what Fran's mum said. She even offered me their spare room. But I blew it, so now I'll have to go back home, which…' I fade out, worried he'll think I'm hinting. 'Shit, I didn't mean…'

'Any friend of Ben's is welcome here. But there's no spare room, as you know.'

Fuck, he does think I'm angling to stay.

'You should proper get away, Geth.' Ben leans forward to face me. 'That's what I'm doing when I've saved the money. I'm thinking Amsterdam…'

Hmm, Amsterdam with Ben? It'd be a laugh, sitting in cafés getting high. But then he'd want to cruise the gay scene and I'd be the sad bastard stoned alone.

'I have got some birthday money – keep forgetting to pay the frigging cheque in. But, hey…'

'Do it!' Ben punches his thigh.

'Where would I go?' How pathetic do I sound?

Ben shakes his head. 'I dunno, jump on a bus, see where it takes you? Find a sense of adventure, man.'

He darts a look at the clock – I can tell he's losing patience. Maybe I should literally piss off into the sunset like he says. But the aimless loneliness of that frightens me to fuck.

Ben starts readying himself to go to work, asks if I want to go with him. 'It's their new LGBT night, you know you want to,' he mocks.

'Don't wanna cramp your style, man.' Feeling awkward with this banter in front of his dad.

'It's a right night whatever for a twink like me. Loadsa tips.' Ben winks, looking pleased with himself.

Rahim frowns. 'Mind you watch out with them queens, Behnam.'

'Dad!' Ben sighs. 'I can look after myself.'

Rahim nods, runs his finger down his sharp thin nose. 'I don't want you to think I'm anti-gay. God knows I have seen enough bigotry.' He looks towards me with his heavy hooded eyes.

I try to hold his gaze, in awe of what he must have been through, even that he's mentioned it.

'There are men take advantage, straight or gay,' he carries on. 'So, I'm wanting Behnam to look out for himself, same as I did with his sister.'

'As in, plenty of Trolls all round, init?' I look at Ben.

Ben does theatrical raising of eyebrows. Is he saying I'm no better because I tried to jump Fran? Wasn't that just misreading the signs?

'Well I'm going to get my protected butt down there.' Ben

kicks his skinny legs in the air before standing up. 'I've got time for a drink, if you're coming.'

The horizon's still bright as we walk along the side of the park into town – smells of mown grass mixed with traffic fumes and the whiff of rotting rubbish. I put my hand in my pocket to feel Gran and Granddad's card and trace the edge of the cheque and the letter from Don next to it. I think about Ben's idea that I should take off somewhere. The smallest shiver of excitement. What have I got to lose?

We turn the corner to go into town and Ben looks at me.

'Hey, our Gethin gone so quiet. Are you all right?'

I nod. 'It was good to talk to your dad, he's sound as they come.'

'He can get a bit serious, but yeah, he's safe.'

'It's like he totally accepts you, and he wants to look out for you, know what I mean? Unlike my mum who is sooo determined I should be something I'm not.'

Ben shrugs, sticks his hands in his pockets.

'It's funny, since I got that letter, I can't help wondering what it would be like to have a dad? Pretty much never thought about it before,' I add.

Ben stops and turns to me. 'I'm earning money, I'm off to uni. I'm not sure my dad would be so accepting of me sitting on my butt all day.'

He presses the button on a pedestrian crossing and watches for the green man.

'Wow, thanks for the support, man,' I shout above the traffic.

Ben shakes his head. 'Not saying it's easy, but there's always someone else to blame.'

'Well I hope you never come unstuck, with your one-way ticket to a higher fucking mathematical plane?' I fling my arms about as we cross the road.

'And it was all laid on a plate for me, wasn't it?' Ben says as we reach the other side.

Ben sets a manic pace into town, with me trailing behind. Little boy told off for being a spoilt brat? I feel tears rising. Fuck's sake.

We reach the roundabout just as a coach turns off for the bus station. I strain to see where it's going but miss the sign.

Ben stops and pulls a half smile at me.

'Look,' we both start at the same time.

'Go on,' he says.

'It's OK, I was considering diverting via the bus station.' I shift from one leg to another.

'Still thinking of taking off?'

'As in I've got fuck all to stay here for?'

'Go for it!' Ben smiles encouragement and leads the way. He knows he's fucked me off. At least he knows it.

'Where are you thinking of, Geth?'

I don't want to tell him, but I might need to borrow some dosh. He may have called me a dosser, but he's a mate all the same.

'As far away as I can get on a bus?' I say, pleased with this get-out.

'Lands' End? John O'Groats?'

'Ecclesfield?' I laugh.

'Tha'll be lucky!'

The ticket offices are closed, but the TV displays show a few more buses yet to leave: Leeds 21:03; Barnsley 21:24; Worksop 21:43; Inverness 21:50.

'Ben,' I grab his arm. 'Where's Inverness?'

'Scotland, you dork.'

'Whereabouts?'

Ben gets Google maps up on his phone and locates Inverness. 'Ten hours through the night. Far enough for you?'

'Hold on.' I find the map on my phone and type in Lochgillan. Wait for it to upload, wondering if I've spelt it right. 'Gotcha!' I say, showing Ben the marker near the top of the North West coast. My heart thumping hard.

'Lochgillan?' Ben looks puzzled. 'Why the hell…?'

I keep him hanging while I look at buying coach tickets online. It's a job to keep my fingers steady on the screen.

'Come on, don't be a bastard!' I mutter at the website.

'Two hours on the bus from Inverness to Lochgillan,' Ben catches up on his phone.

'Yes! It can be done.' I punch the air. 'They email you a ticket.'

'What?'

'Can you do me a massive favour, Ben? Just, if you could transfer me forty quid for the fare? I'll cash Gran's cheque as soon as I hit a bank and get it back to you.'

'You want to go to Lochgillan tonight?' Ben rubs his brow.

'Inverness tonight. Then I'll pretty much have all day to sort out my next move.' I sound a lot more confident than I feel.

Ben hits light bulb moment. 'I get it, you're going to find your dada?' He clutches at my arm. 'Init, bro?'

'Well, kind of. Lochgillan's where his ancestors come from,

and he said, *"I've a yen to make my home there".'* I mime quotation marks around the phrase. 'I literally can't let it rest, like, the idea he exists. I don't even know if I care but I might as well try?' And that is pretty much it. But now I've decided, something's jumping up inside me, raring to go.

Ben's worried look isn't inspiring confidence, however.

'Look, if he's not there I'll have an adventure exploring my ancestral home. You're the one saying I should get away, you and the rest of the universe?'

Ben shuffles, looks at his feet. 'Mate, I'm sorry about what I said earlier. You are fine to sleep on my floor, you know?'

'No, you're right. I need to get my arse moving. And there's a fucking coach going to Inverness in twenty minutes. Gotta be a sign, no?'

'If you're sure you'll be OK?'

I nod. 'If you're cool with lending me the money, we need to get a move on.' I jerk my head to look at the bus station clock.

So, we sit on the bench and piss about making transfer, booking ticket. The email pings in with seven minutes to spare.

'Hang on, two secs?' Ben waves me to stay as he speeds off around the corner.

I watch as the Wakefield coach drops off its passengers: a black woman in tight cream dress with a little girl, eyes wide and dazzled like she's just woken up; white couple in dark hoodies, flashes of nose rings and long dyed hair. The coach leaves in a trail of exhaust and I take a lungful of this scent of adventure, staring at the deepening blue of the sky as the streetlights buzz into action. I can't stop my leg jigging.

Ben comes rushing back, big grin as he produces crisps, a couple of Mars Bars and a bottle of Coke from his backpack.

'Thought you'd need some supplies? And, yeah, take this, you might need some spare cash.'

He gives me thirty quid and I drop the crisps trying to put it in my wallet.

Ben empties out his backpack into his pockets. 'Take the bag as well. I've got another one at home.'

I stuff the things into the bag and get up. I'm literally too choked to speak as fling my arms around him.

'Hey, you'll be giving me ideas, man!' Ben pushes me back, still holding the tops of my arms.

'Thanks Ben, you're the best.'

There's a coach approaching. INVERNESS in LED above the windscreen.

It's real. It's here and I'm off!

Dream Bike – *Jez*

Roar of the engine coming out of the bends. Rush of warm air through the visor. Blurred curve of hills against the snaking road. Eating up tarmac before slowdown through suburban semis. Turning heads as we weave the traffic until Martin pulls the purring beast into the bike shop's car park. He jumps off, shaking his sweat-damp hair as he removes his helmet.

'Fooking hell, that is some bike. Insanely powerful. Fooking lethal.' Big boyish grin. And he's right. This is some ride.

'Sex on wheels, truly.' Slide myself forward to driving position. Look down at the matt black curves, polished aluminium, and those massive titanium covered forks. 'Can you believe they had my dream bike here?'

'Can't believe they let me test drive a brand-new Yamaha VMax.' Martin unzips his leather, wipes his forehead with the back of his hand. 'Fuck it's hot, aren't you ready for taking your lid off?'

I lean forward for the last moment of fantasy riding before jumping off and removing my helmet. How intense is the heat today, banging off the sticky tarmac? That like hot country smell of petrol and chip fat with a whiff of rotting rubbish. Not even a fantasy. I can have my dream bike.

'They've always been good to me here, since I did the Kick Start thing,' Martin says. 'No way would most dealers let you take a bike like that out, especially when there's no chance you're buying.' He moves over to a line of shade by the back wall of the shop and pulls out a pack of Marlboros. Lights up and inhales as he casts his eyes over the bike.

I take off Martin's spare leather jacket and stand next to him against the wall. Take a fag off him and smoke it while I build up to what I've got to say.

'Who says we're not buying?' The words come out like all croaky.

'Yeah right. You're talking sixteen grand, never mind what it would take to insure. Alright mechanics' wages aren't bad, but if you think this is in my league… And before you start I ain't nicking it neither.'

'No, I'm going to give you the money to buy it for me, right, and you're going teach me to ride it.' My heart's thumping. The bike I fell in love with, joked with Ken about buying. Chances of that? And Martin's in town. Go with it, girl. It's meant to be.

He turns to look at me open mouthed. Cigarette burning to the stub in his hand. 'Man, you are fooking joking me.'

I shake my head slowly, draw on my fag and exhale. Look him straight in his pale piggy eyes.

He stares back for a moment, then drops his tab and turns towards the shop.

'I'm taking the keys in and then us'll go for a bevy to cool down. The heat's gone to your conk, man.'

The pub's beer garden is just a yard, weeds straggling out of the cracks. It's rammed, being a sunny afternoon, but I manage to nab a table in the shade as the couple who were there drag their screaming kid away, scattering crisps as they go.

I wave to Martin, coming out with the drinks. He makes heavy weather of crossing the yard in his biker boots and leather trousers. T-shirt with dark patches of sweat. His neck and face puffy red. Yellow hair stuck to his head.

'Fooking jiggered, man, this heat does not suit me.' He squeezes himself onto the bench seat.

'No, you're best served cold,' I smirk. Truth is he's not much of a looker, but he was always my favourite foster brother. And he mostly tried to keep me on his side. Would it be because I was prepared to cover for him?

'I'll gladly sit mesen in a fridge; have all the lasses after me.' He pulls that stupid grin. Takes a long swig of his drink then looks at his glass. 'That's not touching the sides.' He takes another draught. 'Shandy, mind, seeing as I'm driving.'

'Aw, so law abiding!' I laugh, and down some of my drink. Best take it slowly with Martin, like let him chill a bit.

'How long did you say you're in town?' I ask.

'I've got the week off, so as long as me mam's OK with it I'll probably stay while next Saturday or Sunday.'

'And is she? OK I mean.'

'Yeah, she's champion at the moment. She's got a new shrink who she actually likes. Not had a drink for a while, neither.'

'Has she still got that boyfriend?'

'Religious nut, you mean?' He pulls out his Marlboro and lights us both up. He tells me how last time he was there, the boyfriend had locked his mum in her flat to make her dry out. Martin kicked the door in and called the pigs.

'I asked for that copper who knows me, right? The one who got me onto Kick Start,' he explains.

'So, he let you off kicking your mum's door in?'

'Yeah, right pally, asking me how I was doing. Seemed chuffed I'd landed a workshop job in Birmingham.'

'Who'd have thought it? All grown-up and totally legit.' I can picture him when he lived with us. Just turned sixteen and slamming the door on all the do-goody professionals. Mum getting me to persuade him this one had something proper to offer.

'Still find it weird: one minute I'm being done for joy riding and then all of sudden they're putting me through me bike test and training me up as a mechanic. Not what you expect of the cops.'

'Well, you've done yourself proud.'

'Drink to that, Sis!' We clink glasses. 'Big cheer to you and your mam and all.'

Martin's mother has struggled all his life. He was like sent from here to there and back to her until her next collapse. Could have been my life if Alice had lived. How have I never thought that before?

'Know something?' I say. 'Whatever you've been through, you've never said a bad word about your mum.'

He shrugs. 'She's me mam, i'nt she?' He tilts his empty glass at me. 'Time for one more?'

He's off to the bar before I can offer. I lean against the wall, feel its coolness against my back. Alice, fucked from the start with drink and drugs and dead before I could remember. Just blurred images from the access visits. Now Ken's version of her, working its way through like a shard of glass. Not going there. Isn't that the point of the bike?

Martin comes back with two fresh pints. Rubs his sweaty face on his T shirt sleeve. Long swig of his drink.

'Beginning to feel half human.' He smacks his lips. 'Crackin' ride though. Fooking beast of a bike, I'd lose me license soon as look if it were mine.'

'So how about I give you the money to buy it for me? I pay you to teach me to ride it, right, then I fuck off to Scotland on it.'

'You are off your bleeding nut, Jez? Apart from you having upwards of sixteen grand, I don't think so, there is no way you can get your full bike licence in a week, even with Direct Access.'

'But you know I can ride, you said I was a natural.'

'Yeah, that Honda 90 I got you?'

I remind him that he also taught me to ride his 125 round Tesco car park. And that I did my CBT when I was with Stan.

'Stan let me ride his CB 500 on the top roads. It's all still there.' I point to my head, then lean forward, grasping imaginary handlebars. Grin up at him as I counter-steer into a bend.

His frown squeezes sweat into furrows on his forehead. 'Yeah, and I'm betting you haven't ridden since you left Blackburn in a hurry after you got with that crazy Angel character.'

'I had to sell the frigging Honda to pay my fare to Liverpool.'

'Jez, the VMax is over 1600cc, weighs a fucking ton and a half, and accelerates like death. Too fast into a corner and you *will* be strawberry jam.'

'It's up to me isn't it?' First thing I thought of when I got Ken's gold. And it's there in the showroom down the road.

Martin sighs. 'So off you go, buy the bike, get your licence. But you can leave me out of it.'

He downs the last of his shandy and gets up to go.

'Martin, wait.' I pull the mini bank statement out of my pocket.

There it is, clear as you like. Deposit of £21,490 today. Martin stares at it, scratches his head, and stares some more.

'What the fuck have you been up to, Jez?'

'Nowt dodgy like, you don't need to know.'

'Oh, is that right? I'm to put my name to a bike and teach you to ride it illegally and I don't need to know how you've got twenty-one grand.' He picks up his jacket and helmet.

'Martin, please, I've done nowt wrong.'

'Fine by me. I'll not be buying the bike in any case.'

Ken's letter: *Don't let on about it, just use it to enjoy yourself.* But how much do I need Martin if I'm to have the bike? Do I have a choice?

'Please, just hear me out. I'll tell you, right.'

Martin takes another big sigh. Stands clutching his gear. His face a tight frown.

'OK, you can get another pint in, seeing as you're loaded. But nowt you say will get me to buy that bike.'

It's like hearing myself from a distance telling Martin the bare bones of the story. Ken and the gold, deadpan as if it happened to someone else. Martin's face says it all. A likely tale!

I finish the story, all the way to the bank. Silence while we sip our beer. How good was the bike ride this afternoon? Power and speed wiping out all thought in the focus of the moment. Even as a pillion.

I hand Martin the new pack of Marlboro I thought to buy with the drinks. He nods, takes a couple out.

'So, poor fucker's not in his grave and already you've cashed in the gold. What's the bleeding rush?' He lights the fags, hands me one.

'His next of kin have arrived. I'm not hanging round for no family funeral.'

'And they don't know about the gold?'

'No, he said not to tell no-one.'

Martin nods. He knows he owes me trust. My strongest card. Or my only one?

'They might smell a rat if he's left them with nowt,' he muses.

'Yeah, and that's like why I need to get away sharpish.' True, doing a runner from the proper kids has got me moving. But it's not the main thing really.

'So, take a holiday. You could do a world cruise on that money.'

'It has to be a motorbike. Surely you understand that?'

'Why do you think I went nicking them?' he says quietly. Takes a few slow drags of his cigarette.

I almost have him. I just need one more thing. Something I have over him.

'I helped you when you had to hide that bike. I got you the keys for Dad's lock-up, remember?'

Martin scowls. 'I didn't nick that bike, I owed someone a favour.'

'And if I'd grassed you up, you'd have been out of Kick Start.' I take a puff on my fag. Exhale as I eyeball him.

'What the fuck is that supposed to mean?' He stares open mouthed at me.

'So maybe you owe *me* a favour?'

Martin reaches for his drink and necks most of it. Stands up, gathering his clobber again.

'You can fuck right off with your cheap tricks! Blackmail don't suit you and it won't work.' He leans towards me, his face red and sweat-shiny. 'That bike *will* kill you. End of. Get on a plane and come back when heat's off. Go for Direct Access, get your full licence.'

He rolls the jackets tighter under his arm, picks up the helmets.

I stand up. Tears welling. 'Please Martin. I would never dob you in, right? Can we just like talk about it?' I put my hand on his arm, feel the heat of it.

'Like I said, nice ride, Jez.' He pulls his arm away. 'And I'm sorry about your dad.' Then he turns and walks quickly through the yard. Swings wide to avoid a bunch of teenagers. Pushes the door into the pub and he's gone.

Shit. How was threatening him going to help? I take a swig of my drink. Panic rising. You've lost this one, admit it, girl. But I can't give up. Maybe there's a halfway point?

I run out of the pub, down the road to the bike shop. Martin's busy tying the spare jacket to the rack of his Suzuki.

Quick glance down the line of bikes in the window. The VMax outshines them all, but there are a few nice-looking smaller bikes. I turn to see Martin pull his helmet on and switch on the ignition.

'Martin, I'm sorry, I was out of order,' I tug at his sleeve.

He pulls his visor up. 'Just leave it, Jez.'

'No, listen, maybe a smaller bike? Just big enough to get me away?'

He purses his lip. Flips his visor back down, revs his engine.

I lean to face him. Pull my hands in to mimic a really small bike. 'Pleeeeze!' I mouth over the roar.

Martin looks at the shop window and back at me. Cuts the ignition and lifts off his helmet.

'You want me to swing for you, I swear.'

I stand wide eyed. Don't dare say a word.

'We'll have a look,' he says.

Welcome to Scotland – *Gethin*

I wake with a jolt as the coach pulls into a city bus station. Orange glow of streetlamp on rows of empty shelters. Is this Inverness? The clock says 01:10. Still seven hours to go. Idiot.

I stretch my legs into the space in front of the empty seat next to me, and rub my neck, stiff from leaning against the window. There's a smell of stale food, sweat and failed Febreze adding to the skank of my armpits. Fuck's sake, I haven't even got a clean T shirt.

And I'm I hooked straight back into the panic that grabbed me out of nowhere when I was literally high just from getting on the coach. Repeating scenarios of not finding Don, or Don not wanting to know; huddled in a dank Scottish ditch in a howling Scottish gale. Drifting into a sleep that was just a messed-up version of the same. Waking to find I'm on a night bus to nowhere, my mouth dry and sour and in desperate need of more than tepid flat Coke.

When I get a down on myself it's like an addiction. Yeah, there's this tiny voice that pipes up, Chrissakes, you're only going to Inverness…. but then other one hits back even stronger. As in, I've fucked up big-style, Mum hates me, Fran hates me, Ben thinks I'm a waster and he'd be right. Jumping on the first bus I see because it's maybe heading in the direction of some dude who wanked off for my mum?

My tongue sticks to the roof of my mouth. Jesus, I need water. I head for the toilet with the Coke bottle. The coach lights are out, and I bump into a woman slouched into the aisle. She glares at me, lurid in the streetlight, all streaky make-up and clumps of red hair. Pokes her tongue out when I'm about to say sorry.

Suit yourself.

I get to the toilet and fumble for the seat to take a quick slash. The flush doesn't work, at which point it hits me the electrics are off because the coach isn't running. I squeeze soap onto my hands then discover even the water pump doesn't work. Total Idiot. Wipe my soap-slimed hands on some bog-roll and shuffle out still thirsty as fuck. That went well.

Back to my seat and there's a guy all settled with a can of Foster's in the seat next to mine. Why the hell did I leave it unguarded?

He stands to let me past, big fucker, buttons too tight on his shirt. I'm forced to get a bit close, catch the escaping wisps of greying chest hair.

'Craig.' He offers his surprisingly small neat hand as we sit. I give it a half-hearted shake and pretty much feel I have to tell him my name.

'Going far, Gethin?' Craig settles his beer belly and takes a long swig from his can. He's got a Scottish accent, but it's not right hard Glasgow.

'I'm probably heading for Lochgillan, after Inverness?' I try to sound as dull as possible.

'Ah, west coast. You do right. I'm heading up the Moray Firth. My sister's got a B&B there.'

I nod, though it could be another planet for all I know.

'It's a nice enough place, but she's not doing so good.' He pauses and I make a show of looking through my bag, but he drones on about how his sister and her hubby took on this crumbling B&B and the hubby dropped dead from exhaustion within the first year.

'But she's a stubborn lassie,' he adds. 'Reckons she's going to run a gallery now. What does she know about art?'

He nudges me as I pull out my iPhone and stick the earphones in.

'My mum's an artist,' I say without thinking.

'Oh aye, anyone I've heard of?' He licks his bottom lip.

I shake my head, wondering why I mentioned it. I retreat to looking at the music list.

Craig knocks back his beer and reaches in his holdall. The bus starts up and the low lights above the centre aisle flicker on.

He pulls himself up clutching two cans of Foster's. 'Fancy a beer?'

I shouldn't accept, but my brain has already sent signals to my hand to reach out, alerted my smile muscles and instructed my mouth to say, 'Cheers, thanks.'

Craig switches on his reading light and spreads his newspaper. The fucking Sun, wouldn't you just know? There's a picture of some celebrity redhead looking soulful at her reflection in a shiny car.

'No mention of that other redhead up in court just now.' Craig grins up at me. 'Rebekah Brooks? Phone hacking?'

'It's hardly going to be headlining the Sun! As in Murdoch owns…'

'Hypocritical bastards, the lot of them,'

'So why read it?' I mutter, choosing Skepta's *Doin' It Again* from my music list.

'Give you three guesses,' Craig chuckles, opening the paper.

Fuck that! I jig my knee to Skepta kicking in with *Rescue*

Me. Craig gives me the thumbs up then gets back to his tit studies. I swig my beer and turn the volume up.

But the music doesn't stop me fast-tracking to same-old how-pathetic-are-you-running-away-to-find-long-lost-daddy-don't-even-know-if-he's-there?

Google him, fuckwit, the little voice says. For once it wins and I search Don McCalstry Lochgillan on the internet.

What I get is Donald McCalstry, an 1820 Lochgillan post runner; Donald McCalstry, car dealer 59 miles from Lochgillan; and a Wikipedia entry on McCalstry of Lochgillan, with an estate of over 50,000 acres. There's a pipe tune called Lament for Captain Donald McCalstry, and I feel a bubble of excitement rising at the thought that I might literally be related to McCalstry of Lochgillan. Personalised pipe tune and everything? I pause a minute to allow it.

Craig seizes the moment to get in my face, indicating to take my earphones out. 'Eh, hope you've brought your passport, laddie?' He stabs a finger at a piece of news: *Slippery Salmond: Labour Dirty Tricks Accusation.*

'Oh, right,' I say, pleased I've understood what he's on about. 'I've got a few months before the referendum, haven't I?'

'Only got themselves to blame,' Craig continues.

'Who, the Murdochs?'

'Bloody New Labour, bloody Tony Blair. If they hadn't been so busy lining their banker friends' pockets, sending the boys to get blown up in Iraq, and paid a bit more heed to Scottish working folk, that shark of a Salmond would never have brought us to this vote for some cast-adrift Republic of Haggis.'

'So, you'll be voting No, then?' I try to take it all in. Not exactly kept up with the Scottish debates so far.

'Aye, I'll be a bloody Labour loyalist for the good it'll do.'
He shakes his head and turns to the sports' page.

I shove my earphones in and catch a funny thought that
Mum says pretty much the same stuff about Labour, and how
you should vote for them anyway. Hey, I've found her soul
mate.

I get back to Google and look a bit deeper. Skepta starts on
Bad Boy.

I see it halfway down page two. Don McCalstry's Highland
Motorcycle Museum. One mile outside Lochgillan. Fucking
hell, can it literally be that easy?

My stomach clenches as I press on the link. Sepia pictures
of old bikes in Highland settings scrolling across the top. And
the intro blurb.

'This rough and ready collection of British made
motorcycles includes many that are fully functional: some
have run in classic and vintage bike events. The rest could be
described as works in progress, with the workshop in full
view.

The museum is a piece of social history. Bikes are displayed
in tableaux reflecting the age they were made in. From the
soldier and his WAF girlfriend on a 1940s Matchless G3/L;
the family seaside outing in a 1950s Panther sidecar outfit; to
a shiny 1960s Triton outside an Inverness milk-bar.'

Oh My God. OH MY ACTUAL GOOOOOD! I lean back
in my seat, heart pounding so loud I'm worried Craig will
notice. But he's fallen asleep, page three girl spread over his
knees. I switch off the music to try to take it all in.

There are probably dozens of Don McCalstrys in
Lochgillan alone. But it's got to be... *if only there was a job in
that...* somehow, he's found a way to fund his dream. But he

could pretty much as easily be the car dealer? I imagine making a complete tit of myself declaring to the wrong Scottish biker that I'm his long-lost son. I scan the website for a photo of him. There isn't one.

It must be him. At least go and be sure. As in ask a few questions about how he got to open the museum; see if he knows Sheffield? I drift into this scenario: his shock and surprise when I break it to him, moving swiftly to a whisky drenched welcome with tales of the ancient clan.

I look out of the window to see dawn breaking behind the blue-grey hills ahead – the empty road snaking through them. The last thing I see before I fall asleep is the massive blue sign with the diagonal white cross. Welcome to Scotland. Fàilte gu Alba.

'Breakfast,' I mutter to myself walking out of Inverness bus station. It's all pale modern stone round here; the sky reflects off smooth wet paving; sun glinting on shiny apartment blocks. I was expecting dark Victorian stone and castles. I'll get something to eat, find a bank, see about buses to Lochgillan and then, if there's time, maybe a spot of sightseeing?

There's a bounce in my battered trainers. What was I worrying about? The Beginning of a Great Adventure.

I turn another corner and there's a smart looking café advertising Full Scottish Breakfast. You reckon? That should fill the hole that is my ravenous stomach.

The café is all beech and slate with massive artwork in black and white and gold. The smell of coffee is overwhelming, they are actually roasting it in a gleaming steel contraption. I make my way past a group of French backpackers lounging on brown leather sofas and plant myself at a table near the bar. Reach for the menu and study which freshly roasted bean to have for my coffee? Finally look up to see a girl in a brown apron and blond hair pulled into a donut ring to top her chubby baby face.

'Will you be ready with your order, Sir?' she asks in the sweetest Scottish accent.

I grin, liking the 'Sir'. 'I've been up all night, it's got to be the Full Scottish,' I say, rubbing my empty tummy. 'And, let me see, a large latte made with Indonesian Lintong, Madam Popa?'

'Just the thing for a wee hangover?'

'Ah, no, not that kind of night. As in just got off the bus from Sheffield. My first time in Scotland.'

'Welcome to Inverness,' the girl beams.

She retreats with my order and I look over at the artwork on the long side wall. A kind of stylised urban landscape with cheeky black cartoon birds perched on gilded barbed wire, little thought bubbles I can't read coming out of the birds. Looks pretty sick, whatever.

There's a leaflet stand by the plate glass windows and I wander over for something to read. A flyer advertising A Respectful Debate On Scottish Independence. Radical Independence Campaign Youth Planning Meeting. Leaflet from the Highland Council: Have Your Say: Register Now! This referendum seems a bigger deal than I realised. The Radical Independence leaflet is all about an adult-free meeting to discuss the way forward and organise events. Would I even be included now I'm officially an adult? I flick through the leaflet about registering to vote. Would my Scottish ancestry qualify me?

I literally don't notice the girl with the tray until she's right beside me. The full Scottish smells as good as it looks and I'm grabbing a bite of the fat juicy sausage before she's set the coffee down.

'You'll be hungry from your journey?' She smiles.

'Sorry,' I say through half chewed sausage. 'Manners are not my strong point. But I have to say this is place is epic.'

'Och, well it's a social enterprise, you see?' The girl nods, looking pleased with herself. 'It means useless NEETs like me get properly trained and paid to work here, plus we get to design the décor.' She waves at the artwork.

'NEETs?' I'm thinking neets and tatties, but that's some sort of veg, isn't it?

'Not in Employment, Education…'

'Or Training, of course. I'm a NEET myself.'

She smiles doubtfully. 'Well, I'll be leaving you to enjoy your breakfast.'

'Hold on,' I say, gob full of black pudding. Pause to get it swallowed. 'What's your name?'

'Jeanette.' She puts a hand up to her mouth.

I wave the leaflet. 'Have you registered for this referendum thingy?'

'Not as yet, I'm only sixteen.'

'But they're giving you the vote, which is pretty awesome, no?'

'There's a lot of talk about it and I'm going to some meetings to work out what I think. It's a big responsibility, is what it feels like?'

'My father's Scottish. Do you think they'll let me vote?'

She shrugs, looks over her shoulder. 'Well, I'd best be getting back.'

Feeling at least half a stone heavier but still full of the joys, I walk a couple of blocks in search of a bank. Find myself in the old part of town with tall stone buildings housing hotels and banks, including, would you know it, a branch of Abbey on the corner.

'I'd like to cash this cheque, please?' I smile at the dude in white shirt and tartan tie. He looks well young, is this another social enterprise? He studies the cheque, looks at my Abbey card.

'Do you have the money in your account at present?'

'Well, no, it's pretty much empty. So, if I could cash this cheque, I'll pay some of it back in?'

The man shakes his head. 'I'm afraid the cheque will take one working day to clear, which, as it's Friday, means you'll not see any of it until Monday.'

'You what? It's from my grandmother, the same bank as well. All you need is to check her balance, isn't it?'

He purses his lips, like he's genuinely sorry to give me bad news. 'I'm sorry, Sir, there is not that facility.'

I rummage through my wallet. Breakfast set me back over a tenner including the tip for Jeanette. Yep, £21.70 with the bit of change I had in my pocket.

'I've just arrived, I've got nowhere to stay. Surely you can advance me a bit on this cheque?' Literally shaking with the injustice of it.

'Can your Granny not transfer you some money now?'

I imagine trying to explain to Gran about transferring money they've already given me.

'No,' I feel my voice rising. 'No, she bloody well can't.'

The man pulls back, looks to the side of him. 'Shall I be paying this in, the now?'

'Yes. Go on.' I stand to one side while he processes it. 'Fucking bankers,' I mutter. 'Ripping us off for billions to pay for their obscene bonuses. And the fuckers can't cash a grandparent's birthday gift.'

He coughs for my attention. Looking side to side again, like I'm about to firebomb the place. I sign the chit, take my card, and leave.

Fuck-witted useless waste of space. How long have I had that bloody cheque? Moronic stupid dickhead. I pause at a display in the window of Blacks. The cheapest discounted tent is £40. I picture my tent, sleeping bag, cagoule, scattered about my room at home. All I've got is my half-ripped hoody and holey trainers.

Down another stone-building street and I hit the river with the castle looming on the greying skyline. I turn the other way towards some scrubby grassland around an old church. I sling myself onto the damp grass, lean up against a tree, head in my knees, and allow myself to cry while I beat my head with my fist.

I stop even cursing myself with the hot release of tears. I hug my legs and rock myself until literally I'm forced to sit up and clear my blocked nose on my sleeve. I shift against the damp seeping into my arse, move to perch on the bulging tree root.

OK, what are my options? Phoning Mum? Instant no. Getting more money out of Ben? Really not up for telling him I've failed at the first hurdle. Get the bus to Lochgillan and throw myself at the mercy of Don McCalstry? That's if I've got enough for the fare. Supposing he's not there or he tells me to get lost? Sleep on the beach and beg for food? Great plan on the Scottish coast without a sleeping bag and I'm betting they love beggars! Fuck, fuck. Come on.

I walk back to the bus station, passing a Yes Campaign stall – I'm so not interested now. Find out the daily bus to Lochgillan has left. So, I'm here until tomorrow whatever. I pull my phone out, is there a contact I haven't thought of? But it's dead, of course, with all that Googling. What the actual fuck do I do?

I wander back to the café and look through the window at the people happily downing fancy coffees. Half an hour ago that was me. I'm about to turn away when Jeanette walks past the window and waves as she sees me. Fuck it, it's a social enterprise.

I pretend to look at the papers on the newspaper rack, until I see Jeanette moving towards the serving bar. I head towards her and she stops when she sees me.

'Hi!' She smiles. 'Cannae keep away? Sit down, I'll get you a coffee.'

'Actually,' I shuffle from foot to foot. 'I kind of wanted your advice, just for a minute, if that's…?'

'Sure.' She sets down her tray. 'You'll have to be quick though.'

So, I blurt out my dumb shit situation, ask if she knows anywhere I can stay for free.

'I cannae take you home, it's just, me ma, you know?' She frowns.

'Oh no, I just wondered, is there like a homeless hostel or something?'

'There's a drop-in centre, but that's just the daytime.' She purses her lips while she thinks. 'There's some lads camping rough up the river, they might help you. If you walk upstream from the castle, you'll see some wee islands and then a patch of woodland. You'll probably sense the smoke from their fire.'

'Thanks,' I say, touching her arm.

She smiles and pulls back. 'Ask for Skunky.'

It's starting to drizzle, and I pull up my hoody as I head along the towpath, trainers starting to leak. Walking fast, I try to ignore the rising panic at the idea of invading some homeless people's camp. What if they're really hostile? Not exactly the adventure I had in mind. Come on, nearly there. It's worth a try.

Soon enough I pass the islands, with a couple of boats moored alongside. And then like she said, a patch of trees and a thin wisp of smoke rising.

There are a few little tents and some plastic sheeting strung up in the trees. A dude in pink leggings and blond dreads hacking at some branches with an axe; a patchy brown dog yelping with every swipe. I take a wide circle around the dog and reach the fire. There's a few people sitting on logs or rusty oil cans. One of them is slumped back in an old car seat. Black hair in a ponytail with a bleached stripe down the middle, nursing a two-litre bottle of White Lightening. I shuffle forward, hands in pockets, as he waves the bottle at me.

'Hey. What yer after, loping round here?'

'Skunky?'

'And who may be asking?' He grins round at his mates. One of them sniggers as he pokes the fire with a stick. He's stick-thin himself, looks about twelve.

'Jeanette, from the social enterprise café said to ask for you. I'm, like, need somewhere to crash.'

'Ha, that's the social enterprise for you! They ban me from their swanky café, but they're happy enough to send me the waifs and strays.' He shakes his head. 'Got any dosh?' Stained tooth grin at me.

'No, not much. I will have on Monday, but I'm hoping to get to Lochgillan before then.'

'On your holidays?'

'Well, in a way.'

'So, you're no' homeless, just a tourist.'

'But I've only got twenty odd quid until Monday. I've literally got the clothes I stand in. As in no sleeping bag, nothing?' I trace the dirt in front of me with my trainer.

'You're a fooking divvy tourist, aren't yer?'

'What can I say?' I shrug, throwing in a daft smile.

'Och, you were after Skunky and you've found him. You can get some messages with your twenty odd spondoolies and we'll find you a corner to kip in.'

'Messages?' I imagine being a runner for some homeless spy-ring.

'Ha! That's Scots for what you English call shopping, I believe.'

'Oh, right, thanks,' another stupid smile. I glance round, feeling awkward. An African guy with leathery bare feet, carving a stick. The skinny kid on an oilcan poking at the fire. A man in a battered suit staring straight ahead. Nobody looks at me.

'A seat for the laddie, Aiden.' Skunky waves at the kid, who gets up and crashes round the woodpile. Finds a log and stands it next to Skunky.

'Our Aiden's from somewhere in west Fife.' Skunky's exaggerated gestures remind me of Fagin in our Y7 production of *Oliver*. 'Here we have Paoul from Slovakia, Mustafa all the way from Sudan, and Gordon with the dog crossed the waters from Ulster. Me, I'm from the universe, via Glasgee, you mind.'

'I'm Gethin, from Sheffield,' I offer.

Homeless – *Gethin*

I sit on my log watching the smoke in the shaft of afternoon sunlight. Awkward as fuck, like a new boy at school.

'News from the missus, mannie?' Skunky points his bottle at Paoul, sitting across the fire.

He's a small nervy looking bloke, probably in his early thirties, with dirty blond curls and brown pinstripe suit that's too big for him. Mud spattered office shoes. He stares at a well-worn letter on lilac paper and looks up, all confusion.

'Reading it over and over will no' make it any different,' Skunky says.

Paoul shakes his head, goes back to reading.

Skunky turns to me. 'Our Slovakian friend was laid off from the fish farm. Lost his accommodation with the job too.'

'Double whammy!' I say, as Paoul shakes his head.

'Missus,' he moans.

Skunky forces like a *Pirates of the Caribbean* laugh. 'Missus still thinks he's got a job.' He says in a stagey whisper. 'When's she after arriving with the bairns?' He shouts at Paoul.

'Bairns?'

'Kiddies. Missus. When they come Scotland?'

'Next week. What I can do?' He looks up at me, his face torn with worry.

'Can't you, like, say you need time to find a bigger place?' I feel I have to come up with something.

'Missus, she buy ticket. Bringing children also.'

'Dinnae greet now, mannie.' Skunky throws his arms open. 'Something will turn up, never you bother.'

'Bollocks!' Aiden with the stick mutters, stares at me with blank green eyes. His head all small and lumpy under close-clipped mousey hair.

'Well, I suppose it's always worth hoping.' Fuck knows, I'll say literally anything, however dumb.

Aiden gobs into the fire and keeps his eyes fixed on me. Paoul goes back to his letter. The guy from Sudan sits on his oil-can carving a stick with an old kitchen knife and seeming to notice nothing.

'Dinnae mind Aiden. Here, help you chill out.' Skunky winks as he hands me his bottle. I take a swig and he's right – I feel like I need it.

'Aiden's one of those life don't go straight for.' Skunky waves me to take more. This time it goes to my head like I'm about twelve. 'Left home at fourteen, in't it, Aid? Trouble with the polis? Served a stretch…'

'Shut the fuck up, Skunk. Like you're so clever landing up here?' Aiden's still staring at me. It's beginning to spook me.

'Aye, we're none of us too clever,' Skunky turns wistful. 'Mustafa here no' speaks a word. But he'll have seen a thing or two on his travels. Cannier than all the rest of us.'

I glance at Mustafa, wood shavings falling from his ripped combats onto cracked feet, his skin dusty grey, the only colour in his African skull cap. He shows no sign of knowing he's being talked about.

'So, what about you, Gethin?' Spunky continues. 'With your no spare clothes and twenty-odd quid. Bolted in a hurry is it?'

'Oh,' I say, weak as fuck. 'Mainly I needed to get away from my mum.'

'Kicked you out, has she? New fella is it?'

Immediately I feel bad dissing Mum. As if she would ever kick me out.

'No, my mum wouldn't…' Rub my eyes against the smoke, an excuse to avoid their looks.

'So, go on, what's the crack with your ma, laddie?' Skunky leans forward to force eye contact.

'Well, she's been a bit pushy – you know how parents can be?' I give them a what-can-I-do smile.

Aiden looks blank and Skunky raises a massively hairy eyebrow.

'Where's your da, then, son?'

'Well,' I start, not sure how much to tell. 'I've never actually met him, but he lives in Lochgillan.'

'So, you're away to find your long-lost daddy? Fair warms the cockles, eh, Aiden?'

Aiden spits into the fire. Gives me another look. 'How are you at building shelters?'

'Shelters? Yeah. My mum took me and my friend on a bush-craft thing once. We learnt to make shelters out of branches and twigs. Did a bit of that shit for Duke of Edinburgh too, know what I mean?'

I'm babbling crap and it serves me right when Aiden says, 'Let's see you get building, then?'

I wander around looking for a couple of sturdy branches. There are some longish pieces on the pile where the dreadlocked bloke's still chopping. But I'm guessing I need to find my own. I walk further into the woods, passing scruffy tents and couple of shelters made from tarpaulin, crates, scraps of corrugated iron and wooden pallets. There's a strip of carpet outside one of them and a stripy sun lounger.

I get to the edge of the woods in a couple of minutes, there's literally not much of use at all. The only thing would be to cut branches off the trees. As in I'd need an axe that I'd be crap at using. I sit down on a tree stump, hopelessly searching for my next move. I remember the bit of draw in my pocket. I should have bought some tobacco.

Aiden emerges from behind a large holly bush, carrying a bit of tatty plastic sheeting.

'How's it going with the shelter?' he smirks.

'There's not a lot of spare wood around.' I point to the pathetic pile of twigs I've gathered. 'Wouldn't shelter a fairy.'

'Aye, you'll maybe want to use this.' He hands me the plastic. It's a faded orange colour, a good few square metres.

'You reckon?' I smile. 'That'll do nicely.'

Aiden nods, shuffles his foot. He seems awkward rather than hostile now and I am genuinely touched that he thought to help me.

'I've got a bit of draw here, if you've any baccy?'

Aiden pulls out a battered Drum tobacco pouch, perches on the tree stump next to me. 'Go on then, I'll roll us a smoke,' he says, producing a limp looking pack of Rizlas. He sticks them together, then takes a ready-made dog-end and empties it into the paper. Looks up at me, like he's expecting me to be shocked. Which of course I am, well, not shocked, but surprised, yeah?

'Not too proud for someone else's tab?' He takes the grass and tips the whole lot into the spliff. Looks at me as if he dares me to say anything.

Fucking hell, it's literally the best part of a ten bag. Just because he gave me a shitty piece of plastic. But I'm not going to risk getting him riled up.

'We'll go into town later, get you a sleeping bag,' he says, licking up the spliff. He produces an old Zippo lighter and lights up, leaning back as he takes a big toke. He exhales a massive cloud looking up at the sky, then nods and takes another, leaving me to wonder about the sleeping bag.

By the time we get back to the fire I'm like totally trashed. Fucking three tokes were enough for me. I thought I was a hardened pothead, but I'm a complete wuss compared to the malnourished waif Aiden. He goes off to find me some string for my shelter while I stand gawping at the trees, concentrating on staying upright. As if I need a fucking whitey now? I take deep breaths of the dank smoky air, wondering if there's any chance of a drink of water around here. Skunky's back onto tormenting Pauol. I don't want to draw attention to myself.

Someone crashes through the woods on the other side of the fire. She emerges pushing a supermarket trolley rattling with empty cans. A tiny woman in a sleeveless leather jerkin and snake tattooed arms. Spikey dark hair and a heart shaped face. Her skin is verging on yellow and it's hard to tell how old she is. She stops by the fire, kicking at the dirt, non-stop cursing from her rosebud mouth.

'Fucking wanking social shirkers can't even let you fucking alone when they've taken your fucking daughter, fucking five years fucking old and you can't even fucking escape them from fucking Coatbridge to fucking Inverness, the cunts.'

She catches my eye for a second and I see a flash of Emily in her. Something about the shape of her face? Her manic gestures?

'Awright, Minx. Calm yourself lassie, what's going on?' Skunky shifts to face her.

'Come all this way, don't I, to make a new fucking start and that. Off the fucking booze, fucking AA, getting by collecting me cans.'

'Aye, you're doing OK,' Skunky says.

'Wanking social worker on her hols with her bastard girlfriend and their bairn. Dirty lessies are allowed a bairn. There on fucking King Street fucking shouting her head off at the laddie for no fucking reason. Catch me fucking bawling at my daughter like that? I get fucking done for fucking neglect and there she fucking is. Fuck her. Fuck.'

Minx bangs her fists against her thighs with every 'fuck' – so wired it's like she'll snap in two. Paoul walks away but nothing fazes Mustafa who stays put on his oil drum. I move to lean against a tree out of the wood-smoke, feel dizzy and sick and cut up by the weirdest ever notion that this exploding bomb is Emily in a parallel universe.

'Wissht, now, Minxy. Getting yourself all of a lather. Have yourself a sup of this, just this once, to calm you, hen.' Skunky pulls himself up and hands her his bottle.

Minx stares at the label, tilting it as if to drink. Then with a flick of her wrist she slings the bottle onto the fire. The plastic melts and the cider hisses in a cloud of noxious smoke. Skunky backs away cursing, trips on his car-seat and lands on his knees. Minx stands with shoulders tensed, teeth gritted, hands clenched.

'Fuck you, fuck you all.' She roars before turning and rattling her trolley back through the woods.

I take my plastic sheeting to a group of silver birches away from the fire. The smoke's still billowing, and I throw myself down on the sheeting to get under the path of the fumes. Fucking midges aren't put off though, biting my neck, side of my face, pretty much everywhere they can. I pull my hoodie up, tug my sleeves over my hands and lie with as little of my face exposed as possible. Was there ever a time I felt worse than this? These people are fucking out there, man.

I can't breathe with my face pressed against the plastic, plus the sounds of Skunky's complaining and twigs cracking as people move about make my heart pound with fear when I can't see them. I shift to rest my head on my folded arms, look up to see Mustafa standing right there on the edge of my plastic, holding his knife and his carved stick.

I let out a yelp and jolt back with the shock. Freeze on all fours, mouth dry, literally not daring to breathe. Images of drug crazed African militiamen out to scalp the nearest tourist. My eyes dart as he drops his wood and reaches for his pocket. See Aiden approaching with a reel of rope draped around his neck as Mustafa pulls out something metallic.

I gasp as he leans towards me holding out the object. It's one of those like army surplus aluminium water bottles. He shakes it in my face, and I take hold of it, feel the metal cool on my palm. I sit back on my heels, unscrew the top, look at him again.

'Water?' I say.

He stands blank faced, so I risk a sip. Slight metallic tinge, but it pretty much tastes like water. I moisten my lips, take another longer gulp. Never have I so valued water.

I get up to hand the bottle back. Where the hell do you get water round here anyway? As in I don't see no tap or mountain spring?

'Thank you,' I say, mega ashamed of my reaction before. God only knows what he's been through, yet he thinks of me with his scarce water.

'Hey mate,' Aiden makes me jump again. 'You coming into town? We'll grab a bite to eat and get you a sleeping bag. We can sort your shelter later no problem.'

'I've only got about £20,' I whine. 'And I feel really shit, that spliff…'

'Och, you'll no' be paying for much and the walk will clear your head right enough.'

He takes the rope and wraps the plastic round it, stuffs it under a holly bush. I had images of him stringing me up just now. Seriously need to get a grip. But I'm still suspicious of why he's so keen to help me.

'Mine's a large White Lightening, laddie,' Skunky calls as we head to the river path. Well at least that one's not hard to work out.

There's a breeze has got up and blown the low cloud away and the midges retreat a bit as we walk into town. The bushes are dripping with elderflower and the castle in the distance looks almost pink in the afternoon light. Aiden's right – a walk is what I need.

'So, how long have you been living like this?' I try to sound light and chatty.

'Since I got here.' He slashes at the long grass with a stick as we walk. Doesn't look at me.

'I don't know how long I'd last,' I carry on. Too bloody right, I'm still not betting on getting through one day.

Aiden snorts. 'You after finding your da?'

'Well, it was pretty much spur of the moment, to be fair.'

'Aye and I was after losing mine. Soon as I finished on my tag and I could move out of my da's house, I was up here.'

'Where does he live?'

'Cowdenbeath.' He slashes at some more vegetation. 'Shit hole a way north of Edinburgh.'

'So, you were...' I hesitate. 'Was it like a young offenders place?'

'You're not fucking nosy, are you?' he snaps.

'Sorry, just, you literally don't look old enough for prison?'

'At least I'm outa fucking nappies.'

'Fair enough, I'm just a middle class drop-out. What do I know?' I sound pissy, but I do mean it. I may be a NEET, but Aiden and the others inhabit a different world. Perhaps the boundary is thinner than I think? What's to say this couldn't be me if I fuck up much more?

Aiden smokes one of his dog-ends while keeping ahead of me. I'll be blowing some of my precious cash on baccy, that's for sure. Forget not smoking cigarettes, I'll be needing something to get me through and I'm not up for picking up used tabs just yet.

Aiden turns onto the bridge by the castle and stops to throw his fag-end over the edge. I join him, watching the dull green water make sludgy progress towards the sea.

'I'm heading up North West myself in a couple of days,' he announces.

'Really? Lochgillan?'

'Nay, Durness, right up the top. Fella runs a surfing school, has a chippy van as well. Gives me a job flipping the burgers.'

'Wow, that's great Aiden. As in a chance to break out of all this?'

'It's just a scabby summer job. I did it a couple of years back. Did nae keep me outa trouble, did it?'

'So, will you come back here when it's finished?'

Aiden shrugs. 'You don't look ahead too much, living like this. I do what the fuck I want.'

Then you don't want a lot, is what I think. But hey, who am I to judge?

'What about Skunky?' I ask. 'He literally seems to tell everyone's business but his own.'

'Ha!' Aiden laughs. 'Reckons he's a cut above. He was a lab technician or some-such in a hospital. Got caught with his fingers in the drugs cupboard by all accounts. Lost his job, wife. Still thinks he can lord it with us. But I take no notice.'

'Well, I'll buy him his White Lightening.'

'Oh aye, if it's a quiet life you're after.'

Aiden takes me to the homeless drop-in centre, just up from the river. He steers me past a scruffy reception area with a stressed-out woman trying to deal with a guy shouting about needing a doctor. The main room is all Formica topped tables and a pool table at the end. Posters advertising health checks, drug and alcohol counselling, training opportunities, more stuff about the referendum. I feel a fake as we join the queue to the serving hatch where they're dishing up bowls of Scotch broth, though I'm not about to turn down a free meal. Aiden avoids talking to anyone and takes me to a table in the corner.

I put my soup down and notice there's a socket right there in the skirting.

'Hey, do you think I'd be all right to charge my phone?'

Aiden darts a look around. There are a couple of old winos

on the next table and a few lads playing pool, but no-one too close.

'Just keep it low-key if you wanna hold onto your fancy phone.'

I take the seat next to the socket and plug it in discreetly. Maybe not the greatest idea to draw Aiden's attention to my shiny new iPhone, but it's too late now.

We get stuck into our broth which tastes unbelievably good. I've pretty much finished it when a man in an Aran jumper heads towards us with a bunch of leaflets. Aiden stares into his bowl but the guy catches my eye.

'Hi, I'm just coming round with this from Shelter about the referendum.' He shoves a leaflet under my nose: *Shelter Scotland: Make Your Voice Heard.* 'It's about getting homeless people to register.'

'I'm not sure I qualify, as I live in England?' I say. 'Though my dad's Scottish?'

'Ah,' the man smiles. 'It is purely about where you reside, I'm afraid. What about you?' He leans to face Aiden.

'I have no residence. That'll be why I'm homeless?' Aiden gives him his best blank face-off.

The guy explains how it's all about where you habitually spend your time. How everyone's voice will count in this referendum.

'Yeah, I've noticed there's like quite a hype about the issue, and I've been in Scotland less than a day,' I say.

Aiden snorts. 'It'll make no difference. The politicians will do what they want as they always have.'

'Only if nobody challenges them,' says the guy. 'Have a look, give it a thought.'

Aiden grabs the leaflet out of his hand and stands up.

'Come on, Gethin, we've got things to do.' He heads for the door, ripping up the leaflet and binning it on the way.

I grab my phone and follow him out of the front door.

'Fucking do-gooders,' he mutters.

'You could at least listen…' I start.

'We need to get you cleaned up. There's toilets in the shopping centre.' And he's crossing the road before I can say another word.

I follow him into the Gents where he stops in front of the sinks.

'You can wash yourself safe enough in here. The toilets in the centre are minging full of smackheads.'

Standing in front of the mirror, I see my face is streaky grey and my hair has bits of dried leaf in it. I'm shocked how haggard I look, but why the hell would that bother him? He's already lathering his face with soap and water – maybe it's a pride thing. I wash my face and dry it on the paper towels and Aiden even finds a comb to run through my hair, then makes a joke of styling his quarter inch crop. We emerge two shades lighter.

'Don't take much to turn you back into a regular tourist,' Aiden grins as we walk up the street away from the river.

Next stop is the Coop where I buy Skunky's White Lightening, tobacco and a litre of red wine, plus a massive bar of chocolate. Oh, and a large bottle of water

'Stick it all in your wee backpack,' Aiden instructs. 'You'll no' want them seeing those in Blacks.'

I recognise Blacks from when I looked longingly at the tents this morning. Time has stretched something stupid today.

'Right,' says Aiden, pulling me round the corner from the shop. 'There's where we get you a sleeping bag.'

'Aiden, I've got like £6 left.'

'You go in, talk to the geezer about the sleeping bags; you want a lot of detail, right? Togs, all weathers, weights. You're a tourist with money to spend. That's all you've got to do. Keep them talking. You could mention the old HRH?'

'HRH?'

'Duke of Edinburgh? You can't decide which one to buy. You um and you ah until you see me away and still you keep on for another minute. Then you say you need to think about it, what time do they close. Walk out slow. I'll see you back at the river just over the bridge.'

'But, what if…?' I can't even stammer out the fear, the Scotch broth repeating on me.

'You want to be cold tonight? Your bit's easy. Away with you.' He pushes me back towards the shop.

I feel a cold sweat down my spine as I head towards the sleeping bags. Instinctively I start with the cheaper ones, though there's nothing under £50. Then I remember I'm supposed to be loaded so I shake my head and move up to the posh ones. I make a show of fingering the various bags, pulling out the labels and pretending to read them. I cast a nervous glance about, see Aiden come in and start looking at the tents. My heart pounds as he gives me a quick nod to get on with it.

'Excuse me,' I corner the young female assistant. 'Could you help me with the sleeping bags, please?' It's my best middle-class English but immediately I'm worried it sounds over the top.

'Sure,' she seems convinced. 'What kind of price are you looking at?'

'Oh,' I stumble. 'Erm, I want one for all weathers, you know? But I can't work out the symbols on the labels.' I pull my stupid-me smile – standard fall-back position.

She leads me to the top end of the range. 'Here's a popular three-season bag. Down filled, which gives it a wide comfort range…?'

'Sorry,' I have to force myself to hear what she's saying. 'Comfort range?'

'Warm enough for those cold autumn nights, but not too hot in the summer?' She rubs the fabric.

'Ah, yes,' I scour my empty brain for more to say. 'Er, not winter, then?'

'It has a water repellent shell, so good for wet conditions. But probably not for extreme cold. Can I ask what you'd be using it for?'

'Well, you know, I'm planning on taking my Duke of Edinburgh Award,' I say. 'Gold?' I add for good measure though I only did the bronze in Year 9.

'So, you'll be wanting something more like this from our Starlight range.' She moves me up the line, and I resist the urge to look around for Aiden. 'This is filled with Polarloft, with an excellent warmth-to-weight ratio.'

'Warmth to weight ratio,' I nod.

'It's important for challenge expeditions, when you have to carry all your gear.' She explains, like she knows I haven't a clue.

'How much do you want for this one, then?'

'It's retailing at £150, but we might do a discount for the D of E.' She pulls a hand-held device from her pocket. 'Just let me to check that for you?'

I don't know if I've done enough, if Aiden's still in here. We're standing with our backs to the door, so I turn for a quick look and catch a glimpse of Aiden as he grabs one of the cheaper bags and sidles to the door. The guy on the till is busy but my assistant notices me looking and turns just as Aiden's making his exit.

'Hey!' she calls, and immediately the till guy is legging it after Aiden.

'Who was that kid?' My assistant glares at me.

'What kid?'

'I think you know.' She stabs her finger towards my face.

I feel the blood pound in my head. They don't need no lie detector. The guy from the till comes back in, red faced and breathless.

'Little toe-rag got away around the corner.'

The woman narrows her eyes at me. 'He was with you, wasn't he?'

'No, honestly. I don't know who you're talking about.' My voice is squeaky like a kid caught with their hands in the biscuit tin.

'So, you're about to spend £150 on this sleeping bag?'

'I need to think about it,' I stammer. 'Erm, can I come back later?'

'You'll not come back later or ever again. You can think yourself lucky I can't prove you knew him.'

It's as much as I can do to get to the door on my shaky legs and keep walking down the street without looking back.

'You fucking Eejit.' Aiden emerges from behind a bush by the river path.

'I'm sorry, she just turned round. I didn't...' I look down

the path to be sure no-one's followed me. What if they'd got the police to tail me and I've brought them straight to Aiden?

'What were you doing giving me eye contact, Dunderheid?'

'Yeah, I'm right out of practice with nicking, know what I mean?' I'm not exactly wanting to admit the last time was when I was caught stealing sweets aged nine. Mum gave me such a hard time I've literally never done it again.

'No shit! Fucking stick to your mammy buying your stuff and I'll try to keep myself this side of the nick.' He slings the sleeping bag at me then kicks the bush before striding back along the path.

'Oh God!' I run to catch up. 'Do you think they'll report you? Maybe they could identify…' Flash of Aiden on a police line-up with a load of twelve-year-olds.

'It's a bit of petty theft. No' worth their trouble.'

'But if they did, literally you'd be back inside, right?' The lump of guilt catches in my throat.

'Aye, sure enough. Serves me right for being so soft.'

'I don't get it? Why take the risk for a twat like me?'

He stops and gives me that blank stare, his eyes like sea-worn bottle glass. 'Let's just say I'm superstitious?' He walks away.

'Superstitious? What the hell are you on about?' I shout after him.

He stoops to pick up a stick. 'You put me in mind of someone. Dinnae ask, OK?' He swipes at the vegetation.

Back at the camp Aiden helps me to string up the plastic sheeting between a couple of birches for a make-shift tent, with a binbag and cardboard groundsheet. He hardly speaks, but I'm happy enough. The misty damp has disappeared, and the shelter looks almost cosy. I spread my sleeping bag and Aiden leaves me to settle in.

There's no-one near so it seems safe to get my phone out. It had about ten minutes charge, enough for a quick check.

There's a text from Ben sent a couple of hours ago – *Awright mate?* Immediate disappointment it's so brief. I go to check Facebook notifications.

A picture posted by Ben with the caption *On our way to With The Fairies Free Party. Gonna get mash up and forget all examsJ.* There they all are: Fran draped round Jarvis, glitter-flowered face, glossy lips poised to kiss; Jarvis showing off a large trumpet of a spliff; Ben with his arms round Jarvis and Emily, all gold and turquoise face-paint and a garland of daisies; Emily with green fairy wings, pointing a sparkly wand. As far as could be from the Minx girl and I ache with the longing for my lost girlfriend.

I try to imagine being there. As in thinking of nothing more than going mental and feeling the ecstasy induced lurve. But from my far-away hide it all feels mega superficial. And no-one mentions the absence of me? OK, Ben sent the shortest possible text, but I can't help feeling hurt, seeing them now, so happy without me. Not even any more desperate messages from Mum. I have never felt so alone.

The phone conks and I put it away, batting back the tears that I'm too scared to let flow in case I can't stop.

'Gethin, where are you skulking with the bevvies?' Skunky's voice breaks into my misery.

I haul myself up and take the supplies to the newly constructed fire. Skunky's well happy with his White Lightening and Aiden and I settle into the wine and smoke a couple of roll ups. He says very little but I'm grateful for his company. Even Paoul seems to have cheered up, talking about his plan to catch rabbits.

'I set up net, you see? Tonight, when is dark. You will help?'

'Sure, awesome.' I pass him the wine bottle. I'll take the idea of belonging here for now. Never mind how I'm catching rabbits or anything.

It's not exactly proper dark as Paoul leads me up from the river to a lumpy grass field. He's carrying a thick rope over his shoulder.

'Net already there,' he whispers. 'We frighten rabbit and rabbit run to net.'

He gives me one end of the rope and walks across the field until it's fully stretched out. Then he signals me to walk forwards, and he like lifts and thumps the rope on the ground as we go. Sure enough there's a scurrying as a few rabbits hop away at top speed, scattering in all directions. After a bit Paoul drops the rope and runs, beckoning me to follow. I can just see a low net about twenty-five metres long strung up between two trees. Paoul inspects the net, points to something moving. An actual rabbit caught by its front legs, frozen with fear as we approach. Paoul kneels and before I can even register, he's twisted the rabbit's neck and thrown it in his canvas bag.

'There!' He beams at me. I'm totally shocked at how matter of fact this is, but then, if I want to eat meat…

Paoul beckons me further down the net. There's another smaller rabbit, its little body trembling.

'You take this one.' Paoul shoves me forward.

I kneel beside the rabbit to hold it. Its heart flutters furiously as I ease its legs from the net.

'Twist the neck. Do it quick,' Paoul hisses.

I look up at him and then back at the rabbit. I want to tell Paoul I can't do it, when I somehow loosen my grip and the rabbit escapes across the field.

I stare at my empty hands, not daring to look at Paoul, crouched beside me. I hear his heavy impatient breathing. He punches me under the shoulder, and I brace myself for worse. Then he lets out a massive bellowing laugh, rocks himself as he catches his breath.

'Aee you British, so soft to the animals, better than to humans!'

There's not enough rabbit stew for everyone, and I say I'm not hungry, which is true enough. The wine's finished, my tobacco's been passed round, and all I want is to crawl into my sleeping bag with my chocolate for comfort.

'Well, I'll be hitting the sack, then?' I try to sound casual, getting up from the fire.

'Aye, I hope the ground's soft enough for your sensitive bones?' Skunky says.

'Oh, I've slept out in the country a few times, with my mates.' Another pang, thinking of them all out there tonight.

'And then you get the bus home to mammy in the morning, laddie? No,' he holds his hand up to my stuttering. 'Dinnae be ashamed. You dinnae need to hang about with the likes of us. You'll hitch yourself a ride to Lochgillan tomorrow and find that father of yours, will you no'?'

I clutch my stolen sleeping bag, my secret stash of chocolate. I feel about six. Such a fail.

'Good night, and thanks for everything.' I say.

Deconstruction – *Pat*

I jump off the bus into water bouncing off the street and I'm soaked immediately in my canvas pumps and sleeveless top. As I got Charlie's text I rushed out, not thinking of an umbrella. *On way to exhibition with Chloe – meeting Reh there.* Cursing as I splash my way through the torrent. Why the hell do I want to be a bloody artist? I hate showing my work to people I know.

One of the gallery girls sits at the front desk with the inevitable laptop. They are all the same in this trendy pop-up gallery, with their back-combed hair and vintage make-up – eye-contact is obviously beneath them. How is anyone supposed to even know there's a show on, there's no signage and the laptop girl doesn't speak.

I stand at the gallery entrance, absorbing the dry smell of paint and plaster dust while I look around for Charlie and Rehana. The only people I can see are a silver-haired man in a crumpled linen jacket and spotty bow tie, with a woman with a big hooked nose, carmine-pink lipstick and a tight blue dress. They're looking at *Divided Lines* – piles of earth from opposite sides of the Scottish border. The man is holding forth, the woman leaning towards him, seemingly attentive.

'…reductive symbolism of nationalism, the literalism of earth…' the man drones as I walk past. The woman shoots me a you're-a-piece-of-dirt look. I scowl back at her, and she snaps her face shut.

My installation is past the video room at the end of the L shaped gallery. I turn the corner and hear a young girl's voice.

'Dad, do you think I should try…?' It's Chloe, Charlie's twelve-year-old, emerging from the video room with Charlie and Rehana.

I catch Rehana looking at me and quickly averting her eyes. Has she seen my installation? Maybe she hates it.

'You *are* here!' Charlie says. 'I see you got caught in the rain.'

'There's this video, right, of a totally naked girl, like smearing herself in paint,' Chloe tells me. 'Shall I do it, Dad, for my art project?' Cheeky grin at Charlie, head to one side.

'Been done before, circa 1968.' Charlie bats her blond ponytail.

'Waste of paint.' Rehana purses her lips. She glances at my top and turns away again. The top is a lacy antique number from a charity shop. The wet has made it almost see-through, and I'm not wearing a bra. Oh God, no wonder she can't look at me.

I shiver as I pull my arms across my chest.

'Here,' Rehana takes off the peacock blue cardigan she's wearing over her long black robe. 'Put this on, you'll freeze.'

I put on the cardigan and run my hands through my hair, shaking out the water to land in dark drops on the concrete floor.

'That could be like ten second art.' Chloe points to the fading spatters.

'You'll go far, oh daughter. Ten second art about sums it up here.' Charlie points to *Horizon dot com* on the wall behind us: scraps of computer paper printed with coloured spots.

'They'd argue it's all about process, the concept…' I'm

anxious for some reason to defend this work by someone I've never met.

'Process? Concept?' Charlie looks around as if searching the air. 'At best it's a not very clever visual pun.'

I do a quick check that no-one's listening. Charlie is only articulating what I think about a lot of the work here, but I'm afraid of seeming frumpy and out of date in this Emperor's New Clothes world.

Spotty Dick and Hawk Beak walk past to stand in front of *Tonal Detritus,* consisting of two tiny TV monitors on the floor crackling with out of focus visual white noise.

'…hackneyed interpretation of the tonality of the banal…' Spotty Dick drones to Hawk Beak whose face freezes in a look of pained enquiry.

'Is it me?' Charlie asks as we move on.

'What is this Tonal Detritus?' Rehana says with a frown.

'I suppose you could see it as the meaninglessness of information overload,' I suggest.

'It means nothing. Art should communicate surely.' She turns to me as I pull her cardigan closer, buttoning it up over my chest. Her headscarf is the same colour, and she wears a large blue stone on her middle finger. The touches of blue against her black coverings give her a vibrancy in the cool gallery light.

'I can cope with conceptual,' Charlie says, 'but I do want to see some effort, a bit of craft, if that's not too old fashioned?'

'It's just, it's not how they're taught these days.' I don't feel comfortable placing myself above my fellow exhibitors. Even after my momentous decision two years ago to rent the studio, I have remained very isolated from the contemporary art world. The people in my block are mostly jewellers and potters, but I should have made more effort to connect with other artists. The dread of exposure looms close now, and I know I'm desperately procrastinating.

'I quite like this one.' I guide them to *Transition 2*: a shimmering construction of translucent fabric, suspended from the ceiling and stitched to suggest an emerging female form.

'That's right pretty.' Chloe's reaction feels refreshing. She moves to read the blurb.

'... using temp-or-al form and structure to explore the trans-form-a-tion-al potential of trans-i-tion-al spaces.' She stumbles to pronounce the words, lifts her arms in a search-me gesture at Charlie.

'Well, it's beautifully constructed,' I say, impatience rising in my voice. 'You don't have to totally get art to appreciate it.'

Rehana pulls back and Chloe looks down at her gladiator style sandals.

'Sorry,' I say. 'Was I ranting?'

Charlie puts a hand on my arm and steers me gently across the gallery.

'Pat, you don't need to be defensive. What do we know anyway?' He pulls his sheepish apologetic smile.

'I'm sorry. I suppose I'm just so nervous that you'll think the same about my work.'

I look across the gallery; there are a few more people now. A young woman with peroxide hair in a forties twist, dressed in floral housecoat and block heeled shoes. She looks stiff and nervous with a very ordinary looking older couple who I take to be her parents. Two almost identical looking young men: stick thin in black drainpipes, paisley shirts and pointy shoes. Hair brushed to one side and falling in their eyes, one of them blond, one dark haired.

Chloe and Rehana are in front of the *Bedsheets Triptych* now – violently coloured naked body prints on mounted sheets. Chloe giggling behind her hand. Rehana looking grave.

'Rehana's right,' I say. 'Art should communicate. If all it can do is shock for no reason, then, well it shouldn't.'

'All very Brit-Pack and passé,' Charlie says. 'But Pat, I know that's not what you're about. So, you have to take a risk on it, don't you?'

I nod. It's what I would say to someone else.

Chloe comes over. 'Can I go now? I said I'd meet Amy in Primark.'

Charlie rolls his eyes. 'Priorities! Don't you want to look at Pat's work first? You're interested really, aren't you? Your favourite subject?'

Chloe grimaces and twists round on her feet and I feel a lurch of guilt remembering how I pushed Gethin's interest in Astrophysics.

'Let her go,' I say. 'There's no point in forcing it.'

Chloe cocks her head up at Charlie.

'Go on then,' he sighs. 'Don't forget to text Mum to say when you'll be back.'

'Will do, love you.' Chloe all but skips to the entrance, blowing a kiss as she disappears.

Charlie shakes his head. 'OK, that's your scariest critic out of the way.'

Rehana joins us, smiling now. 'I'm sorry Pat, if I upset you just now. It's just, some of this stuff,' she waves her hand towards *Bedsheets*. 'It is not for me, but I'm really interested to see your work.'

I look from Charlie's benevolent smile to Rehana's

intelligent interest and recognise the loyalty of my two favourite colleagues.

'OK,' I grimace. 'Let's do it.'

We walk round the white-boxed installation to the entrance. They pause to read the title label: Patricia Williams: *Anything Goes* mixed media installation. I feel a little leap in my stomach. Perhaps it will be OK.

I follow them in, trying to see the work through their eyes. I watch them take in the six-foot-wide Perspex screen across the middle; the life-sized dancing figures, outlined in thick black paint on the screen, infused with ultra-violet from the strip-light above. I feel a flutter of excitement. I actually made that.

'Look,' Rehana points. 'Their heads are mobile phones.'

'Facebook and Twitter icons for eyes.' Charlie adds.

Rehana scans the splintered spirals of collage on the wall behind, visible through the screen, converging on the figures' phone-heads and filling the outline of their bodies. She moves behind the screen to examine the fractured images of child sweatshops, war blasted ruins, lines of refugees, industrial decay, ravaged rainforest, battered women, collaged with ads for smart phones, make-up, clothes, food.

'We have converted our T shirts to Fairtrade cotton,' Rehana reads from the slogans in the collage mix. 'Human Rights Act: What's not to love?'

Charlie moves to examine the political posters from the eighties, framed in traditional gold stucco and hung at an angle on the white side walls, either side of the screen.

'Hey, I remember that one.' He points to Thatcher in a frame of newspaper headlines: '*MY MESSAGE TO THE WOMEN OF OUR NATION: TOUGH*'.

Rehana joins him to examine the framed poster of my *Lock In* piece: police faces squashed against the photo-montaged wire fence; dancing women slipping in and out like mocking faery spirits.

'I made that after being at Greenham,' I explain. 'I've included it with the other posters to show that, for all our small victories, nothing fundamentally changed.'

'Well, they closed the base at Greenham Common, didn't they?' Rehana asks.

'Yes, but the military industrial complex hardly took a dent, did it?

I take a step back, trying to second guess what they make of it. I'm worried it's too obvious, or that they won't get it. Charlie stares at the *Stop Strip Searches in Armagh* poster as if it's a work of art in a museum; Rehana squints at a slogan in the collage: *Gay marriage: radical legislation for the twenty-first century.* What does she think of gay marriage? Of all the things to worry about: it's just another consumer product, that's the point, isn't it?

'Bloody hell, Pat!' Charlie's grin fills his gaunt face. 'Amazing!'

'You like it?'

He nods emphatically. 'No lack of meaning here: all the shit filtering through the phone-heads, the people dancing through the shit.'

'I'm just trying to show my perception of the world, all its contradictions,' I start, my hands slicing the air. 'So, with the dancers, you see, however we may celebrate our so-called victories, we are tainted by association with the society we live in and the things we take for granted...' I break off, worried I sound too preachy.

Charlie nods. 'And the framed posters. Genius. Like all that we fought for has been absorbed, neutralised.'

'Commoditised,' I interrupt, so pleased that he gets it. 'As with Fair Trade Cotton and Gay Marriage...'

Rehana turns towards us, throwing me off my thread.

'Erm, you know, like, stacked up on the supermarket shelves?' I hear the doubt in my voice.

Again, I'm worrying about Rehana. I'm ridiculously uncomfortable with the mention of gay marriage. Jesus, I think I can take on global capitalism, but I can't say 'gay' to a Muslim? Rehana wasn't around when Gethin was little, and I've always let her assume I'm a heterosexual single parent. So much for being open, Gethin might say.

'Anything Goes?' Rehana levels her gaze at me.

'You know, how everything can be a consumer product, so the Establishment don't even have to bother controlling the left or the counter-culture?'

Rehana tilts her head. 'Maybe in the west, but even then, it only goes so far, doesn't it?'

'Oh, I know, advanced capitalist economies can be marketing illusions of freedom while propping up, you know, the opposite...' I'm rambling into incoherence and will myself to shut up while Rehana takes another look.

She turns to me. 'It is beautifully made. The patterns of the collage, the dancing figures almost like Matisse, isn't it?'

'It has a bit of Matisse's *Dance* in it. But my biggest influence is Hannah Hoch, a German Dada artist. She produced political collage work in the 1920s. I only discovered her earlier this year, at an exhibition in London.'

'I must look her up,' Rehana says.

'The twenties was such an exhilarating time for artists, with the Soviet Constructivists as well,' I warm to Rehana's interest. 'That belief in art at the cutting edge for change. I was inspired by that era when I went to art college in the early eighties. So now I'm trying to peel back the notion of radical art, you see, to examine how possible it is to be a political artist today.'

'Have to say, this is ticking all the boxes for me.' Charlie says. 'Don't you think, Reh? Art that communicates and looks good. It's all we ask for.'

Rehana nods slowly, then she reaches out to clasp my hands in hers. Her smile lights her face, reminding me how young she is.

'I think it's very good, Pat. You know I wouldn't say so if I didn't mean it.'

'Nice one.' Charlie pats me on the back.

After they've gone, I stay in the installation, hugging myself in a rare glow of satisfaction. They like it, they actually like it. It was worth all those countless hours I put into this. It really does look good. They liked it.

Maybe they didn't get it entirely: did they notice the broken golden frame hung empty on the screen? But that's where I've struggled the most: to show how this piece itself is equally meaningless and commodifiable.

What would Gethin say if he were here? Would he think it worth the effort, the time I didn't give him? At this moment I want him to see it more than anything. I could send Grace a text, maybe she could bring him and Francesca along, a way of breaking the ice between us?

I pull out my phone and see there's a voicemail from an unknown number yesterday. My heart jumps. Maybe he used a friend's phone. How have I missed it?

But the voicemail is from Norwich Social Care to say they've booked an assessment visit to my parents on Monday afternoon. 'You are welcome to attend if you feel this would be useful.'

'Bloody hell, Monday?' I mutter, looking round to see the identikit skinny young men coming into the installation. I hurry out past them and stand round the side of the box.

If I feel it would be useful? I asked for the bloody assessment, didn't I? Mum and Dad won't admit they're not coping. I'll have to go.

I'm banging the phone on my hand, and only notice when I hit my knuckle too hard. I lean against the wall. Forget about Norwich for now. See about texting Grace to bring Gethin.

I go back round to the entrance and stand just inside, open a text and think what to say. The two young men are behind the screen. Their stylised clothes and hair make them look like part of the photomontage seen through the outlines of the dancers. A Dada Happening, no less. I have never thought about the effect of people behind the screen. It works on levels I didn't even plan, and I feel again a surge of excitement. I really must get Gethin to see it!

I go back to my text, but I'm distracted by the young men's talk of the death of agitprop.

The dark haired one nods. 'No more than Militant Nostalgia.'

'Naive at best: as if a bunch of hackneyed images can say anything new in this age of information overload.' The blond one waves his paisleyed arm to dismiss the swirl of collage.

That's the point, I want to shout at them. That's why I've framed the eighties posters. But inside my confidence shrivels. Militant Nostalgia? The insult cuts deep. The work is too obvious, or not obvious enough. Either way it has failed.

137

'Deliver us from the Message!' The dark haired one laughs, exposing rows of too-perfect white teeth.

'Art should be asking questions, totally not about answers…' is their parting shot as they head for the exit, oblivious, it seems, of my presence.

The overhead light starts flickering, their dismissals repeating in my head. Militant Nostalgia. All that's left to the 21st century artist. It's what I was saying with the empty frame, isn't it? The obvious question banging for attention. Why do it then? Why bother at all?

I shiver and pull Rehana's cardigan closer round me, flex my numb feet in the wet pumps. How it would be to stand here with Gethin, nerves pitched for his reaction? I shiver again. He'd probably just shrug, art's not my thing. Yeah Mum, he'll say. More of your old politics.

The phone beeps and makes me jump. It's a text from Grace. I open it, heart thumping.

Babe sorry not made it yet to your show, maybe next week? Gethin not with us now, Fran thinks he gone to Scotland. I'm sure he be fine. Try not to worry babe, Gx.

I clench the phone in my fist and feel my stomach knot. Scotland? Why on earth didn't I heed Emily's warning and try to make peace with him?

How many thousand hours in this installation? Militant Nostalgia. Pseudo Radicalism. Is this the sense of hopelessness I've passed on to Gethin, instead of guiding him through his teenage uncertainty? The dancing figures seem to mock my intentions in the jittery light. I could take an axe through their stupid phone-heads. My heart bangs in my chest. I need to get out.

I turn to go just as a woman enters, blocking my way. I

take a step back as she looks quizzically at me through round tortoiseshell glasses.

'You're not Pat, by any chance?'

I nod and pull my arms across my chest, feel myself shrink.

'Gabriella. I'm a friend of Karen's.' She holds out a silver ringed hand with a jangle of bangles.

The hand feels cool and smooth against my clammy fingers. I give it the briefest contact before retreating to hugging my chest again.

'Karen?'

She has a Latin look about her with dark gingery hair in a silver clip, big hazel eyes behind the glasses and a wide expressive mouth.

'Karen told me about your work. I'm meeting her here; she won't be long.' Her smile brings out her crow's feet. She's not young, there's grey in her hair, but there's a sexy rawness to her with the rise of her breasts in a low-cut camisole and the flash of bare leg from her denim skirt.

I feel a rise of panic, made worse if anything by the twinge of attraction. I'm not in a fit state to have anyone else look at my work. I move to stand between her and the screen. Trust Karen to go interfering again.

'Karen didn't say she was coming. I've got to go. Now. Sorry.' I feel the sweat pricking on my brow.

'Well, I'd love to look at your work now I'm here.' She shifts along to peer over my shoulder.

The sweat gathers round my hairline, and I feel the damp of my top against my skin. I wipe my face with Rehana's cardigan sleeve.

'OK, I can't stop you. I'm going now,' I say, heading out of the installation. God, how rude was that? I look back to see her puzzled frown.

'Sorry,' I call to her. 'It was nice of you to come.' And I turn to walk out of the gallery, all the way to the bus stop without looking up, without seeing Karen.

All I want now is to be left alone.

McCalstry of Lochgillan – *Gethin*

The Land Rover drops me by the Lochgillan turn-off before heading down towards Kyle of Lochalsh. I stand clutching my sleeping bag, a cloud of midges literally feasting on my face and scalp, holding my thumb out at the infrequent traffic. Twenty-two miles? Not so shabby.

I've never hitched before and felt the usual kind of idiot when Skunky got Aiden to walk me to the road out of Inverness. But already I'm a pro, as in I can tell the tourist cars that won't stop. My first two lifts being a lorry heading for Ullapool and a local farmer in the Land Rover.

I was dropped off about three o'clock – I could be there in an hour if I get lucky. I zip up my hoody – desperate for a lift just to stop being eaten alive. But then my stomach lurches. What if he tells me to fuck off? What if he's not around? What kind of dickhead shows up penniless on a sperm donor hundreds of miles from home? I could turn now and hitch right back to Sheffield. Yeah, but then what?

I almost don't bother with the foreign registered Renault Espace, but the guy slows down, so I stick out my thumb at the last minute. He pulls into the passing place – two fluffy husky dogs in the back. He rolls down his window and the woman passenger leans forward to get a good look.

'We go to Lochgillan?' he says like a question.

'Yeah, Lochgillan!' I'm bouncing the sleeping bag off my thigh with insane excitement.

I get in the back and the dogs press against the wire mesh for a good sniff. The car is spotless inside and I'm hyper aware of my rank mix of wood smoke and slept-in clothes. If the car smells of dog, I'm overpowering it.

'I am Dirk, and this is the wife.' The guy leans round to grin at me, his face all raw and pock-marked, chunky white teeth with a glint of gold and a fuzz of blond grey hair.

His wife turns, eager thin face and beady blue eyes. 'All the way from Rotterdam!' she says.

'Cool, I'm Gethin.'

'That is good Scottish name, Geth-in?' Dirk tries.

'It's Welsh. My granddad's Welsh?'

'Welsh, ha? All the same Celtish, yes?'

The dogs fidget, still sniffing at me. Dirk shouts at them in Dutch, and they both sit.

'They are good travelling dogs,' Dirk keeps leaning over his shoulder to talk to me. I'm wishing he'd keep more of an eye on the road.

'They travel all round Europe in a trailer for his motorbike,' his wife explains.

'Wow, really?'

'It's a special trailer I built,' Dirk says. 'They have plenty of space. The wife on the back.' He grins then swerves into a passing space as a camper van comes towards him.

'They have their beds, water, everything,' his wife carries on. 'But on the ferry *Dogs Must Be In Cars*.'

'I should have come on bike and the wife drive with the dogs,' Dirk grins. 'Or better still, leave the wife at home.'

I'm saying nothing – I make a show of gazing out of the window as she shakes her head in mock disapproval.

Looking out of the window does the trick though, as in she

talks to him in Dutch, pointing ahead, and he starts watching the road. He puts some music on, Coldplay, I think, which does nothing to pick up the pace of his driving. We're in for a dreary ride.

Then we turn a corner, and the road widens. Dirk puts his foot down and the hills rise before us, the cloud lifting over the craggy tops. I feel a sudden high for the adventure I'm having.

Another corner and we head down the side of a long thin loch, with the bright green hillside and the line of tall pines reflecting perfectly in the water.

The Wife looks up from reading the map. 'Nice, yes?'

'Awesome!' I say.

'Ah.' Dirk grins. 'To be on the bike!'

I have a sudden urge to tell him about Don's motorbike museum. As in we're showing up with Dirk, two huskies and The Wife in tow? Delete that thought.

We're almost in Lochgillan and my eyes are peeled for a glimpse of the museum. I remember it being a bit out of the centre, but with my phone pancake flat I can't check. The road sweeps down to massive expanses of pale sand and the sea spreads to heavy cloud on the horizon. There's like a scattering of whitewashed buildings lining the bay, with stone-built hotels set back from the road. As we come into the town there's a sign for the Heritage Centre.

'Just here will be fine,' I say.

'You meet your friend here?' He leans over, narrowly missing the wall as he turns.

'Er, pretty much…' Let them assume what they want, they've not actually asked me about anything.

'We will be at camping. But the pub for dinner I think, not

the wife's cooking.' He winds down his window as I get out of the car.

'Perhaps I will poison him,' she laughs.

I head to the leaflet stand in the Heritage Centre foyer, but there's nothing about the motorbike museum. I spot the time: 16:35, steel myself to approach the kiosk.

'We close at five.' The woman doesn't look up from counting her till takings.

'I just like wanted some directions, if that's OK?' Panicking now that Don's museum will be closed too.

She looks up, pale eyes bulging behind thick lensed glasses. Curly greying hair and a sparkly nose-ring.

'I was looking for the Motorcycle Museum?'

She raises an eyebrow, looks amused. 'It's not so far. Though you'll take potluck to find it open.'

'Ah, well, I'll give it a try?'

She sketches me a map on the back of a leaflet, explaining it as she goes. 'It'll take you no more than twenty minutes.'

'Does Don McCalstry still run it?' I hardly dare ask.

'Last I heard.' She pulls her arms in tight. 'Let's just say he keeps a low profile.'

'Oh yeah? Why's that?' My heart pounding at this unpromising information.

'Friend of yours?' She shoves the map towards me.

I take a breath. 'Well, kind of…'

'Och, you'll be the first in a while.' She laughs, then goes back to bagging up her change.

I want to ask what the hell she means, but she's muttering her counting. Conversation closed? Nothing for me to do but grab the map and leave.

It's a steady uphill from the village, and already my hair is damp with sweat. I feel rank and uncomfortable, but mainly I'm bricking it. It's like I'm being propelled by some outside force, as in my feet on automatic, pushing me forward. Dreading finding him, dreading not. I pause for a moment at the top: there's a line of heavy-duty mountains on the far side of the bay. Massive, dark, like great rough pyramids. The sea glints dull metal to the horizon. I take a deep breath of damp salty air, hear the screech of seagulls.

My heart thumps as I approach a whitewashed low-rise building, but it's just a couple of bungalows. Then a bit further and I see something like a garage ahead of me. Could that be it? Totally ready to shit myself now.

Getting closer, maybe it's not? A long one storey shack with corrugated tin roof and like battered shop-front shutters padlocked at the ground. No light from the one small window. It would be easy to miss the faded sign hanging from the roof supports.

HIGHLAND MOTORCYCLE MUSEUM

Oh My God! It literally really is fucking well it. I stare at the notice, can't take it in. There's a handwritten sign stuck to the inside of the window.

Opening times are roughly Monday – Friday 10.00 – 4.00, Saturday, Sunday 11.00 – 6.00. If we're not here, try coming back later.

It can't be much later than five and it is Saturday, but still there is zero sign of life. Maybe it's closed for good? I wander round the back. There's a yard with some outhouses and a dilapidated caravan at the side. I pull my hood down, rub my hands through my hair, and force myself to knock on the door.

Nothing. I knock again, then try the door handle. Locked. The tiny windows, curtained with swirly orange and brown, reveal nothing.

The thud of my heart subsides as I make my way to sit on a pile of breeze blocks. I rest my head on my arms.

Now what?

He might be back soon.

Or not.

How long am I going to give him?

He's probably gone away, it's like totally shut up.

So, then what? Idiot.

Fuck.

I pull out my baccy and focus on rolling a fag. I cup my hands to light it and study the deep lines of dirt on my palms, wondering which is the lifeline.

I shift to look out to sea. The cloud has lifted, revealing a smudge of mountains on the horizon. The sea is a pale grey-green now, the sun catching the flickering ripples. I take a deep drag and exhale above my head to keep the midges off.

Come on then, let's make a plan, as Mum would say.

Plan A was getting here and finding him. What the hell is Plan B?

If I stay here, I'll have to find somewhere to sleep, like a cave or an abandoned house? Fuck knows. I've never slept out alone before, I feel I'm wimping out of that one. Plus, what am I going to eat? I suppose I've got enough for a bag of chips or something. I could go to the pub for a half, see if anyone offers to put me up. Maybe they'll know where Don is, even? But that involves explaining how I know him, which I don't.

OK, the alternative is to hitch back to Sheffield. There are still hours of daylight; if I can get to a motorway by dark, I can hang out in a service station. There'll be lorries hopefully? If I get stuck there's always the fall-back position of phoning mum. Get her to pay for a coach ticket or somewhere to stay. I feel such a fail even thinking of including her in the plan. All those wasted years watching Bear Grylls.

I think of Aiden, how I'm lucky that my mum gives a toss. Why I was so angry with her?

I take the last drag of my fag, stub it out and put the butt in my pocket. I've been that well trained.

Gutted as I head back down the road. My fragile sense of adventure morphs into the comedown of failure. I drag my feet, looking out to sea again. Those mountains silhouetted like a distant mirage. Flashing signal of a line of gulls across the wide pale sky. There is such a mental sense of space here. Am I really giving up so easily, after the immense ball-ache of getting here? I trace a couple of plumes of chimney smoke from the little white houses in the bay below.

Fuck it, give it one more night. Try the pub? I'll think of something.

I quicken my pace, a splinter of excitement rising again in my chest. Then I hear the roar of an engine coming around the bend towards me. I jump back onto the verge as an old silver motorbike almost clips me. The rider curses as he passes, shaking his fist at me. Fucking idiot thinks he owns the road. I'm about to set off again when he indicates to pull in towards the museum. Is that? It's got to be! Him!

Fuck, fuck. Plan A.

I run back and get to the yard to see him by the parked bike. He pulls off his helmet, bends down to peer at the engine. Is it him? *Height 5 foot 10.* Probably about right. He's all in battered leathers with tatty fringes. His hair straggles out of a loose ponytail. I'm stupidly disappointed at how old and seedy he looks. What the hell was I expecting?

I walk towards him, literally sick with nerves. Fuck, what do I say? *Hi, you don't know me, but I'm your son...* No. *Hi, you don't know me, but I think I know a friend of yours...* No. I'll just ask about the museum first. Fuck. What if it's not him?

He looks round as he hears me approach, pulls his thick dark eyebrows into a heavy frown.

'Hi!' I smile like a loony as I get near him.

He frowns some more, unbuckles the old leather panniers from the bike.

'We're closed.' He hooks the bags over his arm and turns towards the caravan.

I'm like rooted to the spot, watching him fish out the key and open the door. He looks round, scowling.

'We open at eleven tomorrow,' he says as he turns to go in and closes the door.

Suddenly released from paralysis, I run up to knock on the caravan door. Heart pounding like fuck.

He opens the door just enough to show his face. All wide stubbly chin, plump lipped mouth, a tiny nose and deep-set heavy-lashed brown eyes. Could this really be my dad?

'Do ye nae understand me, laddie?' he says, like proper Rab C Nesbit.

'Sorry, it's just, well, it's you I want to see, actually.'

He pulls the door wide open for a flash, then shuts it back round his face. 'Not a lot to look at really?' There's a flicker of a grin, a chink in the armour perhaps?

A gull squawks as it dips over the caravan roof, making me

jump. Is this the age-worn version of the face I've stared at in the photo? It is. I'm sure it is.

'You'll think I'm mad coming all this way. It was just a spur of the moment thing. As in when I saw the museum on the internet, all those old British bikes, I thought, it's got to be that Don McCalstry?' I babble.

He pulls back from the door, shakes his head.

'I dinnae much care for surprises, but I care even less for suspense,' he growls. 'So, you'll be telling me what you're doing here, and then you'll be on your way.'

'Yes, sorry, no easy way to say...' I focus on the deep vertical lines between his eyes. No trace of a smile now. I look down at my feet in the tatty trainers. 'I think you might be my father?' I say at last.

The words hang as a breeze gets up. A crisp packet scuttles over the yard. I'm wishing I was anywhere...

He gives me the once over until his eyes meet mine. I feel a sudden shock of recognition, like in the shape of them. My eyes transposed to an alien face. Like looking in a distorted mirror.

I open my mouth to say something, anything, but he throws back his head, exposing the fleshy expanse of his chin, and roars with laughter.

I stand like an idiot. Does he have to make it this hard?

'And how in the hell did you work that one out? Because I'm telling you, I dinnae have no son.'

'You donated sperm to my mum, in Sheffield. As in her friend Karen set it up?' I pull out the envelope from my pocket. 'You must remember, you like wrote stuff down for me, I've got your photo.' Suppose I'm wrong after all?

He rubs his hand across his screwed-up forehead then butts it with his fist.

'Karen, Karen.' He keeps on beating. 'Big Friendly Dyke, receptionist at Highcliffe's. Karen.'

'You do remember.' I hand him the envelope.

He pulls out the paper with the photo clipped to it. He purses his lips as he scans it, then looks me up and down again.

'How old are you?' he asks.

'Allegedly you agreed I could have it when I was eighteen, which was…. about a week ago? Seems a hell of a lot longer, though. I've had a few adventures getting here, I can tell you,' I can't stop rambling.

'And you thought I'd be hailing my long-lost son?'

'It's just I wanted to see you, pretty much.'

'Like I said, I'm no' much to look at. Whatever you want from me is no' about to happen.' He starts to close the door.

'Wait!' I put my foot on the step. 'You think I'm like after a dad at my age? It's just natural to be curious, isn't it? Is it such a big deal to talk to me now I've come all this way?' My voice rises with my righteousness.

He pulls his eyebrows into a frown. I have those same straight heavy eyebrows. Can't he see that?

'You've no' told me what they call you.'

'Gethin.'

He scratches his chin.

I'm literally not daring to breathe. He nods his head slowly

'Well Gethin, I hope you like kippers?'

Don pulls back the curtains and the light falls on his living space. It's dead neat and orderly, which does surprise me. There's a sweet little wood stove with a kettle on the top plate, and like a Formica topped table with a tartan tray holding random bits of metal and one of those car pennants with the Scottish flag on a wire stand. He waves me to sit on the narrow bench behind the table, pulls up an old chair without its back and opens the woodstove.

'I'll get this lit, then we'll have tea and a dram?'

'That'll be awesome.'

He starts packing the stove with wood and rolled up paper. His moves are slow and precise, like it's important exactly where each piece of wood sits. I look over at the built-in shelf unit with engine parts lined up where the teacups should be. There's a couple of oil lamps at either end, and a dinky little bed under the window. Everything has its place, and it's all scrubbed clean. You wouldn't think he'd be the house-proud type. Obviously, it's not genetic.

'You've got it all ship-shape in here,' I feel the need to say something, even though I would be happy just to sit and absorb who he is.

He takes some long matches, carefully lights the paper and pushes the stove door to. Then he puts the matches away and centres the kettle on the stovetop, before pulling his stool round to face me.

'Aye, it's pure a ship's cabin. When you've no' much room you need everything neat.' He gets up and unpacks his panniers. There's a packet wrapped in waxed paper, a pint of milk, a bag of potatoes and a loaf of sliced white. He puts it all away in the built-in cupboards, one of them a tiny fridge. He holds the packet up to his nose. 'Wood smoked kippers from down the road. We'll have them in a wee while.'

'Thanks, I do genuinely…I mean, I should have written or something…' I start.

He waves me to stop. 'You may as well eat now you're here.

I don't get many visitors, so you'll excuse the lack of airs and graces.'

'I'm just interested in who you are, that's all.'

'Dinnae be getting ideas over a plate of kippers,' he growls. He gets all Rab C when he's riled. Otherwise his accent is lilty and clear.

He sits back on his stool, rubs his chin. 'Your ma's a pal of Karen's, you say?'

'Yes, they were, like, together when I was little.'

'Hmm, she was a quality lassie, that Karen. You owe your existence to her, son, because no fucker else would have persuaded me to part with my spunk.' He eyeballs me as he says this.

I pull back, gob-smacked by his bluntness, that he called me 'son'. Weirdest ever to think that he is my flesh and blood.

'Aye, Karen.' He goes back to musing. 'Maybe it helped that she was a dyke, but she was one of the few pals I've ever had.'

'You met her at work, is it?' I'm trying to imagine this unlikely happening.

'She was a receptionist where I worked in Sheffield.' He pauses, like his brain shifting a gear. 'I was no more one for people then than I am now. Always on the wrong side of folk. Or they on the wrong side of me.' He glares, as if I'm about to disagree.

I shift on the bench. 'A bit different to Karen, then. She's, like, totally friendly with anyone. It used to embarrass me, as a kid.'

He laughs. 'About as opposite as you could imagine. But she took no crap, and I liked that. The lads would make some lesbo joke and she'd laugh along with them, then chuck the joke back at them with interest. Make them seem small.' He scratches his chin again. 'She took me as I was, stood up for me when I wasn't popular. Rare thing, that.' He falls into silence, staring blank at the kettle.

I look out of the window above the bed. It faces right onto the sea and the charcoal outline of the distant mountains.

'Awesome view!' God, I sound like an idiot.

'Aye, I've no need of a TV.'

'What are those mountains on the horizon?'

'That, my laddie, is the Isle of Skye.'

I feel a tremor at him calling me 'my laddie'. It's what guys like him call young men. But he's also my dad, whatever he says.

Don takes a bottle of whisky, a glass tumbler and a china teacup out of a cupboard.

'You can tell I'm no' used to visitors.' He pours the golden liquid. 'One whisky glass to my name.' He smiles at me, with a dimple just like mine.

I swear I can feel my cheek twitch as I beam back at him while he sets the teacup in front of me. Can you believe it? He has my dimple!

I take a sip and run my tongue around the whisky. It's all caramel smoky, sending a delicious warmth to my guts.

'Like it?' He shows me the bottle, 'Caol Ila forty-year-old. I didnae come to the top end of Scotland to drink Bells.' He laughs.

'What made you move here? Apart from the whisky.'

Don pulls his frown lines in. 'I ran out of room for motorbikes.' He looks deadpan at me.

'But you're from Lochgillan, originally, isn't it?'

He takes a jolt back, like I've said something offensive.

'It's just, you said on this…' I pull his letter out again.

'Then you'll know all about me already.' He waves the letter away.

'Oh please. I'm just curious.' My voice wavers and I'm stupidly close to tears.

He takes a sip of his dram, closes his eyes for a minute while he savours it. I take some breaths, try to keep calm.

Don opens his eyes and nods at me. 'We moved to Glasgow, where my mother was from, when I was a wean.' He talks like it's almost too much effort to explain. 'My father ran the petrol station up here, but he had grand ideas of making his fortune as a second-hand car dealer in the Big City.'

'Is that like how you got into motorbikes?'

'Motorbikes were my thing, nothing to do with me da,' he growls.

Fuck's sake, sooo touchy.

I sip the whisky and feel the warmth relax my worn-out body. I'm about to risk another question when Don looks up at me.

'I found my first bike under a flyover when I was fifteen, but always had a thing for bikes. I remember as a kid up here, seeing the bikers coming through of a summer…' he pauses.

I zip my lips shut, hoping he'll say more.

'It takes a biker to understand,' is all I get.

'Well, obviously, I can see they are mega important to you,' I try.

'Me da hated bikes. Maybe saw them as competition for his business. He thought I'd become a Hell's Angel or something. At any rate, my idea was to get away as soon as possible. Which, aged seventeen, I did.'

'Where did you go then?'

'Sheffield.' Don starts making tea. The kettle's steaming and the caravan is all toasty warm. When am I going to tell him I've got nowhere to stay? I take another sip of whisky. Not thinking about that now.

'Why Sheffield?' I ask as he hands me a tea.

'This pal of mine, Mick, used to work for my da. Taught me all I knew about bikes, did Mick. He took me to Sheffield to check out this rare bike.' He pauses, sips his tea. 'Well the lad he bought the bike off had a room for rent. I'd had a huge barney with my da the night before and it seemed like as good a time as any, so I stayed.' He stares at me like warning me not to question? 'Ended up I got settled there. Did my mechanic's apprenticeship. Worked in the workshop for years, where I met Karen.'

'Well, I'm very glad you did.' How weak does that sound?

'I'll bet you are. And it's only that I owed her a favour, really. It was around the time my mother died. I was pure cut up, and Karen had a way of getting me to talk, kept me sane, I'd say…'

He scowls down at his feet as he falls into silence. I hardly dare breathe, like I've caught him off guard and he'll clam up the minute he realises. I'm surprised to hear him talk about Karen like this. To me she's always been in-your-face jolly, not exactly the obvious choice for someone like Don to confide in. But if she hadn't been there for him, I wouldn't exist. Weirdest ever.

Don breaks the mood, slapping his legs to get up again. 'Kippers?' he says.

I watch him prepare the fish, heating them in milk on the stove while he butters bread. All with that precision care. What would it have been like to grow up with him? I'm betting he'd have made a grumpy sod of a dad.

155

The kippers take literally all Don's attention as he carefully pulls the fish apart and wraps each mouthful in bread. I've eaten nothing all day and I've never tasted smoked fish so good. Thinking I could eat another five, I mop up the juice with my bread, looking out of the window as I eek out the last bites. There's like a bank of slatey cloud building up on the horizon – it's hard to tell where Skye begins and ends. Rays of lemon sunlight stream up out of the cloud and the sea has darkened.

'Awesome, this scenery changes like every five minutes?' I say.

Don grunts, still absorbed in his food. I watch a group of birds swoop black arrows across the pale sky and listen for the faint hiss of the sea while I wait for him to finish. Building up some jittery excitement for what I want to ask him next.

Eventually he gathers the plates and pours more tea and whisky.

'I saw on the internet about the McCalstrys of Lochgillan. Are you officially one of them?' I go for it as soon as he sits down.

'McCalstrys of Lochgillan eh?' He pulls his shoulders up tense.

'Yes, as in they're big landowners around here, it says…' I pull my phone and charger out and look around for a socket.

'You'll no' find such mod cons as electricity here.' He waves at the oil lamps.

'Ah, never mind. So, you're not related to the local landowners then?' I try again.

'We may be distant rellies, but to folks here I'm pure a minging Glasgee scunner and I get nae invites to Broomdale.' He spits out the words, proper Rab C again.

'Broomdale?'

Don takes a gulp of whisky and scowls at me like a challenge.

Fucking hell, sooo tetchy. What was it I read about the McCalstrys of Lochgillan?

'There was something about them being good clan leaders, not evicting their tenants during the clearances, is it?'

He snorts as I say this.

'That sounds pretty awesome to me, like something to be proud of?'

I look up at him, heart thumping. I'm excited these people are my ancestors. Why can't he indulge me and talk about it?

'Me grandda liked to boast of his links to the noble clan. But they weren't so keen when me da tried to tap them for a business loan. Aye, they think a lot of themselves.' Don holds me in his gaze.

Is he like studying my features? Has he actually noticed I've got his eyes?

'Folk around here have a lot of nonsense to talk,' he says, all slow and deliberate. 'I'll thank you not to go about bragging of your relations to the McCalstry clan, or to me for that matter.'

I'm literally squirming with the sternness of his stare. I nod just to get him to look away.

He goes to fill the kettle and stoke up the stove. 'Enough of the bloody McCalstrys.' He sits back down. 'What about yourself?'

His look is a challenge again and I'm pissed off with its power. What the hell is there to say? I sip the whisky, shift my feet.

'Not a lot to tell, I'm nothing special.' How pathetic does that sound?

Don smiles for the first time in ages. And there it is, my dimple again. 'That'll be something we have in common then.' His eyes softer now. Not so bad looking after all.

I feel a strange comfort in this like solidarity of failure. Without Mum to add, *of course you're something special*, then outline all the reasons I'm not.

'But you've got this epic motorbike museum?' I say.

'Aye and it's bankrupting me.' Don stares past me.

'But I've seen it online. Such an awesome idea, as in, I don't know a lot about motorbikes, but I really like all that old stuff…' I gabble.

'You don't want to believe everything you see on the internet,' he interrupts.

'I knew it was you when I found it on Google? You said in your letter, like about your passion for old bikes? *If only there were a job in that…*'

'Aye, I made a fair bit of money before I came here, rebuilding the British bikes that no beggar cared about in the seventies. Now you get old bikers gone respectable, wanting to turn heads with a shiny old classic at the weekend. Pay through the nose for someone else to tart up the chrome, retune the engine.'

'So, what gave you the idea of the museum?' I'm feeling smug with how neatly I've got the conversation back on him, but I'm still treading carefully.

He nods his head slightly as he thinks. You can pretty much hear the cogs whirring.

'These bikes are a part of the history of everyday folk. So, I had the idea of showing them as they were: transport for a family trip to the seaside; café racers, highland scramblers, all that. I managed to scrape enough to open about four years ago.'

'Sounds sick! I can't wait to see your museum. You should be dead proud.'

'Aye, well pride never paid the bills, and it doesn't make enough. I'm out of capital before it's finished.'

'Couldn't you like get a grant or something?'

'Oh aye, a grant. You have nae idea how things work here.' He jerks his head around the caravan, like he's heard something suspicious.

I've obviously hit yet another sore point. What about that woman at the Heritage Centre, hinting that Don had no friends? I'm desperate to know what that's all about, but somehow, I sense now's not the moment.

'I'd still love to see the museum,' is all I say.

'It's open to the public.' He starts twirling the car pennant flag from his tray, like that ends the subject.

Fuck's sake, why can't he just show me now? And I remember again I've got to tell him I've nowhere to stay and no money. I put it off as another question emerges.

'So, are you for Yes in the referendum?' I point to the spinning flag.

He plants the flag firmly back on the tray. 'Och, someone gave it to me with the idea of flying it on the bike.'

'So, you're not that bothered, is it?'

He considers for a moment. 'I'm aye bothered. It would make my day to see Scotland give the Global Establishment a wee kicking, but it'll make no difference flying the Saltire or anything else. Them in power will fix the vote if that's what it takes, they'll nae let go of milking Scotland.'

'Whoa, and people call *me* Negative? They can't actually fix it, can they? As in, there'll be a lot of scrutiny, isn't it?'

'Aye, they will manage well enough with their biased

media. It's no' an even fight, for sure.' Don finishes the last of his whisky. Sets his glass down slowly.

All the more reason to fight hard, is what I want to say, but still I'm struck by how like me he sounds with his what's-the-point attitude.

Don pushes his stool back abruptly and stands up.

'You'll need to be getting to your lodgings, Gethin.' He looks through the window. 'The cloud's rolling in again.'

'Yeah, well, the thing is…' I get up to move nearer to him and knock the tray full of metal bits which crashes down, and I watch in Slow-Mo as its contents scatter all over the floor.

Don holds himself rigid as the last nut rolls into a corner. Then he kneels to pick up the bits, inspecting them one by one. Teeth clenched, the veins on his forehead literally fit to bust.

'I'm sorry,' I bend down to try to help.

'Leave it!' he shouts. His face all red and glistening sweat.

I retreat round the table, feeling totally useless, barely daring to breathe. He finishes picking everything up and carefully lays the tray over the sink.

'Those pieces were in a particular order,' he mutters. 'It's no good. I dinnae do visitors. Blabbing me business, never works, never…'

'I've like made a big mess of this. As in I've only got a few quid until this cheque clears on Monday. I genuinely didn't realise when I set off, idiot, obviously…' I blurt it out, my voice thin and trembly.

Don shakes his head at me. 'No, no. You cannae stay here. You've seen me, you've dragged out my tales. That's it. I did some lesbian chick a favour, that's as far as it went.'

He shoves some more wood in the stove, slams the door shut.

'My mum is not some fucking chick!' I lean across the table towards him, the searing heat of anger surging through me. 'And that wasn't "it". You agreed you could be traceable when I reached eighteen.'

'You want the honest truth? I didnae give it a thought. Karen left work for her teacher training and I wasn't even sure if the chick conceived.'

'How can you not have thought? Sperm meets egg makes baby? As in person, flesh and blood?' I shout, shaking now. 'Fuck you! Bastard!'

I grab my bag and sleeping bag. Sling them over my shoulder and head for the door. Blood banging in my head.

'Don't worry. I won't be troubling you with my inconvenient existence anymore.'

I open the door and nearly fall down the step with the force of slamming it.

I stomp through the yard and onto the road. I'm still shaking, incandescent. Why write that fucking note for me? As if I'm just like some favour for a 'lesbian chick'? Fucker. I head towards town. I'll do that trying the locals in the pub thing. I'm too angry even to be worried now. Fuck him. Fuck him.

I turn the corner and I can see the houses spread around the bay. The streets look quiet as fuck, no cars, nothing. Saturday night and it's high season. There'd better be people in the pub.

I hear the roar of a clapped-out engine, glance back to see a tatty pickup truck. It pulls in just past me and the driver gets out. It's him, beckoning at me. I'm not moving. He hurries towards me.

'I may no' be the most sociable of buggers, but I'm no' a

bastard,' he says as approaches. 'I'll take you to the campsite; I can lend you a tent.' He fishes in his pocket and pulls out some notes. 'There you go, you can pay me back on Monday. It's enough for the campsite and some food.'

Still not moving. Don't want his fucking tent or his money.

'Come on, laddie. You need a place to stay. You may as well do a spot of sightseeing, now you've come so far.' His accent is soft and lilty again.

Every part of me wants to tell him to go fuck himself. I'll make do tonight and get the hell out tomorrow. But then a little voice reminds me that I did turn up on him out of the blue with no money. Now he's trying to help me out. I take a deep breath, hear the sea breaking on the shore below and feel the salty cool of the air. Fuck it, I do have a right to stay around, why should I be too proud to take a loan from him?

Another breath, shrug of my shoulders. 'OK, thanks,' I grab the money and make my way to his truck.

Road to Nowhere – *Jez*

Swinging round the bend coming out of Chatburn I catch the fat arsed Mondeo in front of me. The A59 straightens across open country with nowt approaching. Drop down a gear and hit the throttle while the Harley roars past him and the road is my own. Fucking natural or what? Up a gear and hit sixty in seconds. After the nervous drag through endless Greater Manchester, finally got the overtaking thing. Got my map on my tank bag. Got my swanky panniers and dinky little tool kit. Tent, sleeping bag, everything I need. The bike eats the road. Got my Harley Sportster Good-as-Dream-Bike.

Slowing down for the thirty through Gisburn, it's like I could walk faster, could brew a tea on the natty petrol stove. Through the village, turn along the Ribble valley, taking the whole line of cars as soon as the speed limit comes off. Road curving through open country heading for the Dales. Confidence growing with every car I take. I think of Martin riding with me while I practiced. Forced to agree I had a knack for it, though it was all down to his choice of bike for me. Sexy in its own way with curvy black tank and the gold Harley signature. Shiny engine. Gleaming double exhaust. Martin laughed when I said it's more understated than the V Max. First time he'd heard a Harley called understated. Whatever, he was right, it suits me, and it handles like a fucking dream. A dream bike that's real and live between my legs. Way To Go!

Cool air whistles through the visor, flashing lines of trees, open fields, grey stone wall. Whiff of manure and damp ditches. Speedo showing eighty. Martin said, keep off the motorways, keep to the speed limit, don't attract attention. But I can see a frigging mile off on this road. Eye out for cameras, I'll be fine, right? Would insult the bike to go any slower.

Past the sign into North Yorkshire – Yay! The road dips down to the river and a café with a couple of bikes parked among some ragged looking flags. Suddenly I'm starving.

I order all-day-breakfast and make my way outside. Sit with my back to the bench table to face the bike. Light a fag and stretch my legs out while I gaze at it in awe.

Weather's cooled in the last day or two, but it's still hot in my leather. I pull it off to reveal my new biker-chick top. Catch the eye of the guy on the next table. Middle aged, tad overweight, shaved head, and right piggy eyes. Wearing one of those red and white Gor-Tex jobbies that bulks him out. Obviously been waiting for my attention as a cheesy grin spreads over his blobby face.

'Going far?' he asks.

'As far north as possible,' I say, watching sunlight flash off the bike exhaust.

'Aye, it's a good ride up to the Lakes from here.'

I turn to face him with a smug grin. 'Right to the top of Scotland.'

His eyes take in my new leather trousers, squeaky new jacket and shiny helmet. Only my battered pink Docs, which I wasn't about to ditch, show any sign of wear.

'Been riding long?' he smirks.

'Well, not really.' Should've kicked the leathers up a dusty road! I stare at the bike again. Leave me the fuck alone.

'That your Harley there?' he persists.

I nod, can't help smiling. My Harley.

'Suits you, yeah,' he muses. 'Not sure the Basic Rule will apply to you.'

I turn and frown at him.

'The Basic Rule of Motorcycling: behave as if you're invisible and all car drivers are stupid. But they'd have to be pretty dumb to miss you.' He chuckles.

I tense my shoulders and look away. I'm used to being in old combats and T shirt. Not learnt to deal with this biker chick look. Fucking creep!

'Aw, only teasing, love. Nowt wrong with looking the part is there?'

I shrug, pull out my phone. The café girl comes over with my food and I turn to face the table.

'Well, you should still know the Basic Rules.' He gets up cradling his helmet. 'Anticipate the worst. Car drivers don't see you, no matter what I said; they don't use their mirrors, and most don't know the Highway Code. What you have to do…'

'Yeah, there's a lot of dicks on the road,' I say, getting the music up on the phone. Spin my finger to land on Amy Winehouse as the girl sets the food down. Get stuck into my bacon while Amy starts with *Rehab*.

'Nice to meet you,' he hollers, pulling on his helmet. 'Good to see more lasses riding. You take care now.' His squished face manages what passes for a quite nice smile before he makes for a big red and white Honda that matches his jacket.

Amy sings *No No No*.

The A65 starts to bore me through tame country skirting the Dales. Ready for more of a challenge at Ingleton. Detour onto a little road alongside the long bulk of mountain. The road climbs steadily as I drop a gear for the wide bend taking me up, then dipping and rising into a sharp hairpin. Drop another gear, lean into the next bend, straighten, accelerate, over to the other side for another sharp bend. Up and up – open moor spreading dull greens and rusty browns into the distance. The road straightens and I change up to top. Truly I am in the zone. No traffic, scenery belting past, wind streaking my face. Amy with *Back to Black* stuck on a loop.

Soulful cry repeating the chorus of *You Know I'm No Good.*

Alice in my head with no warning. Pale thin face. Those eyes, both fearful and empty. The only image of the mother I will never know.

You Know I'm No Good. Was that Alice deciding not to find Ken when she was pregnant?

Flashes of Ken's story repeating as the bike bombs across the moors.

Sat at the bar looking into an empty drink…

Small and sad, all I wanted was to look after her…

Thin arms covered in bruises…

Like she was trying to forget herself…

Bloke in me couldn't help it…

All I will ever have of her: a blurry photo and Ken's guilt-ridden mitherings.

Amy comes through, right on cue, *He Can Only Hold Her.* What happened to Alice to make her like that? Unbearable that I will never know. Why didn't I probe Ken more?

What if she hadn't died when I was little? Why has that might-have-been never occurred to me? Is there owt of her in me? She took Ken home on a whim – I looked after him at the end, right?

The moors spin past – blurred through frigging tears. Riding on automatic.

Amy laying it on now with *Wake Up Alone.*

Those frightened blank eyes. What the heck was behind them? Did she die alone? How else?

Suddenly the bike's juddering – I've slowed right down to thirty, catching traffic stuck behind a caravan. Managed the brakes instinctively but not the gears. Glance at my foot changing down; see the loose chippings, how close to the side I've drifted. Look up and see the silver Toyota just in front of me swinging over to take a left at a junction I didn't even notice.

I hear my horn, not as loud as it should be, slam on the brakes, feel the skid of the back wheel throw me. Oily gleam of puddle in broken tarmac. Thud of the dropped bike. Smell of rubber and petrol. Visor steaming up. Scrape of the road sliding on my side to the lumpy edge. Damp cool earth as I scrabble on hands and knees to land helmet face down on the bank.

Head pounding breath echoing. Condensation refracting grey-brown grass. Fuck, the bike! Got to rescue the bike. Push up on my hands to roll to the not-hurting side.

'Are you OK there?'

Lift the visor to peering face of a man with dark hair hanging over his eyes. I nod, feel the weight of the helmet, push onto my knees to get up.

'Here.' He offers his shiny-clean hand.

Sharp pain in lower ribs as he hauls me up. Stagger to the bike lying back wheel into the road. Bend to grab the handlebars and wince with another shot of pain. The guy leans over and pulls it up in one easy move.

'You want to watch what you're doing, young lady.' Smug in business-man-on-holiday casuals.

The paintwork's scratched on the tank and the front mudguard's dented. Tears well for my precious bike. He looks for the side-stand. I try to take the bike from him, clutching at my side.

'I can manage,' he snaps. 'You were far too close to that car. You didn't even notice him indicating left.' He heaves the bike onto the stand.

I look around – just the one car with the hazards on behind us.

'No, he didn't stop, but that doesn't…'

'Probably didn't even notice me come off, right, that's how much he was looking.' I hear the shake in my voice, heat of tears. I turn to wipe my face with my gloved hand, still holding my side with the other. It hurts to breathe.

'Whatever. You're lucky you're not badly injured. Nothing broken, I take it?'

'I'm frigging walking, aren't I?'

'I should call the police. Shame I didn't get the car's plate.'

Sharp intake of painful breath. 'No, please, don't,' I plead.

He looks doubtfully at me. Shit, don't show you're bothered.

'Honestly, there's no need. As you say, it was my fault.' I try a weak peace-making smile.

He shrugs, Adam's apple wobbling over his polo shirt. Rattles his keys in his pocket.

'Do you want me to stay to see if the bike's working?' he asks, gazing over at his car.

'No, I'll just sit on the bank for a bit, have a cig. I'll be fine,' I say, casual as I can.

'You shouldn't be on that bike, but I suppose that's your funeral. Just bloody make sure it's not someone else's.'

I give him a nod, knowing he's right.

He turns and gets into his car, pulls back onto the road and he's away. Thank fucking God for that. I take some shallow breaths holding my side.

My legs wobble as I clamber onto the scrubby bank and sit on a clump of thick moorland grass. Grapple with my helmet strap. Try again with gloves off. Hands shaking as I fish the cigarettes from my inside pocket. The packet's squashed – fumble desperately for one that's not broken. Please. I just need a frigging smoke. Find one that's only bent – more frustration trying to light it. Hit of the smoke straight to my head, dizziness overwhelming the pain of inhaling. Still, I clutch at my left side. Maybe I've broken a rib. Fuck knows.

The Basic Rules from the bloke in the café. Idiot, I thought I knew better. Stick Amy on the iPhone, why don't you? Because you are *such* a natural motorcyclist? Forcing Martin to get me this bike against his better (yes, better) nature. What would he think to me not even noticing a simple left turner in a queue of traffic? If that guy had called the police! Maybe he still will. What if he like memorised my number plate?

I inhale too deeply, making me cough, splitting my side with pain. Slide my hand under my jacket, feeling for any damage. Nowt sticking out, maybe just a cracked rib? My left leg hurts when I touch it, hopefully just bruising. My leathers have scrape marks all down them. You wanted to look less shiny and new, right? Scratched up bike to match, how's that for Street-Cred, girl?

I lean on my elbow to look at the poor battered Harley. The

guy was right: I shouldn't be riding it. Shiver as I finish my fag, suddenly cold. Fucking Amy Winehouse dragging me into an emo-trip about Alice. The bike was my escape and now it's obvious I can't handle it. Twist of disappointment in my gut as sharp as the real pain. How much did I have riding on this trip? I stub my fag into the peaty damp soil. Position myself to lie back with my head resting on a grassy tussock.

Massive amount of sky up here. Thin clouds drifting towards the distant flat-topped mountain. Smells of damp earth, trickle of a stream beyond the bank. A tiny bird hovers high, trilling its song. I could sink into the earth and drift with the clouds forever. The bird makes a sudden dive for the moorland. I shiver again, cold seeping, brain numbing. Close my eyes to drift in it.

The roar of a passing motorbike jolts me to sit up. Panic checking the Harley hasn't gone. It leans on its stand, mud-spattered and abandoned, still a dull shine from its damaged tank. Am I really giving up on my pride and glory that easily? Get back on the horse, is what they say. I take a painful breath. If I just ride carefully, find a campsite, make sure the bike's OK. Think about Martin and Stan and their tales of scrapes and falls. Every biker comes off at some point, usually when they get too cocky, right? Less of the Invincibles, more of the Basic Rules. No more frigging music. No more head fucks.

I push myself up and stagger to the bike, still clutching my side. It goes through me how sad it looks. I pull out my phone for a picture to mark its first knock.

Fuck, the screen glass is smashed. As if! I gulp down the tears as I stare at the screen. All the pieces are held in and it seems to be working. I take a picture featuring the scratched tank. The image is visible under the smashed glass. It'll do. I re-zip the jacket on the tighter setting. Feels better like that around the ribs.

Turn the ignition, heart pounding, please, please God. It sputters with the spark and dies as soon as I give it throttle. Try again, the same. Come on now, where there's spark… Again. Yes, the engine roars. Yay! I mount the bike and study the map on the tank bag. Just a few miles away from Hawes. There's got to be a campsite around there. Engage the clutch and slip into first, nervous as fuck as I indicate to pull out. Easy does it, up to second, slow around the bend, straighten into the road ahead.

There's a low cloud rolling in as I come down from the moors and I whoop out loud at the campsite sign. Made it to safety in one piece! Got back on the horse, right? I park the bike and haul myself off, my left leg stiff and sore as I limp to the campsite shop. I register for the night, buy more fags, a few cans and some chocolate, and spot the extra strength painkillers to complete the supplies. The woman directs me to a secluded spot down by the river. I pull off my helmet, hear the gurgle of the brook over the stones. It's like this place was waiting for me. Refuge from the danger road.

Putting up the tent, for the first time, with an aching body strapped into sweaty leathers, in the humid midgeyness, knocks a fair bit of shine off my temporary high. But a simple little tent will not defeat me now, so I pop some painkillers and keep at it. Finally, it's up and I haul the panniers to my pale blue shelter on the river's edge. I had thought of going to the pub to eat, but not up for any more friendly advice from blokes who think they know better than a novice bike-chick. Especially when the bastards get proved right. Got my supplies, including a tin of ham and pea soup if I fancy tackling the dinky stove. Count my blessings: the police don't appear to be on my trail.

For now, I'm cool with lying in the porch, head propped on the panniers, with a can of beer and a fag from the new pack. The early evening light shines through the trees as the cloud clears and the midges retreat. I'm aching and totally knackered. Yes, I managed a cautious ride for another few miles, but my confidence has bombed. Barely sixty miles today and I'm shaky as fuck. Great start, gal! Finish my fag and roll up my hoody to cushion my side. Take another slug of beer and lie back, drifting into the play of light on leaves.

I wake to full-blown moonlight. A breeze rustling through the silhouetted trees. Every bone in my body aches and the night air seeps cold. Fuck, how long have I been crashed for? I fish out my phone, the pain in my rib waking up as I move. 23:15 and the phone's low on charge. Time for bed, right? I pull out my sleeping bag and find the wind-up torch that doubles as phone charger and radio. Way too much effort – there's enough light from the moon to drag off the leather trousers and crawl into the sleeping bag. I open another can of beer, rest it in my boot to stop it falling over. Attack the chocolate and down more painkillers.

All I want is to go back to sleep, but now the day's events are repeating on me like bad food. I drink more beer, finish the chocolate, shift round to smoke a cigarette. Catch myself wondering about Ken. Have the proper kids staged the funeral yet? Fuck's sake, I need distraction. All I have is the wind-up radio. I lay the fag in the little tin ashtray and start to wind, holding it with my left arm pressed to my side.

Giving it all I've got with my right arm, counting to a hundred to keep me going. Just about finishes me off, but it's stopped the bloody mithering. I turn on the radio and try to tune it while I finish my fag.

A lot of crackle and white noise, but eventually the strains of some music. I lie back, propped on the panniers, drink some more beer.

I can't place the intro though I know I know it. Then the electro drum kicks in and, of course, it's Talking Heads: *Road to Nowhere*. Takes me back to the Classic Rock bar in the days of Stan. The radio just about lasts the song out. Fucked if I'm winding it again.

All I can do is lie with my aching side strapped up in my leather. Close my eyes, the sound of the brook merging with *Road to Nowhere* in my head. Image of a ribbon of tarmac snaking over the horizon and beyond. Just being on the road, even if it's strewn with obstacles, even if it's going Nowhere, right? Riding it now for as long as it takes.

Who Do You Think You…? – *Gethin*

I wake to a dull pink light seeping through the red of the tent, after an uncomfortable night of fitful dreaming. As in searching for something with Gran in their house, everything like covered in dust and cobwebs, walls crumbling, windows blanked. Granddad waving his stick and shouting, 'No, you fools, you should be looking in Scotland.' Fumbling through the fading dream logic to waking, realising I am in Scotland with only a deep pit of disappointment. It feels early, though I've no idea of the time, my phone being dead, and there are raindrops on the tent door. I am so not up for rain today. Not up for today, full stop. I pull my sleeping bag over my head and cocoon myself back to oblivion, successfully putting off the need to pee.

Next thing I know the tent is beaming red heat and my bladder is calling time on excuses. I pull on my rancid jeans and unzip the door. The air is sweet relief from the me-stench and the sunlight bounces off the wet grass. I walk across to the toilet block, taking in the sweep of this site on the dunes, swifts darting through the still air, the sea flat and blue and the unreal feather line of mountains on Skye. I stretch out my arms and pull back my shoulders to take in a lung full. Awesome or what? Could life be possible after all?

Half an hour later and I'm still on a high, topped up with the cheese and ham baguette and can of coke that was breakfast from the camp shop. I take a path over the dunes, long dry grasses brushing my arms, dropping down to acres of sandy beach. I bend to touch the lacy edge of an incoming wave, retreating hastily to avoid wet trainers and licking the saltiness from my fingers.

I take a path leading up to the heathland behind and bounce across the mostly dry pinkish bog-moss, clumpy heather and tiny bright ferns. Birds dart everywhere – little chirpy ones jumping out of the heath, others with thin legs and sharp bills, poking at the mud by the stream. Swifts, sparrows and seagulls are about my bird knowledge limit. Karen had a fit of taking me birdwatching before she settled on bowling. But all I can remember was a bunch of baby grouse chicks one day. Funny how little I think of her, considering I owe her my existence. Did she actually force Don to write that letter, the one he gave no thought to?

'Stop it!' I shout, leaping through a patch of wet bog. Can I just allow myself to enjoy this? Push through several wet trainer moments before hitting some meadow-land teeming with wildflowers: all splashes of pink, yellow, purple. The tiniest sapphire blue flowers as I climb a hummock, the highpoint of the heath.

The view up here is epic. With my back to the sea the land rises to craggy hillside. Another quarter turn and there's the heavy-duty mountains the other side of the bay, brooding solid chunks of matter. Turn 180° to face the sea and Skye in the distance; then the last quarter turn to the valley floor dotted with highland cattle and a sprinkle of white houses. Thinking of my phone like charging up in the campsite shop. That 360° photo app would be awesome for this. I'll have to come back and take the photo and I dunno, stick it on Facebook I guess? Like anyone would be interested. I sit on a rock facing out to sea and watch as Skye disappears behind a smudge of cloud. Suddenly I feel lonely as fuck.

A couple of hours later I'm in the coffee shop at the head of the bay. It's like a lefty-hippy throw-back, as in dark red and green paintwork; random piles of books about Scottish politics mixed with alternative therapy manuals and local history; posters advertising yet more referendum debates. An overpowering smell of cinnamon.

'Where do you hail from?' The woman behind the counter asks, totally cut-glass English sixty-something.

She smiles as I tell her, tossing back her silver bob, like trying to look interested.

'How about you?' I add. 'You don't sound very Scottish?'

She laughs. 'No, I haven't absolutely *gone native*. But the locals are super welcoming of us retired English ex-pats.'

I nod, wondering how that fits with Don's world?

I order a latte and a cinnamon scone and sit overlooking the bay. Switch on my newly charged phone. The coffee isn't exactly as strong as it might be, and the scone is on the heavy side. To top it all my phone has no signal. Not that anyone would be trying to contact me. I sip the coffee and try to wash down the claggy scone.

The hand on my shoulder makes me jump, spitting coffee over the tablecloth.

'Geth-in!' I look up to see Dirk the Dutchman. 'I am right, Geth-in?'

I nod, suppressing a smirk at the pronunciation of my name like an out-of-the-way guest house.

'I said to the wife a few minutes ago, "We will see our young friend today, I feel sure."' He beams his tooth-filled grin and

I find myself smiling back. 'She is spending my money as usual. Ah, there she is.'

The Wife skips around the tables, waving a handful of books.

She nods at me. 'You find your friend yesterday?'

'Erm, yes, he's busy working right now.'

'Ah, there is plenty to occupy in here.' She spreads her books on the table.

'Plenty to bore me stupidly.' Dirk throws back his head like in mock despair.

The Wife smiles at me. 'Look at this, *James McCalstry's Lochgillan Stories*.'

I grab the book, a sharp stab in my guts at the mention of McCalstry. The blurb promises tales of intrigue, deception and cold-blooded slaughter, recorded in 1886 and providing a fascinating mythic backdrop to the clan still dominant in the area today.

'Wow, that doesn't look boring to me.' I'm already tempted to spill the beans on my McCalstry origins.

'Not to me either,' The Wife smiles knowingly at Dirk.

'Ah, the wife feels a special connection,' Dirk explains.

'My great grandfather was a McCalstry,' she says with a smug smile. 'From Argyle, but still, we are all one *clan*, you see?' She pats me on the shoulder, like she already knows about me. I'm weirdly pleased to know my connection is stronger than hers without having to brag about it.

'So now I have the tales, we must to the ancestral home, no, Dirk?'

'Ah, well, the dogs need a walk, that much is true.' Dirk winks at me, like I'm in on humouring The Wife. 'And what about you Geth-in? You will come with us up the Broomdale?

They say there are many rare plants, you can help me convince Else we can identify them, no?' Dirk flashes his gold toothed grin.

'Else. You have a name?' I surprise myself by not instantly finding an out for this trip.

She holds out her hand to me. 'And you will do me pleasure to come with us?'

I shake her hand and nod my agreement. God knows, the McCalstry connection or just desperate loneliness, but right now I'll take adoption by this crazy couple. And I'll get to see Broomdale, which is, remember, *my* ancestral home, not hers.

Dirk and Else fuss like over-protective parents with the dogs once we've parked at the foot of the glen. I feel a spare part as I lean over the bridge and watch the river seeping into stewy marsh as it meets the shoreline.

Eventually we are dog-leashed and setting off up the glen where the river runs fresher through banks thick with yellow flowered bushes. I'm about to identify this as gorse, when I get a flash of inspiration.

'Broom!' I point at the plants. 'That's why it's Broomdale!'

Dirk beams his approval, and I allow the satisfaction for a few seconds. Else meanwhile has mastered the art of walking and reading out loud, and I mean loud.

'*Black Mordoch McCalstry of the Cave received this soubriquet because, being a wild youth, he preferred to reside within the Torridons, hoping to get a chance of slaying his enemy Leon MacGallieatirs.*' Else reads in a monotone Dutch accent, pausing now and again to nod at me.

I'm literally losing the plot before it starts as she ploughs endlessly through this story of Murdo hiding here and sailing a galley there, gathering a band of fighters and finding his old nurse and a load more ins and outs before eventually slaughtering his enemies somewhere up the coast. I smile and nod like an idiot, while Dirk snorts and raises his eyebrows, which of course encourages Else to read more. Meanwhile the dogs pretty much throttle themselves on their choker chains in reaction to the snail pace walking.

The path skirts the wooded hillside which is indeed lush with vegetation: primitive looking fern-like specimens, low lying bushes with white star flowers, a patch of little purple flowers Dirk decides are orchids. Banks of trees rise up the hillside, trailing lichen and swinging creepers. Else continues her endless tales of whales and drownings in lochs, of fishing smacks loaded with weapons and whisky, kidnapping, murder, and trickery of every sort. Her dull monotone literally destroys any interest the stories may have had for me, not helped by the thickening clouds of midges further into the glen.

Eventually our path crosses a driveway that leads through some stepped grassy banks to Broomdale house. There's a PRIVATE – NO ENTRY notice on the gate but you can see the manor house with its line of chimneys and random gables.

Else pauses and we stare at the house and the blank of its mullioned windows. It couldn't feel less welcoming.

Then she starts up again, 'Angus McCalstry, renowned archer, was said to have enticed his enemy's daughter with his extraordinary physique, bringing her to his grand new Broomdale house…'

'Maybe we can claim a whisky from your clannish folk?' Dirk says to Else while winking at me. 'They owe us this small, how do you say, kindred spirit?'

I manage a hollow laugh at Dirk's joke before moving to lean against the gatepost. Am I in some nightmare episode of *Who Do You Think You Are*, where my claims to ancestry are side-lined by the pathetic routine of these lowland imposters? Meanwhile my own father won't acknowledge me as kin.

'Ah, Geth-in. How do you think to call on the wife's family?' Dirk moves to give me a hefty nudge.

'If they get their Scottish independence, perhaps they can support me for dual citizenship?' Else steps forward waving her book in my face.

Something snaps in me and I jump away from them, shake my fist at the NO ENTRY sign.

'Looks to me like they've closed their ranks.' My voice rises with the emotion I can't control any longer.

'Oh, we only make a joke,' Dirk reaches to touch my arm.

Else comes around the other side, face creased with concern, trailing the dogs who position themselves in front of me. They are creeping me out big style. How desperate was I choosing even temporary adoption by these loonies?

'Whoa,' I hold my arms out. 'I just need to go now, guys, OK?' I glare at them both and they back off as I turn to the path towards Lochgillan.

I've worked up major thirst by the time I get to the hotel bar, and I'm slapping a tenner down for a pint of Tennent's before I even notice who's serving me. I down a few gulps and finally look up to her staring through bottle-thick glasses. I've seen her before; I remember the nose-ring.

'Ah, you were at the Heritage Centre? I swear this place has about two people in total.'

'My husband manages the hotel, so I help in the bar, as well as at the Centre,' she explains. 'You were after finding the motorcycle museum, as I remember?'

'Oh, yes.' I look down into my drink, remembering Don's warning to keep quiet about him. 'It was like closed, as in nobody there.'

'Aye, that'll be nothing unusual these days.' She pulls a little knowing smile. 'Did you say you knew the fella that runs it?'

'Not exactly. Just, like, a friend of my mum's used to know him and kind of suggested I look him up?' I shrug.

'Hey, did you hear that, Robbie?' She moves down the bar to a guy reading a newspaper.

He looks up, all blue startled eyes in a ginger-bearded face. 'Sorry Laura, I was that deep in this article.'

'This young man's mother was a pal of Don McCalstry,' Laura nods as she emphasises the name.

'Oh aye?' Robbie gives me the onceover.

'Oh, no, not my mum, her friend,' I say, feeling awkward.

'Not that it's any of my concern who he's pals with,' Laura mutters, moving out to the back with some empty glasses.

I drink my beer, smiling as I'm betting Laura had something going with Don, catching Robbie's eye.

'Och, your ma will tell you he's nae such a bad soul,' he leans closer. 'In my opinion, he's his own worst enemy.'

I want to ask what he means. But Laura comes back into the bar just as two serious cycle-types come in, hauling a pile of panniers, and Robbie retreats to the bay window.

I finish my pint while the cyclists ask Laura about a room for the night. She takes them out through a side door and I'm about to try talking to Robbie again, when a different barmaid appears.

'Can I get you another?' she asks.

I meet her glance and her face lights with the most rosy-cheeked full-lipped smile. I study my empty glass to cover the rising flush I'm feeling.

'Ah, that so didn't touch the sides,' I say. 'All your bracing Highland air and the Mighty Battle with your Scottish midges.' I look up with what I hope is a winning smile.

She rewards me with a throaty chuckle. 'I'm not Scottish, am I?' She moves to pull me another pint, her sleek dark ponytail brushing the neckline of her skimpy black top.

'Oh, no. Actually, you don't sound it?' Foolish grin now, and literally aching with the relief of someone nice to talk to.

She pushes the drink towards me, and I take a sip, scratching for the next thing to say.

'So, what brought you here?' Lame, but it'll do.

Her dark grey eyes meet mine as she thinks about this, sending a shiver through me.

'The wind?' she says.

Aw, sweet answer. I raise my glass to her, drink more.

Laura pokes her face round the door behind her. 'Can I borrow you for a moment, Rosa?'

Sweet name as well, I muse as Rosa asks if she can get me anything else before she goes.

'I'll have a whisky chaser as well.'

'As we're in Scotland.' We both laugh in unison.

The whisky hits the spot, numbing the emptiness I've been fighting, aided by the glow of Rosa's attentions. I shift position to take in the public bar with its dark wood panelling, sepia pictures of old crofters and fishing boats. The cyclists are back, talking to Robbie. I stare out of the window and slip into a fantasy walk on the beach with Rosa, talking, laughing, waiting until it's pretty much unbearable before brushing her hair away from her face, her lips finding mine, soft and slow. I feel myself stirring and shift on the barstool, forcing myself to listen to the cyclists boring Robbie with tales of their trip.

'We've done three hundred miles so far,' one of them says, after a long-winded explanation of their route.

'That's in less than four days,' says the other.

'Which when you consider the terrain?' says the first. 'I mean, it's not quite the Bradley Wiggins….'

'No,' says Robbie.

'I've been counting the referendum posters,' the first guy says. 'So far it's two to one in favour of independence.'

'Aye,' says the other. 'That'll be because the No people are scared to show.'

Robbie shakes his head. 'It's the Westminster politicians with their Project Fear stories about economic collapse if we go it alone. But as soon as folk challenge this they're accused of intimidation. Och, it's time we stood on our own two feet.'

'Well, it's a worthy ideal, but it is a risky business. There'll be a run on the banks, so they say.'

'All bluster,' Robbie spits his disgust. 'We're one of the richest countries in the world, don't you know? We can more than afford to go it alone.'

I'm just finishing my second pint when Rosa makes a welcome reappearance. I order a refill with another chaser and ask if she'll qualify for a vote in the referendum.

'I've been told I can register as I'm resident here. I'm not sure it's right though?'

'Why not? If you're planning on staying, it affects you the same, no?' I down my chaser, start on the beer.

I tell her how I'm pretty much gutted I can't have a vote, even though I'm half Scottish. How it's like an infectious excitement that it's got everyone so massively fired up. I do a bounce on the barstool as I talk, grin up at her.

'It is a big thing, that's for sure.' Her gorgeous smile goes straight through me again.

It's a tricky balance with girls, rushing it can be counter-productive, but already I'm thinking of asking when she finishes work.

Then she drops her bombshell. 'My fiancé says I need to stop thinking like a tourist, if I'm settling here.'

I lean forward, open mouthed, looking for a trace of sheepish in that smile. Literally not a hint.

'He's doing the evening shift at six, so you'll meet him if you're still around,' she adds helpfully.

'Fiancé?' I stammer after a large gulp of beer to numb the plummeting disappointment.

'Crazy, isn't it?' she's like totally oblivious. 'My mum thinks I'm too young.' Rosa starts polishing glasses. Keeps on about her mum refusing to congratulate her.

I drink some more and stare into the glass. Here we go a-fucking-gain. Gethin Getting It Wrong With Girls. Trouble is, ninety percent of girls are way too attractive for their own good, but they act like they don't have a clue about it. The way they push up their tits in their little lacy bras, widen their eyes with their smoky makeup, and get you thinking everything's a come-on when it's totally not.

I slap myself down for this sexist thinking, but the fact is I find girls hard to fathom. Take Sonia, the first girl I properly got with: losing our virginity together at her suggestion, then her saying the next day we should just be friends. Making me worry like hell it was because I came too soon, even though at the time she said it didn't matter.

I look up and Rosa's right in front of me, tits nicely lined up at eye level. I rest my fucking case. Shaking my head, I look quickly away, thinking of Emily.

With Emily I thought I'd finally got it right, as in I gave her so much space she had to ask if I fancied her. I can still see her lying on the grassy bank in the park, her little knowing smile, eyes half closed, the rise and fall of her breasts with her breath: 'So, what are you waiting for?' Being with Emily was like nothing I'd ever known; tender and responsive, sexy as hell. But I have literally no idea why she dumped me, and it still hurts like fuck. I polish off my pint, followed with a deep sigh.

'Are you all right?' Rosa's concern sounds so genuine it brings tears to my eyes.

Fuck. No. I don't trust myself to speak. She lifts my empty glass and I nod, handing her the whisky glass too. Fuckit. At least I didn't actually make a move on this one. What a great fucking day I'm having.

The cyclists shout cheery goodbyes and Robbie retreats behind his newspaper.

'I haven't upset you now, have I?' Rosa asks softly as she sets down my drinks.

You'd think she'd want rid of me? I don't fucking get it.

'I'm just an idiot, don't take any notice,' I mutter.

'I hope I didn't, you didn't?' She steps back. 'I was only being friendly.'

'It's OK, I'm not good at reading women?' I down the whisky, slam the glass. Feel like some piss-head American movie character.

'Well, you'll not be the first, will you?' Rosa starts polishing up the bar.

'You needn't worry, as in I'm not going to be hanging around much longer.' I take a long draft of beer.

'Oh, there's no rush. It's nice to have someone to talk to, it gets that boring on the afternoon shift.'

I'm not convinced she means this, but I'll take company on any terms right now.

'So, are you up here on your own?' she asks.

'Couldn't be more so,' I slur into my glass. Oh God, how maudlin does that sound? I feel suddenly pissed as fuck. I should go before I make any more of a tit of myself.

'What brought you here, then?' Somehow, she sounds like she is actually OK with listening to me.

'Hah! Whole reason I'm here, as in here right now, like a failed mission to find why I'm here, as in here at all, maybe?'

Rosa shakes her head. 'Sorry, I don't…'

'Yeah, not 'splaining myself. Fact is I came here to find my dad? Literally never met him. Mum never met him, just got delivery of his spunk.'

'Delivery?' She frowns her total not getting it.

'Sperm donor?' I lean forward in a stagey whisper. 'Mum's a lesbian, see? Immaculate Conception Me.'

She shifts away a bit, carries on polishing.

'Sorree, too much information?' I drain my glass, ready for the off.

'Just unexpected, I suppose. So, have you found him?' Reassuring smile again.

'Yeah, the bastard doesn't want to know. He's one of the McCalstry clan – a bit up themselves, it seems. He runs the motorbike museum?'

She shakes her head. 'I don't know many folk around here, my fiancé may…' She glances at the clock.

'Ah, no, I'll spare you the embarrassment.' I look at my empty glass. 'Time for one more, then I'll be off?'

'Maybe you've had enough for now?' she says quietly.

'Aw just the whisky, then, for the road. Don't worry, I'm sooo not going to be hanging around?'

She purses her lips but gets me the drink anyway.

'I'm sorry you've not had a good experience in Lochgillan,' she says, softer again.

'Yeah, well, no chance of father-to-son advice on handling women, eh?' I say with a stupid grin. I am joking, aren't I?

'Hmm, how many boys you know get advice on women from their dads?'

'Perhaps it pretty much happens, you know, by osmo-o-mo-sis?'

'I'm not sure.' She hesitates. 'Some dads, I often think you'd be better off without them?'

Deep sigh. Thinking about Jarvis with his string of worse-than-useless stepdads, Aiden in Inverness? Ben's dad's lovely, but it's hard to think of many that are. And, to be fair, the chances of Don saying anything useful on the subject of women is, like, a total zero? And yet there's still a big but here.

'I hear that such a lot,' I say, still trying to work out what my point is. 'I'm not saying it's wrong, but it's a cop-out. As in I hope if I have children, I put a bit of effort in, not just Quick Sperm-Squirt and Job's a Good 'un.'

Rosa blushes as she turns away to polish the other end of the bar. Robbie looks concerned in my direction.

'He knows all about him.' I wave my arm at Robbie. 'Own worst enemy? What the hell was that about?'

Robbie walks towards me. 'Come on now, laddie. It's time you took a rest.'

I look round to see Rosa hovering by the staff door. OK, I've literally blown it and it's nearly fiancée o'clock. I drain the last of the whisky and feel it stoke my fury as I make to leave. Then I see through the window Dirk's Espace pulling into the car park.

'Shit, no,' I run back to the bar. 'Please, Rosa, is there another way out?' I plead with her. 'There's like some people coming I totally don't want to see.'

Rosa looks nervously around her and beckons me to follow her through a storeroom to a door leading out to the back yard. 'You can cut round by that track.' She points to the far end of the yard. 'It'll bring you out farther up the road.'

'Thanks,' I yell as I hurry across the yard without a backward glance.

I get to the gate and struggle to unhook the chain. Give it a shake and then notice it's padlocked. Fuck's sake. I'm A Waster Get Me Out Of Here. I start to climb over, lose my footing and end up sprawled on the muddy path. Jesus fucking fuck.

I haul myself up and rub at my thigh where I landed. Feeling bruised and sore, I wipe my dirty grazed hands on my jeans and kick my way down the road. How come I had to sneak out like I have no right to be here? That's the fucking message, let's face it. Forced to hang out with loony Dutch couple just to glean a bit of knowledge about my heritage. Making an idiot of myself while I drown my sorrows. If Don would just acknowledge me, I wouldn't be avoiding like half the population of this fucking place.

I hit the road and find myself heading away from the campsite. What the hell am I supposed to do with myself now?

Maybe it's the righteous anger pushing me on, but it doesn't seem long before I reach the museum. All shut up dead just as before. Maybe it's all a front for a high-quality skunk farm. Ha! If only.

I stumble across the yard towards the caravan. Feeling a sudden desire for a bit more Dutch courage, though obviously not the Dirk and Else variety. I should have brought them with me – Hi Don, meet some more distant rellies?

My stomach takes a leap at the sight of his bike parked up. Fuck Dutch courage, I'm fuelled enough.

The caravan's not exactly showing much sign of life, curtains drawn on the little windows. Fuck it, I know you're there. I bang on the door.

Nothing. I bang again. Put my ear to the door. Not a peep.

I take a step back. Maybe he's gone out without the bike? But I see his pick-up parked behind the museum. Unless he's gone for a drink?

I'm about to give up and then I notice smoke coming out of the tiny metal chimney. He is in there, too chicken to let me in. What the fuck does he think I'm going to do to him?

Back to the door, walloping it with my fist.

'Don, it's Gethin. Let me in for Christ's sake!'

Nothing. 'Fucking hell, I just want to talk. You can't actually shut me out for no reason.' I bang again. 'What the hell have I done? Did I even ask you to write me a letter?' Bang bang. 'Fucking tossing bastard. Fucking let me in!'

Nothing. I step back, my head spinning. My fist hurts and my leg aches. Do not believe he could do this to me, feel a great sob convulse through my body. I stagger across the yard and out onto the road.

Home Visit – *Pat*

Judith the social worker perches on the edge of the lumpy chaise longue, weight poised on the balls of her feet, as if ready for a quick escape. My parents, stiff in their formal clothes, sit either side of the hearth. In between her tick-box questions Judith peers over half-moon glasses, her snub nose wrinkling as she takes in the threadbare Wilton carpet inadequately covered by the Poundstretcher rug; the marble fire surround with the grate filled with toffee wrappers; the cobwebs hanging from the candelabra light fitting.

OK, I want to say, this place has seen better days. But you're a social worker, for God's sake. And it's not as if she's so immaculate herself, wearing creased draw-string trousers and scuffed Mary-Janes.

'So, how are we for personal care?' She tosses her greying bobbed head from side to side at my parents in their winged chairs. Dad frowns and pulls his arms over his chest while Mum's lips tighten.

Judith taps her clipboard with her pen. 'No worries with bathing? Paying a visit? Come on, David, no need to be shy.'

Dad takes a sharp breath, straining in his tight shirt. 'I manage my own ablutions, thank you.' He pulls at his old Magdalen College tie. Mum said it was pretentious to wear the tie, but he said he didn't want to be taken for a fool or let his Welsh accent give the wrong impression. Now he tugs it away from his red raw neck, his face puffy with the simple effort of breathing this stuffy air.

'And would that be your assessment, Clarissa?' Judith turns to Mum. 'Is it Clarissa, or do we call you Clari?' she adds, as if to a toddler.

Now it's Mum's turn to flinch before pulling herself upright and glaring her disapproval at the upstart.

'I'd rather be addressed as Mrs Williams,' is her haughty reply, and for once I'm with her.

Not that it cuts any ice with Judith. 'Ah, we like to be more informal nowadays.'

Mum purses her mouth, exaggerating the cracks in her orange lipstick. She has made an effort too, in her pale pink pleated skirt with matching short sleeved jacket. She has lost so much weight lately that her clothes swamp her and the amethyst brooch on her jacket, one of her family heirlooms, is missing a couple of stones. Her dry bare legs are covered in liver spots. I am still not used to seeing her look so vulnerable; haven't adjusted to the shift in my role with them. Back in the days, when I saw the family as a tool of patriarchal oppression, I kept contact with my parents to the minimum my engrained guilt would allow. Now I can't imagine abandoning them, however problematic our relationship.

'My husband is very proud,' Mum says eventually. 'He will manage as long as he is able.'

'Proud, that's a fine one, Clari, coming from you.' Dad grips the arms of his chair, his face turning a terrible purple.

'Dad,' I lean forward. 'I know this is hard for you, but your health isn't good now, you are both going to need some help.'

'We'll say OK for personal care.' Judith ticks her boxes, studiously ignoring me. 'What about preparing meals?'

Mum fidgets with her rings, loose on her bony fingers. 'My husband is quite particular about his food, he's a meat and two veg man, you could say.' She tosses this statement with a little laugh.

'None of your foreign muck,' Dad says, in his liltiest Welsh accent.

'But Dad's on a low-fat diet now. You said you need help with this, Mum.'

Mum pushes her rings, wobbling the slack skin of her arms.

'Your mother's not stupid, Pat.' Dad scowls at me. 'Oxford educated, same as me, you know?' He turns to Judith, adjusting his Magdalen tie.

'No-one's saying either of you is stupid,' I snap. For God's sake, I want to shout, where's the working-class socialist historian, pulling all this Oxbridge crap?

Judith fixes us with a look of infinite patience. 'Perhaps some help with the shopping?'

I sink back into the chaise longue. Can't this idiot woman see the dynamic here? My father with severe heart failure, barely able to move around the house, refusing to admit defeat. Mum, once glamorous faculty wife, anxious and shrivelled to half her size. The way this Judith takes everything they say at face value. Are these the only old people denying their neediness?

The room closes in on us, ivy encroaching on the stuck sash windows. The heavy closeness of the day intensifies in here, the stale air musty, a hint of rotting food. My determination to get them some help is disappearing in a wave of hopelessness and lurking depression. I just want to get out of this house that has been a symbol of my claustrophobic isolation since we moved here from North London when I was twelve.

'Well, I must say you are managing very well, Clari,' Judith pauses to smile at them both individually, 'and David.'

I shrink from the idea of butting in. Have I given up already?

Judith shifts to face me. 'I think we can look at a home carer, perhaps a couple of sessions a week?' she says, as if in confidence.

'I'm sorry,' Mum still not missing a trick. 'I didn't catch that.'

Judith turns back to them. 'We'll have one of our support workers call in twice a week. A bit of help with the shopping, advise you on the cooking, that kind of thing.'

The way she puts it, it's a fait-accompli and I have to admire her skill: neither of my parents say a thing. Perhaps she realises the main thing is to get in, the care can always be increased later.

Judith moves seamlessly to the knotty subject of finance. There will be a visit from the financial assessment team.

'But, surely it's free of charge?' Mum's impeccably posh voice is incredulous.

Judith explains that it's means-tested. 'We don't, of course, take the value of your home into account.'

She looks around, as if only now taking in the relative grandeur of the shabby room. It's too much for them, this Georgian pile. But this won't be the moment to be mentioning downsizing.

'All those years of paying the rates, do you know what we pay on a house like this?' Mum barks.

'It will all be taken into consideration.' Judith packs her clipboard into her canvas briefcase.

'And quite right too,' Dad says. 'It's called redistribution, remember, Clari? If we want everything free, we should pay more tax. Can't have it both ways.' Only my dad could make a socialist argument *for* charging for elderly care and I can't help but love him for it.

'I thought you were all for taxing the bankers, not raiding old people's life savings,' Mum argues.

'Bankers. Inherited wealth. The lot.'

'When you think how I lost all that money,' Mum whimpers.

Judith stands up, evidently not interested in their argument.

'I'll get the OT to come and see about some adaptations. But you might want to consider moving to somewhere smaller.' Judith looks pointedly around the room. 'It would make life easier and realise a lot of capital.'

'For you to get your hands on,' Mum starts.

'I'll be in touch,' Judith makes for the door.

'We are not selling the house, whatever *she* thinks,' Mum says.

'While I have breath, I'll wipe my own arse,' Dad adds, almost simultaneously.

I set the tray down on the coffee table and pour them both some tea.

'I don't think you realise how difficult things are for me and your father,' Mum says as I pass the plate of Sainsbury's Basic shortbreads. I get a whiff of BO from Mum and wonder when that suit last went to the cleaners.

'Why do you think I'm trying to get you some help?' I complain, setting the knitted cosy back on the pot. 'You heard what the social worker said, you're going to have some home-care. Now let's talk about something else before I have to go back.'

'Oh, but you've only just got here. We simply haven't had company for weeks.'

'Clari!' Dad bangs his fist.

Silence. The clink of cup against saucer and the faint noise of traffic from the distant outside. He still has the power to render me and Mum speechless, though she adopts an air of indifference as defence. And I am as usual irritated at being an unwilling participant in their unending power games. I look at the pictures on the mantelpiece: Jonathan's graduation; me with Gethin as a baby; Gethin with his telescope. I draw a deep sigh at the sight of his ten-year-old face grinning pure delight.

Dad seems to follow my gaze. 'So, how's my favourite grandson?' As usual he breaks the tension when he decides, arbitrarily, it's time to do so.

'He's cashed his birthday cheque, I see,' Mum adds straight away.

'Has he?' I say, heart beating. Well, of course he has.

'I hope he's spending it wisely.'

'As long as he's enjoying himself, eh, Pat?' Dad smiles for the first time today. Somehow it makes him look even older and wearier.

'I think he's taken a trip to Scotland.'

'Oh?' says Mum. 'Edinburgh festival?'

'No, the Highlands, I believe.'

'You don't sound very sure,' she accuses.

'He is all right, isn't he?' Dad leans forward.

'He's eighteen. I'm not in charge of his life anymore.' My voice tightens as I feel this sudden sense of him controlling his own destiny, for good or bad, without me.

'I would think that was the last thing you should try and be.' Dad frowns.

That's rich coming from you, I want to say and almost do when Mum jumps in.

'Oh, Pat, you haven't fallen out, have you?'

It's like being six, telling her about a playground squabble. Somehow, they still have this way of holding me to account for anything concerning Gethin.

I swirl the last of my tea round the china cup. I can't possibly tell them about Gethin storming out over Don's letter. The grief they both gave me when I explained how he was conceived still haunts me. Dad's Presbyterian mutterings of unnatural practices. Mum's total hysteria: how can I think of this thing as a grandchild? Provoking Dad to turn on her: no child will ever be turned away from our household or talked of as a thing.

I remember being so overwhelmed by that show of his innate humanity, giving him a hug, tears in my eyes. I trust you will do right by the little one, he said. As for how it got here, we will not speak of this again. And in my gratitude, I accepted this price for their total and uncritical devotion to my son.

'Pat?' Mum pushes for an answer.

'It's been hard, you know, since he dropped out of sixth form,' I start. 'He seems to have lost all motivation really. I can't get him to find a job, or another course.' Saying this I feel that I have somehow let *them* down.

'Is he still staring at the sky through that telescope?' Dad asks.

I look at the happy face on the mantelpiece and bite my lip to hold in the tears.

'No, he hasn't touched it for a couple of years, you know?' I see Gethin lolling about on his unmade bed, plugged into some game on his laptop.

'Perhaps you pushed him too far. He's a young man, wants to enjoy himself.' Dad's comment hits hard.

'That's just not fair,' my voice trembles. 'All I've done is nurture Gethin for who he is, encouraged his interests.'

Dad scowls as if he doubts this is true.

'You know *he* badgered *me* for a telescope until I managed to scrape the money together with your help. It was his idea to be an Astrophysicist.'

'Have you been too hard on him, Pat?' Mum joins in the attack.

'I never particularly pushed him at school. I really don't know what you mean, I was hoping for some sympathy here.' I can feel the tears welling, how can they still get to me like this?

Dad waves his hand as if to calm the atmosphere. 'There's no point trying to control what Gethin does. After all, we should know, we had little enough success with you.'

I feel as if I've been punched in the stomach and I can't get my breath. 'Little enough success?'

'Oh Pat,' Mum's dismissive tone. 'You've hardly had a glittering career, have you?'

Instant portal to feeling I've always been an irritating inconvenience, at best, for Mum. As a child I decided Mum hadn't wanted another baby after Jonathan and resented me because of this. Wait 'til I tell your father, was her regular refrain, and he would whack me out of duty to her, for answering back, for being late home, for stealing food from the fridge. 'And that's your measure of success, is it?' I attempt a fightback. 'Like Jonathan, you mean?' I nod towards the mantelpiece photos – her golden boy with his Oxford first in PPE.

Mum smiles as if reluctant to agree.

'For all the good that did the godless Tory rascal.' Dad pulls at his tie again, his face reddening.

Ah, the old family dynamic. The constant mealtime clashes with Jonathan boasting his debating society victories: arguing controversial right-wing positions, but also pitching for the triumph of reason over superstition and religion. Mum hailing her brilliant son, bringing the argument to a bitter three-way. Then when I got caught skipping Sunday school when I was nine, how I screamed at Dad that he'd taught me to question everything, but I wasn't allowed to question God. Dad turning pale, his eyes filling; silencing me with the pain I'd caused him.

But now this talk of my lack of success. Unbelievable after all this time. I'm not going to let that go, am I?

'You know when you moved us here from London,' I start, 'art was about the only thing I could relate to, but you never thought that was worth encouraging, did you?'

'Oh, it didn't take you long to find some misfits to slouch about with,' Mum true to form now, every statement a barb.

I think about driving here today on the A11 – that long straight road through fields of cabbages and pigs, still throwing me back to how I felt then.

'Did you even stop to think how hard it might have been for a twelve-year-old from London to relate to the regular kids round here? Most of them had never been on a train, would gawp at a black person, you know? So, I hung out with the screwed up social rejects and painted desolate landscapes.

Mrs Toller, the art teacher, was the only person to encourage me.'

I fumble for a tissue, cursing the tears that have broken through my defences. How is it OK for them to gang up on me like this? Why can't I stand up to them, even now, without crying?

'We only worried about the unsettled lifestyle,' Mum says. 'Really, there's no need to get upset.'

'You were concerned that I wasn't hitting the top grades at school. Art was a bourgeois diversion, wasn't it, Dad?' I try a swipe back.

'Working class people fought for the right to education.' Dad bangs his fist again.

That was always his line: no child of mine chooses ignorance and decadence. No child of yours chooses anything, I'd retort in a flurry of door-slamming.

'Do you know, Dad, it wasn't until I went to college that I was even aware of art as a progressive force? What socialist wants a world without art?'

Dad pulls his breath in, and I worry that I've hurt him. For all his intransigence, his beliefs are strongly felt, and I hold a grudging respect for that.

Mum on the other hand, only ever interested in me fitting her image, gets right in there with another dig. 'But then you dropped out of art college, didn't you Pat? All that camping out at Greenham Common.'

'You never got it, did you, anything about Greenham? We were constantly harassed, evicted, our shelters destroyed, our possessions shredded, just standing up for what we believed in. But you saw it as some lesbian drop-out camp.'

'Oh Pat, it really wasn't that simple,' Mum starts.

'Wasn't it? Everything I did was a pointless rebellion to you. When I told you about my relationship with Gaynor, it was all about what people would say: how I was wasting myself, too pretty to be a dyke?' I feel my throat tighten; I can hardly believe I'm getting into this. But there is a righteous rage keeping me going.

Mum pulls back as if preparing her retort.

Dad glares across at me. 'There's no need to be upsetting your mother, now.'

'Oh God.' I sigh. 'You know, that was all you ever said, Dad. You never really gave me credit for taking a stand in my own way.' And I can still feel the desolate disappointment in my firebrand socialist dad, backing up my mother's hysteria. Why was I never able to challenge this?

'I always admired your spirit, Pat,' Dad says quietly, reaching for his cold tea.

'Well, why didn't you show it, then?' I almost whisper. 'Greenham was both one of the best, and the most difficult times of my life.'

It comes to me: Gaynor on the roof of her car, screaming manic abuse at the bailiffs. The women surrounding her, singing *Which side are you on? Are you on the side of suicide? Are you on the side of homicide…?* Me, trying to connect with that incredible power of our chanting to rattle the authorities, but feeling a sick dread inside, wanting Gaynor to climb down and give them the car, scared for her, scared I was losing her. *Are you on the side of genocide? Which side are you on?*

'We put everything on the line, you know, Dad? Not just the physical comforts, we were living our politics, examining our every action. I didn't find it easy, I tried to use my art to

200

contribute. It was life-changing, Dad, you never tried to understand that.'

Dad swills his tea around in his cup, looks at it with distaste.

Mum shifts in her chair, starts to push up on the arms. 'Is the tea still hot in the pot?'

'It's OK, Mum.' I take her cup, my hand shaking it on the saucer. 'I'll do it.'

Mum lowers herself down, wincing slightly. Is her back hurting again?

'Are you OK? Do you want some painkillers?' I hand her the tea.

'Just a twinge when I got up, I don't take drugs unnecessarily.' Her best martyr voice.

I throw out the dregs of Dad's tea in the kitchen. Why on earth am I arguing about the past with these totally illogical old people? The point was Gethin, wasn't it? I come back and pour Dad a fresh cup.

'I'm sorry, I shouldn't have brought up all that stuff. I suppose I'm just wondering, why is it different when Gethin drops out?' I ask, calmer now.

Silence. Mum looks at Dad who sits scowling with his chin on his chest. Then she glances up at the photos on the mantelpiece and back at me, self-satisfaction twitching the sides of a smile.

The air seems to thicken as it hits me – they are saying it is no different for Gethin. That I am no better at allowing him to be his own person. I want to scream and throw my cup against the wall. How dare you compare my parenting to yours?

My chest tightens; I can hardly breathe. Dad lets out a snort as he falls into a doze, and Mum leans back in her chair, still smiling. They will always win whatever I say.

I have to get out of here before I suffocate completely.

Motorcycle madness – *Jez*

All of ten minutes on the road this morning and the purple-black cloud hanging over the mountains tips its contents into the wind aimed directly at me. Fuck's sake. Like riding through a waterfall – the road a steaming inky blur. Drop my speed, only to be taken on the straight by a souped-up Honda Civic. Splashing me to fuckery. OK, with your windscreen fucking wipers! Need to invent them for crash helmets – way to a cool few million? Fuck, another soaking from a frigging Ford Transit. The Shame, to be taken by a van! No fun in this at all.

Covered a load of miles yesterday, up through the borders to Jedburgh, taking it cautious. Pumped up with pain killers, ribs bound tight in stretchy bandage. Keeping concentration after the shock of the day before. Let go a bit once I hit the Highlands. Roaring up the side of Loch Ness, sun glinting off the flash of dark water. Keep riding fast and far and the thoughts won't catch you. But now with the pasting from the elements, side still aching like fuck, I'm thinking, know what, I could take a day off. Maybe even a B&B. Don't want to run out of roads, right? Coming into a bend, drop a gear, lean in careful, but still nearly lose the back wheel. Next place I get to we'll call it quits.

The road twists up lined with dark pines then opens to a clear run high above the coast. I can sense the sea more than see it. No sign of civilisation yet. Then the low bulk of a one storey building. Catch the dull gleam of corrugated iron roof, slow down to read the sign, pull in, raise the visor. HIGHLAND MOTORCYCLE MUSEUM hanging on rusty chains from the roof.

Chances of that? Gotta be a sign. I park up, clip my lid to the bike. Squelch my way to the entrance, wringing the water from my gloves.

The door creaks open, taking me to an empty booth pasted with old motorbike adverts. There's a bell on the open hatch and a hand-written sign:

Adults £8, small, old and poor people £4. Please ring bell and WAIT.

I unzip my jacket to let out the body-steam. Damp seeped through to my T shirt. Pool of water around sodden boots. I ding the bell and wait as instructed. Take a quick scan of the place.

The booth opens onto what looks to be the rest of the museum. Gleaming line of polished bikes along the far wall. Rusty engine parts stacked on shelves. The floor space broken up with displays and the far end cordoned off with police tape for like a workshop stuffed with half-built bikes. Rhythm of drips into tin buckets adding to the drumbeat of rain on the roof. Ring the bell again and just starting to wonder if anyone's about when I hear the drop of a spanner and the geezer emerges from the workshop.

He walks towards me wiping his hands on dirty overalls. His focus somewhere distant as he looks right through me, frowning slightly. Flash of sinister American Road Movie with hammering rain for effect.

He lets himself into the booth and gives me the onceover in my still-only-a-bit-worn leathers. Pauses for a millisecond to clock my tits before looking down at the electronic till.

'That'll be £8.' He peers at me from under thick eyebrows. I hand him a tenner and he purses his lips with concentration as he pulls off the till receipt.

'I'd'a thought you'd have one of them old money tills, right, with the big silver keys?'

'Aye, I got talked into this on the grounds it does everything bar the shopping.' He pulls a wry smile. Looks me in the eye. Nice deep brown eyes, as it happens, but his skin is rough as fuck and he's got to be at least twice my age. Not a chance mate.

'However, it doesn't fix bikes and there's not a deal else for it to do.' He waves towards the empty museum.

I move forward to look around. 'You got any old Harleys?'

Proper big grin now, sets his cheek off twitching. 'Ninety-five percent of Harleys ever made are still on the road.'

I shrug, not getting it.

His lips quiver as he breaks the punch line. 'The other five percent made it home.'

I nod my inward groan.

'So, what have you got out there?' He moves to the little window.

'It's a Harley Spor…' I start.

'Sportster 1200.'

OK, smug git, we know you know it all.

'It's a good-looking bike, right?' I say.

'Aye, all chrome and no knickers. Why do Harley riders chrome all their parts?' Pause for me to shrug. 'Makes them easier to spot on the side of the road.'

'Yeah, very funny.' I move away towards the line of display bikes.

The bikes start with a 1910 Triumph: like a bicycle with a long thin petrol tank strapped below the crossbar, tiny engine at the bottom of the frame. Move along a few more, reading the quirky potted histories. 1926 Royal Enfield with like proper footplates and leg guards: *This model is especially suitable for ladies' use, or for the gentlemen who do not wish to wear motorcycle clothing.* A weird little 100cc Corgi, like a glorified lawnmower: *Wartime machine for paratroopers, not very successful as the wheels were too small.* Pause in front of a frigging beautiful 1956 Velocette, all curvy black and shiny chrome. The geezer makes his way across.

'Now here's something might interest you.' He beckons me to a display featuring an old-fashioned trials bike with big rutted tyres.

'Nice,' I say. 'What is it?'

He points to an enlarged sepia photo of a woman dressed in leather tunic and cloche hat. Smiling demurely by a similar bike. *Miss E Sturt. Scottish Six Days Trial Silver medallist with her 1930 Scott 596 Sprint Special.*

'Wow! A woman racer!' I look across to more photos of 1930s riders ploughing through bog and rocky moorland.

'The Six Days Trial used to come through Lochgillan, and this,' he points, 'is the very same bike.'

'The one she won on?' I'm all wide eyes.

'Aye. And it still runs, though it needs a bit of tinkering.'

The bell rings from the booth and I turn to see a lanky young man in a bright red cagoule. Hair dripping like hasn't bothered with the hood. The museum geezer gives him a brief glance and turns back to me.

'Oldest motorcycle trials event in the world, started in 1909 pausing only for two world wars.' He gabbles on with too much detail about the gruelling slog through the Highlands. I glance at the young man, making his way towards us, pausing a few yards away. The geezer's back stiffens as he makes a point of not noticing.

'I'm after doing a bit of a display about the Trials, mock-up landscape, you see?' He waves his hand to illustrate.

'Yeah, you should do it, right?'

The lad steps forward, waving a tenner. 'Excuse me.'

The geezer crosses his arms in tight, pulls his heavy lined frown.

'Am I OK to come in?' the lad asks nervously.

'We're open to the public,' the geezer snaps. Grabs the money and heads for the booth.

The lad stands in front of me. Wet hair plastered across his forehead. He wipes the back of his hand across his eyes. Moves along to the next display. I shift to stand near him, looking at the fifties Panther and sidecar stuffed with a family of manikins against an old seaside poster. The sidecar holds kids in chunky jumpers with plastic ice-creams. Mum in headscarf and sunglasses on the pillion seat. Dad in battered leather and weird Tommy helmet with earflaps.

'What's with old fashioned families being so frigging smiley?' I ask.

The lad jolts to look at me – quizzing with heavy-lashed eyes. Pulls out his phone and takes a photo of the tableau.

'Pretty much the only smiley I'm going to get,' he mutters.

The museum geezer approaches with the change.

'It's OK thanks, Don. I've got my money now.' The lad moves towards him. 'I can pay what you lent me, and I'll get the tent back to you – I just, well thinking I might stay another night.'

He's so hesitant, pleading almost. Want to shake him, tell him to man up. I concentrate on reading the blurb about the sidecar family.

'It's a free country, rumour has it,' Don says, turning to go back to the workshop.

I read about how in the late 1940s ordinary working blokes could buy an ex WW2 bike, paint it black over the army green, and bolt a sidecar to it. Giving the family freedom to get out of their smoky industrial shithole for a picnic. Trip to the seaside once a year.

The lad opens his mouth but says nothing. Catches my glance for a moment. Dark eyes peering through strands of wet hair. His face has a bluish tinge, his cheeks as though they are sucked in. Then he blinks, turns away.

'Are you OK?' I ask.

'Oh,' he looks around the museum. 'Maybe I'll take some more photos.' Pulls a nervous straight-lined smile. Moves to point his phone at the nearest line of bikes. 'Can't actually stop me.'

I watch him photograph the next display: a sixties Triton café racer by a milk-bar mock-up. Rain still pelting the metal roof, dripping into tin buckets. Clink of Don's tools echoing through the space.

The lad continues round until he's level with the workshop. Don gets up with a spanner in his hand. I sidle over to some nearby bikes.

'Look, I'm sorry about the other night. I was drunk, you know? I just want to talk to you, as in so many questions…' The lad plucks at the police tape and Don stiffens.

'I've got nothing to offer you, Gethin,' Don's voice is strained. 'I'm sorry for your wasted journey.'

Gethin. Yeah, a bit elfin. Suits him, right?

'Wasted? You lay a trail and then you serve me a blank, is it?'

'I should no' have laid it, that's the truth.' Don wipes his spanner on his overalls and takes a step back.

'So, why did you have me in for kippers and whisky? What, are you worried about the locals talking? Your mate Robbie in the pub reckons you've only got yourself to blame. Whatever the hell that means?'

'I thought I warned you not to go about gossiping,' Don hisses.

'I didn't say a thing.' Gethin's voice rises. 'I asked that Laura the way here the other day, and then she was there behind the bar, introduced me to Robbie.'

'You'll take no heed of what she has to say.'

'You're not ashamed of me, are you?'

Don takes a couple more steps backwards, shoulders pulled up tight. Gethin points his phone at Don, leans into the tape and takes a shot. Don lurches forward and grabs Gethin's wrist. Prises the phone away, snapping the tape.

'Hey!' Gethin reaches forward. 'Give me my fucking phone!'

'I'll no' be one of your family snaps.' Don buttons the phone into his top pocket.

'You can't cut me off from my roots. And you can't take my phone.' Gethin looks round. Catches my glance. Throws up his hands.

Don stands with arms crossed. Lips set tight.

Gethin shoots me a can-you-believe-it look. I attempt a sympathetic smile.

'He's taken my fucking phone!' he shouts.

I shrug. I should leave them to it, right? But I'm kind of hooked in and want to know what's going on. Could be father and son?

'I'm guessing Don maybe needs a bit of time,' I suggest, moving slowly towards them.

Don clenches his fists, face reddening. 'Look at all this!' He waves at the jumble of bike parts in the workshop. 'I've no room for anything else.'

'As if I'm like an inconvenient pile of junk?' Gethin looks down at himself and then across to the workshop. 'What do you reckon?' He turns to me. 'Can you see the family resemblance?'

And suddenly I can, it's the eyes, the shape of the sockets, the heavy lashes. 'I can see you might be related,' I say.

Gethin laughs, 'As in me and the scrap metal? But yes, he's like supplied half my genes. Big of him, eh?'

Adopted. Knew it.

'You'll no' shout your way into my life,' Don says, arms tight around his chest again.

Gethin does his big-eyed thing at me. What the heck does he want me to do about it?

'You can't make someone let you in, Gethin,' I try.

'You think it's OK then? To spread your sperm and fuck the consequences?'

I shrug. 'I don't think about it, not having any sperm.'

'Oh ha, ha. What the hell has it got to do with you anyway?'

Fuck's sake, how is it a good move to get clever with him? I take a step back. 'I'm sorry. Just thought maybe I could help.'

'As in you could tell him to give me my phone back?' Gethin shakes his head, quieter now.

Don takes the phone out, turns it over and over. 'You'll

have it back, laddie. But the lady's right, you'll agree to go now.' He fiddles with the screen, frowning.

'Just fucking give it me.' Gethin's voice rises again as Don keeps messing with the phone.

'Here,' I hold my hand out. Flick the camera open and delete the picture of Don. 'Gone.' I hand it to Gethin.

'What the fuck?' Gethin shouts. He points the phone as Don raises his hand to cover his face. Then Gethin turns and marches towards the door, kicking at the Scottish Trials display stand. The display wobbles for a few seconds before toppling against Miss E Sturt's bike as Gethin slams the door behind him.

Don walks slowly to the display and sets it right. Goes around adjusting the bike's position. His body is set rigid. The rain has stopped hammering the roof, but there is still the random drip rhythm. I watch him for a few minutes. Rooted to the same spot.

He finishes with the bike and looks up at me. 'You can bugger off out of here and all. Interfering little bitch.' He chucks a spanner to clatter on the floor as he retreats to the far side of the workshop.

Blood banging in my head. I take a breath to steady it. Then I step forward to go and notice some old helmets lying to the side.

Don clanks away with his back to me and I grab one of the helmets before I've had time to think. Hold it in front of me as I walk out of the door.

The Harley stands shiny wet, bouncing pale blue from the clearing sky. I retrieve my helmet from the clip. Strap the spare helmet to a pannier. Start the bike, heart leaping with its familiar roar.

Top of the World – *Gethin*

I kick my way through a line of puddles. Fuck Bastard Fuck Bastard. That's it, is it? Brick wall? No contact? Tossing Motherfucking Shitting Bastard.

My brand-new walking boots hold out against the wet and even now I'm pleased about this. After spending pretty much all yesterday down and mooching, following my drunken outburst, I woke this morning and remembered my cheque will have cleared. Thinking I can get him his money, see the museum, grovel apologies, I walked into town in the pissing rain, grabbed some cash and passed by a sale of outdoor gear in the community hall. Proper Berghaus Gor-Tex jacket and Hi Tec walking boots with change for £60. New kit and money in my pocket. Laugh out loud how I thought this would make a difference.

Skye's mountains emerge pale grey from the clearing cloud. The sea's still choppy with flecks of white surf breaking up the surface. White horses, Mum used to call them. I feel a lurch in my stomach remembering walks along the cliffs in Wales, that time we spotted a colony of seals. Tears in my eyes for when things were so simple.

ET Home Phone. A flash of my favourite film as a kid: as in that image of the alien's finger beckoning me to safety and comfort. Fuck it, I will ring her. There's zero signal on my phone, of course. I'll find a phone box. All I want now is to crawl home and spend a long time under the duvet.

The road bends inland and I wipe the tears away with my

sleeve – Gor-Tex not exactly the best for this. Then I hear it, the roar of a motorcycle engine behind me. My heart pounds. It's him, coming after me, like the first time. The grumpy old sod's already regretting it, we'll go back and have more kippers.

I'm barely breathing as I stare at the bend and the noise comes closer. Hold on, I don't want him to think I'm waiting. I carry on walking, willing myself not to look back until the bike passes and pulls in just in front of me. I hurry to catch up and it's only as I get near and the rider lifts their visor that I realise it's not him at all.

I'm stopped in my tracks, literally winded with disappointment.

'Gethin?'

How the hell does she know my name? Then I clock the pink Docs – it's that biker girl who was in the museum.

She takes off her helmet. 'It is Gethin, right?' She jumps off the bike and offers me a cigarette from a battered packet.

'Y… yes,' I hesitate, waving no to the cigarette.

She lights up and I instantly regret turning one down.

'Just wondered if you need a lift anywhere. I've got a spare lid.' She points to a battered looking helmet strapped to her panniers.

I run my hand through my hair and scratch my head. I just want to be left alone. She takes another drag and sees me following the path of the cigarette.

She holds out the pack again. 'You know you want to.'

So, I take a cigarette and lean forward as she cups her hand round her lighter. I can smell her damp leathers backed by a hint of musky perfume. I take the first drag and watch as she leans back against the bike. She can't be much than five-feet-tall, but she's chunky: all leather clad thighs, and big tits judging by the bulk of her jacket.

'Sorry, never said, I'm Jez.'

I nod, awkward as I take another drag. I'm guessing she's in her early twenties. The leather almost guarantees sex-appeal, but she's not really my type. Good. We'll leave well alone then.

'Are you OK? You were obviously upset back there,' she starts.

'And it's your business how?'

'Yeah, kinda hard to ignore?' She looks like she's challenging me to disagree.

'You deleted my fucking photo. What gave you the right?'

She shrugs. 'I guess I was just taking the heat out.'

'You reckon? Some kind of peacekeeping force, are you?'

She grinds her fag out with her pink boot, then looks up. All baby-faced despite the nose-ringed tough girl stance. As in big blue eyes and big round cheeks, button nose and pouty lips.

'OK, it was spur of the moment, right?' Is there a chink of shame behind the pout? 'You were on to a loser with him there, I was like caught in the middle.'

'You had literally no idea what was going on.'

'So, I came after you to see if you were alright, offer you a lift?' She pats the seat of her bike. I don't know a lot, but it looks well handsome, all shiny chrome and black paintwork.

'Nice bike,' I say.

'Goes a frigging dream on these roads. Go on, let me take you to where you're staying at least.'

She switches on the ignition, gives it some revs as the engine roars. I'm tempted. It's only a couple of miles, it would be fun. She un-straps the spare helmet, cocks her head like a question.

'I've like never been on a motorbike before, I don't know what to do,' I say, lame as fuck.

She shoves the helmet at me. 'Sit like a sack of potatoes. Hang onto me. Relax. You don't have to do anything.'

She gives the bike some more revs. The air fills with shimmering exhaust. I stand frozen between excitement and fear.

'I'll take it slow, I promise,' she shouts over the noise.

Fuck it, why not? I pull the helmet on, fiddle with the fastening. She comes to help me, her face squashed up in her helmet. She fixes the buckle and pulls the strap tight.

'OK, where to?'

She pulls out and I grip the sides of her jacket, look over her shoulder at the shiny black road. We wobble a bit to start with, but she takes it slowly enough and the bike steadies as we climb to the bend. I feel my bum slip as she leans for the corner, tighten my hold on her jacket to pull myself back to centre when the road straightens. She puts the brakes on to descend into Lochgillan and I slide into her, my body pressing against hers as she slows to a halt at the lights. I try to wriggle myself back into position while she plants her feet on the ground.

'Stay still until we move!' she shouts. 'Use your feet to brace yourself. Relax!'

I freeze, embarrassed at being like rammed up against her, with the lights seeming to be on red forever. At last we move, and I can push down on the footrests and pull my arse back on the seat.

Through the town and I concentrate on the sack of potatoes thing, manage not to slide so badly at the next corner. Then we're speeding up on the road out and I feel the rush of cold air round my neck. The sea glints at the corner of my vision, the rising land on the other side flashing green, yellow, purple. The bike throbs between my legs, my bare hands literally frozen to the sides of her jacket. I'm suspended in the moment. Go with it!

We're there in no time and I hang on like fuck as she bumps over the rutted road to the reception. She pulls up and gestures for me to get off.

I slide my left foot down to the ground and try to pull my right leg over the panniers, grabbing her shoulder to steady myself and landing in a heap on a patch of scrubby grass. I pull myself to stand, steaming up inside the helmet. I can't get it off, as in my hands are frozen solid. She parks the bike and comes to my rescue, unbuckling the helmet.

'Still in one piece?' Her squashed face filling the space.

'Just need to work on my getting off technique?' I grin.

'All in good time, right?' A bit flirty, is it? 'Whereabouts are you camped?'

I walk down the track through the dunes with her riding behind. The bike skitters on the loose chippings and she curses as she steadies it with her feet on the ground. I point to my tent on the bank and she rides up the grass to it.

'Nice spot.' She unzips her jacket, looks out across the dunes to the sea. The storm clouds have settled over the dark mountains to the south and the view of Skye is sharpened by the high sun. The wind rustles through the pale dune grasses. She takes a deep breath and shakes her head, flipping her dark ponytail.

'Yeah,' I say. 'I'm guessing there are worse places.'

I watch the play of cloud shadows on the sea, the black shape of a bird bobbing on the waves. The awesome vastness punches the guts out of me with the loneliness of being here.

Jez crouches by the tent to light a fag, cursing the wind. I get down beside her to provide more windbreak and she leans into my body. I glimpse her full cleavage, her leather clad hips, catch her scent again and feel that twinge of arousal. Shit, no, concentrate. She lights the fag, then hands me one, lit from hers. I get up and focus on the sea.

She stands and smokes beside me, saying nothing. The wind takes literally half my fag as I inhale deeply, hooked straight back into the ache of being excluded by Don, like it's built into the landscape. I can't stay here. I finish the fag in a couple of minutes, building resolve as I turn to the tent.

I feel the bulk of her behind me as I pull at the pegs.

'You off already?'

'I need to get a move on so I can get a bus out.' There's a little bird hopping about on the grass, moving closer like it's expecting some pickings.

She bends to look quizzically at me.

'At the museum? That was my father.'

'He didn't seem keen on having you around, that's for sure.' Her body's like foreshortened as I look up at her, her face looming large.

'I met him a couple of days ago, as in for the first time. He invited me in, started telling about his life, all that. Then suddenly he doesn't want to know.'

She nods.

'I only want to talk to him, I'm just curious, is all.'

She nods again, says nothing.

'He might have known I'd turn up sometime. Do I look like such a liability?' I pull more pegs as the tent starts to subside. The bird is joined by another, pecking at the daisies.

'Well, he needs time, I guess,' she says.

'Fuck that, he's had eighteen years. He doesn't want the locals gossiping. Pathetic.'

'And you need another parent right now, do you?'

I pick up the tent and shake out the sleeping bag and assorted empties onto the grass. The birds fly up with a frantic flapping, then land to pick amongst the stuff.

'No,' I shout. 'I don't *need* a fucking parent, but I'd like the chance to explore, well the idea of him being, you know, where half of me comes from?'

I tug at the poles to release them from the flysheet, kneeling on the side to prevent the wind whipping it up.

'At least you know he's alive,' she says, pointedly. 'Why mither about it now?'

I glare at her as I fold the poles and slap them into their bag.

'Well thanks for the friendly advice,' I snarl, righteous anger rising. 'Fucking easy for you to say, isn't it?'

She pulls back, her arms over her chest. I start folding the tent, half lying on it to stop it blowing away. She watches me struggle then crouches to take one side.

'You don't know that it's easy for me, do you?' she says, handing me her half.

She looks down as I start to roll the tent. No, I'm thinking, I know literally nothing about you, and that suits me fine.

'I'm adopted too, right?' she says.

I start stuffing the tent in the bag, supressing a smug grin as I turn to look at her.

'I'm not adopted, OK?' I say, like she's a child. 'As in my mother's a lesbian and that wanker was actually her sperm donor. OK?'

Her face turns thoughtful, like she's processing the info. 'Fair dos, it's not the same. But it's not a lot different.'

I take a deep breath, at least she's not phased by the sperm donor thing, and I realise I am kind of interested. 'So, did you trace your birth parents?'

'They're both dead.' She crosses her arms over her chest again.

'Sorry,' I mutter, picking up the sleeping bag and casting round for its cover. Why am I apologising? Did I bring this up?

She scoops the cover from where it landed behind me.

'I did meet my real dad, just a few weeks before he died. Came up here to escape thinking about it, I guess.' She tenses her shoulders, suddenly all small and vulnerable.

'Smart move bumping into me, then?'

'Good distraction. The way I see it, every closed door opens another…' She nods like she's convincing herself. 'So where are you heading now?'

I stuff the sleeping bag into its sack. 'I'm going home. In fact, can I ask a massive favour?'

'I'm heading north, which isn't homeward, right?'

'No, I was just wondering if you could take the tent back to Don. Oh, and some money I owe him.'

Jez does a thinking pose with her finger on her mouth. 'I'm heading to Durness, right at the top. You could take that open door and come with me?'

My jaw drops. 'You what?'

'Seize the day while you're up here? It's only about 120 miles and I'm told the roads are wicked past Ullapool.'

I shake my head, this girl's a nut. 'Thanks, but I'll pass. I pretty much want to get the fuck back home.'

'And what will you do when you get there?'

'Go to bed?'

'Crawl back to Mummy, right?'

I shake my head as I pull out the £50 for Don from my wallet and hold it out to her with the tent.

'No, you take them, I'm heading north. How often do you get to be in spaces like this?' She spreads her arms wide, then starts up the bike and pulls her helmet on.

I freeze, still holding out the tent and money. I was actually starting to enjoy the ride. I need to get out of Lochgillan, but do I need to go home? What the fuck have I got to go home for?

She lifts the side-stand on the bike and gives it some revs. The exhaust fumes fill my lungs with the sense of adventure.

'Good luck, Gethin!' She waves a leather gloved hand then manoeuvres the bike round.

Something snaps in me as I lurch forward, flapping my bags. She carries on turning like she hasn't noticed. I tap her on the shoulder.

'OK,' I say. 'Let's hit the Top of the World!'

I swear I'm a pro by the time we reach Ullapool. Jez suggests I put my arms right round her rather than clinging to her jacket, keeping my arse back and bracing with my feet and thighs. I get the hang of straightening myself out after, not during, the bends. I start to embrace the blurred rush of scenery, the blast of cold air, the throb of the bike. Adventure, what the hell? Awesome!

We pull up at a hotel on the Ullapool seafront and park

next to a couple of little Honda bikes laden with luggage and a guitar strapped on top. I manage a more graceful descent from the beast and can't stop grinning as I pull my helmet off.

'Epic!' I say, blowing into my ice-block hands.

We pass a family tucking into mounds of fish and chips on our way to the bar.

Jez smacks her lips. 'Fancy some of that?'

'You reckon? As in I could eat a fucking whale.'

Jez attracts the barman's attention. 'Two large fish and chips.'

'Certainly.' The barman sounds Eastern Europe. 'Have you come far?'

'Just Lochgillan today,' I say. 'We're on our way to the top.'

'Ah, Cape Wrath?'

'Durness,' Jez scans the beer pumps.

My phone starts dancing vibrations in my pocket. 'Hey, signal!' I shout.

The only actual message is from Emily, the rest are Facebook notifications. The top one catches my eye: *Fran has changed her status: in a relationship with Jarvis.* 'You are fucking joking me!' I feel the crash of all that is certain. That is just wrong.

'You will see Cape Wrath, very wild place,' the barman continues, pulling a pint.

'Jesus!' I move to Emily's message. *Thanks for telling us you fucked off to Scotland. How's Daddykins? Your Mum's not happy. E.* Fucking hell, where do I start? As in, thanks Ben for snitching on me? Thanks for the caring message, Emily? Mum not happy? She's not exactly the only one. Oh, and Jarvis and Fran? Brilliant.

'Gethin? What are you having?' Jez takes a gulp of dark amber beer.

I frown at her. 'Should you be drinking?'

She tosses her head, flicking her ponytail. 'I'll be fine with one. Chill.'

I'm too distracted by Emily's message to care. 'What is that?'

'Pint of Heavy.'

'Heavy it is, then.'

We take a table next to a young couple dressed in matching biker suits. He's all round face in a fuzz of baby beard, fingers like fat speckled sausages. She's thin as anything with wispy blond hair and sharp blue eyes.

Jez takes herself to the toilet and I take another look at Facebook. A different Fran notification: *Big Up to my parents getting married.* Fuck's sake only a week ago we were in trouble for mentioning such a thing. Probably more chance for Fran and fucking Jarvis. I literally don't want to know any more. I remember my 360-degree photo, my one proud moment from Lochgillan yesterday. I upload it to my status and try to think of a tag line. Something a bit elusive to show them I'm above their petty bollocks.

'Those your baby bikes outside?' Jez asks the young couple as she sits down.

'Och yes, we are babies,' the girl sounds coy. 'We just passed our CBT – this is our first long trip.' That way of talking as if they're joined at the hip – fucking couples can get on your nerves.

'Only took us three days from Aberdeen,' the guy says. 'What are you riding?'

'Oh, a Harley 1200 Sportster?' Jez brags. She takes a gulp of her beer and licks her lips.

'Nice. Are you the rider?'

Jez nods, totally bursting smugness.

'So, what's CBT?' I ask.

'Compulsory Basic Training,' the guy says. 'You have to do it before you can ride any bike. Then you move to the full test for big bikes like the Harley.'

'That's the theory.' Jez grins.

'No,' the girl bends forward, all seriousness. 'It's the practical, the theory is separate.'

Jez nods knowingly into her beer.

The barman comes over with the meals. Massive piece of battered fish and piles of chunky golden chips. I set to with the salt and vinegar and a good dollop of ketchup. The fish is about fifty times tastier than usual, awesome with the crispy chips. I wash it down with a long gulp of beer and take a few more mouthfuls before the question on my mind surfaces.

'So, you've done your CBT and full test then, Jez?'

'I did my CBT years ago.'

'And your full test?'

She raises her eyebrows, all mock innocence.

'You haven't got your full licence, is it?' Wouldn't you just know it?

She loads her fork with food. 'Not as such, but I got some frigging good training,' she says, dead-pan casual.

'But, it's illegal!' The girl's eyes widen.

'Jez?' I pitch in.

Jez piles the food into her mouth and makes a deal of chewing and swallowing before she speaks. 'It's whether I'm safe that counts, right?'

'As in having proper training, passing a fucking test for road-worthiness?'

'I was taught to ride this bike by the best motorcyclist I know. The rest is just paperwork.' She takes another mouthful, calm as fuck.

'Jesus, as if you'd take me on the back. What if we crash?'

'We're not going to crash.'

I look over at the baby bikes couple. 'Tell her, will you?' I sputter, barely able to speak.

The guy just pulls his lips in and shakes his head. The girl yanks her hair back and leans her face into Jez.

'Supposing you injure someone, you're not insured!'

'So, I spend the rest of my life paying the compensation. My funeral.'

'Your funeral?' I shout. 'Mine, more like.' I see a sudden image of Mum getting a call from the Highland police.

I look at my food, the smell reminding me I'm still hungry, but now I'm too wound up to eat, which makes me even angrier.

'Soon as I've finished this, I'm off for the bus.'

Fuck it, I'm not leaving with an empty stomach. I wash down a mouthful with a gulp of beer, though even that seems to stick in my gullet.

Baby Beard signals to his girlfriend for them to go. She gathers her things hastily, follows him to the door.

'Fuck's sake,' Jez mutters. 'Motorcycle Moral Majority or what? No chance of being head-hunted by Angels here.'

'You are so out of order Jez. I expect they want to be well away before you hit the road. And I will be too. Fucking loony.'

Jez eats without saying anything. I manage a bit more, take

out my phone again: the landscape from all directions. I type in the caption: *Lochgillan: Awesome with not a person in sight.* Maybe loneliness improves with practice, it can hardly get much worse.

'Did you feel unsafe on the bike, Gethin?' Jez interrupts my maudlin musing.

I pull back from the sinking pit and try to think how it was. 'Well, a bit, to start with. But that was mainly me. The point is…'

'The point is to feel safe, right? My foster brother taught me to ride this bike. He was confident I'd be OK. And riding up here has, like,' she hesitates, 'well, I've learnt a lot.'

'But you're not insured!' I insist. She is so not going to talk me into getting back on the bloody thing.

'Does insurance make you safe? You see plenty of shit riders who've passed their test. If I get caught, that's my look-out, right?'

'But why not just take the fucking test?'

'I didn't have time. Martin gave me a "crash course".' She makes finger speech marks.

'Oh, ha ha.'

'I've ridden a 500cc before, this isn't much different. He thinks I'm a natural.'

'Oh, and how many blow-jobs did that cost you?'

'Now who's being funny?' She looks into her beer.

Shit. I cannot believe I said that! Just when I had the moral high ground.

'OK, that was uncalled for. Sorry.' I hold my hands up. Fucking idiot.

She shrugs, starts looking around, like avoiding looking at me.

'Why did you have to get away in such a hurry?' I ask. How come it's suddenly me that's wrong?

She drains the last of her drink and looks up at me, her face more weirdly innocent than ever. 'You wouldn't understand,' is all she can come up with.

'Try me.'

She pulls her jacket on. 'Don't want to talk about it, right?'

'OK, as in none of my business. But it takes the piss, not telling me you're not legal on that bike.'

'Well, you know now. So, are we hitting the road or saying goodbye?'

I shake my head. 'Seriously takes the piss, Jez.'

She focuses on her zip, then looks at me. 'What do you want? Big grovel? I can't run off and do my test now, can I?'

'No, just, well…' my argument is literally falling apart even though I'm right.

She tucks her helmet under her arm. 'I know what I'm doing with the bike. There's no traffic and about one policeman for every hundred square miles. We've only got seventy to go.'

I look at the photo I posted on my phone, remember the high of the ride up here. I don't do reckless, but do I really want to face Fran and Jarvis, Emily, never mind Mum?

'Hold on a minute,' I say, my heart thumping as I change the caption for the photo: *Expanding horizons in the Scottish WildLands.*

What the actual fuck have I got to go home for? I take a deep breath as I pull on my cagoule and pick up my helmet.

'OK, I've come this far.'

My hands are a lot happier in the Gor-Tex gloves we bought in Ullapool. Thirty miles in and I'm relaxed enough to actually enjoy it. I count the Independence Referendum signs at the side of the road – it does seem to be two to one for the Yeses and I'm even excited for that. The road skirts round the loch sides, twisting up through forested hills, emerging onto scrubby moorland and massive cloud-studded skies, down again to another loch, another forest, the road narrowing to single track. I could count the cars we've seen on one hand. Jez is taking it slower, perhaps it's the 'not legal' conversation. Now I'm wishing she'd go a bit faster.

The road dips to a little ford between two lochs and she slows the bike, lifting her legs as we splash through, whooping while accelerating up the hillside, the forest closing in on both sides. She slows and I follow her lean into the left-hand bend, catch a whiff of pine, the criss-cross of the trees' dark shadows, hear her scream before I see it, standing in the road about ten metres away, its eyes catching the beam of the headlamp. A deer, smallish, but Big-E-Fucking-Nough!

Jez bangs on the horn and slams on the brakes, my face ramming into her jacket. I smell the leather, tighten my grip as the bike shudders, glint of the deer's eyes zooming closer, the surface of the road rising as Jez slings the bike to the right, but the gap looks too narrow and the moment is frozen. Wish I'd called Mum. Will Don regret? What about Emily? Scream of the horn, smell of burning rubber and we're inches from the deer when suddenly it moves across the road and the bike skirts past it, juddering as Jez pulls back to keep it upright. She slows right down, punches the air.

'Yeeeeeeesssss!'

I signal for her to pull over at the next passing space. She turns off the engine and lifts her visor.

'Unbe-fucking-lievable!' She shouts. 'Are you OK?'

I'm shivering clammy, shaking my head as my visor steams up. Somehow, I manage to get off the bike and I stand frozen, looking through the mist at the bumpy surface of the roadside.

She comes to put her arm around my shoulder. 'Frigging near miss, that.'

I feel sick, start fiddling with the helmet buckle. Must get air. She pulls me to face her and takes the helmet off for me. I lean forward with my hands on my thighs, sweat dripping off my nose and plastering my hair to my forehead. A cooling breeze whips up across the treetops. I inhale the pine-clean air, focussing on not throwing up.

'At least there'll be no insurance claims from a deer!' Jez jokes.

I don't respond, take more breaths.

'Aw, come on Gethin, it was shit scary, right? But you gotta admit I handled it well? Nothing damaged but our jangly nerves.'

I nod, still not daring to look up. She fetches a bottle of Lucozade Sport from the bike and hands it to me. I stand up slowly and take a draft from the bottle. The orange fizz feels cool in my gullet and lifts the empty feeling a bit. I pass her the drink.

'I was never one for white knuckle rides. I shouldn't have agreed to come.'

She takes a slurp then hands it back to me.

'You hung on, I got us through,' she says. 'We're only about thirty miles away. I'll take it really slow, though I was already, which is why we're OK.'

I look up and down the empty road. 'I don't suppose I have much choice. But I'll be getting the bus home from Durness.'

She pulls out her fags and lights us both one.

'Let's smoke this. Then we'll ride at a snail's pace. You're doing well, right?' She sits herself down on the roadside. Pats the space beside her.

I crouch down to join her, watch the light between the trees through my cigarette smoke. And I feel a lift of something like more than the welcome hit of nicotine. Despite the fear, there's this rising excitement for life that I haven't felt for a long time.

'And I was about to suggest you went a bit faster!' I laugh. 'You're turning me into an adrenalin junkie.'

She lights up with the biggest gap-toothed smile and I could snog her face off right now. I'm glad of my cagoule to cover the sudden hard-on but can't help my massive stupid grin.

Rescue Remedy – *Jez*

It's a day to make your heart dance like a Happy House loony. Top of the world is where we're at. Tents perched above the sandy bay. Sea spreading brilliant blue. Nothing to stop it until America. I stretch out for a lung-full of warm salty air. Proud glance at the battle worn Harley – sun flashing the mud-spattered chrome.

The sides of Gethin's tent move as he lumbers around.

'What the heck are you doing?' I shout. 'It's an amazing day. Let's go explore!'

More shuffling as his boots emerge from the flysheet and he hauls himself out. Blinks as he pushes back his floppy dark hair. He stumbles forward and trips on his bootlaces. Plonks himself down to tie them then sits and groans with his head in his hands.

'Too much of the Heavy? Och aye, young folk noowadays, nae got the stamina.' My best fake Scottish.

'Yeah, whatever.' Refuses to be amused.

'Aw, this air's gotta be the best hangover cure, right?'

He makes a pathetic attempt to stand and falls back again.

'Come on.' I offer him my hand and haul him up. Not difficult, he's skin and bone. 'Let's have a run on the beach, clear the cobwebs. Then we'll mosey on round the village – see what's buzzing.'

'I'm not running nowhere,' he moans.

'OK, mardy arse, a stroll, right?'

He shuffles beside me as I head towards the path to the beach.

'Even you can't feel bad for long on a day like this.' I grin at him.

'You reckon?' He manages to twitch his dimple.

I stride ahead then pause at the top of the stone steps cut into the cliff. Watch the sun catching tiny lines of surf. Flash of gulls dive-bombing the sea.

I think of last night's sesh in the pub by the campsite. It took a few pints and a couple of whiskies to absorb the massive drama of the deer. For me, a total thumbs up, bigging me up from that lapse a couple of days ago. And the whole adrenalin rush kept Gethin right high well into the sixth pint. But when he started on maudlin ramblings about Donor Dad Don and his lack of male role model, I pleaded exhaustion and retired to my tent. Leaving him to sink another few, no doubt.

Down on the beach I splash my Docs through the line of the incoming tide, skipping along the length of the bay. Turn back to see Gethin lurking among the dark rocky outcrops. Laugh to see him startled by a dog hurtling towards him.

'Come on, let's explore the village,' I say as I approach him. 'Maybe score you some paracetamol, right?'

We walk along the road and stop at the signpost on the cliff top. Tall white pole with about fifteen signs pointing in different directions. Landwards it's London 886 km; Rome 1926 km; Lands' End 1018 km. Out to sea there's New York 4695 km; Tokyo 10668 km and North Pole 3057 km.

'Fan-fucking-tastic!' I say, pulling out my phone. 'Stand underneath it.'

He moves into position and as I frame the shot, he points to the sky.

'The only way is up!' he shouts.

I pat him on the shoulder. 'Yay, Go Gethin!'

A smell of frying drifts from a burger van parked in a lay-by. Suddenly I'm hungry as fuck.

'Let's get some chips.' Gethin reads my mind. Links arms to pull me towards the van.

There's a young lad with shorn mud coloured hair, flipping burgers. Thin pock-marked face frowning. He doesn't look up, so I cough and ask for chips.

'Oh, right.' He fetches a plastic tub and slings a couple of shovels-full into the fryer. 'Be a few minutes,' he says, finally looking at us. Sea green eyes you'd swear were designer contacts, but he's not remotely the type. He steps back as he sees Gethin.

'Fucking hell, you stalking me, man?'

Gethin stares at him, light bulb hits. 'It's Aiden, is it? Inverness?'

'Yeah man, you're the soft kid almost got me nicked in Black's. Did you find your Da, then?'

Gethin lowers his head, saying nowt.

'Kinda sore subject,' I explain. 'So, what's the story with Black's?'

Gethin shuffles his feet. 'Let's just say Aiden helped me when I like dossed with him and his mates in Inverness?'

'Didn't take to the homeless life, did ya?' Aiden smirks. 'Well you were best away from it.'

'So how come you're here?'

'I told you I'd a job here, didn't I?' He gives the chip basket a shake. 'Luxury accommodation: I kip on the front seats, so I'm guard dog as well.' He bares his tobacco-stained teeth with a snarl.

'Hey, a step up from sleeping under plastic,' Gethin sounds awkward. 'Does he pay well?'

'Minimum wage, man, but I get me nosh and all, so no

complaints.' Aiden pulls up the chip basket and shovels them into two polystyrene boxes. Shoves them towards us.

'That'll be a fiver. Help yourself to sauces.'

I hand him the cash and shake a load of salt and vinegar on my chips. A little underdone, but I'm saying nowt. Gethin eats slowly, studying a leaflet from the counter.

'Vote YES for a better deal for the Highlands!' he reads. 'Have you taken up the cause now, Aiden?'

Aiden slaps a burger into a bun with some onions.

'The gaffer is pure on it,' he says through a mouthful. 'Latest is he wants to get me spray painting a fucking cliff-side with the Saltire.'

'Sick!' Gethin starts.

'Like I need to get nicked for criminal damage.'

'Yeah, no,' Gethin awkward again.

A phone rings from the back of the van and Aiden rushes to answer it.

'Aye,' he mumbles, 'Fucking hell, whales? How big are they? Right. You reckon? OK, I know where you mean. Aye, nae bother, I'll be fast as fuck.'

He ends the call and turns to us, green eyes wide, cheeks sucked in.

'Sorry guys, I've gotta run.' He darts to switch off the grill and remove the tray from the counter.

'Something about whales, right?' I ask, curious as hell.

'It's Iain, the boss man. He's a volunteer coast guard as well.' He pulls the counter up on its chain and bolts it to the sides. 'The boatman at Cape Wrath just spotted a pod of pilot whales stuck in the Kyle.' He pulls the roller shutter half down. Comes around to the front to secure it with a padlock.

'What's the Kyle?' Gethin asks.

'It's like a wee channel just along the coast. The whales swam in there and now they're stuck.' Aiden bangs the padlock against the shutter. 'Fuck this, bastard thing.'

'Here,' I take the padlock and ease it through the lock.

Aiden nods and takes his keys. Grabs an old puffer jacket from the van. 'Right, I'm away. See you around.'

'Wait,' Gethin touches him on the arm 'So, what does your boss want you to do?'

'I'm to drive his boat round on the trailer so they can start and help the whales now.' Aiden throws his keys from hand to hand.

'Will they need any more people to help?' Gethin asks.

'They're waiting for the marine rescue team,' Aiden says, turning to set off.

'So, maybe we could all muck in until they get there?' Gethin walks backwards to keep up with him.

Aiden stops, scowls at Gethin. 'They didnae ask for no chocolate fireguards.'

'Aw, can't we just come with you and see?' Gethin says, all little boy excited, setting off his dimples and those gorgeous eyes.

'Can't do any harm, right?' I say, picking up on Gethin's enthusiasm.

'With this dunderheid?' Aiden says scornfully. He throws his keys in the air and catches them. Then he shrugs and signals for us to follow him down the road.

The boat's already on the trailer hooked up to the pick-up truck. We squeeze into the passenger seats beside Aiden and he hurtles onto the narrow road out of Durness. Changes gear to take a corner, then ramps it up again. Glances across at Gethin clinging onto the seat front.

'Don't be worrying, me da was a stock car racer, you know?' He grins, leaning forward over the steering wheel.

'As in that's meant to make me feel better?' Gethin forces a nervous smile.

'He taught me on the track when I was about eleven. I've driven all sorts.' Aiden swings into a passing place to the honk of the car coming towards us.

He so doesn't look old enough to drive. Maybe I'm not the only illegal on the roads up here!

We're there in a few minutes and Aiden rattles up alongside the beach. The channel is about half a mile wide. Edged with sandy dunes, curving round to the rising hills so you can't see the open sea.

'Look!' Gethin points as we jump out of the pick-up.

There on the water's edge: two long sleek shapes draped in wet sheets. Couple of guys in Hi-Viz jackets.

We stop for a moment, taking it in.

'Fucking Hell, Those Are Whales!'

We follow Aiden as he rushes towards them. 'Iain! Iain!' he hollers as we get close.

Iain comes to meet us. 'Keep the noise down, guys. The whales are distressed enough.'

'Aye, sorry.' Aiden shuffles his feet. 'I've brought the boat, and, well, these hangers-on...'

Iain looks us up and down. 'You can help us keep these two comfortable while Aiden and I get the boat going. There are about twenty more in the Sound, can you see?' He points to where the water separates around a sand bank about fifty metres from the shore. Then I see the black fins bobbing through the surface.

'Wow!'

'There might be more on their way,' Iain says. 'They may have been chasing prey, or something frightened them into the Kyle. Either way they need to be turned around before low tide, or they'll all perish.'

'Will we get the boat down, then?' Aiden says, his leg jigging impatience.

'Aye, and you two can help Stewart here with these whales. There's the navy bomb disposal men and a marine rescue team on their way. But we haven't much time so we'll do what we can the now.'

Stewart's a hefty geezer, busting out of his padded Hi-Viz. Grey eyes too small for his big round face. He shows us how they're keeping a channel around the whales and filling it with water. Sits me near the whale's head and tells me how to dig round it with my hands. Instructs Gethin to fill a watering can from the sea to pour into the channels and onto the sheets to keep them wet.

Gethin stares at the whales like he's paralysed.

'Go on, then!' Stewart hands Gethin the can. 'Let's get on with it.'

Gethin runs to the sea while I scoop like crazy around the whale's sleek black head. Its mouth is fixed in like a resigned grin and its eye stares blank. Huge dark pupil in a pale grey iris. Massive brain in that frigging enormous head. The size of its suffering – I can hardly bear to look. Concentrate on my shovelling as Gethin comes to fill the channel.

Stewart directs Gethin to pour some water over the whale's head and the whale pulls its eyelids shut for a second. I'm thankful as fuck to see proof that it still lives. But it goes through me again. Unbearable.

'What are their chances?' Gethin asks.

Stewart scoops sand from the side of the other whale. 'Statistically not high. They die of dehydration, or their bodies collapse under their own weight. Sometimes they drown if they can't move and the tide comes in and covers their blow holes.'

'But there is like a chance?' Gethin's voice is shaky.

'I'm just the ferryman,' Stewart sounds unsure. 'We'll do what we can. The team will bring floatation devices. It's no' easy though.'

Gethin heads back to re-fill his can and Stewart and I carry on scooping. I focus in on the rhythmic splat of wet sand as we work. Notice a faint high-pitched whistle and try not to think what the heck that might be.

'What about the others out there?' Gethin comes back with more water.

Stewart explains that some of them are stuck on a sand bank and they're going to try to move them and turn any that come in behind them. 'There's a theory that the pod members follow each other's distress calls,' he adds. 'But nobody really knows. Some blame the military testing from Cape Wrath. They dropped a few 1000 lb bombs in the sea recently.'

'What?' Gethin looks horrified as he pauses his water pouring.

'Training exercise. It's the only place in Europe they're allowed to drop live bombs. They aim at the wee island off the Cape, but inevitably a few go in the sea.'

'But aren't whales really sensitive, to sonar and stuff?' Gethin asks.

Stewart shakes his head. 'Who knows the effect it might have? But the bomb disposal crew are coming to help, so you could say we're lucky they're here.'

'Fucking military,' Gethin mutters. 'It's obscene.'

'Aye, well cursing will no' save the whales,' Stewart says. 'Let's just be getting on with the job.'

We carry on working in silence. The faint slap of the sea hitting the shore. Mournful cry of the gulls. Distant whistling from the Sound.

'That's their distress call,' Stewart informs us, matter of fact.

Jesus, this is more than I can take. Come on, girl – like the whales have any choice but to bear it.

I move to scoop around my whale's head again. The great staring eye gives no clue if this is doing her any good. Decided it's a female, have I? Kidding myself I'm connecting, right? Just shut the fuck up and carry on scooping.

More people arrive from the village, wanting to help. Stewart gets two of them digging channels around his whale. Hands another watering can to the third. At least the activity and low muttering of the people drowns out the distress sounds.

Iain comes across the beach to us. 'We're taking the boat out to help turn the whales, if you want to join Aiden and get kitted out with wetsuits in the van.' He turns to the roar of two large dinghies coming into the Kyle.

'It's the military guys.' Stewart stands to watch.

Each boat holds four men in wetsuits and padded lifejackets. Iain waves to them as he heads back to the concrete jetty.

Gethin shoots a questioning glance at Stewart.

'Go if you want, we've a team here the now.'

I place my hand on the wet sheet above my whale's flipper. She blinks, like she's responding.

'Jez?' Gethin nods towards the boats.

I keep my hand on the whale. Stewart pours water over her head and I watch her shut her eye again.

'Come on, Jez.' Gethin's face shines adventure. No hesitation whatsoever.

'I'll be back,' I whisper to the whale, then follow Gethin and Iain to the jetty.

Getting into wetsuits in the back of Iain's surfing van takes the frigging piss. Like pulling on a rubber skin. Iain crawls around showing us how to ease them over every joint, pull tight round the crotch. I cringe as he pretty much does this for me, insisting the suit is not too small for my chunky thighs, while Aiden smirks, already suited up. I emerge red-faced and twice as bulky. Waddle in the weird rubber socks to the jetty.

It takes about two minutes to cross to the whales in Iain's boat. Gethin and I sit in the middle while Aiden makes a point of ignoring us, looking out from the front seat. Iain at the back with the outboard motor.

The nearest whales are grounded on a submerged sandbank, some on their sides, some on top of each other, others swimming round the bank. The guys from the dinghies are wading waist deep, shouting instructions. The whales' eerie whistling pierces through.

'Jesus,' Gethin whispers as we link rubberised arms.

Iain explains that we need get in and try to shift some of the whales while we're waiting for the marine rescue. The tide's rising and if they don't move, they will drown. Gethin and I lumber into the water and follow Aiden wading slowly towards a beckoning guy.

'Aw, freeze your baws off,' Aiden shouts as the water hits crotch height.

And he's right – the wetsuit isn't as much protection as you'd think. Strange pinpricking as the cold seeps through. Legs like lead taking forever to walk a few metres.

The guy signals us to a whale lying on its side facing away from us. Water lapping halfway up its body. The guy holds a rolled up yellow mat that we need to get underneath the whale. He positions us to hold onto handles along one side of the mat. Then he starts to unravel the mat. Dips down under the water to pull it along. His mate follows him at the other corner, and they emerge a few seconds later.

'Again, pull hard!' the guy shouts to his partner. They dip down to come up a bit farther along the whale's side. 'That's good, again.'

Gethin and I grip the rope handles either side of Aiden. Hands freezing in the wetsuit gloves. The guys haul the mat and the whale moves a few centimetres, flipper waving helplessly.

'Again!' They heave and heave and suddenly the whale slides towards us and starts to turn. A shining black wall of flesh coming for us, and I tighten my hold for all I'm worth. Aiden shouts as the whale advances and splashes into the open water. Then he loses his balance and slides under the surface, still gripping the mat. I can't frigging see him, just the flailing mat and the massive bulk of the half-submerged whale.

I stare at the spot where Aiden fell. Gethin looks round frantically. Moves along the side of the mat.

'Stay where you are!' the guy yells.

'Gethin, careful!' I scream as he ducks down under the mat.

The guy lunges towards us as the ripples settle from where Gethin went under. I lean forward, my eyes straining to see beneath the water's surface.

The whale shifts its shiny wall and I hang onto the mat and steady my feet. Cold shiver in the small of my back. Time stands still as the guy approaches. Face strained and anxious. Distant shouts from the other boat. Pierce of the whales' whistle. Smell of rotting fish and diesel. Bitter taste in my mouth mingles with the salt on my lips. Stomach hollow with fear. Forgetting to breathe.

Suddenly the water parts and rolls off the hulk of Gethin rasping for breath and hauling Aiden onto his shoulder. Aiden splutters, face ghostly green, and the guy grabs him under the arms and drags him onto the boat with Iain. Gethin stands shivering next to me.

'For God's sake.' I grab his arm. 'I thought we'd lost the pair of you, right?'

He looks at me, hair plastered to his face. A bit of seaweed hangs from his ear like some merman's jewellery. Opens his mouth to speak but can only shake his head. I squeeze his arm tight with the relief I feel.

We make our way to the boat, like wading through treacle, still clinging to each other. Iain helps us get on while Aiden sits shaking pale and blue lipped.

'Aiden, what happened? Are you OK?' Gethin asks.

Aiden's eyes are blood-shot but his skin is a slightly pinker green. 'Dunno… got caught up in the mat… panicked,' his voice breathless. 'I can't swim, you know. Jesus, I pure thought I was gone.' He rests his head in his hands. The lumpy line of his skull looks right fragile under his thin fuzz of hair.

'Gethin did well to drag you out,' Iain says.

'I pretty much just grabbed him; we weren't like in deep water.' Gethin can't hide his beaming proud grin.

'Good on you, either way!' I encourage.

Aiden nods, manages a tight smile.

'We'll get you all back to shore. I should no' have brought you. It's too dangerous.' Iain pulls the throttle to start the outboard.

'I'll be right,' Aiden says. 'It won't happen again.'

Iain laughs. 'We're rescuing whales, not teenage heroes, and the marine team have arrived now.' He points to a few people unloading equipment out of a van. A couple of dinghies being made ready to launch. 'We'll get you warm and you can help on the shore again if you want.'

Aiden hangs his head, looking shamed.

'Dinnae fash,' Iain says. 'At least you were up for it and good for you.'

'Absolutely.' Gethin doesn't sound superior at all.

I nudge him with my bulky elbow, and he leans into me, his wet hair tickling my cheek.

'We'll be guiding the floating ones out in an hour when the tide's right,' Iain says as we get out of the boat. 'Go and get changed, see if someone's got a hot drink for you. You can come along in the boat then if you want, as long as you promise to stay in it.'

Aiden stamps his feet on the jetty, squelching water as he goes.

'That'd be grand Iain' he says. He looks over at me and Gethin, shakes his head. 'Will there be room for my pals as well?'

'Of course, laddie.' Iain laughs. 'With you owing your life to them.'

Back in the van Gethin and I start trying to peel Aiden's wetsuit off, still lumbering about in our own.

'Here, I've got your sleeve, just yank your arm out, there, no. Try again. Yes! Fuck!' Gethin tumbles backwards with the counterforce of Aiden's arm release, landing in my lap.

'Jesus!' I shift to the squeak of rubber on rubber. 'Give me leather any day.' I laugh at the idiot look Gethin pulls on his upside-down face while Aiden wrestles with his suit trousers.

I push Gethin off and tug at the ankle of Aiden's suit. Gethin peels from the waist while Aiden takes the weight on his hands.

'Aw, the smell's enough to send you, isn't it?' Gethin sniffs at the dank scent of rotting seaweed with a hint of stale pee.

'Aye, it's pure perfume, man,' Aiden says as we wrestle him down to his wet underpants. He looks skinned and exposed with his limbs glowing pale in the dim light.

'Here,' I grab a blanket from a pile in the corner, drape it over Aiden's shoulders as he tugs it round him. His face peeps out. Ghostly white and thin.

'Aw, I was just getting excited there.' Gethin keeps on arsing about, pulling now at his own suit. Rolls over splayed out on the van floor.

'You all right, Aiden?' I ask, ignoring Gethin.

Aiden nods. 'Aye, that was a bit of a shock, in the water.'

Gethin sits up. 'Sorry, I'm being an idiot.'

'Nah.' Aiden tries a smile. 'Just thinking it was worth risking getting nicked in Black's to have you save me life and all?'

'Don't be daft, the other guy was there as well,' Gethin says

'It was you pulled me out. We'll call it quits, shall we?'

'Sure.' Gethin grins. 'Which reminds me, something you

said in Inverness, when I asked why you bothered helping me?'

'I said I was superstitious.'

'I reminded you of someone?' Gethin wraps a blanket round his shoulders.

Aiden rocks like an old man in his wrappings. 'Aye, you put me in mind of my brother who died. The way of your face, uncanny…'

Gethin's eyes widen. 'Shit, sorry, I'd no idea.'

'It seemed like bad luck not to help you. Softheaded bollocks, but then…'

'When did he, like, die?' Gethin shifts to lean against the side of the van beside Aiden.

'Five years ago. Stepped under a lorry. Eighteen years old, same as you, int it? No-one knows if it was an accident or…' Aiden pulls his blanket tighter.

'Shit. That's terrible, did you hear that Jez?'

I nod, pull my knees to my chin. Hug the cold rubber around my clammy body. The talk of death freezes my brain around the image of the whale on the beach. I need to move.

'Would you boys give me a bit of privacy getting this skin off?' I ask eventually.

They jump to, gather their clothes, and pull on their jeans. Leave me to struggle alone.

It's a trip on the boat herding the twenty or so whales out of the Kyle. The rescue team up to their chests in water pushing them to turn in the right direction while the boats contain them. I sit at the front, my hair wet with the salt spray. The sun glints on the black fins bobbing forward. Whales still whistling their distress. We edge to the bend in the Kyle and the open sea, beckoning its creatures to safety.

Gethin's in his element, gesticulating at the whales heading out. Even Aiden's lost his hard-boy edge with his straight-lined smile. Leaving me, arms held tight round my churning guts, wanting to howl out loud as I battle the flashing images of death. Alice's haunted face. Ken zipped in his black bag. Aiden's brother splattered under the lorry. And the whale I left stranded on the beach. Those great eyes watching without hope.

Light and Shade – *Pat*

Dappled shadow across the brickwork. The bricks a sooty kiln-red, shining pale violet from the chalky deposit near the bottom, echoing the pot of pansies with their deep orange centres. My hand moving pastel across paper, smudge of indigo where the pointing has gone.

The late afternoon sun warms the back of my neck as I sit on my tiny terrace at the top of the metal backstairs to the flat. There's a scent of damp earth from the watered pots, a hint of jasmine, someone's fried dinner. It's been a while since I've sketched like this. I can't stop the thoughts from surfacing, but I can at least give them less attention.

Reducing the world to shapes and colour. A hazy memory of the old apartment block where we lived until I was four: the blocks of colour cast onto the marbled floor from the stained-glass panel above the main front door. Skipping between them, like a fairy playing hopscotch, as Dad would say.

I drift into images of my early days. Lying on the sofa with Mum after lunch, the itchiness of the green baize upholstery, smell of milk and stale crumbs. *Listen with Mother* on the wireless, the theme tune called *Dolly* that she could play on the piano. Jonathan home from school, pulling upside-down faces through the triangle of his legs. Dad reading me stories of exploited Victorian children: *The Little Match Girl, The Water Babies,* along with the nonsense of Edward Lear sounding so funny in his sing-song Welsh accent.

And Mum, after the sofa days? I see her as if from a distance, acting the stylish, witty faculty wife. Then when it was just the family, she would find something to moan about, to blame me for. Retreating into my colouring book patterns to block her threats of punishment.

I bring my attention back to the sketching, the orange against the blue. Turn the page now, closer into the brickwork.

When I was about fourteen, in a rare moment of intimacy, Mum told me of two miscarriages between Jonathan and me – how she'd been desperate for another child, had hoped for a girl. Shattering my assumption that she'd never wanted me and confirming that I was a massive disappointment because I wasn't a clone of her perfect self.

Surely Gethin has better memories of me. What about our sofa days, watching ET when we first got the telly? Taking him stargazing up on the moors, blanket spread, hot chocolate and toffee? Talking, always talking, his whys stretching back to the origins of the universe. Until one day he stopped. Or did I just make it impossible for him?

Curve of paint-can flower-pot intersecting the brickwork. I have sketched through the crunch-points of my life. I was sketching at Greenham when Gaynor was released: the *Which side are you on?* song threaded through the circle of women surrounding tiny bailiffs. Gaynor had Nora with her, a Christian from Violet Gate, who'd been her cellmate. Gaynor was unnaturally calm, talking about God being the spirit within as I carried on sketching. Now I stab at the paper with the still raw wound of knowing that day I'd lost the love of my life.

This was my therapy when I first moved here, fighting

post-Greenham, post-miners' strike, alone in the fucked-up world depression. I would sit here sketching over and over, looking for that intersection of shape and colour of the Russian Suprematists that inspired me as a student. It provided some solace against the hopelessness, but I felt dead to any new inspiration, even after Karen helped lift the depression.

In the end Gethin became my source of hope. The idea of him sparked by my mother complaining she felt excluded from her friends with their married daughters expecting children. 'Who's to say I won't have a child?' I retorted. That set her off on a tirade, of course, but it planted the germ of the idea in me. Before then I'd assumed I would stay childless. So, it really was about rebelling for the sake of it. The thought rises like a shock wave, and I throw my pastel off the terrace in frustration. So much for the mind-stilling therapy.

'Whoa, flying missiles!'

The shout from below makes me jump, the sketchbook sliding off my lap as I leap up to lean over the rail. 'Karen!'

She holds the pastel stick like a trophy. 'You'll need better ammunition than this to keep me away!'

I pull a tight smile. I'm not at all sure I want to deal with Karen right now, but I crave relief from the aching loneliness.

'Come up, I'll put the kettle on,' I call down

'Just the thing!' She brandishes a large cake tin.

We settle on the sofa in the living room, with large slices of her chocolate and raspberry gateau. I pour the tea while she glances round the room.

'Wow, Pat, it looks so different in here. What have you done?'

'Oh, I cleared a load of stuff for Gethin's party; it's all piled up in my room.'

'You can actually see your quirky style without the piles of crap everywhere.'

I look at the rugs on the scuffed polished floorboards: the deep red Persian at an angle to the blue and brown sixties swirls; the pale Moroccan runner between the windows. Then the eclectic mix of pictures: the Hannah Hoch collage poster next to my moody teenage Norfolk landscape, and my Greenham picture *If You Go Down to the Woods*, with the women dressed as animals leading the soldiers in a dance through the barbed wire.

'This room invites quirkiness, you know,' I say. 'The way it curves around the corner above the shops.'

'Yes, that side wall coming out at an angle,' Karen adds.

'I loved this flat as soon as I saw it, I was so lucky to get it.'

'It's always suited you.'

I catch myself feeling grateful she's here. Why was I so pissed off with her? I take a forkful of her delicious cake and look around the room again. I cleared all my ornaments, leaving just Gethin's dragon collection on the corner unit, and the gilded plaster cherub sitting fat on the mantelpiece.

'I should move my clutter back in. Now it's just remnants from the life Gethin doesn't want anymore.'

'Hey, come on now.' Karen leans over, touches my hand.

'He spent all his pocket money buying that cherub for me from the school fair, you know,' I say, my voice choking.

'Pat, you're mourning the loss of your little boy. It's only natural.'

'Where did I go so wrong?'

'He's growing up, that's all.' She pulls me to her, her arms enclosing me, my head resting on the soft cushion of her breasts. My body caves into the comfort, and I let the sobs come as she rubs my back. Gethin, my Gethin, what have I done to you?

Karen hands me a tissue as I emerge dripping. I laugh at myself as I fill it in one blow.

'I was worried about you, Pat. I was going to ring, but I didn't want to give you a chance to turn me away, plus I hoped some of my famous cake might help.' Karen hands me my plate and I take a mouthful of its creamy sweetness.

'Thanks,' I say, licking my fork. 'I'm so sorry I was angry with you, none of this is your fault.'

'Shh, I know you well enough. Not as if it were the first time, is it?'

I purse my lips, not really wanting to think of all our arguments about Gethin before we split up.

'I wanted someone to blame. And I was sitting out there just now blaming my mum for the idea of me having a child,' I say with a half laugh.

'At last, something to thank her for!'

'It was a reaction to her disgust at the concept of lesbian motherhood. What kind of reason is that?'

'No way was that the main thing. You talked about it for weeks, questioning the old feminist line that children simply tie women to domesticity.'

'Yes, some of the Greenham women's dilemmas about whether to leave their children and live at the camp or settle for a less radical lifestyle with them. Heartrending. But after that exchange with Mum the other argument surfaced: that having children was a chance to raise a new generation with the principles of equality and freedom.'

'There you go – a thoroughly considered decision.'

'So, I had Gethin to give my life purpose, with the added bonus of pissing off my mum. And even that didn't work once he came along and entranced her.'

'Ah, there are worse reasons for wanting children.' Karen sounds impatient. 'Look at how you were with Gethin: the constant hugs and laughter, the daily I love yous. Where was that with your mother?'

She's right, but that doesn't change how things are now.

Karen tops up our tea, sits back to drink some more.

'It hasn't been like that for a few years,' I say eventually. 'Really, the only way I can get him to engage is to provoke an argument. Like when we spent half his GCSE year rowing about whether he could have a laptop, which he won by getting backing from my parents. Then we argued when he predictably played games on said laptop half the night. I tried reconciliation, taking him to London, the Planetarium, and a nice meal out. And then we did talk, it felt good at the time, him encouraging me to take on the studio. But somehow, we never addressed what was going on for him and it soon blew up again. Over and over.'

'You're too hard on yourself, teenage boys aren't easy. You could be one of a dozen people I see at parents' evenings. And that's just the ones who give a shit.' She gives a little half smile.

I try to smile back to cover the stab of pain as I remember what troubles me the most. 'You know, I saw my parents the other day and it somehow turned into them laying into me, the failure of my life as they see it.'

'No change there. Is it any wonder you blame yourself for everything?'

'But Karen, it made me realise I've been doing the same

with Gethin. Putting him under pressure to achieve, not valuing him for who he is.'

'Well, he wanted to be an Astrophysicist, didn't he?'

'He liked mapping stars, and he read bits of Stephen Hawking. But I got carried away, buying him books he never read, pushing him to do science A levels when even the teacher said he lacked the commitment.'

Karen raises her eyebrows. 'Like I said, he won't be the first.'

'But I wasn't even listening to his doubts, asking what he wanted for himself, you know?' My voice rises with exasperation. I don't want to hear that this is commonplace. 'Seeing my parents brought home what a sham my so-called radical parenting has been. Living vicariously through my son, and then being disappointed with him.'

I pause to swallow the swelling emotion. My Gethin is a disappointment. I have said it.

'Now it's too late, I've lost him, Karen.' I reach for my tea, give my eyes a surreptitious wipe with the back of my hand.

Karen passes me another tissue. 'Pat, believe me, he won't forget all that you gave him.'

I shake my head, unable to speak.

'It's a difficult time for both of you. His eighteenth marks a big life transition.'

'But I just chose to ignore it. All I could do was stress about my art and shout at him. On his birthday I said I was proud of how I conceived him, as if that makes any difference. Now I just want to go back and tell him I am simply proud of him. Except I'm not exactly, am I? Not so much proud as worried. And disappointed.'

Karen shifts round to face me. 'Pat, you seriously need to

give yourself a break, you're torturing yourself and that's not going to help.'

'I was trying to do some sketching to stop myself thinking, but it didn't really work,' I start.

'That reminds me.' Karen squeezes my hand. 'My friend Gabriella came to your show. By the time I got there you'd run away, like a scared rabbit, is what she said.'

'Oh God.' I pull my hand away. 'That was so rude, please apologise to her. I'd just overheard some awful criticism of my work, I couldn't face…'

'Well, you can apologise yourself, she's sent you a Facebook friend request.'

'Facebook friend? Why on earth…? I met her for less than two minutes.' My voice in a panic rise now.

'She's an artist too. That's why I suggested your exhibition. I thought she might have intelligent things to say, unlike me.' Karen does her can't-help-it shrug.

'How do you know her?'

'She's running a mural project at school. She's a cool lady. Have a look at your Facebook.' She gives me a friendly punch.

I look at my phone and sure enough there's the friend request. I touch her profile photo to fill the screen: sitting on a sunny hillside, big sunglasses, light glinting red on piled up hair, dark lips parted in an inviting grin that makes me catch my breath.

Karen looks over my shoulder. 'Aw, she's gorgeous. Go on, accept!'

I bat her back. 'Stop it! I don't have Facebook friends I don't know. What does she want from me?'

'For God's sake, Pat.' Karen directs her best schoolteacher

look at me. 'She likes your work; she wants to connect. Look at her page, go on!'

I scroll down her page, the usual raft of lefty memes sprinkled with shares of art and exhibitions. Then I see a collaged image of sixties social housing, rising in a shard-like tower poised to topple into the broken surface of reflecting water below. *My latest, a bit of a departure.*

'Well?' Karen asks.

I smile up at her. 'She's a lefty artist alright. And she uses collage. This is quite good, really.' I pass her the phone.

'Praise indeed!' Karen shakes her head as she touches the screen a couple of times.

'This is her artist page, see? You should have one. Promote yourself!'

I scroll down to look at more work. Woman with gleaming kitchen sink for a head, another with clothes cut away to reveal a bar of Lux soap. Both in glossy fifties advert style.

'Hmm, a bit obvious perhaps,' I muse, 'but who am I… it is nicely done.'

'Friend her!' Karen demands.

I look again at Gabriella's profile picture. She likes my work. She actually likes it. I press Accept.

'I've got to go, sweetheart.' Karen scrapes up the last of her cake. 'I'm meeting Julie at seven.'

'Julie?'

'Oh, I so told you about her. The school secretary lady?'

'You're incorrigible.'

'Gotta do something to blow this schoolmarm image.' She goes to the mirror above the mantelpiece, sucks her lips in and blows herself a kiss.

'Thank you for coming. I don't deserve you.'

'Aw, enough. We'll get together again soon, hey?'

I walk with her onto the terrace. She turns to give me a hug and kiss on the cheek. Then she stands back, fiddles with her bag strap, awkward for once. 'I let you down, Pat, I'm sorry.'

'I said I don't blame you for Don's letter.'

'No, I mean with Gethin, over the years.' She looks up at me, worry lines around her violet swirled eyes.

'You let Gethin down.' I start rearranging the pastels on the table.

'Yes,' she says simply. 'I see that now. I allowed it to get to me, not having a child of my own.'

'I can't believe you didn't tell me about that.'

A couple of breaths of silence between us. Then Karen shrugs and steps forward for another hug before turning to go.

She looks back at me from the top of the stairs; her face its beaming self again.

'Message her!' she commands.

I watch her go, then look over to the gardens backing onto the yard, stretching on up the hill. Birds singing their midsummer business – you wouldn't think you were in a city. It's like being abroad on a warm evening, the sounds somehow softened: a passing motorbike, murmur of neighbours with their doors open. I take a deep breath, try to calm the bubbling restlessness.

I turn to the sketch book lying blank page open on the little table. I arrange the pastels back in the box and look up at the gardens. Deep red umbrella of the Japanese Acer offset by the white globe of Mock Orange behind it, framed on the other side by cascades of yellow Laburnum, triangles of conifers leading upwards. I sketch out the shapes, trying not to think.

Something has lifted in me. A slight shift in the weight of depression so heavy it almost hurt to breathe. It feels fragile: I've had a good cry, some tea and sympathy. The comfort of reconnecting with Karen. Nothing has actually changed, has it? Gethin has taken himself away from me, hurtling into adulthood but so ill prepared. The blame still falls on me.

I feel the familiar stomach lurch at this thought. I grab the dark green pastel and fill the shapes of the conifers bearing down. The sun goes behind a cloud, dulling the contrasts. I take the yellow, jab the spikes of Laburnum.

My phone, I've left it inside. I wander back in. I could send Gethin a message, just to say I'm sorry, hope he's OK. I find the phone, my heart jumping as I see I have a Facebook message.

Pat, so glad to be fb friends. Wanted to say how excited I was by your installation. I'm into political collage too – rare to see something as finely executed as yours. Would love to meet, share ideas, ART, etc. Best, Gabriella.

Wow. She really does like my work. Oh my God.

I wander about the flat in a rise of jittery excitement. Into my bedroom where the Gethin collage has tortured me with the terrible blank space at the end. I lie back on the unmade bed, feel the lumpy edge of the pillow, the smell of unwashed sheets. How much time have I spent here weeping for the loss of Gethin, the crashing disappointment of the exhibition, for the mess of my future?

I'm in no fit state to meet up with some artist who's obviously established and confident.

Karen's voice in my head: Message her.

I sit up and open my phone to another Facebook message. My God, this woman doesn't hang about.

Hey, hope you don't think I'm being pushy, but just occurred to let you know about an exhibition at the gallery attached to my studios. I'm not in it but will be there tomorrow eve for opening – promises to be good. Let me know and I'll look out for you (eagerly!) G

Blood-dee hell. Tomorrow evening?

I get up and look in the mirror. My face looks drawn, my eyes still puffy from crying. How did I get to be so old? Not that she's that young, come on. With a bit of make-up, the right clothes… Who am I kidding? I've got nothing to wear, I feel about as sexy as a dishcloth. Who said anything about sex? Oh, for God's sake. I move away, sick of the endless inane internal dialogue.

Back on the terrace I look at the sketch and take the purple pastel for the line of Acer intersecting the Mock Orange. My heart's thumping insanely and my focus drifts to the phone. I look again at her message and notice there's a link to the exhibition. I skim read the blurb: four artists responding to a post-industrial northern city. Oh, why on earth not? I type my response: *Exhibition sounds tempting. Thanks.* Send before I have a chance to change my mind.

The reply comes straight back. Jesus, is she really that keen? *Great, I'll be there from about 7. See you soon G.*

I take a few deep breaths, pick up the pastel and finish the Acer just as the sun breaks through with a shaft of light through the conifers. I take the yellow and draw in a bright triangle piercing the dull green tree shapes. Lay down the pastel and nod my satisfaction.

Then I pick up the phone and send Gethin a simple message.

A Midsummer Night – *Gethin*

Durness beach shines psychedelic as the tide goes out, reflecting lemon sun in violet sky, the jagged rocks casting long purple shadows over the sand. I take a photo to prove I'm not tripping.

'Wow!' I turn to Jez, big grin spreading. 'Awesome doesn't even describe…'

She stands on the cliff beside me, arms hugged round her chest. She nods her reaction, doesn't speak.

'I tell you what, I'm not ready to leave this day. How about we light a fire on the beach? We could cook some sausages, get a bottle of whisky?'

There's a flicker of unease before Jez forces a smile. 'Whisky could be good, right?'

We reach the shop along the road with five minutes before closing. I dash round collecting sausages, French bread, chocolate, firelighters. Jez stands staring at the newspaper headlines.

'Epic, they've got Caol Ila.' I call from the whisky section. 'Twelve-year-old. Sweet!'

Jez moves to join me. 'Frigging should be at that price.' She points to the £35 tag.

Can I really spend that on a bottle of booze? 'Fuck it.' I sling it in the basket. 'Not every day you rescue a whale?'

Aiden's at the till buying some cans and tobacco. 'Hey pal, you're looking well supplied,' he says.

'We're having a fire on the beach. Fancy joining us?' I pat

him on the back, feel the sharp line of his shoulder bone. He's all wrapped up in an oversized hoody.

He darts a look at Jez who's back at the newspaper stand.

'Come on, the more the merrier!' I sound like someone's uncle, or older brother maybe?

Aiden and I collect bits of driftwood and pile it up like white bones on the gold sand while Jez sits smoking on a rock. The air feels soft and balmy – our every movement like mega significant in the unreal light.

I start to lay the fire near Jez. Aiden settles on another flat rock and pulls out the makings for a spliff.

'Ah, good man!' I give him the thumbs up.

'Aye, I'll see if I can trust you to the fire.'

My Woodcraft Folk training finally comes through as I find enough small stuff to break up over the firelighter. The sound of the wood snapping is as exaggerated as the light. The orange flames lick the white scoured wood, smoke mingling with the salty air. I spread out the sleeping bag to sit between Jez and Aiden.

'Hey.' I gesture at the fire. 'Not bad effort, is it?'

'Aye.' Aiden passes his big fat doobie. 'You'll be after the fire-maker badge as well as the lifesaving, now?'

I feel myself colour, though his sarcasm is spot-on. I take a long drag, try to think of a response.

'Fuck me,' is all I can manage as the smoke massively hits the spot. 'Your jays need a public health warning, man.'

Aiden exaggerates inane nodding at me, making me snort giggles as I exhale my next drag, collapsing coughing on the sleeping bag. I get up on all fours, carrying the spliff in my mouth to give to Jez.

'Hey, be warned,' I say.

Jez nods, deadpan. I pull back, feeling the idiot now, put a couple of larger pieces on the fire as Jez gives a little shiver.

'Come and sit closer,' I offer, patting the sleeping bag beside me.

She shrugs. 'I will in a bit.'

'As in, closer to the fire, not, you know…'

She gets up to deliver the spliff to Aiden, gives me a sweet sad smile as she returns to her rock.

There's something I'm not getting here. I turn to Aiden, strangely seeming the easier of the two right now.

'A fire-side seat for you, sir?' I grin up at him.

'Aye,' he says at last. 'I'll warm myself a wee while before I'm away.' He sits beside me, picks up a stick and traces circles in the sand, reminding me of when I met him in Inverness. Sooo wary and hostile then.

'Hey, you don't need to go yet, do you? As in we haven't started on the whisky, and there are sausage sandwiches to come.'

'I'm fair shattered from the day.' He passes me the spliff, keeps on spiralling the sand with his stick.

I take a toke and reach for the Caol Ila, admire its amber glow against the light.

'You have to sample this, man?' I pull the cork and take a slug, spread its awesome peaty sweetness around my mouth. I pass Aiden the bottle and get up to hand Jez the spliff.

She stares into the fire while she smokes. Her face in profile glows with baby innocence, sending a quiver through me.

'Are you OK?' I try.

She turns with that sad smile. 'Just going for a walk along the beach. Won't be long.'

260

Aiden makes to get up. 'I'll be away now, anyway.'

'No, don't hurry. I just need a little stroll, right?' Jez touches my arm as she turns towards the sea.

I give up. Perhaps I'll find out what's eating her later.

Aiden hands me the bottle. 'That's a rare dram, thanks.' He leans back on his elbows.

'That's OK, bro.'

He darts his head to give me his green-eyed stare. 'Whad'ya call me?'

'Sorry, I didn't mean,' I stumble. 'But it's the weirdest, since you said I remind you of your brother...'

He takes a breath, stiffens.

'Do you miss him?' I ask. Idiot question.

'Maybe I've paid my dues, spending time with you.' He takes up his stick drawing again.

'Dues?'

He gives me another full-on stare. Goes back to the stick.

'You have the look of him, but you're nothing alike. My folks were forever fighting and drinking and drinking and destroying. He was the one looked out for me when I was wee.'

'I'm sorry, I don't know what to say...'

I chuck another log on the fire. It sends up orange sparks, flames pinkie-blue over the bleached wood.

'Say nothing. Last time I saw him we argued bad.'

'How old were you?'

'Twelve. He was eighteen.'

I look at him, so small and thin, like he stopped growing with his brother's death.

'There is no way it was your fault; you must know that?' I say, feeling clumsy.

He pokes the fire, says nothing. Then he drops the stick, pulls out his stash and lays it on the sleeping bag.

'I'm away to get some kip. You have the rest of this, and we'll definitely call it quits.' He forces a grin, pats me on the shoulder as he gets up.

I look out to the shoreline to see Jez heading back towards us, pink Docs glowing. Aiden waves and she gives a double thumbs up, silhouetted against the sky.

'Have a good night, the pair of you.' Aiden gives me a sly wink.

I focus on rolling another jay while Jez returns, held in the interval between these two weird companions. I'm still on a high, not just from the weed. As in the day like nothing I have experienced before, and now strangely moved by Aiden seeing his dead brother in me. Jez makes her slow way back, looking down like she's deep in thought while crossing the ridges of wet sand. Something troubling her for sure.

I finish rolling just as she arrives and present it to her with a flourish, along with the whisky. She accepts both with a smile and returns to her rock. I lean back and look at the sky staining blood orange as the sun starts to set. Still not a cloud.

'Perfect end to a spectacular day, wouldn't you say?'

Jez takes a slug of whisky and hands me the bottle. I drink some more, keep on talking.

'I felt such a sense of, I dunno, purpose, today. Like totally with something that's not about me?'

'Yep, that might be a novelty.' Jez laughs.

Wow, reaction. Keep on with that, then. 'I've been drifting for a while now. As in dropping out after bombing in my AS exams, then my girlfriend dumping me for no obvious reason. Sinking into hopelessness, you could say, no sense of direction.'

'Maybe there's like no sense *in* direction?' Jez hands me the spliff.

'Hmm, yes, but, well, know what I mean?' I take a toke, not at all sure of what *she* means. 'Aw, too stoned, spinning into senselessness. I did have a point…'

I stare into the fire. Aiden's stick is now a creature with a long smouldering snout.

'I suppose the trip up here, looking for Don,' it comes to me as I say it, 'was the first thing I've done, like a positive action? Outside the comfort zone, all that?'

'And you end up taking a ride to the top of the world with a crazy woman on an illegal bike. Risk drowning yourself rescuing whales. Hardly what you were expecting?' She looks at me as she talks, her face glowing in the firelight. But her voice lacks its usual spark.

'Ha, but even getting here was a trip. As in, sleeping out with proper homeless people.'

'Proper homeless?'

'Yeah, makes you feel lucky, know what I mean? There was this guy from Sudan, God only knows what his story was. And this Slovakian dude who'd just lost his job and accommodation and his wife and kids were coming to join him. I helped him trap rabbits, only, well, it didn't exactly go too brilliantly…' I tail off, aware I'm rambling way from the thing.

Jez nods, lips pursed. 'Yeah, I've worked with Eastern Europeans, picking cabbages in Lincolnshire. Hotel work as well. They get paid jack-all and send it all home, right? A rabbit can brighten up the cabbage soup.'

'Oh, well you know all about it, then,' I say, a bit deflated. Then I remember. 'Yeah, but the point is, the point is…the whales. It's like, to come up here and to know I am in some way a part of it, and then have Don shut me out like that…hmm.' I muse on this as Jez reaches for the spliff. 'But the thing now is the whales, how awesome would it be to be able to do something like that properly? Like one of those marine scientists?'

'Or a navy bomb disposal expert?' she says, deadpan still.

'Ha, yes, not so good. But know what I mean? As in I could get some science A Levels, train as a marine biologist. I reckon I'd be motivated.'

Jez gives a snort, shakes her head. 'How about those sausages?'

'Yeah, sorry.' I spread the burning wood with a stick for Jez's cooking pan. Drop in a bit of butter followed by the sausages. They spit and sizzle as I move them round.

I leave them to cook and lean back. The beach spreads pale violet to the dull slate of the sea, a few stars pricking through the velvet blue sky, though it's like eerily light on the horizon.

'You can see the Plough already, Polaris, and the evening star, Venus, of course.' I point upwards. 'I wanted to be an Astrophysicist when I was a kid – I had a telescope and everything. That like childhood belief in your own special future, know what I mean?'

Jez pulls herself up, serious eyebrow raising at me.

'I went off the whole idea when it started to involve mega maths,' I add.

'Yeah, and you are so very middle class, aren't you Gethin?' Jez pulls a patronising smile. 'You look at some stars, you're going to be an Astrophysicist. Help rescue some whales, it's marine biologist.'

'Wow, prick my bubble!' I shoot her a resentful glance. 'Isn't it good to know what you're aiming for?'

'Yeah, Follow Your Dream! Like life is just one straight path upwards. If you don't make it, you didn't dream hard enough, right?'

'Fair enough, I totally get that there's like shit-all chance of most people making it. But, still, I've found it hard, literally not having a reason to get out of bed, beyond scoring some draw or getting through the next level of Oblivion.' I feel a sinking dread of the fug of stale smoke and bedclothes that has been my life in the past few months.

'How much less misery and disappointment would there be if people just took from the moment without expectations? At least among those with enough to eat?'

'Hmm, very Buddhist,' I say, not convinced.

'It's not fucking Buddhist. It's fucking life.' Jez grabs my stick and jabs at the fire, sending the frying pan wobbling.

'Watch it!' I steady the pan with my sleeve over my hand.

She pulls back, traces patterns with the stick in the hardened sand.

Fuck it, I'm so not arguing with her in this mood. I give the sausages a turn with a knife, start cutting up the French bread.

'It's how I've lived my life, at any rate,' Jez starts, calmer now. 'I used to play this game with my stuffed toy tiger, Zooey.'

'Is it? I don't have you down as a stuffed toy kind of gal.'

'Best frigging friend I ever had. I'd spin round fast in the park, holding Zooey by the tail, then throw him and head off for whatever adventure that direction took us.'

'Hmm, bit like Dice Man?' I say, vaguely remembering some talk of a dude who lived by the throw of the dice. 'So, did you find adventure?'

'Sometimes.' She shrugs. 'I adopted a stray dog once. Spent all my sweet money on cans of Pal. Another time I found a wallet with a like porny photo in it. Thought about blackmailing the owner, until I got bored with the idea and binned the wallet.'

'What happened to the dog?' I'm finding it hard to keep a straight face.

'Ran away,' she says, matter of fact.

'Rollercoaster adventure, then.' I laugh.

'It got better as I got older. It's about being open to any chance experience.'

'Well, I'm pretty open to the eating experience right now. So, I declare these sausages cooked!'

I chuck the sausages into the bread, hand one to Jez and start to lay into mine. A few minutes of total concentration.

'So, where are you like right now, Jez?' I ask as I surface.

She jerks round. 'On the beach, right? Eating a sausage sandwich.' She clamps her teeth around the bread.

'Well, you haven't exactly seemed all here this evening.'

She gives me her attempt at an ironic smile.

'Hey, I'm not all insensitivity, is it?'

'It kind of got me right worked up, with the whales I guess – that distress whistle…' She pauses for a deep sigh, flicks me a look.

I return her gaze, saying nothing.

'I got into this dumb shit, talking to that whale on the beach, right?' she carries on. 'Told her I'd be back, but after all the kerfuffle with Aiden and everything, it didn't, I didn't… now I can't let it go that I frigging left her there to die.' She shivers before taking up her stick patterns again.

Weirdest, just like Aiden with the stick thing.

'It upset you,' I say, gently.

She glares at me.

'As in it was upsetting,' I babble on. 'Knowing we couldn't rescue them all. They seemed so, well, stoic I suppose?'

'Like they had a choice? Like when they talk about someone's *brave fight with cancer*. It's bollocks, you have no control over what kills you.'

Heaveee. Yes, it is terrible to think of the beached whales. But I'm so wanting to stay on my high.

Jez reaches for the whisky and has a swig then hands me the bottle.

I take a gulp and swallow slowly, working the whisky round my gums, deep glow spreading through my insides. We don't speak while I concentrate on rolling another spliff. Just the sound of the fire cracking, the faint hiss of the waves, warmth of the fire through my jeans.

'You told me you were adopted, Jez.' It pops up as a way of changing the subject. 'How did that happen?'

She turns to frown at me, her face pale in the frame of her dark wisps of hair. Then she drags her stick through the embers. I chuck another log on and wait.

'My adoptive mum fostered me as a baby. Then I came up for adoption, so she took me on.' Her tone is guarded.

'OK, so you were the only child, is it?'

'No, she already had a daughter of her own and then she had another when I was about seven, plus piles of foster kids.' She pokes more at the fire.

'Wow! So, it was like,' I try to picture this, 'a mini children's home?'

Sharp deep breath, impatient. 'She'd like foster one at a time, two at most if they were siblings.'

'Was she a single parent then?'

'You don't want to know much, do you?' She glares at me.

'Fucking hell, Jez, I'm just trying to get to know you?' I hand her the spliff. 'Take this, chill.'

She inhales deeply, holds it a moment before letting the smoke out, staring at the ground.

'We can talk about something else – I was just curious, is all,' I say.

'You're OK, it's not a big deal to tell you really.' She attempts a smile, making me want to hug her. 'Our dad worked away a lot. It's always been right hazy how he makes his money. Bit of this and that. Half of it dodgy. But he'd turn up and we'd get treats: cinema, bowling. Always the latest telly.'

'Hard for your mum, though?'

'I think it suits her. She loves kids and she's a good homemaker. He contributes in fits and starts.'

'Hmm, my mum used to say it was often better being a single parent, but then she only had me, which was piss easy, of course.'

She laughs. Hey, result!

'He's fun to have around, but yeah, she likes having the control. They met when he was escaping being forced into an arranged marriage in Liverpool, right?'

'So, are they like, Asian?' I ask, hoping I'm not making stupid assumptions.

'My dad's half Indian. His father was in the Indian navy, jumped ship and married a Liverpudlian. But then he wanted to arrange my dad a traditional Indian bride.'

She hands me the spliff, stirs the embers. Their glow intensifies, pulsating orange and purple.

'So, did you, like, get close to the foster kids?'

'I kinda learnt not to,' she pauses, thinking. 'There was this kid my age, Helen, we'd have been about nine, sharing a bedroom. We like competed for who was the hardest. One time we snuck out to this Victorian cemetery in the middle of the night. Right overgrown with ivy and shit, broken tombs…'

'Bloody hell, scary as fuck!'

'Yeah.' She grins. 'We were daring each other to rob the graves, right? There was this tiny raised tomb for a two-week-old baby. We pushed at the stone, and it shifted a couple of centimetres. Imagined some monkey-sized skeleton, all curled up like a foetus in a jar. We were just about literally shitting ourselves. Hard-girl duo resigned on the spot. Ran fast as fuck out of there.'

'I would so not have set foot in the place at night?' I shiver at the thought of it.

She sniffs a little laugh. 'Helen used to say we were like sisters. She had the notion that my mum was going to adopt her too. I remember lying in our bunk beds – half dread, half excitement at the idea. I felt a bit hemmed in by her, right?'

'So, I take it she didn't become your sister?'

'No, she ended up back with her family. I felt let down and relieved at the same time. Taught me not to trust that kind of closeness. There was Martin though, when I was in my teens. He's the lad who sorted me with the bike. Nearest to a proper brother, I suppose.'

'What about your birth parents?' I decide to push it.

Instant tension. 'I told you, they're both dead.' She lifts her stick, the end crimson. She bangs it on the sand, sending sparks.

'You met your father before he died, isn't it?'

Silence. I light the spliff again.

'What about your mother?' Hope I sound gentle.

She stiffens, takes a breath, and holds it. I look up at my exhaled smoke joining the thin wisps from the fire. The stars are coming through now in the deepening blue of the sky, though it's still amazingly light on the horizon.

'She died when I was in foster care, right? That's when I was adopted.' She looks hard at me with those big heavy-hooded eyes. Daring me to know how to react?

Which I don't. 'Fucking hell, I'm sorry Jez.'

She shrugs, 'I never knew her, right?' She reaches for the last of the spliff. 'Ken, my father, told me a bit about her when I met him.'

'So, I mean, how did you even meet him? Did you like know he was dying?'

'Not when I first turned up. He thought I was the district nurse.' She sniffs that little laugh again. 'I'd borrowed my mum's navy raincoat, maybe that was it?'

She tells a story of how the nurses showed up before she'd been able to explain to her dad who she was. Big kafuffle and confusion: it was their first visit and all. Turned out he had terminal cancer and a few weeks to live.

'So...long story short, I moved in and looked after him until he died.' She blurts, like a confession.

'Just like that?' I say, literally stunned at the whole idea.

'Not quite. I visited a few times. Then I found him collapsed on the stairs – that's when I decided to stay for the duration.'

'Wow, that is so hard core. Sorry, it's just, not exactly an everyday story.'

She smiles through the firelight at me, her face softens with it.

'Tell me about it! But there was really no-one else. He'd discharged himself from hospital, refused to have anything to do with social services. He was a mardy old bugger, but I kind of took to him. Maybe I get that stubborn independence from him, not from Al, my adoptive dad. Perhaps it's all genetic after all?'

'Genetics don't mean shit.' I tense up as I say this.

'Could've fooled me,' she retorts.

I let this go, as in I'm more interested in her story right now. 'Did he have any other kids, then?'

'Yeah, he called them the Proper Kids…'

'Proper Kids? As if!'

'Whatever, they're grown-up and weren't interested. His wife left him years ago. So, he had no-one, and I had nowt else to do.'

'So, you were literally there when he died?' I form a death-bed picture like from one of Gran's costume dramas: all white lace coverlets and darkened rooms. Probably not?

'Yes,' she says quietly.

I take a drink and hand her the bottle. Stare into the fire and pick out a clutch of blinking goblins with fat square heads.

'He was all drugged up – it was quite peaceful.' She takes a swig. 'The whisky reminds me of him. I was giving him shots on the little sponges he had to moisten his mouth. *Teacher's*, mind. He was too tight to buy owt flash.'

'That must be the weirdest – to know someone for a short time like that, and then watch them die?'

'It's funny, you feel nothing and something at the same time. It's like, I'm not grief stricken, right? I hardly knew him.'

'But you had those few weeks, that must have been intense.' I feel suddenly ridiculously jealous of this experience.

'Like I said, I learnt as a kid how not to get attached.'

'So that's your defence mechanism?' Shades of Mum coming through here but seems about right.

'Yeah, whatever,' she says dismissively.

'That's me in my place.' I reach for the bottle.

She looks thoughtful as she adds, 'Well, I'm not exactly feeling nowt. Just don't know what the heck I am feeling. I'm more fighting the stuff popping up about my mum.'

'Your real mum, is it?'

She pauses. 'I always knew she died when I was little. She was a druggie which was why I was fostered. I'd never thought a lot about it, but listening to Ken made it more real, I guess.'

'So, you literally had your father talking about your dead mother while he was, er, dying?'

She pulls something out of her inside pocket, hands it to me. 'He gave me a picture of her.'

I lean towards the fire to get some light on it. A blurry close-up of a young woman. Tiny face in a halo of piled up blond hair. A little pointy chin. I look at Jez biting her pouty lips. It's hard to see anything of her in this image.

'Wow,' I say softly. 'That must have been something, to see her actual face, like for the first time?'

Jez leans forward, crosses her arms to clutch her thighs and rocks on the balls of her feet.

'Thing is, I thought I had a memory of her, from the access visits before she died. But it's not, it's not the same as the photo.' She gulps the air and buries her head in her hands, her body shakes with a suppressed sob.

'Hey, it is OK to cry, you know?'

'Like maybe I've remembered the frigging social worker all along? And now I keep thinking about how she died.' She rocks as she allows another sob, then she stiffens, pulls herself in tight. I move to give her a hug. Then I'm not sure, reposition myself on the sleeping bag.

She wipes her eyes with the back of her hand and pushes her hair away with a weak hint of a smile. She's like a lost little girl and the sadness of it is overwhelming.

'It's like a hole inside me that she never occupied, and the flash of her face… Proper grief might be easier to deal with, right?' She bites her lip again.

'Come here,' I pat the sleeping bag. 'Let me give you a hug.'

She stares at the fire, takes a sharp breath. Shit, she thinks I'm hitting on her.

'I don't mean,' I start.

'It's OK.' She smiles her little smile and sits down next to me. She leans towards me and I put my arm round her shoulder, feel the soft weight of her body against mine as I tighten my grasp, trying to ignore the horny stirrings.

'So that's why you're belting around Scotland on an impressively cool illegal bike?' I try gently teasing.

'Ken left me some gold, told me to have an adventure. What could I do?' She looks up, eyes widened in mock innocence.

'Gold?'

She shifts to rest her head on my shoulder, and I tense up against my hard-on.

'He left me a kilo bar of gold bullion,' she says slowly, like for maximum effect.

'Sick! Gold bullion? Fucking hell, what does that weigh?'

'Erm, a kilo?' She laughs, poking my chest.

273

I relax my hold on her. 'Duh, I suppose I mean how big is a bar that weight?'

She holds her hand in the shape of a rectangle about fifteen by ten centimetres, immediately bringing dick jokes to mind, which obviously I don't share.

'Wow, that's like a fairy tale. Have you still got it?'

She leans back into me and I grip her shoulder again, still awkward.

'No, Numpty. I sold it to buy the bike, right?' She strokes my chest and I tense up.

'Duh again! As in you wouldn't get far riding a lump of gold?'

'Nah, a lump of polished steel's a better bet.'

I shift away from her, thinking we seem to be over the upset bit. But she pulls her knees up to her chest and shakes her head in a little shiver.

'Aw Jez, I'm just trying, you know, to lighten things?'

She looks up at me, fearful almost, her reddened eyes glistening, her lips parted, showing the gap in her teeth. It goes through me to see this tough girl so vulnerable.

'Just hold me a bit longer, Gethin,' she asks quietly.

I shuffle to put my arm around her, start rubbing her back between the shoulder blades. I still feel dead awkward, my movements mechanical. She wriggles her shoulders, and I shift up to rub her neck, watching the rhythm of her breath moving her breasts. Feel that un-asked for stirring again. She turns to lift her face to mine and plants a kiss on my lips.

I freeze, desperately trying not to respond. She pulls back and I take my arm away. She cocks her head and raises an eyebrow.

'Don't you fancy me?' she asks.

I feel a wave of panic in direct proportion to the twitching arousal. 'Nno, I mean, yes, it's just, know what I mean?'

'What?' She shifts to face me with her back to the fire, resting her weight on her hand in the space between my outstretched legs.

I lean back on my arms, hoping she can't see my hard-on. 'You're upset, I don't exactly want to take advantage?'

She nods slowly, moves herself a bit closer.

'I'm always getting it wrong with girls, like, misreading signals. It seems simpler not to.' I'm burbling now, rapidly losing ground as she moves her hand to brush the inside of my thigh. I don't move a muscle.

'You're never a virgin, right?' The tip of her tongue rests on her bottom lip. Mocking.

'No,' I try to laugh this off. 'I have, you know, had a couple of girlfriends. It's just, well lately, I pretty much always seem to fuck up.' Bollocks, bollocks, here we go.

She strokes my thigh again, coming close to brushing my groin. I take a sharp intake of breath.

'Not asking for performance of the year. Just a bit of mutual comfort would be nice…'

She flicks her hand to touch my boner then moves to lie on her side to face me. I turn towards her, and she takes my face in her hands, strokes my hair away from my eyes and plants her lips softly on mine. I abandon resistance and take the cue for a long slow kiss, running my fingers through her lush thick hair falling out of its ponytail. She unzips my hoody, the soft weight of her breasts through her T shirt against my chest. Then she runs her hand along the line of my trousers, and I groan in anticipation.

Then I remember myself. Freeze as she undoes the button on my jeans. 'I haven't got a condom. We can't go all the way.'

'Aw, so well-brought-up,' she teases, working to squeeze my erect dick. 'Don't worry, we'll manage,' she says as I let out another moan.

I move my hand up under her T shirt and grab one of her tits through the lacy bra. Another long kiss and we're rocking together now. I tug at her belt buckle and she pauses to undo it, pulling off her tight leathers, her pale legs soft in the firelight. She bends to pull my jeans down, kissing my legs as she goes. Comes back to hold my dick. Strokes it against her juicy pussy. Moving her swollen clit against it. I squeeze her tits and we kiss hard until she brings herself to a long slow climax. She moves to lie beside me, still pumping me, just when I can literally hold back no longer and shout the relief when I come.

'Respect!' I gasp when I've got my breath. 'As in I may not be a virgin, but I've never had a girl do that with me before.'

She gives my balls a gentle squeeze and pulls the other sleeping bag over us. We lie with our legs intertwined, her hand still holding my limp dick, my hand cupping her soft breast as I drift into the salty smoky scent of her hair, the kiss of the waves on the shore and the image of the sleek black-backed whales heading out to freedom in the open sea.

Cavern – *Jez*

Wake to the rhythm of rain on tent. Stretch my legs in the warmth of the sleeping bag. Gethin's gentle snores like the backing track for the patter. Remembering being woken at dawn by the rain on the beach. Scooping up our stuff and running barefoot up the cliff-path. Decamping to Gethin's tent – more whisky and spliff and plenty more snogging and stroking before falling asleep. Heads together, Lauryn Hill through one earpiece each.

My head bangs if I move it, but I'm happy just to lie in this cosy haze, his warm bulk beside me. Another stretch. Close my eyes. Another drift.

'Aw, Fuck's sake, it's pissing it down!'

Roused from my doze to the sight of Gethin's bare arse as he pokes his head out of the door.

'Morning, gorgeous.' He slides to lie on his front beside me. Kisses his fingertips. Plants them on my lips. I pretend to bite, and he pulls away with a mock growl.

'Not sure it is morning to be honest.' I reach for my phone. 'Ah: 11:54, right? We have six minutes.'

'Mustn't waste it!' Cheeky look as he reaches to tickle me round the midriff.

'No, you'll regret it!' I shift to get him under his armpit.

'Enough! Truce!' he cries after several minutes of tussling. Holds my wrist in a tight grip. 'Aw, that's made me hungry. Let's go to the pub for a bacon butty.'

'Hair of the dog?'

'I was like thinking of pig myself.' So pleased with himself. Have to smile.

Yesterday's massive open space has shrunk. Cloud touching the ground and muffling even the sound of the sea. We hurry, heads down, hands in pockets. Smell of damp waterproofs adds to the mix of beer and cooking fat as I push open the pub door. Country and Western on the juke box. Babble of people through the warm fug.

Gethin studies the food menu. 'That's got my name on it.' He points to the All-Day Scottish Breakfast Bap.

My stomach rumbles in reply.

'Shall we make that two All-Days?' he says as the barman approaches. 'And are we going straight for the Heavy?'

Think about it for all of one second. 'Yeah, fuck it. Two pints of Heavy.'

'And, for the gentleman?' the barman teases.

We sit by the window alongside the pool table in the big open bar. All seventies bare brick and pine panelling. Fake beams and horse brasses. A middle-aged couple shouting at each other as they finish their game.

'You cannae defend that kind of talk.' The woman slams a ball into the pocket. Straightens to walk around the table. 'It makes no difference whose side she's on.'

'If she's being called a traitorous bitch, it's no more than she deserves.' The guy pushes his ratty thin face at her.

The woman shakes her Barbie blond head. 'So, she's fair game because she's famous and female? I tell you, it does your cause no good.'

She leans to take the next shot. He gives her tight jeaned arse a playful slap.

'Och, sling yer hook, ignorant bastard!' She kicks a high heeled boot back at him as she pots the next ball.

'Yay!' I can't help cheering, just as the breakfast arrives. The baps are righteous and we both focus on demolishing them.

'You've a healthy appetite,' Iain appears at our table. He pulls up a stool and sets his pint down.

'All this outdoor adventure,' I say through half a mouthful. 'How are the whales today?'

Iain purses his lips and sighs. 'The ones on the beach perished overnight. They're still clearing the carcasses. It's a terrible shame, though we did well to get the twenty or so back out to sea.'

I drop the remains of my sandwich. Sit frozen.

'Oh My God, that's so sad.' Gethin shakes his head.

'Aye, we'll no' be out on the surf today. Doesn't seem right.'

'I so wish we could have been more use,' Gethin says.

'Better to think of the ones we did help. As far as we can see they're off and away now.'

Iain's words seem to comfort Gethin. But how wrong is it to be here drinking beer, those whales dead on the beach? Why the heck didn't I stay with her at least?

Iain lowers his face to meet my gaze. Washed-out blue eyes in pale circles from his surfing goggles. 'Nature's a cruel thing, hen. There's no help getting maudlin. Will we see about a dram in a minute? Nothing else for it on a dreich day like this.'

I force a smile. 'A dram is probably the way to go.' I try to claw back that chilled feeling I woke with.

Meanwhile Middle-Aged Barbie has finished thrashing her partner at pool.

'I'll chalk that one up for the ladies, will I?' She brushes her hands down her pink fleecy sleeves.

'Aye, if it pleases you, it'll be short lived.' He slings his arm around her.

She moves to tap Iain on the shoulder. 'Will you tell our Danny here, there's nothing to gain from this trolling of JK Rowling we're reading about?'

'Oh, right, I saw it in the headlines yesterday,' I say. 'JKR getting hit with sexist tweets for coming out against independence.'

'Well, she has a right to her opinion, you'll agree with me there at least, Iain?' The woman sits down with us.

'Aye, Sheila, there's no need to cheapen a healthy debate and give the media what they're looking for.' Iain says.

'Well, the bitch has cheapened things for the Better Together with her million squids. Be awright if we could all do that, Iain?' Danny leans over the back of Sheila's chair.

Sheila jolts her head to shift him. 'There's the lottery millionaires have donated to the Yes people. And she's making some sound points, like how we're to support our old people when the oil and gas runs out.'

'All these are arguments that can be debated,' Iain says as Danny looks about to butt in. 'And an independent Scotland stands more chance, in my opinion, of developing new policies for sustainability and social care away from the money grabbing Westminster cronies.'

'Well, you've no' convinced me to take the risk, though you've more chance than this dunderheid.' Sheila tosses her head back to bump Danny's chest. 'Come on then, you great hulking mannie, let's see you even up the score.' She drags him back to the pool table.

'Hmm, with friends like him, I'm guessing Yes don't need enemies.' Gethin leans to whisper to Iain.

'Och, there'll aye be nutters on both sides. But the British media love to brand us all as louts. The reality is ordinary Scots like Sheila here, fiercely debating stuff they never even thought of before, and mostly with respect'

'As in, it's got to be about more than JKR?' Gethin suggests.

'Too right! And it's time we raised that dram for the whales. Another pint for the chaser?'

Iain heads for the bar just as Gethin's phone beeps. I stare out of the window at the milky blank while he reads his message.

'Do not believe.' Gethin shoves his phone under my nose. 'My mum apologises!'

Hi darling, hope you OK & enjoying Scotland. Sorry I've been difficult. I love you. Mumx

'That's nice. Guess it took a lot for her to send it, right?' I say.

'Yeah, I am slightly touched, I have to admit,' his voice shakes a little. 'I'll reply in a bit.'

He stares at the phone. Jumps as it goes to standby. 'Back in a minute.' He beams up at me, strokes my hand as he heads for the Gents.

Through the window I can just make out the fence at the cliff edge. A man in a dark coat walking a black dog through the greyness. Nowt for it but to take a dram and some more random company. Stop me dwelling on the whales. I let out a long sigh just as Gethin appears. All one big grin.

'Hey, look what I got!' He flicks a pack of condoms in my face.

'Bit presumptuous?' I'm not even half joking.

'Just taking precautions.' His dimple twitches and I resist smiling back. How is he right cute and annoying at the same time?

Iain comes back with the drinks just as Aiden appears, the smell of outside clinging to his oversized hoody. Iain makes a play of looking at his watch.

'Aw, no-one's buying burgers. They're all in here the now,' Aiden snaps.

'I'm joshing you, laddie. Here, get yourself sorted and come join us.' Iain hands Aiden a tenner.

Danny slaps Iain on the shoulder on his way past. 'Och, it's lucky the question won't be won on a pool game, or the Nays would have it here!'

Iain looks over to Sheila, leaning smug on her cue. 'Aye, you'll need to up your game, mannie.'

'So, you're pretty much a hardcore nationalist, is it?' Gethin leans towards Iain.

'You English may think it's a thistles and shortbread Bonnie Prince Charlie re-run. But it's more about being governed by people we've voted for than some misty-eyed nationalism.'

'Yes, I don't blame you, as in getting shot of the Tories? But you'll be landing us poor English with them forever.' Gethin takes a slug of his beer.

'Nobody's forcing you bastards to vote for them,' Iain says. 'But you'll see it all over, like a Scottish awakening. Community buy-ups of land or buildings – employing local people and ploughing back the profits to improve their lives.'

'Social enterprise, is it?' Gethin's all knowing. 'There's this awesome café in Inverness that does that kind of thing, like training up local kids, a homeless drop in…'

'Aye, devolution has helped a lot of that, with the Land Reform Act and community right to buy. There's an unstoppable momentum the now.'

Aiden comes back with a pint and chaser to match ours.

'It's what I keep telling our young friend from Cowdenbeath here. We have a chance to make a difference,' Iain carries on.

'So, has he convinced you to register, Aiden?' Gethin asks.

Aiden shrugs. 'Wearing me down maybe?'

'Aye, I hope so. Look at how the Scottish government have started with reducing the homelessness,' Iain says.

'Can't say I've noticed,' Aiden sounds weary, sups his beer.

'Och, you'll no' engage, that's why. With our own government and full control of the finance, think how much more could be done.'

'They'd send me back to me da, I'm no' eighteen yet.'

'No' if you don't want that. They're giving you the vote, aren't they?'

'Makes sense, you've got to admit?' Gethin joins in. 'As in if you don't vote you can't complain.'

'Awright, awright!' Aiden holds his hands up. 'I came in for a break!'

'Fair enough, laddie,' Iain nods.

'Too fucking right,' I say.

Gethin positions his glass dead centre on his beer mat. 'I have to say all this makes me proud to be half Scottish?' His very best superior tone.

Aiden smirks into his beer. I bite my lip to stop me laughing out loud.

'OK, I'm guessing it'd take a while to be accepted as a Scot round here,' Gethin adds. Bit more sheepish.

'Och, you're all strangers to the Highland way of thinking,' Iain says.

'But everyone's been mega friendly.' Gethin looks puzzled.

'They'll aye be friendly but keeping their guard. They think I'm weird because I lived in California.'

'But you're from here, isn't it?'

Iain leans in, conspiratorial. 'They call me Beach Boy – rumour has it I might be gay.' He grins, waiting for a reaction.

Gethin rises to it, of course. 'But that's so wrong, just because you surf, and then, well, who cares if…'

'Hiring Aiden confirms it all,' Iain winks while Aiden blows him a mocking kiss.

Gethin shakes his head in moral outrage.

'Och, come on,' Iain turns serious. 'Will we raise a dram for the whales?'

We down our drams, stay quiet for a minute. There's a numbing glow from the peaty sweetness, but I can't be thinking about those whales for long.

'I'm going for a cig,' I announce.

'Good idea!' Gethin grins at me.

I'm the first out as they sit making rollups. Take a breath of earthy dampness before lighting up under the roof overhang. I lean back on the wall, watching the drip from the gutter.

'No, mate, I'm like just the passenger,' Gethin says as he piles through the door. I signal to him and pass him my lighter.

'Cheers. Aiden says he's staying in the warm as he's just got here.'

'Aye, I'll go back with him in a bit,' Iain says.

Gethin exhales his smoke into the white air. 'But I was just telling Iain about your bike. Harley Roadster, is it?'

'Sportster.'

'Mean machine. And you rode it all the way up from Bolton?'

'Blackburn.'

'These Lancashire towns,' Gethin mutters. 'But yeah, I literally only hopped on for the last hundred miles or so from Lochgillan.'

'Lochgillan? There was a Motorcycle Museum there at one time,' Iain starts.

Gethin freezes. Stares panic at me.

'It's still there,' I keep my tone neutral. 'Right interesting, tons of good stuff.'

'What do you know about it, Iain?' Gethin's voice sounds strained, but Iain doesn't seem to notice.

'Oh, things you hear.' Iain takes a puff of his cigarette. 'The fella who runs it was a bit like me. Went away and came back to aggravate the locals. Except it's mainly good-natured banter with me.'

'Not with him, then, is it?' Gethin asks.

'The talk was his museum was attracting unsavoury types, greasy bikers off-roading and littering up the beach. You know how folk go on.'

'Can't say the place was crawling when I was there. Though I'll have been one of them, right?' I say.

'Aye, you'll have set the tongues wagging for sure,' Iain jokes. 'But then he's got a reputation for the young lassies, so they say.'

'Is that so?' Why am I not completely surprised?

Gethin looks horrified. 'Well, it's all probably malicious gossip, like you say.'

'Something about him getting a local lassie pregnant a

couple of years back, and her family going in and busting up the museum. Which is why I wasn't sure he was still there.'

Gethin turns to look at me wide-eyed.

'Well, the museum's a bit scruffy but it doesn't look smashed up or owt. I hope he keeps it going to be honest. Can't imagine there are many places like it. It's right quirky, you know?' I'm rambling to fill the space.

'Oh aye, good luck to the fella. Folk like to embellish, and here am I spreading the muck.' Iain stubs his fag out. 'But truly I take everything with a shovel of salt.'

Gethin stands with his eyes focussed somewhere distant. I rack my brain for a change of subject.

'Well,' Iain looks from me to Gethin. 'I'll do a stint on the burgers and give Aiden a proper break, poor laddie.' He downs the last of his pint. 'I'll be seeing you around before you're away on that bike?'

'Sure!' I raise my glass at him.

Gethin grunts his goodbyes and stays standing still. I light us both another fag. Replace the gone-out rollup between his fingers. He looks at his beer and cigarette as if he doesn't know what they are. Then he turns to me.

'Fucking hell, Jez, did you hear that?'

'I was right here.'

'It makes sense, doesn't it? As in Don being so grumpy? Everyone against him like that?'

'You don't know how he treated the young lass.'

He takes a puff of his cigarette. 'From what Iain says it doesn't take much to be ostracised round here.'

'Most of it light-hearted banter, he said.'

'Well, it didn't exactly sound light with Don,' Gethin insists.

'No, that's what I mean, right?' I give up.

I look out to the sea. There's been a slight breeze and the cloud has lightened. Someone's bashing out the Skye Boat Song on an accordion in the pub. So, not misty eyed at all!

'Let's take a walk along the road, Geth. Get some air.'

A signpost outside the pub points to Smoo Cave, 0.5 miles.

'Sounds good,' I say. 'We might even make it before the weather changes again. You know what they say if you don't like the weather in the Highlands?'

Gethin trudges along beside me. Head down.

'Wait ten minutes,' I give the answer.

No response.

'Gethin?'

'Sorry, what?'

'Forget it. It's good to be out, right?' I stretch my arms to the sweep of sky and sea. Shiny wet road winding through the moorland. No bugger about. Sound of our boots and the faint hiss of the sea as the road dips down to skirt the beach.

'I've got to go back and talk to him.' Gethin stops and turns to face the village.

'What? We're on our way to the frigging caves.'

'No, later, tomorrow. We've so got to go back to Lochgillan.' He shoves his hands deep in his pockets, shakes his head.

'What difference does it make what Iain said?'

'He's like an outcast. I don't know, he had me in for kippers, then literally brick wall, like he's scared?' He pushes his hair away from his eyes. Gives them a sneaky wipe.

Fuck, he's crying.

'Come on, let's keep walking.' I take his arm.

He leans into me. Kicks at the tarmac as he goes.

'I need to think how to approach him, you know? I'm such

a fuck up, you've no idea, it's like everything I touch…' he starts, his voice shaky. Then he stops and turns to face me. 'Maybe *you* could talk to him. Tell him about finding Ken? He sounds at least as grouchy as Don, but he let you in, isn't it?'

I take a breath. 'What am I going to tell him? You're gonna nurse him when he's dying?'

He steps away from me. 'It's not about dying, is it?' he hisses.

'No, you're right.' I feel bad now. 'What do you reckon it's about?'

He starts walking again. Still kicking at the tarmac. 'I could have a little sibling out there, have you thought about that?'

'Fuck's sake, Gethin, it was all malicious rumours a minute ago.' Hopeless sinking at the thought of him chasing some unknown baby relative.

'There could be a child. You'd have more chance of getting through to him, isn't it?'

'Because I'm a young lass, right?' I snap at him.

'Do not believe you're falling for the gossip.' He turns to face me. Walks backwards into a puddle. Reaches his hands out to steady himself.

Think of how Don looked at me, eyes pausing on my tits. Nothing unusual, girl. Not worth pushing it. 'I'm just not up for talking to him, that's all,' I say quietly.

Gethin strides on ahead, cursing to himself.

I carry on walking. Out of nowhere I get this picture of knocking on Ken's window that first time. Peering through the nets, except this time I find, maybe I'm told by his neighbour, that he'd died before I got there. What would that have felt like?

We turn the corner, and the sign points us off the road for Smoo cave. There's a car park and the low whitewashed building of a hotel. Then a deep inlet in the coastline with a fenced pathway running down to a bridge and along the other side. Gethin heads down the path without waiting for me. The wind blows his hair, and he pushes it back as he walks. His movements right jerky and quick.

The bridge crosses a fast-running brook that pours into a hole in the cliff-side. All I can hear is the water, but Gethin doesn't even pause to look. Charges up the path on the other side. Disappearing as it curves down.

I follow as fast as I can. Reach the turn and see him at the mouth of the massive cave at the bottom of the cliff.

By the time I get there he's vanished again. There's a shaft of light coming through a gap in the roof of the cathedral-sized chamber. The craggy rock is Day-Glo green with moss where the light reaches. Air thick with moisture and the roar of falling water I can't see. No sign of Gethin either.

'Whoa Jez! Up here!' The cry echoes over the sound of the water. I make my way along a wooden walkway over the river to another chamber. Cling to the creaky rail to avoid slipping on the slimy boards. And there it is, the massive roaring waterfall pounding into a deep pool at our feet. Gethin grips the rail at the side. Grins when he sees me.

'Awesome!' he shouts. I nod.

We stand for a few minutes in the presence of the water. Powering hard into the dark pool. Wiping all thought.

'How about a spliff?' I suggest as we return to the main chamber. Could be a good move to chill him now, right?

Gethin nods and wanders out. Finds an old wooden platform, like an abandoned jetty, on the grassy bit at the side. I sit next to him. Watch the river, just a shallow trickle here. The vegetation at our feet is bright and lush. Everything smells sharp and freshly watered.

Gethin lights the spliff and takes a few hefty tokes before passing it to me. 'Aw, that's better. What a place, eh?'

'It's good to be out exploring again, right?'

'Totally!' He smiles at me. 'I'm sorry, I was out of order back there, but I properly want you to know I am so glad I jumped on that bike.'

'Despite being illegal and nearly ramming you into a deer?'

'You reckon? I love your recklessness – I'm so not a risk-taker.'

'Well, you risked coming to Scotland in the first place, didn't you?' I take a drag, lean back on my elbows.

Gethin considers for a moment. 'I've literally never done anything like that before, as in spontaneously jump on a bus to nowhere. No luggage, no ready cash. No idea where I'd stay...'

I hand him the spliff and he smokes a bit. Deep in thought.

'That's mostly how I've lived my life,' I say. 'I first left Blackburn aged seventeen. More on the run, right, from this Hell's Angel geezer I got involved with after dumping my nice safe boyfriend, Stan. Going with the random adventure, as per usual. Maybe I'm more afraid of staying put.' Is that actually true? Or do I think I have to provide some psycho-babble reason for how I am?

'But look where it's taken you?' Gethin leans round so he's half facing me. 'As in you found Ken and you didn't run from him dying. And then you spend his gold on the great adventure of that bike...'

'And pick up a fucked-up eighteen-year-old lad, right?' I joke.

'Obviously, the biggest risk of all!' he adds, dimple twitching. He passes the spliff to me. 'Seriously, though, I'm glad you've been able to open up with me. All that stuff about your real mum, I could see how painful it is for you.' He leans closer. Holds me in a steady gaze with those dark pool eyes.

'Yeah, well, it was the whales that got me worked up,' I mumble.

'Even that, I'm literally only starting to feel it now. Thinking about what you said, how crap is it we didn't even go back to the whales on the beach?' He moves to rest his hand by the side of my thigh.

I shift away from him. Really can't go there.

He moves to close the gap again. His knee jiggling as he speaks. 'But it's brought us so close, that like shared experience. And I am so inspired by how you found a connection with Ken – I properly need to take a risk with Don, know what I mean?'

So much for getting frigging stoned and laid back. His intensity is freaking me out.

'Look, you're reading too much into everything. It's all spur of the moment with me, right?'

'So, you nurse your dying dad and find out painful shit about your mum. Totally nothing deep about that, is it?' He squeezes my thigh as he moves his face closer. Lips parted. Ready to kiss.

I shove the spliff at him. Get up and take a step back.

'Just get off my bleeding case, will you?' I hiss.

'What the fuck?' He kicks his heel hard into the ground. 'So sorry for giving a toss.'

I pull my arms tight across my chest. Can't explain. Just don't want this.

'Afraid to stay put, is it?' he persists. 'In case you find you give a fuck about something?'

I clench my teeth against the rising desire to get the heck away.

'Jez?'

'I can't do all this picking over wounds, right?' I say, angry at being pushed. 'So maybe, yeah, time to move on again.'

'Well, excuse me for putting my shoulder in the way for you to cry on.' He gets up. Takes the last toke. 'I may be a fuck up, but at least I'm open about it.'

He throws the butt at me, clambers up a little shale path on the grass bank behind us.

I light a fag, my hands shaking. Sit back on the jetty. Let him go. We had a good time, leave it at that.

'Tell you what, Jez?' he shouts from above. 'Never mind the shoulder, what about the joy-stick? Was that a close enough ride for you?'

I look to see him halfway up the cliff, doing a wanking gesture before he disappears behind a boulder.

Smoke my cigarette to calm the thumping in my chest.

'Fuck You, Jez! Fuck Fuck Fuck You!' His cursing echoes round the inlet. The last word turns to a scream and then a couple of thuds.

I run up the shale path, steadying myself on the steep bank to the boulder. Heart banging.

'Gethin! Where are you? Gethin!'

Move round the boulder. See skid marks on the grassy slope. Scramble down on my arse until I see him. Splayed out his back on the sandy ground below.

'Gethin, I'm coming. Don't move.'

The bank flattens out to a ledge with a sheer drop of about ten foot. Too high to jump. I scrabble up to re-join the path. Start running down and slide a few feet until it's safe to jump. Run around the cliff base to him.

'Geth, for God's sake, are you hurt?'

He doesn't move, doesn't speak. I crouch down, heart thumping faster.

'Gethin! Can you hear me Gethin?'

Nothing, but I can see the faint movement in his chest. Get close to his face and feel the breath.

'Listen, you're going to be alright. I'll phone for an ambulance.'

His face is waxy pale and motionless. How the heck will they get an ambulance down here? I pull my phone out. They'll know what to do. Squint at the shattered screen glass. No signal: Emergency calls only. My hand shakes as I bring up the keypad to dial 999.

Industrial – *Pat*

I'm worn out and ready to give up, traipsing unfamiliar streets backing onto the river. Past warehouses with boarded windows; whirr of a welding workshop still in operation; then a trendy wholefood café and smart city living conversions. The river, contained in stone-built banks, moves sludgily around islands of silt and rotting branches occasionally sprouting new growth with the rustle of bird life. The cool brackish smell combined with diesel and rubbish hits me as I cross the road bridge for the third time. My good-as-new sparkly red pumps are starting to rub and it's a bit chill in my silk top. Seven o'clock and the small amount of confidence I had in this evening is fast disappearing. What on earth was I expecting from an invitation to some unknown gallery from some woman I met for thirty seconds?

I turn into the next street and notice a line of parked cars and a sandwich board with a poster half hanging off it. I swear I've been down here already, but now I see it's the sign for the gallery that I must have walked straight past before. I stare at it, my stomach jittery, still tempted to back out. A taxi pulls up and a young woman jumps out and helps an older woman pull herself up. The older woman beams at me from under her purple felt hat as they make their way to the entrance.

Go on, at least there'll be someone else there. I give them a minute to get ahead before taking the metal staircase into the depths of a dilapidated factory building, graffiti on its breeze block walls. It's hard to believe there's anything here.

Then I hear the music, leading me along a passage lined with piles of junk, to a dim light at the other end. And there it is: the entrance to a hidden world. A long factory room with a glass roof letting in the soft evening light. I hang back for a moment, taking in the lines of paintings and the gleam of sculptures; people with plastic beakers of wine grouped round the exhibits, their chatter and laughter competing with the music; smell of fresh paint only partly hiding the hint of mildew. It looks something like a proper exhibition, and I realise how low my expectations have become since Cuttin' Edge. But I'm wary of crossing the threshold, standing out as the intruder to this world.

The music is clashing, avant-garde, industrial. It suits the venue and makes me feel less conspicuous. I take a step in and look around for Gabriella but can't see her. Bloody hell, don't tell me she's not going to turn up? I feel a wave of panic as I head for the make-shift bar. A guy in a black brocade frockcoat and highly decorated trilby pours me some wine.

'Cheers,' he lifts his cup to me. His short-trimmed beard has flecks of grey and I'm guessing he's around my age. The trilby sports a long bronze-coloured scarf and there are silver jewelled spiders glinting from the rim. 'I'm Alex, one of the artists,' he says.

'I'm Pat.' I take a quick gulp of wine. 'I had no idea this place was here, you know?'

He lifts his hat to me with a grin. 'Glad you found us.'

'I'm supposed to be meeting someone,' I say, looking around.

'Well, would you like me to take you round while you're waiting?' Alex asks. 'Or by all means go by yourself.'

'No, you take me, if that's OK?' I surprise myself by accepting his offer.

He takes his hat off with a mock flourish.

'Do like the outfit!' I smile.

'Ah, you have to make the effort.' He glances at the ranks of jeans and T shirts. 'Not that anyone else has, apart from you, of course!'

I look down at my purple silk top, black skinny jeans, and the sparkly pumps. I agonised over the outfit, remembering Gabriella in her lacy camisole. Now I worry I'm overdressed.

Alex starts the tour with his semi-abstract paintings of industrial ruins morphing into shiny soulless structures.

'It's my response to a northern city in a post-industrial age. And I take my palette from the moors and rocks around.'

I can see what he means, looking at the landscape in front of me, with its layered muted blues and umbers, ochre and burnt sienna. It could be a natural rocky gorge, or a decaying cityscape.

'I do like that. There is so much to see in it. Refreshing in an art world where painting seems to be a rarity.'

'Ah, tell me about it,' he says.

I cast another look around for Gabriella as he moves me on to another exhibitor's sculpture, made from what he calls industrial sweepings. Creatures modelled from assorted nuts and screws, bottle tops and micro-chips, set on plinths around a massive crocodile made of tractor tyres.

'It's beautifully worked,' I say, admiring the use of the tyre tread to form the croc's scales. I think of Charlie bemoaning the lack of craft. 'It's good to see art that is so, well, grounded, I suppose.'

A tap on my shoulder spins me round. It's Gabriella looking flustered but gorgeous in a brown silky shift-dress.

'Pat, I'm so sorry.' She gives me a polite peck on the cheek, hint of musky perfume and sweat.

'Don't worry.' I feel my heartbeat rise. 'Alex has been looking after me.'

'Ah, he's a good-un.' She pats him on the arm. 'Honestly, I invite the woman, she hardly knows me, and then I'm really late.'

'Well, that's not like you at all, Gabriella,' Alex mocks.

'Shh.' She gives him a playful punch and I feel ridiculously jealous of their easy banter.

'Pat's an artist, too,' Gabriella tells Alex. 'Really exciting political collage.'

'If that's not a contradiction in terms,' I say, awkward with the attention.

'Why should it be?' Alex says. 'I hope I get to see your work too, Pat.' He takes a bow with his hat, moves to talk to someone waiting for his attention.

'Oh, I am so pleased you are here.' Gabriella's eyes shine behind her glasses. 'Let's look round together.' She touches my arm, sends a shiver of excitement through me.

She takes me to another set of metalwork sculptures, constructed out of old cutlery, bicycle chains, tools. We pause in front of a large owl made of feathered knives and forks.

'So, this gallery is connected to your studios?' I ask.

'Yes, the studios are on the other side.' She points to the entrance, the light catching the line of her forearm, the glint of her bracelets.

'Well, I'm impressed. I love this sense of art emerging from the ruins of the past, so rooted in this part of the city.'

She nods slowly, moves a strand of hair behind her ears, her fingers stroking the line of her bare neck.

I catch my breath, look away. 'It just highlights for me the emptiness of most of the work at Cuttin' Edge,' I mutter, as if to the owl.

'Well, your work shone out at that place,' Gabriella insists.

I pull a nervous smile, drink my wine.

'Seriously, why do you think I found you on Facebook? You were in such a hurry to get away, I didn't get to say how much I admired your piece.'

I feel flushed with this rare attention. 'Your friend request was so out of kilter with my mood, to tell you the truth. But I think curiosity got the better of me.'

'While ever we have curiosity…' She flicks her tongue over her bottom lip. 'Come and see my studio!'

She steers me along the dark graffitied passage to another top-lit area partitioned into low walled studios.

'Here we are.' She leads me through a wooden gate to the faded orange sofa along one side. 'Make yourself comfortable, I'll get us more wine.'

She rummages through a cupboard while I look around. There is work hung on every available space and piled up at the back, but the picture on the easel attracts my attention. A large collage of overlapping images of poster-sized magazine women, painted with a thin strip of translucent yellow, like cellophane wrapping.

'Wow!' I say as Gabriella emerges with half a bottle of wine. 'I like that image. Is it finished?'

She cocks her head to one side, looking at the picture. 'I think so.' She pours us both some wine.

'The way the images overlap, interchangeable, unreal in their wrapping,' I say. 'At least, that's how I see it.'

She takes a step back. 'I've been working around deconstructing constructed images of women. Not that it's particularly original.'

She laughs, nervous now, which surprises me. It seems I'm not the only one uncomfortable with showing off my work.

'Well, it's more considered than some of the feminist art I admired at college in the early eighties,' I say.

'Oh, those visceral vaginas and menstrual celebration!' She sits down next to me on the sofa.

'Yes, Gaynor, my first girlfriend, had a huge appliquéd vulva on her bedroom door.'

She raises her eyebrow, suppressing a smile and I take a breath at my mentioning a woman lover. And it comes to me, I dreamt of Gaynor last night, beckoning through piles of discarded collage, her face glowing in the halo of her blond hair, then morphing into Gabriella. The detail is hazy, but the expectation of reaching Gabriella is palpable.

'But it was necessary at the time,' she continues.

I pull my attention back. 'It always embarrassed me, you know. Pure prudishness – I blame my puritan father.'

'Ah, and would you say you're still prudish?' she teases.

I pull back, my arms around my chest, in a gesture of uptightness that isn't entirely a joke. 'Let's say I was more attracted to the cleaner graphic style. People like Barbara Kruger and Louise Nevelson. Though back in the days, I wasn't beyond daubing words like WANKER across my careful photo-montages.'

'Angry woman art!'

'Absolutely. Subverting male establishment ideas of artistic merit. My tutors called it infantile, sacrificing the art for the message. I probably still do that, you know.' That haunting hopeless failure from my work at the exhibition.

She shakes her head, the light from the roof glinting on her glasses. 'I want to start a group of women political artists. Your work fits perfectly. It's so beautifully done, a lot of complexity there.'

I stare wide-eyed at her. 'I…I'm…really?'

She sips her wine, keeping me in her gaze. 'You don't believe in your art very much, do you?'

Something shrinks inside me, that terrible doubt. 'Militant Nostalgia.' The dreaded phrase.

Gabriella looks puzzled.

'Just some feedback I got.' I swill the wine in my cup. 'The images are hackneyed; they can no longer have any impact. It's pure self-indulgence, you know?'

'We live in a very jaded age, don't we? Nothing shocks, nothing is new. It's very hard to be ground-breaking, my work is no more so.'

I remember how I thought the images on her Facebook page weren't especially original, but it didn't stop me admiring her work.

'I find it hard not to think that I've been wasting my time,' I say weakly.

'What better use of time can there be? How much poorer would we be without our creativity, our soul-food?'

I think about the buzz I've had at times with my work, how it was when I first got the studio. Taking my dancing Greenham women and weaving them as negative space through collage of destruction and exploitation. Feeling I was onto something new as I constructed barbed wire dresses cut through to reveal the same collage.

'Oh, there are creative highs. But that doesn't mean it has any intrinsic value.'

'It has value when it connects with others.' Gabriella's tone is impatient. 'You felt it in the exhibition just now. I felt it with your work.'

I stare into my cup. I am excited that she includes my work as an example of the power of art. But still the doubt looms huge.

'I do know what you mean, and I sense it with your work too.' I look again at the image on the easel. 'And I have felt poorer, as you say, when I've had no creative expression. But, to tell you the truth, I feel these past couple of years could have been better spent supporting my son.'

'Ah, the Old Mother Guilt.'

I grimace. 'I do get the feminist line. But my son just walked out on his eighteenth birthday. No contact, no nothing. I pushed him too hard, he dropped out of sixth form, all I've done is go on at him.'

'Oh, they all need a bit of space at that age.'

'I gave up on him, you see?' My voice shakes with the difficulty of admitting this. 'I hid my disappointment by throwing myself into my art. So now it seems tainted.'

'It's difficult for young people. There's no clear sense of direction for many of them.'

'He needed to be able to talk about that, some guidance.'

'Well giving up your art won't help him. Art broadens your mind to possibilities.' She looks round her studio and then back at me. 'At least, that's what I'm banking on,' she adds with a grin.

I can't help smiling at the innuendo. I sip my wine and try to focus.

'When I was his age, art was my passport to the wider world, you know? I painted expressionist landscapes of the Norfolk fens, desperate bands of melancholy, slashed with dark rain. Then my art teacher took me to London and introduced me to load of screen printers: all heavily Andy Warhol, to tell you the truth, but it stopped my sinking isolation, made me braver.'

'So, it's helped form who you are.'

'Gethin hasn't got anything like that.' I feel a lurch in my stomach as I understand the truth of this. 'He's lost his passion.'

'You have to let them find their own way and trust you have given them enough tools to do so.'

'Yeah, well, I wish it were that easy.' I feel myself tightening at her glib suggestions.

She takes a breath, raises her eyebrows. 'Believe me, I know it's difficult. My oldest went to university with flying colours and then crashed in his third year and was at home doing nothing for two years.'

'I'm sorry, I had no idea,' I say, foolishly.

'Well, he's coming through it now. Then my second son dropped out of sixth form like yours, hanging about doing fuck all. I had such a go at him one night, you know, overbearing Mum. The next morning, he got on a flight to Naples, and it was two months before he got in touch.'

I stare down into my cup. Of course, Gethin's not the only troubled youngster. Am I over-reacting?

'Giving up my art wouldn't have helped either of them,' Gabriella continues. 'In fact, the older one's helping me with my website design.' She pauses, leaning into her knees. Her bare legs are blotchy with a few age spots and there are raised veins around the line of her feet in their sling-backs. Their imperfection moves me.

'Talking of which,' Gabriella reaches to top up our cups. 'Is your work anywhere online? Your Facebook has virtually no art on it.'

'I suppose lately I've thrown all I have into the one installation. Trying to say everything at once, you know? My son also helped me with a website, but I was so disappointed when not even my friends looked at it, I haven't kept it up.'

'You have to push it, Pat. Find other artists' pages, connect online.' She leans towards me, holds me with her gaze, flecks of gold in the hazel of her eyes.

'I'd rather join your collective, you know?' I say before I've even thought it.

'Do both! We have studios to rent. The facilities are basic, but it's probably cheaper than where you are now.'

'I'm about to be made redundant, I'll have to give up that place anyway.' My eyes widen to that opening of horizons.

'What better way to invest your pay-off?'

I shake my head, pull my shoulders up. This is all going a bit fast. I could be committing my redundancy money before I've even finished work. But the buzz of this place, this woman, is something I've not felt in a long time and I refuse to slap it down.

Gabriella takes off her glasses and leans back into the sofa. I sit forward, sipping my drink, allowing the sense of possibility to seep through with the wine, expanding with every breath, a tingling sensation of coming alive. I shift to rest my head against the sofa next to her. Her big expressive smile lights up her face, her eyes caressing, naked without the glasses.

I catch my breath, holding the surge of desire, my lips parting as I moisten them. I think of Gaynor, dancing to *Love and Affection*, the radiance of her face in that moment we first kissed, turning into Gabriella in my dream.

I put my beaker down, trying to regulate my breathing. I should get up and go while I still can. I'm not ready for this, am I? I sit back up – she still holds me in her gaze. I move towards her, my hand brushing her leg, feel its warmth through the silk of her dress. There is no way I'm backing out now.

She draws closer, her breath soft on my hand as I stroke her cheek, close my eyes as our lips barely brush. Slowly building up for more, my groin throbbing as she runs her tongue over my lips. I feel the softness of her hair falling around her neck, sink into the sweet fullness of the kiss.

The vibration of my phone in my pocket makes me jump. I pull back, look at the screen. It's an unknown number.

'I don't know who it is, it might be important,' I start.

'Take it.' She smiles. 'There's no rush.'

I answer the phone.

'Is that Mrs Williams?' A Scottish woman.

'Yes?' Who would call me Mrs Williams?

'This is Raigmore Hospital, in Inverness.'

You can run… – *Jez*

The early morning light hits hard after the dimmed night of the hospital. It bangs off the washed grey Inverness pavements. A pink tinged pigeon with a dirty scrap of bread. Bob the Builder yellow of the dustcart. Like the day after Ken died: everything too candy brash. What you on about, girl? Gethin hasn't died. They said he was stable, right?

The taxi pulls into the bus station and I pay with the fake looking money. The driver points me to the white curvy bus.

Five frigging hours to Durness, via Ullapool. It'd take about two on the bike. But the bike's in Durness.

My bus is even called the Bike Bus. Yeah, there are a couple of cyclists. All Lycra and fleeces, loading their bikes onto the bus's special trailer. Also, an old guy in raincoat and flat cap, battered brown suitcase. Middle aged woman fussing over much older lady, matching anoraks and beige slacks. I buy a cappuccino from the stand and get on the bus.

There are plush reclining seats with tables like in a train. I sink into the upholstery. Sip my coffee.

Was I going to sit and watch someone else die? The question flashes electric current. What am I talking about? No-one's dying, right? That shrunken world of the hospital: beep of machines, subdued voices, hushed footsteps. The still bulk of him lying there. When they said his mum would be there soon, I was like, right, I'll get out the way. No problem.

The engine starts up and I'm glad to be moving. It's not long before we're on the main road alongside the river out of

Inverness. I close my eyes, flash to the image of Gethin lying among the tubes with the bubble of the oxygen machine. What is it about finding people to look after? Really not my plan with this trip. How come one look of those lost boy eyes sent me chasing him with a stolen crash helmet?

The road pulls away from the river just as it starts raining. I finish my coffee and recline the seat as far as it will go. Sleep would be good.

A wave of loneliness hits like nausea. How would this trip have been without Gethin? Hurtling to a kind of critical mass after Ken died – that was only, let's see, about ten frigging days ago. Gethin looked after me as much as I did him, right? Shift my position for better neck support. Drift into that night on the beach. How sweet was he, his heart on his sleeve? OK he's a self-obsessed middle-class kid – won't be the love of my life. But he did, actually, help me. Can't I hang onto that without the image of him unconscious punching in every time I close my eyes?

I do fall into a rumbling kind of sleep, woken by the warmth of the sun as we drive alongside a long loch. The clouds have cleared, and the flag blue of the sky bounces off the loch. Reflects in each raindrop still clinging to the window. Can't wait to be back on the bike. Follow the road wherever it takes me.

You gotta run, run, run, run, run… from that Velvet Underground album Mum plays. How does it go?

Fag break in Ullapool. Stand on the front staring blank at the sea. *You gotta run, run, run, run, run…* Smell of the sea in my hair as I get back on the bus. *Run, run, run, run, run… Tell you whatcha do.*

This time I'm dozing most of the way. Blur of grey and

violet and flashes of blue to remind me I'm still in Scotland. *Run, run, run, run, run* – echoes of the song as I drift.

It doesn't take long to take down the tents and pack up the panniers. Back on the road, I pause to look at the signpost pointing in every direction. That photo of Gethin with the thumbs up: that was the day of the whales, right? The world at his feet and he made it half a mile up the road before being air-lifted to Inverness. I take a breath. Where to go now? Could head around the top to John O'Groats, then down the east coast. That'd bring me to Inverness before long. So, I'm going back, right? Can't just fuck off, not knowing if he's OK.

I swing the bike round when I see Aiden running towards me, waving his arms madly. Fuck, wasn't reckoning on having to talk to anyone. Shouldn't have hung about.

'Jez, I was no' sure it was you.' His thin pale face peers into my visor.

I pull off my helmet. 'Hey, Aiden.' Give a weak smile.

'I heard they took Gethin in the air ambulance. Is he awright?' He pulls at his hoody.

'How the heck did you know?'

'You hear about everything here.' He looks around him, his movements jerky. 'Is he…?'

'They say he's stable. But he only came round for a short while.'

'So, he'll be right, yeah?' His eyes widen. I'm surprised again by their vivid green.

'Yes, I mean, I hope so.' My chest tightens – realise I don't know. 'They said the first twenty-four hours are critical – keeping a right close watch on him.'

'Christ, he's no' going to die?'

'No, just well… could be some damage.'

'Brain damage?'

'Let's hope not, right?' I fiddle with the strap on my helmet. 'I'll probably go back there later. But his mum's with him now, I think.'

Aiden nods. Scuffs the ground with his trainer. 'At least I did no' argue with him,' he mutters.

'Argue?'

He looks up, his face pinched. 'Aye, you see I rowed with my brother, last time I saw him before he died. I was telling Gethin about it the other night. He said I should no' blame myself, but if I'd done that again…' he tails off, keeps scraping the ground with his foot.

My insides plummet as it hits me that Gethin and I were arguing when he stormed off up the cliff-side. I tighten my grip on the helmet as we stand in silence. Want to get away, but I'm like paralysed with fear and guilt.

'Well, I'll leave you be,' Aiden says, pulling at his sleeves again.

I nod, bite my lip against the prick of tears.

'If you could, let us know. I'll give you the number for the burger van.'

I pull out my phone and he dictates the number.

'Tell Gethin I've promised Iain I'm voting in this referendum thingy. It may make no difference, but you never know.'

'Aw, he'll be wanting to steal your vote.'

We stand awkward another moment. Then he pats my arm and walks away.

I start out on the road to Tongue, heading for John O'Groats. I should be back in Inverness before it's too late this evening. Right now, I crave the bike ride to stop me thinking.

Massive lurch in my stomach as I pass the road off to Smoo Cave. How was that only yesterday? Carry on for a couple of miles, the road turning up the side of a long sea inlet. Can't stop thinking about Gethin. The bike focus thing not working. He asked me to go and talk to Don. Practically the last thing he said to me, right? So why am I heading in the opposite direction?

I pull into a lay-by. Light a cigarette and sit for a minute. Why not go the whole hog with this story? I smoke and watch a gull glide the wind current in an arc above the sea-loch.

Must have helped to have made up my mind – the ride to Lochgillan totally keeping me focussed on the road. All about the bike. Throb of the engine. Rush of cold air. Flash of light on the loch-sides. Blur of green and purple as I lean and turn and the bike eats the tarmac. Unwelcome thoughts to the winds. I hit Lochgillan with no idea as to how I'm going to tackle Don.

Coming out of the pines, up and round the bend, catch a glimpse of the museum on the straight. Afternoon light batting off the roof. No other vehicles as I park up in front. I lock my helmet to the bike and shake my hair loose. Pull on my shades – maybe better if he doesn't recognise me right from the start?

Push my way into the entrance booth and ring the bell. Seems a lifetime since I stood here with the rain dripping into tin buckets. I count it back – only three days. No buckets now. But the clutter of bikes, displays and assorted junk is just the same.

Such a déjà vu when he comes out of the workshop wiping his hands on his greasy overalls. That far-away look of his. Then I see him clock my leathers and glance out of the window to see what I've parked there. Yeah, the only way in is through the bikes.

'Harley Sportster 1200?' he says, taking my entrance money. 'You've been here before. I never forget a bike, not even a Harley.'

'That's right,' hoping he remembers the bike better than me. 'Thought I'd take another look at the lady trials racing champion.' I walk towards the display.

'Ah, yes.' He joins me in front of the old trials bike. 'Miss E Sturt's Sprint Special. That's supposed to be my next project, to get the bike working.' He takes a breath and holds it in, pursing his lips.

'Then you'll need a spunky lady biker to trial it, right?'

He looks me up and down. Faint smile flickering. I turn to the display, not ready to be recognised. 'Leather knickerbockers and flying ace helmet. I'll be cutting a pace through the bog.'

'Aye, we can all dream,' he muses. Then he jolts himself out of the moment and turns away.

'Got any more like her in your collection?' I ask. Desperate to keep him talking.

He cocks his head with a thinking frown. 'Can't say I have. Even these days you don't see many lassies riding solo like you.'

'Ah, I'm not a run-of-the-mill lass.'

'Aye, you don't seem like your average. What got you into bikes?'

'The Harley's like my first proper bike.' I toss my head, flicking my hair over my shoulder.

'Well, that lump of polished chrome did no' cost nothing. Land yourself some sugar daddy, did you?'

I look at the photo of Miss E Sturt. Demure smile hiding who knows what. Now's the moment.

'Not that sort of daddy,' I start. Tell him about Ken and the gold in the briefest, most matter-of-fact way I can manage.

He looks straight ahead. Rubs his chin as I tell my story.

'I've perhaps heard stranger tales, but no' for a while.' His deep-set eyes soften – hitting me with the flash of Gethin in them. 'Stroke of luck him leaving you that gold, eh?'

'I wouldn't be here without it, right? But I was chuffed to have that time with him before he died, whatever.'

'Ah, well, yes…' he shuffles his feet, looks towards the workshop.

'He'd have made a crap dad.' Don't let him escape! 'But I was right glad to know him. Got to be worth more than a flashy motorbike? Not that I'm complaining.'

He pulls his arms tight to his sides. 'Aye, you could do worse, even than a Harley.' He looks away. 'Must get on. Bikes won't fix themselves.'

I push my sunglasses up onto my head. 'You don't remember me, right?' It's the now-or-never moment.

He frowns, taking a step back. 'I told you, I never forget a bike.'

'I was here when your son came looking for you. I deleted your photo from his phone?'

He stops, eyes wide open. Panic mode. Then he turns and makes towards the workshop.

'We'll be closing shortly.' He steps over the police tape.

'I've got your tent.' I move towards him. 'He asked me to get it back to you.'

He turns and stares at me. 'Who?'

'Gethin, your son, right? I've spent the last couple of days with him in Durness.'

Frozen moment. Him staring. Me forgetting to breathe. Think of Gethin lying out cold on that hospital bed. Have to push this.

'Then you'll know I told him I dinnae need no son,' he says slowly, folding his arms over his chest.

Heart banging. What the heck do I say now?

'You can fetch me my tent and be on your way. Like I said, we're closing.'

Air smells fresh, washed with a recent shower. Light sparking off the distant sea. I stand for a minute in a patch of sun – warmth on my face. How am I going to Inverness without trying everything? Un-strap the tent and go back. Don locking the museum door. He sees me and stands, hands by his sides. Deflated and pathetic. How painful is this for him?

'Here,' I say. 'Thanks for lending it to him.'

He takes the tent. Nods and bites his lip. 'Tell him thanks for returning it.'

'He would have come himself, right?' Choking on the words. 'But he's like had an accident. Fell off a cliff in Durness.'

He jolts at this, eyes bulging. 'He's all right then, is he?' A tremor to his voice.

'I, I don't know.' Tears pricking. 'It's just, he asked me to talk to you, before his accident. I thought there's no harm. Just to talk, right?"

'You say he fell?'

'Lost his footing. Fell a good ten feet. Knocked himself out.'

We face each other a metre apart. Him clutching the tent

and frowning at the ground. Me fixed on the distant line of sea behind him. Straining against the tears. A breeze whips up, blows my hair in my face. I brush it out of my eyes, giving them a wipe while I'm at it. He catches my movement, looks up at me. Gethin again in those questioning eyes.

'Dinnae go greeting on me, big biker lassie like you,' he says at last. Trace of a smile?

I take a breath. Pull a smile back.

'Let's have a walk,' he says.

We take a path to the beach, skirting the golf course. Sandy bay in the curve of dense green bushes and grass. Silvery pools from the outgoing tide. Fishy smell of rotting seaweed and the cry of a gull. No bugger in sight though it's only about five. We walk towards the rocks on the far side of the beach. Stretch my arms – take a lung-full of air.

'Do you know what?' I break the silence. 'I still can't get over the massive amounts of space and air up here. So few people.'

'Aye, that's the best bit.' Don picks up a flat white stone. Turns it over in his hand as he tells me how he spent his time here as a little boy, with his hide-out in a cave on the cliff-side. I try to picture him as like a mini Gethin, trapping small animals, doing a spot of fishing, building a fire…

'I'd feel like I was the only person on earth,' he says, looking up at me. The pain of the memory like etched in his face.

'So, how is it any surprise that Gethin wants to feel his connection to this place?'

'His connection?' Don picks up his pace towards the sea. 'I was transported to Glasgow aged seven, had to fight my way in the alien city. Me da busy ruining us all with his moneymaking dream, me ma chronically depressed in the tower-block. It was the thought of this place got me through.' He stops and turns to me. Spitting out the words. 'Gethin has some misty notion of a link to the clan and a load of old stories he knows nothing about.' He walks on fast again.

I scurry to keep up. 'Look, OK, Gethin has no real claim to this place. But how is that a reason to cut him off? God's sake, the lad's in frigging hospital.'

'He'll still get nae invites to Broomdale via me.' He keeps turning his stone over.

'Broomdale? What the heck's that?'

He scowls, picks up another stone as he walks. Says nowt until he reaches the water's edge.

'I know what you're thinking.' He stops before the frilly curve of the incoming sea.

'Oh yeah?' I watch as he skims his stone to bounce five times.

'You found your da while he was dying. Don't get me wrong, I admire your spirit. But you think it should be the same with Gethin, and I'm telling you, it's not.' He takes the other stone and gets seven bounces. 'See, I didn't get his ma up the duff and then bugger off like your father, did I?'

'You know nowt about it. Fuck you!' I walk away from him. Kick at the wet sand as I go. What about the lass he supposedly got pregnant? How fucking dare he?

I get about twenty metres away before I think to calm down. Come on, girl. Not helping to make it all about me. Stand still and stare at the sea. He catches up with me. Skims another stone.

'You have no right to criticise Ken,' I say quietly.

'All I'm saying is he has some responsibility for the wean

that is you. Me? Just helping some lesbo bird I never met.' He shakes his head.

'And that makes a difference to Gethin how? Half his frigging genes are yours, right?'

He shoves his hands in his pockets. A wave comes in closer and covers his boots. He splashes on through to the rocks.

'Genetics dinnae mean jack-shit.' He stops to shout in my face. Isn't that what Gethin said? 'How bothered was his ma about my genes? She wanted a bairn without a man, and that is what she got.'

'So how come you wrote that stuff about yourself?'

He flinches at this. Purses his lips and walks on.

'You thought the kid might want to know about you, right?'

He carries on walking.

'You could have left it like totally anonymous, right? But you gave him hints at who you are. How are you surprised when he wants more?'

He's clammed shut, but I know I've got him. It's about the other kid, got to be.

He stops at the edge of the headland. The tide filling a rock pool at our feet. Salmon-pink anemones clinging to the side. Their tendrils move with the motion of the sea.

'Gethin showed me what you wrote. Not like you were hard to find.' I challenge him again.

He kicks his boot into the rock. Stares into the swirling water.

'Aye, I'll soon be moving to the city, instead of being a sitting duck idiot for every bugger to chuck their worst at.' He rubs his chin as he speaks. Head lowered. Shoulders pulled in.

I watch the ebb and flow of the water. How the heck do I get him to tell me what's going on?

'You sound like me,' I say as it occurs to me. 'I'm always on the run, right? Left my last job in a hurry when the boss went bankrupt without telling me. Same time as deciding he was in love with me. And once I got Ken's gold, it had to be the bike. Couldn't wait to be away on it.'

'Well, you've got some guts, hen, I'll say that for you.' He looks at me at last. Face drawn and weary.

'I wouldn't have the bike without Ken, right? So, it leads back to him. No escaping what's in here.' I tap my head. Clocking the truth of this.

Don picks up a driftwood twig. Pokes the end into an anemone, which clamps itself around the stick. 'Who says I'm after escaping from my heid?' he mutters.

'Right, so what is it? Something between you and the folks round here?'

'What have you heard?' He glares at me.

'Nowt, just things you've said, right? The folk in Broomdale? Is that like your family HQ?'

'There's a distant connection. My father and the Laird are third cousins twice removed or some such. My grandfather liked to boast of our clannish connections, but we mean jack-shit to the Laird.'

'Is that why you're so hostile to any mention of them?' I meet his scowl. Holding eye contact.

He turns and heads for a rocky ledge away from the tideline. Sits and stares ahead of him.

I light myself a cig. Walk over to offer him one. He shakes his head, disapproving. I stand smoking feeling an idiot. How do I get him to tell me about the young lass?

'Och, the Laird keeps himself aloof, that's nae bother to me. It's the ordinary folk cause me grief around here,' he says at last.

'Why's that, then?' I take a couple of drags. Will myself to give him time. The image of Gethin stone cold on the beach flashes through me again.

'The old crofting families, they like to moan well enough about English folk with their trendy coffee shops and second homes sending the land prices rocketing. But that's as nothing to how they see a bit of Glasgee trash bringing in a load of greaser bikers to lower the tone.' He rocks on his ledge. Staring out to sea.

'Can't say I've seen the place crawling with bikers,' I say.

'No' the now, but when I first opened the museum was quite popular. The locals were glad enough to help me bring in different tourist money.' He pulls his lips tight.

Bend to put my cigarette out on the damp sand. 'So, what happened?' Pocket the butt. Step towards him. 'I'll get it out of you, right?'

He takes a deep breath. Shaking his head as he exhales.

'You're no' one for giving up, are you?' Glimpse of a smile?

'Resistance is futile.'

'Sit down.' He pats the flat rock beside him.

Do as I'm told. Wait for him to talk.

'There was this young lassie, Ruthie. From one of the crofting families, two older brothers, they'd already taken against me.'

He pulls a sheepish grin and I nod. Wey-Hey, we're getting there.

'She was a bit of an odd one, shall we say. A tad overweight, awkward in company. She started hanging around the museum that first summer – four years ago now. She'd sit at the side of the yard, watch the bikes coming and going, then ask me about what I had on display.'

'That pleased her brothers, right?'

'Aye, you can imagine. I'd tell her to get away home, but she'd be back, wanting to help. It seemed better to give her a few odd jobs than have her lolling about drawing attention. And she had this way of getting on with things, no' saying a lot, no' being in my way...' He leans forwards, elbows on thighs, chin in his hand.

'How old was she?' I have to ask. Though I'm not sure I want to know.

'Seventeen.' He raises his eyes to level with mine.

'Right.' I flinch at the thought of it.

'You're thinking it's no' right, a man my age. And I tell you I'm no' proud of what happened.'

'Go on then.'

'Well, I closed the museum out of season, but I still had a lot to do. Ruthie kept coming when she was supposed to be at college. She took on some of the display work, she had a knack for that. We were two odd bods who let each other be. That's all there was to it for a while.'

I look out to the dull gleam of the sea. Yeah, I can see the attraction for a misfit teenager. Don's gruffness could lull her into feeling safe. However...

'You'll find it hard to believe a lassie like that would take an interest in me.' Like he reads my next thought.

I pull back. Nowt to say.

'Buggered if I know why.' He pulls a tight smile. 'It was nothing I'd planned. She was helping me with the manikins, in the sidecar display?'

I nod.

'Her idea, them manikins, she put a lot of work in getting the right clothes and everything. One night we were working flat out for the Easter opening, and this massive storm blew a section of the roof off. We were out there with the ladders, battling to fix it down – got soaked right through. I invited her into the caravan to dry off.'

'Of course, you did.'

He frowns. 'I had no idea of touching her. I lit the stove and got the whisky out and we had a good crack about what the manikins might be up to. I can see her now, sitting in my old shirt, her awkward way of moving, and I saw how bonny she was for the first time.' He scowls up at me. Like he realises he's opened up too far.

'So, there was nowt for it but to take her to bed?'

'You can see it how you like, it was never my intention, and that was the only time.' He pulls his arms over his chest, closing up.

Think about the blokes I've slept with. Apart from Stan, who was more like a friend. All the rest being right dodgy geezers, employers trying it on, one-night stands. It's the age difference that gets me with Don's story. What about Ken and Alice, then? Assume she was a lot younger, right? Just the once with them as well, according to Ken. How was that so different? But the main question is what the heck any of this has to do with Gethin? Another stomach lurch thinking about what might be happening with him now.

'I'm not judging,' I start, busting to get to the point. 'Just trying to understand, right?'

'You'll be the first in that case.'

'Why, what happened?' Force my impatience down.

'Didn't see her for ages after that. I blamed myself, felt foolish, you know? Come the summer there were reports of Ruthie hanging out on the beach with some of the bikers. I told myself to forget about her...' He sighs, rubs his chin, stays silent for a minute.

'You must have missed her, right?' I suggest.

'The next thing was I came back one night to a brick through the window, tyres slashed on my bike and PAEDO in red paint on the museum wall.'

'What the fuck?'

'I heard from Robbie, my pal from the pub, that Ruthie's brothers had been saying that I'd got Ruthie pregnant and they were going to do me.'

'So, what, you just painted it out and carried on?'

'More or less. Except everyone wants to get involved, don't they? Next thing, up trots Laura from the Heritage Centre: she was helping me with my funding returns and used that as an excuse to come nosing about. Tells me Ruthie's not saying who the father is, but everyone thinks it's me. I told her where to stick it.' He leans forwards on clenched fists. Quiet confession hardened into pure anger.

'Maybe she really wasn't judging, right? Just trying to help,' I suggest.

'No? Well, she got me banned from the pub. Though I might have got lairy...'

'So, what happened, to Ruthie and the baby?' What will Gethin feel about this sibling now?

Don takes a deep breath. 'This is why I don't talk to nobody.' Shakes his head at me.

'What?' I hold my hands up. No frigging idea.

'You're assuming I've left her to get on with having my wean.' He jumps to his feet and turns to face me.

'I'm just trying to understand, right?' I say quietly.

'Anything I do gets distorted, twisted. And you're asking

me to take on a long-lost son?' He's shouting now, his face shiny red.

I stay still. Lip buttoned.

'Och, what's the use?' He slaps his thigh with his fist. 'I'm away out of here as soon as I can now.'

'And it's still yourself you'll have to live with,' I call as he strides back across the beach – trailing boot prints in the wet sand.

I watch a group of thin-necked black and white birds swoop down to the pools left by the outgoing tide. What the heck do I do now? Can't believe I came that close to the nub of Don's story. Maybe I am judging him, right? Like I can judge Ken if I stop to think about it. But maybe Ken did the right thing by me? I had a decent childhood – would I have wanted it different? How does any of this affect how Don is with Gethin?

Big sighing breath as I look at the time on my phone. Half past six. I'll need to get a move on to get back to Inverness by any reasonable time. I so want to find out how Gethin's doing, but I've no signal here. I walk towards the path back up to the road.

The Harley's tank glints as I approach the museum. Pat the seat as I look across at Don's caravan.

'Won't be long,' I whisper.

There's movement behind the caravan curtains. I take a deep breath. Knock on the door.

He opens it immediately. Filling the little doorway.

'Aye,' he says, softly now. 'I figured you'd be back.'

High Dependency – *Gethin*

Thick brown suffocating fog. I push through, reaching for the surface. Hear voices, gasp a breath, and sink again. The pressure of the fog increases as I thrash against it, sinking further. Then a hand stretches towards me, and I lunge to grab it, feel the pull upwards and the gulp of air.

'Mum?'

Strip lights overhead hurting my eyes. Shut. Grip the hand.

'Gethin? Are you awake?' A sing-songy voice, unfamiliar. 'Do you know where you are?'

I turn my head to the voice and moan with the sharp jolt of pain.

'Take it slowly, it's all right.'

I peer out as my brain rearranges itself. A young smooth hand on mine, sparkly silver ring. Not Mum.

Still the light hurting. Blue and green interlocking shapes on the curtain.

'Am I in hospital?'

The hand moves as she steps back, all dainty in her nurse's uniform. She smooths the bed, takes the clipboard from the end.

'That's right, you've had us worried the while. I just need to do my checks before you drift away again.'

'Aaahh! Fuck!' I move my head to follow her, my brain sloshing against my skull.

'Keep still now. You've had a big knock. I just need a wee look in your eyes.'

She comes into close focus. I can see the blobs of her mascara, faint gold fuzz above her pearly-pink lips.

'Open wide.' She shines the light into each of my eyes. 'OK, that's fine.'

I close my eyes, spots of black dancing against luminous green.

'Just doing your blood pressure.' I feel her fastening the band, the hiss of pressured air, the band tightening.

'Am I in Sheffield?'

Her laugh like water down stone steps.

'Do I sound like a Yorkshire lassie?' She releases the air. 'No, you're in Scotland. Inverness. You had a nasty fall and you've been in and out of consciousness the while. Rest now.'

I lay my head back on the pillows, focus on a soft gurgling fish tank noise.

'Will I draw the curtains back for you?'

Interlocking shapes retreat. Line of beds opposite, one with curtains still drawn.

'Why am I here?' My mind dredges through porridge soup.

'You're concussed from your fall. You're on High Dependency for observation, but you've no need to worry. Your mam will be here soon.'

'Mum?' A surge of comfort at the thought.

The nurse moves away. 'Hello, Christopher? Do you know where you are?'

I shift my head slowly to the left. Nausea ripples like a Mexican wave. There's a square of pale sky in the plate-glass window, a mass of fluffy cloud in the middle. I trace the face of a goblin in the cloud, but the strain hurts my head.

Shut my eyes and hear the sing-song of the nurse, 'What day is it? Who's the prime minister?'

The gurgle of fish tanks.

Fog clears to mist swirls round my head. Squelch of feet sucked into the bog, trying to get to the other side. 'Do you know where you are?' Voice muffled and distant. Scotland, I want to say, tongue heavy. Why am I crossing this sinking bog?

'There he is!' The voice distinct and crystal.

I open my eyes to Mum, peering from the door of the ward. She looks shrunken and worn in her parka. Her face creased and tired. Old.

Then her eye catches mine and lights with a smile and she's Mummy come to the medical room after I banged my head ducking out of a rugby scrum. That glow of safety as she hurries towards me, her eyes filling as she leans for a light-touch hug.

'Don't cry, Mum.' My voice falters.

She bites her lip, perches on the bedside.

'I've been so worried, Gethin. Thank God, you're…'

'How actually did you get here?' The wrong question.

She does her patient Mum smile, strokes my hand, her fingers raspy. 'I drove through the night, though I was probably over the limit when I started. I got here on Red Bull and coffee, really.'

'Red Bull?'

'I was fighting being mesmerised by the lights on the motorway. You know, when it feels like a computer game? Not good.'

I drift into a picture of Mum driving a Red Bull F1 car on the Xbox. As in crashing at the corners because she's crap at it.

'…didn't know where you were or what was happening, then I got that call. Gethin?' Her worried face looks far away. 'What on earth happened, Gethin? Why were you in Durness?'

'Whoa, easy with the questions.' I look beyond her to the

window. The cloud has darkened and spread. I stare at it, trying to work things out.

'They say you fell off the cliff in Durness, you were with a girl on a motorbike or something. I thought you were searching for Don, that's what Emily said,' Mum fills my head with gabble.

'Will you shut up confusing me with the third degree.' I bang my hand on the bed, my head vibrating. There was a girl: wide blue eyes, pouty mouth, lines of silver earrings. Who was she?

The nurse approaches. 'Try not to get him too excited, Mrs Williams.'

Mum tenses up. I close my eyes.

Silver bulk on the ocean floor – swimming down to it but whenever I'm in touching distance it retreats – running out of breath give it one last push and grab at the handlebars – an old motorbike – but he's pushing down on the seat, face behind the helmet screen, mouthing NO – blood banging roaring in my ears. Got to get to the surface, but I can't let go of the bike. I tug and lunge to get away. Gasp at the air as I break through.

'NO!'

'It's OK, Gethin. Gethin breathe!'

Mum squeezes my hand, face crumpled with worry. I take another breath and another.

'You dropped off again. Had me worried for a second.'

'I was underwater, I literally couldn't breathe?' I try to explain.

'It's the concussion, they say you just need to rest, you know?'

I try to pull myself up on the pillows. Mum rearranges them and I lean back. The people in the beds opposite all look half dead, as in, bandaged heads, tubes and dials. There's a tube in my arm, leading to a drip.

'They're just rehydrating you; it's going to be OK.' She seems to catch my thoughts.

I shut my eyes, the image of his No-saying face still wavering 'He's not my father, is it?'

'You found him! What did he say? Has he upset you?'

'Mum, please!' I pull my hand away, though I am strangely comforted by how she annoys me in all the usual ways.

'I'm sorry. I've just been so anxious.'

I can hear the hurt in her voice, but I can't relate to it. What is it about Don? Everything's so far away.

'I found him in Lochgillan. He's got an old motorcycle museum, pretty sick place, like, really quirky…' I pause as an image of the museum starts to form.

'Ah that's great, Gethin. I don't have an issue, you know…'

'He's set up these scenes, like smiley motorbike families in the fifties and shit…' I trail off, an image of Jez standing next to me looking at the display.

'Where's Jez?' I ask.

'Does he have a daughter as well? The girl you were with in Durness?'

'What the hell are you on about? Just shut up a minute, will you?'

She pulls back into hunched shoulders.

'Has he got a daughter?' I clutch at a thought just out of reach.

'I only wondered about the girl,' Mum says. Not helpful.

Where were we? Me and Jez in the mist. Someone talking about Don?

'He's like in trouble. But he doesn't want to know me.' The image of his face: he has my dimple.

'Oh, Gethin, I'm so sorry, I just assumed…'

'Maybe I've got a sibling, Mum?' I remember now, a local girl pregnant.

'The girl on the motorbike?'

'No! Not Jez!' I shout. 'A baby, but I don't know where.'

'Oh, Gethin.' Mum's disappointed voice.

I wave her quiet, shut my eyes. Flash to standing with Jez by the waterfall, the overwhelming roar of it.

'I was angry with Jez. Where is Jez?'

'I don't know.' Mum squeezes my hand again.

I turn to the window. The cloud has thinned to a shining blank white. My thoughts blur into the distance.

I drift into a more regular doze, still conscious of the nurses, the random beeping of machines. Mum shifting position, rustling in her bag, sniffling. After a while I'm like aware of her above everything, and when I look, I see she is crying.

'Mum?'

Her eyes are ringed red in dark circles. I feel a sudden wave of nauseous fear.

'Mum?'

She blows her nose and pulls an unconvincing smile. 'I'm so sorry, Gethin, really.'

'You haven't done anything, is it?' I hear the rise of desperation in my voice.

Mum does a lot of being anxious and going on, but she doesn't do crying. Then I remember, when I was about ten, finding her in tears on the phone to Gran. I said I didn't think she ever cried. And she'd laughed, 'Not with you I don't.'

'I've let you down, Gethin,' she says now, wiping the tears she can't seem to stop. 'Just when you've really needed me, all I could do,' she pauses to control her voice, 'was nag at you.' She snuffles into the already dripping tissue.

'Ach, more tissue!' She grabs at the box on the side and has a good wipe.

I shift to bring myself more on a level with her, my brain sloshing a bit less now. But I literally don't know what this Upset-Mum is about.

'You were so angry on your birthday, you know?' Mum looks pleading at me. 'When I gave you Don's letter. I handled that, everything, so badly.'

My mind lurches to that storming scene. I can see myself kicking the table, the owner walking towards us, me slamming out of the door. But I can't locate the feeling and it's making me uncomfortable to see it upset her.

'Mum, it's OK.'

'No, Gethin, let me just say this.' She looks at me, steadier. 'I've been going over and over how I've lost touch with you.'

'Maybe I've just been growing up, know what I mean?' I interrupt, thinking that being in touch with Mum wasn't exactly that important in the last couple of years. Friends did that stuff now. At least some of them did, some of the time.

'You know, I went to see Gran and Granddad last week and it made me realise that all those middle class values I rebelled against – being measured by success in a worthwhile career, all that nonsense – I've ended up pushing on you.'

'I thought Granddad was a socialist?'

'He thinks it's criminal to waste a good education when

workers have had to fight for any knowledge that helps them think.'

'Well, to be fair, people my age, we do like take a whole lot for granted,' I say. Then I think of Aiden, literally living from day to day, grabbing at rare chances like the burger van.

'As in, the middle-class ones like me do,' I qualify.

'Well, let's just say Granddad has no time for mooching about sorting your head out, man.' Mum smiles as she makes her sort of joke. 'But I had such ideals of how different I would be with you. And then I got carried away with the idea of you being an Astrophysicist.'

'Well, it's not like I wasn't into it. I loved the telescope.'

'But I put too much pressure on you…'

'It was the maths, pretty much. I wasn't up for working that hard, not exactly your fault.' My skin prickles with discomfort. Even though I so resented the pressure at the time, her self-blame trip is unbearable.

But she's on a roll. 'And when you dropped out, it feels like I gave up on you, Gethin?' Her voice shakes and she pauses to take a deep breath.

'I've been such a crap mum,' she whispers, setting off a churning ache in my stomach.

I glance at the square of sky again. It's cleared to sheer blue with a few fluffy clouds chasing across it. I imagine lying on my back on a bank of grass. Maybe sharing a spliff with Jarvis on the field behind school. I think about his mum prioritising her crap boyfriends; Jez and the endless rounds of foster kids; Emily saying she'd die for a bit of parental expectation after I said I craved neglect. That feeling when Mum walked in here, that like total security I have never had to question.

I look at her now, literally trying not to fall apart all over me.

'Mum,' I start, not sure what to say. 'The fact that you actually even give a fuck…'

I grin to cover my awkwardness and she bites her lip, before allowing that wide mouth to break into a smile. She touches my hand, nodding.

I allow her to hold this moment for a few seconds before reaching for a drink. I take a sip of the tepid water, run my tongue round my dry lips.

'Could murder a cool beer!' I say.

'Oh, I don't think they'll allow…' she starts, so typical.

'Mum!' I shout. 'Take a joke, will you? Fuck's sake!'

The nurse comes hurrying over.

'It's OK,' I say. 'We just need a sense of humour transplant for my mother, if you have that procedure?'

'Ah,' the nurse beams. 'We've used them all on the doctors round here.'

'You reckon? Like it!'

'Good to see you more lively, Gethin. We've a side room become available. Don't ask how, I only sold them your kidney,' she does a stagey whisper. 'But we'll be moving you away from this lot now. Give you and your mam a wee bit of privacy.'

Mum pulls a questioning frown. 'So, how long do you want to keep him here?'

'We'll see what the doctor says tomorrow. But he's doing well, and he doesn't need the High Dependency bed now. No-one gets the side room for long, I can tell you.' She pats me on the arm. 'Someone will be along shortly to get you shifted, Gethin,' she says before scooting off round the ward with her checks.

'Hello, Christopher. What day is it?'

'Who's the prime minister?' I say at the same time as Mum, making her giggle like a schoolgirl.

'Hey, they did the transplant after all.'

'Transplant?' Mum looks all horrified.

'Aw, fucking hell, Mum.' Suddenly very weary.

She shuts up for a bit and I listen to the oxygen burble, trying to ignore the headache I've just noticed. The sound starts to remind me of that irritating whale music Grace used to play. Must tell Mum about whales. I'm sure it's relevant to whatever we were talking about. What were we even talking about? Aw, stop thinking!

'Gethin Williams, is it?' A foreign sounding voice.

I look to see a giant of a man, with a big red face, handlebar moustache, thick hairy arms poking out of overalls, broad hands holding onto a wheelchair.

'Time for move,' he says. I'm guessing Eastern European.

'Wow, I'm sure I can still walk.'

'Why walk – you ride?'

I start to shift my legs, but he waves me to stop, beckons the nurse over.

'Right, ready?' She pulls back the bedclothes and I see I'm wearing hospital pyjama trousers, though they've left my T shirt. They've taken my boxers off too.

'Don't worry, we've got your jeans,' the nurse says.

'Run off with my underwear?' I joke.

'Irresistible! But you'll knock 'em dead in these!' She slips synthetic hospital slippers on my feet.

'Now, swing your legs over and steady yourself on my shoulder. That's it.'

I get myself to a standing position, surprised how weak my legs feel, my head woozy.

'Let's walk you to the end of the ward, and then we'll use the chair.' She takes my arm. 'There's a bag with his stuff in that locker,' she points out to Mum, 'if you want to bring it along.'

I feel about ninety, leading the procession in my beige slippers, hanging onto the nurse's arm. We get to the ward entrance and I'm thankful for the wheelchair.

The nurse helps me onto the bed in the side room. I lean back on the pillows and look out of the window. The brightness hurts my head and I turn away from it, rub my temples.

'Will I get you something for your headache, now?' the nurse asks.

I give her a weak smile. 'I bet everyone wants to marry you, I want to marry you!'

'I'm that spoilt for choice.' She laughs.

Mum fusses putting my stuff away, pouring me water.

'It's OK.' I wave her away. 'Just need the drugs, yeah?'

'I should leave you to rest a while, really.'

'In a minute, Mum. Hold on.' There's a thin thread of something I wanted to say. I lean back and get an image of Jez in the firelight. When was that? Was that it?

The nurse brings painkillers. 'Why don't you take a wee rest?' She looks at Mum who hastily gathers her bag.

The thread slips away. There is only Jez.

'Where's Jez?'

I drift into a soft greyness and give up thinking, better to sink and be carried by the warm cloud. All is emptiness, allow the drift.

I open my eyes a couple of times; they have drawn the

slatted blinds across the window. I take a sip of water. Drift again.

'Gethin?' Mum's voice, touch on my hand. I focus on her face, her blue eyes piercing the dim light. I feel a surge of gladness that she's here.

'You've got a visitor.' She's like when she's springing a surprise on me as a kid.

She turns and I see, hovering behind her, that fat-cheeked baby-face with pursed lips holding back the biggest grin.

'Jez!'

The grin erupts as Jez lunges towards the bed, landing with her arms around me, the weight of her boobs on my chest before she pulls back to look at me.

'Oh my God, I actually made it back in time to see you!' Her eyes glistening.

'Fucking hell, Jez, I'm not about to snuff it, is it?'

She takes a breath. 'No, that's not... but it was frigging scary when you fell off the cliff.'

'Was I literally out cold?'

'They brought this air ambulance. Right exciting.'

'Aw, I don't even bloody remember. Did you take any photos?'

'Yeah, Gethin, it was all about the YouTube experience.'

'You videoed? Awesome!' I see myself strapped pale and motionless onto a stretcher and winched into a helicopter. Jez beside me in the cramped space, camera shake and roar of the propellers lifting off over the tip of Scotland.

'Idiot! As if.' Jez punches me in the arm.

'Oh.' I sulk as the image collapses.

Jez shakes her head, still that barely suppressed grin. I am so totally happy to see her, but something's bugging me.

'You were lucky Jez was there, that there was an air ambulance at all,' Mum pipes up.

'OK, thanks for that, Mum! The thing is… what the thing is…'

'You mustn't get upset.' Mum's pleady voice is such a wind-up.

'Maybe I'm upset that I woke alone in a hospital bed with literally not a clue how I got here?' I glare at her and Jez in turn.

'Gethin, I'm sure Jez–' Mum starts.

'Shut up, Mum!'

'It's OK, Pat,' Jez says.

'On first name terms already, is it?' I snort at their sisterly bonding.

'Just listen a minute, right?' Jez gives me her best eyeballing.

I pull back, not exactly sure what I'm arguing about.

'I was with you in the ambulance. You were out cold, but you came round a bit when we got here.'

'I so don't remember that.' I'm still accusing.

'You were quite sick, so they gave you something for the nausea, then you went into a heavy sleep. I thought you were unconscious again, but they said you were stable, and your mum was on her way, right? Thought I'd go to Durness for the bike. Leave you in peace.'

'Well, no-one told me any of that,' I mutter, ashamed now of my outburst.

'You've had concussion,' Mum says. 'You're bound not to remember everything.'

I close my eyes. Something I was going to say to Mum, and I've forgotten what that was.

'I took the tents down, packed up the bike. Decided to go and see Don, like you asked me,' Jez says, quietly, so it takes a moment to sink in.

I open my eyes and stare at her. She sits rigid, holding her breath.

'You went to Lochgillan? You talked to him? How long have I actually been here?'

'I left early this morning. Didn't take that long. You were upset, in the pub in Durness yesterday, right? Iain told us that stuff about Don?'

'Was that yesterday? With that couple playing pool?'

'Yeah, it seems an age ago to me, and I haven't fallen off a cliff.' Jez smiles.

'Did he talk to you? What did he say?'

Jez looks nervously over her shoulder at still-hovering Mum.

'It's OK, Mum. Sit down will you?' I shuffle to make room on the side of the bed.

'He got some girl pregnant and her family like smashed up the museum,' I say as I remember it. 'Did he tell you about that?'

Jez leans forward, her thighs twitching in their leather, her hair straggling round her neck. I catch my breath as I trace the glistening line of her cleavage.

'I had to fucking squeeze it out of him.'

'So, I've got a little sibling, is it? I bet it's a girl.' I see a tiny female version of me with dark page boy haircut, in a yellow dress, sucking a strawberry ice-lolly. Where the hell did that come from?

'No Gethin…'

'A boy then?' I'm properly disappointed. 'Don's been

denied access, so he doesn't want to see me because I remind him of it?' I feel a twang of jealousy for this kid he cares about losing. 'As in, sperm donor child doesn't count.'

Silence. Mum shifts on the edge of the bed, tensing up her shoulders.

Jez takes a breath, her hands pushed palms together between her thighs. 'Gethin, will you give me a frigging chance?' She looks me in the eye. 'I'm trying to tell you, there is no sibling. No baby. Nowt.'

Whoa. I feel knocked dizzy by this. 'I don't understand?' My voice is small now.

Mum leans forward. 'Let Jez explain.'

'There was this seventeen-year-old lass,' Jez starts. 'She helped Don out at the museum. He reckons they only slept together the once.'

'So, the rest was all malicious gossip, just as I thought, is it?'

Jez snorts a little laugh. 'Oh, she was pregnant all right. He told me how her brothers came and smashed up the place. Painted PAEDO on the museum and stuff.'

'PAEDO! I thought you said she was like seventeen!'

'Yeah, young enough if you ask me,' Jez says, then waves me down as I start to protest. 'Alright, calm down, not a paedo, right?'

I take a breath. 'What happened to the baby?'

'It took me a while to get it out of him, I tell you.' Jez pushes a strand of hair out of her eyes.

As she lifts her arm, I see a little butterfly tattoo on her shoulder. I never even noticed it before. I would more have expected a serpent or something.

I nod, keep my lips shut tight.

'So, after Don getting beaten up some more by the brothers, Ruthie, the girl, comes to tell him it's not his baby.'

'You what? Fucking hell, how come she let everyone think it was?'

'She'd refused to say who the father was. The brothers decided to blame it on Don. In fact, it was some Dutch biker, and she was hoping he was coming back for her, right?'

'So how did she even know who it was?' I say, impatient.

'Apparently, she had her period after sleeping with Don. Got knocked up the following month. Her brothers guessed because she was throwing up all the time.'

'Fucking hell, what a bitch, to let them blame Don like that.'

I can feel Mum tense on the bed beside me. 'She was very young, Gethin, remember?' she says quietly.

'Yeah, as in a year younger than me? I'm hoping I'd have more guts than that.'

'You'd know all about being alone and pregnant with bully boy brothers kicking off?' Jez growls.

'OK, sorry, carry on.' I pull back into my pillows, totally shown up, ashamed of my reaction.

'Well, this Dutch geezer never turned up. So, Ruthie took herself to Inverness and had a termination.'

'Oh my God, no baby?'

Jez goes on to explain how apparently this Ruthie said she couldn't face bringing up a kid on her own in that community. And then how after she'd got rid of the baby she decided to get away and got herself a nannying job in Germany. I feel like a delayed reaction in taking this story in, still absorbing the fact that there is no baby.

'So, what, are the brothers still blaming him for it all?' I ask eventually, wondering why this is still a big deal for Don.

'I don't exactly know. He's so tetchy, right? Thinks they're all against him there.'

I remember that guy Robbie, saying Don was his own worst enemy. 'So, am I just a bit of gossip too much for him, then?' I ask, my heart thumping.

'No, I don't think it's that,' Jez weighs her words carefully. 'He thinks he's best keeping away from people. Like any time he lets his guard down, it all goes pear shaped.'

I nod slowly, still taking it in. I think of how he was that first day with the kippers. OK he was gruff, but he actually shared a shred of his life with me. I feel a sudden welling of tears.

Jez looks at me, head cocked to one side. 'He did ask me to let him know how you are.'

'Right, what a shame I haven't died to make him feel really bad.' I grin, blinking furiously.

'Oh Gethin!' Mum pulls a weak smile. Guessing this whole thing is the weirdest for her. As in, suddenly it's all about the guy she never met whose sperm she squirted into her body. We have never needed him.

'He's just a bit scared, I think,' Jez says.

'Scared? What of?'

'Getting too attached?'

'Attached?' I run the word around my battered brain. Emily talked about Attachment Theory before she dropped out of A level psychology. She reckoned she had an anxious-ambivalent attachment with her mother.

'I'm not sure I'm looking for parental attachment, to be fair?'

I look from Jez's quizzing eyes to Mum's pursed lips, the obvious question like forming in the space between us?

'What the hell am I looking for?'

'Only you can answer that,' Mum says quietly.

I lie back and try to work it out. I think about Don's museum and all those stories about the clan, the big house, the history. I was seduced, isn't it, by the idea of having a solid connection to such an awesome place? These past few days I've felt more alive than I have for ages. But it hasn't exactly been all about Don, not even mostly. It's about the landscape and Jez and the bike and the referendum and the whales. The whales.

And I start to tell Mum about the whales, Jez filling in where I'm too garbled.

'Aw, Mum, they are such awesome creatures. It was totally overwhelming seeing them so helpless and distressed. But the fact that we could help a bit… we actually got one whale off the sandbank even though Aiden nearly drowned.'

'You rescued Aiden too, right?' Jez butts in.

'Ha! Aiden thinks I'm his dead brother, isn't it?'

'What?' Mum sounds exasperated.

'Forget it. The whales is the thing. As in, it got me thinking about doing like training in Marine Rescue, or something.' I feel the rising excitement of this idea.

'Well, I expect science A levels would be involved.' Mum can't help herself looking pleased.

'Yeah, no promises there.' I fold my arms over my chest. Like literally deflated by this all too familiar exchange.

'Oh, I don't want to put you under any pressure.' Mum sounds defensive.

I can see the corners of Jez's mouth twitch as she brings her hand up to hide her smile.

The nurse pops her head round the door, taps at her watch. 'Time our invalid settled for the night, guys.'

'Really?' I literally have no clue what the time is.

'It's gone half ten,' Jez points to the clock. 'I didn't set off from Lochgillan 'til about half seven. Did it in an hour and a forty flat.'

'No deer in the way, is it?' I tease.

Jez shakes her head.

'I'll give you ten minutes,' the nurse says.

There's a faint glow coming through the drawn blinds. 'Is it still like light out there?'

'It will be,' Jez says. 'Practically the midnight sun here, right?'

I remember the night on the beach, the light sitting on the horizon, competing with the stars.

'Let's have a look, before you go.' I shift my legs to the edge of the bed.

'Gethin, be careful now,' Mum warns.

'Aw, come on, I can make it to the window. Give us a hand.'

I swing my legs to hang over the bed, signal Jez and Mum to either side and throw my arms over their shoulders while I stand. We walk a slow shuffle to the window and Jez pulls up the blinds.

The sky is a dusky blue patterned with mackerel cloud and the pale glow of the sun slipping behind the buildings. Beyond the neat rows of modern housing, the dark mounds of a golf course lead to the glint of the river. There's a bank of trees downstream which could be where the homeless camp was. My eye follows the river past the floodlit castle, widening as it heads out of eyeshot, to the sea.

'I tell you what?' I pull Jez and Mum closer. 'There's so going to be a lot more getting out and living for me. Whatever happens with Don hardly matters compared to that.'

I lean my head on Jez's shoulder and smell the sexy saltiness of her. 'Seize the moment, is it, Jez?'

'Totally!' She gives a thumbs up.

'I'll go with that.' Mum squeezes my arm, and it feels like she actually might mean it.

Finishing Pieces – *Pat*

The music is strangely seductive with its clashing industrial tribal drumbeat. It holds me in this moment sitting at my worktable, the air warm and soft through the open window, the shine of the copper beech framing the edge of my vision. Gethin's life collage spread in front of me and the image filling my laptop screen. A landscape of open sea, dark mountains, craggy heath and shining valley: 360° on one picture plane. I ache with the lonely beauty of it, discovered amongst the endless pictures of young people draped over each other. *Expanding horizons in the Scottish WildLands.*

I catch my breath, thrown yet again into flashback of that dry mouthed terror as I drove to Inverness. It was the time I caught him toddling into the path of a reversing lorry; the time he and Francesca disappeared from the pub garden.

The tap on my shoulder makes me jump, a little involuntary scream as I turn to see Gethin.

'Fucking hell, Mum, I did knock. What's with the heavy industrial?'

'Oh, something this friend lent me. How to Destroy Angels. It's the guy from Nine Inch Nails, who I have at least heard of, and his wife, whose name I forget.' I'm wittering to cover being caught out with the collage he doesn't know about and his Facebook page on my laptop.

'Hmm,' he's distracted, obviously, by the collage. The laptop has conveniently switched to standby. 'What the hell is this, Mum?'

I'm struck, not for the first time, by this tall good-looking man-boy of mine, pushing his hair out of his eyes, his puzzled frown giving an air of thoughtfulness that seems somehow new to me.

'It was meant to be a surprise, you know? I wasn't expecting you back so soon.'

'Yeah, well, Ben had to go to work.' He moves closer to the collage. 'Wow, I remember that severed finger. As in I tried to frighten you with it.'

'You succeeded, running in screaming with a ketchup covered tissue. I could have a heart attack just thinking about it.'

'My Top Gear chart? You actually hated Top Gear.'

'It was all part of you.' I pull a nervous smile.

'So, how long have you been making this?'

'I started when you were a baby, as a piece about your conception. Then it became more a record of your childhood – stealing bits and pieces as you cleared them out.'

He scans the length of it again. 'Liking how you literally start with the syringe. Is that the actual one?'

'The one and only.'

'The way it like expands out of that...I remember those drawings: I was obsessed with gore and guts, isn't it?' He points to sharks dripping the blood of hapless pirates.

'That and the spaceships.' I indicate the rocket drawings I have heading for the star charts, trailing orange and red crayon.

'Hmm, it's clever how you've done that.' He looks thoughtful again. 'I had a properly good childhood, isn't it?'

I nod, look down at the blur of collage. Was I really such a bad mum? The music beats in loud. *Listen to the sound, of my big black boots.*

'Heavy stuff, Mum.' He laughs.

'So, how did your day go?' I ask, wanting to keep him here.

'Oh, yeah, guess what?' He seals his lips in a daft grin.

'Something about Ben?'

'Yeah, kind of.'

'He's seduced you into finding your gay side?' I joke.

'Ha! Not bad Mum.' His dimple twitches and I want to hug him. 'If anyone could tempt me, it would be Ben, for sure. But it's pretty much not like that with us.'

'I give up, then.'

'I've got a job. As in working at Ben's club.' His smile fills his face, little boy proud.

And now I do hug him. 'Oh, Gethin, I'm so pleased. Just, well, for your sake, you know?' I pull back still holding onto his arms, tears pricking.

'Yeah, well, it's just a scabby nightclub. But the guy's sound enough. I'll probably look for a day job too. I pretty much want to save up as much as I can, know what I mean?'

'It's a start. Well done you.' I squeeze his arms. 'Hey, sit down a minute.' I throw my clothes from the spare chair to the bed and hurry across the landing into the kitchen.

He's studying the collage when I come back with the Cava. I pop the bottle before he can say anything and pour us both a glass.

'Having you back more or less in one piece is special occasion enough. The job's a bonus, eh?' I clink my glass against his. 'Here's to my grown-up son!'

He nods his smile at me.

'There, something else for the collage.' I brandish the cork. 'I've been trying to finish it. It was meant for your eighteenth, you see?'

'Not a lot since my GCSEs, is it?' He looks me straight in the eye, no smile now.

I take a breath. 'I'm sure there are things, I just stopped looking, you know?'

'As in a few burnt out roaches, maybe even a couple of used condoms.'

'Oh, Gethin, it's not that bad, is it? I've just been looking on your Facebook page, seeing as we're *friends* again.' I fire up the laptop to get the photo.

He shuffles forward, nods slowly. 'I was actually quite proud of that.'

'It's beautiful, it looks such a stunning place. I'll print it off.'

I busy myself sending the image to print. Then I remember that I also have things to tell. Come on then, get on with it.

'I've been meaning to talk to you about my job, Gethin. I was just waiting, you know, 'til you were fully recovered.'

'Oh? What about it?'

'Well, it looks as though we're going to be made redundant. The Council are cutting our funding.'

'Shit, Mum, I had literally no idea.' His eyebrows meet in a deep frown.

'It's no real surprise. The local government spending cuts are massive, you know. Services like ours are seen as a luxury.'

'But you help lots of old people and shit,' he protests.

'It's cheaper for the Council to tag it onto their existing services.'

He shuffles in his seat. 'I don't know what to say. Other than, that's crap?'

'To tell you the truth, it's not necessarily so bad for me. I'll get a decent payoff as I've been there a while, and it's maybe time for a change.'

'Yeah, makes sense. Any ideas?'

'I'd really like to make a go of my art full time.' My heart pounds at putting this emerging plan into words. 'I've found this artists' collective – their studios are cheaper than mine, plus I'd be less isolated.'

'Oh yeah, where's that?'

'Down by the river at the back end of town. One of the artists does feminist collage… she's been really encouraging.' I feel myself blush as I say this.

'And is she responsible for your new taste in music, by any chance?' He smiles amusement at me.

'Well, yes, she lent me the CD.' I feel ridiculously caught out.

'It's about time you met some new people,' he says simply. 'Go for it!'

'It's a big risk. I only met them a week ago, the night I got the phone call from the hospital. But I wanted you to know it's there as an idea.'

I take a big gulp of wine to curb the jittery feeling this is giving me. Despite the drama of Gethin's accident, the attraction of Gabriella's collective has taken hold of me. And I shocked myself by thinking of sleeping with her even on the drive to Inverness. Since we've been back, I've been obsessing with financial calculations whilst trying to convince myself that sex with Gabriella is not part of the plan.

'Hey, Mum, don't over-think it.' He raises his glass and we clink again. 'Here's to both our futures!'

I pour us some more and we drink in silence for a moment. The copper beech glows in the late afternoon light – the air fresh and sweet since last night's rain. I focus on my breathing, feel my shoulders relax. It is after all such a relief to have told him.

I take the 360° picture and place it near the end of the collage, lay the Cava cork beside it, leaving some empty space after the GCSE photo.

'What else have we got?' I go back to his Facebook, click randomly on an image.

'Hey, me out getting wrecked with the gang, is it? What a surprise!'

I look at the photo: Gethin, Ben, Francesca, Emily, a couple of others. Red eyed and wasted at some underground music night, pointing peace-signs at the camera. 'Well, you're having a good time, by the looks of it.'

'Aw, you're not printing that?' He holds his head in his hands.

'It's not as if you're murdering babies, is it?'

He shrugs. 'You could like scan this, if you want.' He pulls a photo out of his wallet.

It's the picture of Don that came with the letter. It sends a shock wave through me, seeing it again, those eyes so like Gethin's.

'Did I tell you I took a photo of him on my phone? He went ape-shit, so Jez deleted it.' He bats the picture against his hand.

'I do hope he agrees to see you again,' I say, suddenly hit by the hurt of it all for Gethin.

'Jez rang to tell him I was OK. Apparently, he might write to me.' He places the photo in the middle of the landscape picture. 'That's how I see him, as in right at the centre of that awesome place.'

I look at the picture of Don again. So strange to put a face to the other half of Gethin's genes. And I thought it was all about me.

'Do you think you would have liked a father involved in

your upbringing? I mean, I know other lesbian mothers with donors that were very present. Was I selfish to deny you that?'

He takes a drink and wets his lips as he thinks. Then he looks me straight in the eye. 'I've thought about it, while I was up there. You know, if I could have used a "Rail Mole Model".'

I smile and wait for him to carry on.

'But, in the end, I never knew any different, did I? So, I can't say I actually missed it. And there are literally plenty of guys that make useless fathers, so why would I have wanted that?'

'I suppose my main concern was that you would feel a stigma from having a lesbian mother,' I start.

'So not an issue, Mum.'

'I know, you say that, but I remember the head-teacher when you first started school, saying, "Oh, don't worry, we have all sorts here, prisoners' children and everything."'

Gethin snorts his laughter. 'You are joking me.'

I shake my head. 'When you think, Gethin, the age of consent was still not equal for gay men, and Section 28 was still the law. Now we have a Conservative government legalising gay marriage.'

'Yeah, things have changed a bit. My generation are like more accepting of difference. The way we see it, there's just like a continuum of sexuality, sexual identity. Literally, we don't care who anyone is, where they're from, all that.'

'Still, I should have thought more about your need for some kind of father figure.' The familiar lurch of regret.

'Mum, we can't go back and start again, can we? Cut it out with the bloody guilt-fest.'

'I'm sorry, I'm over-reacting.' I sound so pathetic.

He takes a breath. 'You seriously need to chill out, Mum.'

He drains his glass, takes the bottle to top us up. 'Come on, bottoms up, isn't it?'

I do as I'm told, pass him my empty, then fetch the photo of Gethin and his friends from the printer. They seem so innocent, the way they pile together like that, confident in their new-found righteousness. And now I'm presented with this growing up Gethin, this sharing of wine and talking as equals. It's a struggle to keep up, but I'm glimpsing a future relationship beckoning. It's up to me really, not to blow it.

Gethin watches the play of light on his glass as he twiddles it in his fingers. 'For the record, Mum,' he says eventually, 'I am genuinely glad to have found Don, to have put a face to that half of me. He did let me in for a couple of hours, he did actually give me that. And I hope I do see him again, go back to Lochgillan, all that.' He pauses to take a sip of wine. 'But no way do I feel I need him. Never did, why would I now?'

'Perhaps it was good that Karen pushed for your right to know who he was.'

He nods. 'You should have her round some time. As in I could quiz her on what Don was like when she knew him.'

I smile at the idea. 'I'm sure she'd enjoy giving you the low-down.'

'I'll tell you what, though, I am totally loving Scotland. Not just the landscape, but, you know, the people, with the referendum and all that, there is so much energy, a sense that change is possible?'

'Interesting time to be there, though I have my doubts about Scottish independence. Mostly I don't fancy the idea of what we'll be left with in Runt UK or whatever.'

'Perhaps it's time we pushed for our own change, know what I mean?' He pulls a half smile, seeming to recognise that's so much easier said than done. But there is a spark about him I haven't seen for years. And I'm not about to dampen it.

Gethin grabs the picture of his mates and places it in the gap on the collage. 'Aw, did I tell you about Fran and Jarvis? So unlikely. Ben says they're a total sop-fest.'

'Perhaps they can head for a double wedding with Grace and Sebbie, if we're talking unlikely couples.'

'Come on, Mum. No way will Fran be letting Wasteman get in the way of her designer career. As for Grace and Sebbie, apparently, they've worked through a lot of shit and realised after all this time that they want to be together much more than they don't. That's well mature, isn't it?'

I nod, amused at Gethin's appreciation of this middle-aged maturity. I really should get in touch with Grace. She has been a proper friend, whatever I think of her choices. I take a sip of wine and look at the picture.

'So, the jury's still out for Fran and Jarvis. Is there a sugar daddy for Ben?' I joke.

Gethin shakes his head. 'Fucking hell, Mum! For a lesbian feminist who's been single for about a million years, you don't half go in for fairy-tale endings. Ben has this like High Maths Gay Hip-Hop Persian Prince thing that will take him places I can't even dream of.'

'And what about Emily?' I watch his expression tighten.

'Hmm, she wants me to go for a drink. Fuck knows why – she's so been hard on my case lately.'

I think about how Emily was on the phone, taking my side against Gethin for reasons I didn't try to fathom. But now it comes to me. 'Well, at the risk at sounding old-school, I think Emily would like you back, you know.'

Gethin's eyes widen, his face colouring. He shakes his head.
'You don't think so?' I prompt.

'She's got a funny way of showing it. Honestly Mum, she's rivalled you for getting at me.'

I feel a stab of hurt at him saying that. Ignore! 'She doesn't seem to be letting you go, put it that way.'

He nods, thoughtful. 'I do really like her. I was proper gutted when she dumped me and I'm not over it yet.' He pauses, as if playing with the idea of Emily now. 'The thing is, she's totally screwy. Part of me would love to get back with her, but she's too, well, needy. I don't exactly need needy right now. As in I'll let her down and feel like an arsehole.'

'What about Jez?' I ask.

He smiles, a big broad smile. Ah, so handsome. 'She has actually made me a proposition.'

'Oh yeah? Not marriage, I take it?'

He snorts his laughter. 'That would be so the opposite of Jez. I don't fancy her as much as Emily, but she is sexy, and she's turning into a real mate, know what I mean?'

'That sounds like just what you need.'

He nods and goes into thought mode again.

'So, come on Mum, what about you?'

'Me?'

'Yeah. As in, you've finished bringing me up, embarking on a new artistic career. You split up with Karen when I was about seven, with no love interest since, as far as I'm aware. About time?'

I take a drink to cover my blush. 'You haven't told me about Jez's proposition yet.'

'I'll tell you when you answer my question. What about this artist woman, lending you CDs and liking your work?'

I feel the blood rush to my face. Hopeless to try to hide it.

'Go on, what's she like? Have you got a photo of her?'

'Of course, I haven't. Her name's Gabriella, but it's her work, the studios that interest me.'

'Yeah, Mum. Right.' Gethin makes a show of suppressing his amusement.

'OK, I'll admit she's bloody gorgeous. But we met for coffee yesterday...'

'Ah, it's all coming out now!'

'And, if you'll listen, I said I would be interested in joining the collective, and her political artists group, but we basically agreed that's as far as it's going.'

'You what? How actually does that work?'

I think about how it did work. I told Gabriella that I didn't want to blow it, and she smiled and said I was a lovely lady – she could snog me right now – but nothing has to happen if I don't want it to. And I admitted I wasn't sure if I was relieved or not.

'We agreed there's no hurry, we've got lots of art to discuss, we'll leave it at that for now,' is what I tell Gethin.

He nods knowingly, and I get a flash of Gabriella leaning to kiss me, a wave of longing I'm so unused to feeling.

'Ah, so tempted,' I say, bursting into teenage giggles. Gethin catches the mood, laughing with me.

'Go Mum!' he says, as I start to calm down.

He takes his iPhone, scrolls through the photos and passes it to me. It's a selfie of him and Jez on her bike, both grinning stupidly from their helmets.

'Can you print that?' He hands me the lead for the phone.

I plug it into the laptop and download it to print. 'So, Jez's proposition?'

'She's like done a deal with me. As in she'll get herself legal on that bike, while I earn enough cash to join her on some travels in a couple of months. We're talking Eastern Europe, maybe.'

I nod slowly. Terrified of the idea of him on the back of a bike, and not liking to think in what way it wasn't legal. I'll have to force myself not to fuss it.

'Jez reckons I should learn to ride as well,' he carries on, not helping my fears. 'I dunno, maybe. But there's something quite cool about being a male pillion for a sexy female biker, don't you think?' He raises his eyebrows, so full of himself.

Ah, I do love him. And I'll admit to being pleased that he's choosing to get out and live for a bit rather than committing to more study that he may not be ready for.

'I'm excited for it. As in I haven't been abroad since we hired that Spanish villa after GCSEs.' He takes a swig of his wine. 'And that was all about getting trashed around a pool, which even then seemed kind of pointless.'

I hand him the picture from the printer. 'Well, Eastern Europe on a bike with Jez sounds much more interesting. I'm almost jealous,' I say, only half joking.

Gethin grabs a magic marker and holds it poised above the collage, his dimple smile filling his face. Then he draws the lines of a road heading out, splitting off into multiple directions as it reaches the end of the calico. Places himself with Jez on the bike at the start of the road.

He grins at me. 'There you go. Finished!'

About the Author

Penny Frances has an MA Writing from Sheffield Hallam University and writes accessible literary fiction. She has had numerous short stories published in literary magazines, both print and online. She was a prize winner with the Southport Writers Circle Open Short Story Competition and has been shortlisted for the Bournemouth Writing Prize, Ilkley Literary Festival Competition and Flash 500 Short Story Competition.

Originally from London, she has lived in Sheffield since 1985, balancing the demands of writing, day job (with the Council), and family. She is now in the process of moving to Scotland with her husband. Being married to an artist helps keep alive her interest in art, and annual visits to Scotland (sometimes on his motorbike) have provided the impetus for this novel, along with her experience of being a single parent to a son, conceived in 1996 with donor self-insemination.

Learn more about Penny on her website:
https://pennyfrances.wordpress.com
or find her on Twitter: Penny Frances Writer
@PennyWightwick

If you have enjoyed this book, please consider leaving a review for Penny Frances on Amazon and Goodreads to let her know what you thought of her work.

Printed in Great Britain
by Amazon